The Homecoming

By Rosie Howard

The Homecoming

The Homecoming

ROSIE HOWARD

Allison & Busby Limited
12 Fitzroy Mews
London W1T 6DW
allisonandbusby.com

First published in Great Britain by Allison & Busby in 2018.

A CIP catalogue record for this book is available from
the British Library.

First Edition

HB ISBN 978-0-7490-2212-9
TPB ISBN 978-0-7490-2283-9

Typeset in 11/16 pt Sabon by
Allison & Busby Ltd.

The paper used for this Allison & Busby publication
has been produced from trees that have been legally sourced
from well-managed and credibly certified forests.

Printed and bound by
CPI Group (UK) Ltd, Croydon, CR0 4YY

For my father – who always wanted to go into a bookshop to buy my book and so nearly did

CHAPTER ONE

It began just as Maddy approached the roundabout at the bottom of town.

The blue, dawn light, which had heralded her arrival at the hospital, had warmed now to the bright sunshine of a fine autumn morning, burnishing the turning leaves of the trees lining the streets of Havenbury Magna and contrasting their richness with a cloudless sky. The air was crisp, the traffic was light after the early-morning rush and pedestrians greeted each other in the street as they went about their daily routines. There was nothing to fear here. No monsters hiding in the dark. No nameless terrors. And yet, as she drove past the docks, turning right to climb the steep high street, her chest tightened and her breath caught in her throat. Gripping the wheel tight, she focused her eyes on the ruined castle at the top of the hill. Breathe slowly. Relax. *Calm, calm*, she chanted in her head, but it was no good; by the time she turned her little car into the narrow lane leading to the car park behind the Havenbury Arms, icy sweat had drenched her and her feet juddered on the pedals as her legs shook. Gasping and sobbing for air she stalled the engine and yanked on the handbrake, resting her head on the steering wheel as she waited, despairing, for the panic to pass. Gradually, the raw terror ebbed away, leaving her weak and tearful in its wake.

And this – she thought to herself as she wiped her cold, dripping hands on her shirt and climbed unsteadily out of the car – *is why I haven't been back.*

She stood, quaking, as she took in her surroundings, concentrating on the feel of her feet on the ground, the sharply cold air pouring into her lungs as she carefully, consciously, slowed her breathing. She was glad no one from the high street could see her.

She may have been alone in the little car park at the rear of the pub but she was not the only one using it that morning. There was already a grubby old Land Rover and a sleek, new navy BMW with an ironed, stripy shirt hanging from a hook above the back seat. The car park was for customers only but a few locals sneakily used it when the pub was shut to avoid the heinous charges in the bigger council one up the road, which annoyed Patrick, the landlord, no end.

Drawing herself upright with determination, Maddy wiped the cold sweat from her top lip with a still-trembling hand and locked the car.

Letting herself into the back hallway, the familiarity she expected was marred by a sense of something amiss, and she swiftly recognised the reason for her disquiet. There was someone in the bar. Two people. They were talking loudly enough to indicate they felt entitled to be there. Which they absolutely weren't.

'Of course this would originally have been two rooms,' said one voice confidently. 'Good size ones too, so taking out the bar and putting the wall back would be a small matter . . . I'll be the first to admit a couple of improvements wouldn't go amiss.'

The second man made some reply she couldn't quite catch. She peeked through the door from the kitchen and spied the top of Dennis's shiny bald head barely clearing the bar he stood on the far side of.

'I don't know what sort of timescales you are working to,' he continued, addressing the man outside Maddy's field of vision, 'but Top Taverns is expecting to be able to let the place go by New Year at the very latest – most likely in the next couple of months, if I'm honest,' he added in a lower tone, tapping the side of his nose knowingly.

'And precisely how does Top Taverns think it's going to do that?' Maddy demanded, as she marched into the bar to confront the little man.

'What the hell . . . ?' Dennis blustered, as she placed herself in front of him, looking down from a height advantage of at least six inches. 'Ah, it's Maddy, isn't it?' He looked nervously up at her. 'S-sorry to hear about poor old Patrick. Such sad news.'

'He's not bloody dead. And you've not been to visit him. Too busy shoving your nose in here to bring him a bunch of bloody grapes, which, might I say, is a little rich given the way he slaves to fill your pockets.'

'Well, not actually *my* pockets, obviously, although I appreciate Patrick is a loyal partner of Top Taverns, and also,' Dennis added a little more confidently, puffing out his chest, 'I slightly resent the suggestion I am "shoving my nose in" given I am the regional manager for this pub, as I believe you know very well, although I haven't seen you here very recently.'

A low blow, thought Maddy, although admittedly she

hadn't seen the loathsome Dennis since that summer three years ago.

'I'm not likely to forget your little visits in a hurry, though, am I? Interesting, though – to hear you talking about improvements – because I can't help but notice that Top Taverns hasn't felt moved to do anything about the deterioration,' she said, remembering the peeling paint outside and the slime running down a wall from a long-neglected gutter.

'Patrick has a full-repairing lease, as I am sure you are aware,' said Dennis, spitefully, knowing she wasn't, 'and I am bound to agree with you that there is work needed. I have been strongly advising him it's something he needs to be thinking about now his lease is coming to an end.'

'Coming to an end?'

'Yes,' he replied, glad to have caught her out. 'Patrick's lease runs only until the end of the year. Renewal is a possibility, of course, but . . .' he waved a hand vaguely and let the sentence hang in the air between them.

Loath to let Dennis get away with thinking he had won that particular bout, Maddy steered the conversation elsewhere. 'And who the hell are you, anyway?' she said, turning her fierce gaze to the other man for the first time.

He seemed irritatingly unmoved by her fury, leaning one elbow on the bar with casual grace whilst treating her to a leisurely appraisal. It wasn't clear if his lazy grin was generated by amusement at her anger or approval at her appearance, although she doubted it was the latter. She was still wearing the jeans and flannel shirt she had thrown on in London, before driving down through the night to reach Patrick's bedside.

The shirt, an old one of Simon's, had shrunk in the wash, the cuffs turned back into thick wodges of fabric to reveal long, slim forearms, with a fading tan. Cropped jeans ended in narrow ankles and her bare feet – she hadn't wasted time on socks – were slipped into creased leather deckshoes. Under scrutiny she pushed back her wavy brown hair with unconscious grace, but it fell instantly over her face again, hanging down over one eye, like a Shetland pony's mane. After a night filled with worry and no sleep, and rattling from the panic attack she had barely overcome, Maddy wiped impatiently at the tears that sprung to her eyes, turning the action into a general face rub so the stranger wouldn't see her sudden distress.

'As the lady says,' he drawled, turning his attention diplomatically to Dennis, 'it would appear that reports of Patrick's death have been exaggerated, so . . .' he paused, 'we find ourselves de trop.'

'Right-o.' Dennis wavered, clearly feeling he no longer had control over the conversation. 'I need to get back to the office so, if you prefer,' he nodded his head in the man's direction, 'we'll convene another day.' With barely a glance at Maddy he trotted out of the bar, fiddling with his mobile phone as he went.

'Ben Faraday,' said the man at last, holding out a hand for Maddy to shake. The wavy brown hair flopping over his face could have looked effeminate but his tanned skin had the tough, lined appearance of being out in all weathers and made him look anything but soft. Maddy took his hand, which was so large it encompassed her. She had to resist a desire to reach out and see if his biceps were huge too.

'Arse,' said a baleful voice.

They both jumped.

'Dennis?' said Maddy uncertainly, looking at the door he had exited through seconds before.

11

'Butt crack,' the voice observed, morosely.

This time they both turned towards a shrouded dome in the corner.

'Pirate.' Ben laughed.

'Oh my goodness!' she exclaimed, going over to drag the cover off the cage. 'Pirate the parrot. Hello.'

Pirate was thrilled to have the blanket removed.

'He-llo,' he replied, as if butter wouldn't melt. 'More tea, vicar?' he queried, running first this and then that way on his perch, turning his head to one side and giving Maddy a beady look.

'He's in the bar?' she said. 'That's not like the old days.'

'He was banned because of the smoke for years, but there's no smoking now so Patrick thought he may as well have the company. Although I'm not sure it's doing much for his vocabulary.'

'I wouldn't worry. He's sworn like a trooper all the time I've known him and it wasn't the company he was keeping then.' Maddy tickled the top of Pirate's head through the bars of the cage, making him edge closer and shut his eyes in rapture. 'Actually, we wondered if he had Tourette's.'

'Knickers,' commented Pirate, seemingly in support of her hypothesis.

'I'm sorry about Patrick,' said Ben. 'How is he?'

'How well do you know him?'

'He's a good friend. I wasn't in last night so had no idea he had been taken ill until this morning. As a matter of fact, I was just coming up to see if there was anything I could do to help when I bumped into lover boy Dennis. Quite a charmer, isn't he?'

'Patrick isn't well at all, but he's asked me to make sure the pub opens as usual,' she said as she shepherded Ben towards the back door. 'I'd love to sit and chat but I do have rather a lot to do.'

By this time they were both in the little courtyard and, thanks to all the beer kegs clustered on the ground, Ben was too close for comfort. Impatiently she went to shove a barrel aside with her foot.

'Gaahhh!' she shrieked as her foot buckled against the immovable keg. 'Sodding hell!' she added for emphasis, going on to swear with an inventiveness and fluency that would have made a navvy blush as her leg punished her for her carelessness.

'So, it's not just Pirate with the extensive vocabulary,' observed Ben, having waited patiently until she ran out of steam. 'Interesting display of masochism.'

'I thought they were empty,' she muttered, rubbing her foot. 'This is where we leave the return barrels for the drayman. Oh sodding hell again, I suppose he delivered this morning when there was no one here to unlock the cellar. Otherwise he'd have put the full ones in there. At least he took the empties . . .'

'Right, give me the key to the cellar,' said Ben, rubbing his hands together.

'No really, you don't want to—'

'Yes really, I *do* want to. If not for your benefit, then for Patrick's.'

'OK fine,' she said, ungraciously, although privately relieved. The full barrels were unbelievably heavy. It was all she could manage to shove one a couple of feet out of the way to get a new one online when they blew. Getting them down the ramp to the cellar was going to be impossible without a bit of borrowed brawn.

She took the padlock key from its place on the nail inside the door and opened the trapdoor to the cellar. Not wanting to risk any further injury to her feet, she left Ben to it and went to do a recce of the bar area. Unlike the days when she had helped out to fund herself through her degree, it was obvious the room had not been cleaned thoroughly in a long time. The glasses were washed but the shelves were grubby on close inspection, something Patrick would never have allowed to happen in the time she had known him before. The long, wooden bar top was grungy from too much cursory wiping and the chair rungs were dusty where she had made a point of wiping them with a damp cloth once a week. She decided to put aside time for a thorough clean. In the meantime, though, she straightened the chairs, dished out some beer mats and checked the pumps were all set to go.

She went out to check on Ben just as he was pushing the last keg into place. His hair was flopping over his face again but, other than that, there was no sign of significant effort, which impressed her. Not only would she have ultimately failed, she would have got dirty, red-faced and sweaty doing it.

'I suppose you think you've earned yourself a cup of tea.'

'That'd be nice.' He straightened and smiled at her.

'Earl Grey, Jasmine, Lapsang souchong?'

'Builder's tea would be fine.'

'As in PG tips, or are we talking six sugars and a large chipped mug with a picture of a naked woman on it?'

'Strong – milk – no sugar. Although the mug sounds interesting now you mention it.'

Maddy explored the kitchen and found Tetley's tea bags, two cleanish mugs and some milk which was just the acceptable end of the fresh/off continuum.

'So, how do you know Patrick?' she asked as they sipped.

'I might ask you the same question.'

'You might, although strictly speaking I asked you first. But – seeing as you seem fairly helpful . . . Patrick is an old, old friend of my mother's. Plus, he looked after me when I was studying here.'

'So you were at the college? Don't look as if you graduated long ago.'

She hadn't graduated at all, but she sidestepped deftly. 'I left three years ago, more or less. I've been in London running my own business.'

'Good for you – you're young for a successful entrepreneur . . .'

'Yeah well, not that successful – not rich yet, anyhow,' she admitted. Her partner – in both senses – Simon was always trying to persuade her to 'big it up' a bit when talking to prospective clients.

'Anyhow,' she added 'your turn.'

Ben cradled his mug thoughtfully. 'The pub's been my local since I moved back here a couple of years ago. Plus, Patrick's a good bloke. As a matter of fact, I'm coming back to my roots. I've got friends from my childhood around here, so it feels like home. I probably worked my way through my most irritating teenage behaviour at the Havenbury Arms. It took a while and poor old Patrick was very tolerant – kind of a cross between a father and a cool uncle. Now I'm back because of the college.'

'You're a bit old to be a student, aren't you?'

'I'm thirty-two. Not too over the hill yet, I hope. Anyhow, I'm not a student; I'm a lecturer, if that makes it a bit better.'

'Sorry,' she said. 'I honestly don't mean to be rude. My

social skills seem to deteriorate a bit when I'm tired. What are you lecturing on?'

'Psychology.'

'So you're here, on the Havenbury Magna campus, then?'

'Yep, you?'

'Yes,' said Maddy. 'I was . . . business studies and marketing. Strange we didn't meet before.'

'Not really. If it was three years ago I was away in the army. Ships that pass in the night and all that. It's nice, the campus here,' he went on. 'Better than the main city one. Small.'

'That's what I liked about it too,' said Maddy. 'Horrible, grotty student halls, though.'

'They've gone. It must have been just after you left. Big chunk of funding. Knocked down. Rebuilt. Everyone gets their own en suite bathroom and everything, apparently. Although I haven't seen inside any of them myself,' he added hastily.

She was shocked. It was weird to think that the place she remembered, the one that featured in her nightmares, didn't exist any more. She should go and look – or maybe not.

She suddenly realised Ben was staring at her.

'So,' she said, giving herself a little shake, 'psychology, eh? Must be an interesting subject to teach.'

'It is, although I am sort of studying too. I'm here to write my doctorate, amongst other things.'

'Will I understand if you tell me what it's about?' said Maddy, intrigued.

'I'm sure you would, unless I am a very bad lecturer.' Ben laughed. 'I wouldn't presume to bore you with the details, but basically it continues the work I started when I was in the army – strategies for early interventions and management of post-traumatic stress disorder.'

'PTSD?'

'That's right. I'm looking at the efficacy of hypnosis in the resolution of dissociative amnesia, particularly.'

'Making people remember through hypnosis,' mused Maddy. She gave a convulsive shudder.

If Ben noticed he pretended not to, the same as he had decided not to notice Maddy's trembling when they were talking to Dennis earlier.

'Yes,' he continued, 'I developed an interest in the subject when I was on active service. I couldn't help feeling, looking after the mental health of my men, that some sort of immediate support on the ground would help reduce the number of men who find it difficult to come to terms with what they experience out there.'

'Your men?'

'I was a major in the army. You sort of feel responsible for the men because . . . erm . . . you are,' he admitted, rubbing his forehead. 'Anyway, enough of that now. Don't you need to open up?'

She checked her watch. 'I suppose so. God knows where the bar staff are. Has Patrick been running the place on his own?'

'There's a guy called Kevin.'

'Kevin Brown?'

'Rings a bell; not sure. Is he a friend of yours?'

'No!' she replied, turning away and busying herself straightening a bar towel that was already straight.

Chapter Two

The lunchtime session was busy. Lots of regulars had already heard about Patrick being taken ill and the ones that hadn't soon did. As well as serving the drinks in Kevin's absence – clearly he had decided a day off was in order – Maddy had to fend off questions that she didn't have the answers to. Asking her own questions as a form of self-defence, she learnt that, for several months, Patrick had been in the kitchen doing the food, leaving Kevin to run the bar pretty much single-handed.

She also discovered that Kevin didn't seem to have a large fan club, which was something she could relate to.

After having been woken by the phone call from the hospital at two that morning Maddy was exhausted. As a result she felt she probably hadn't been enthusiastic enough about greeting people who hadn't seen her for three years and appeared to be pleased to see her now. Trouble was, they all wanted to know what she had been up to since last being in Havenbury Magna. Worse, despite being much more recent, the drama of Patrick's illness was very nearly matched by the drama of Maddy's departure. People were plenty keen to wallow in both equally.

Being busy conveniently prevented her from engaging in

long conversations about awkward topics but there was no escaping her kindly tutor, Linda, who discreetly took her to one side when she was forced to leave the security of the bar to collect dirty glasses.

'Maddy, how are you? You've not kept in touch like you promised.'

She blushed. 'Hi, Linda. I know, I'm so sorry . . .'

'I'm so disappointed for you,' Linda went on. 'If you could just have filed your dissertation like we discussed at the time . . . your marks were so strong, even missing the final exams, you'd have scraped a Third at least.'

'I know, I know,' said Maddy, blushing. 'But that's life, eh.' She smiled brightly. 'Must just . . .' she added, and scooted back to the relative safety of the bar. If only she hadn't picked such a small, friendly campus. The very thing that made Havenbury Magna attractive to her and her anxious mother was her downfall now. Three years wasn't long enough for people to have forgotten. Not nearly.

The lunchtime customers had gone and, just as she was loading the last of the glasses into the dishwasher, she heard someone open the door.

'Closed, I'm afraid,' she called, without turning around.

'What, not even a cup of builder's tea?'

'Oh. You again.'

'Would you be more pleased to see me if I said I'm here to give you a lift to the hospital?' Ben asked.

'Not really, it's not as if I haven't got a car of my own. How do you think I got here?'

'You look done in.' Ignoring her rudeness, he took the damp cloth from her as she limped wearily around, giving the tables a wipe. 'You're obviously too tired to drive safely, and I was planning to go and see Patrick anyhow.'

'Oh, okay then.' Maddy sat down with relief and rubbed her ankle.

'Is that from kicking the bucket this morning?'

'Kicking the barrel, actually – the whole bucket thing means something else entirely – and isn't tactful either, under the circumstances.' Suddenly self-conscious she realised the ugly purple scar tracking down it was clearly visible. She pulled down her trouser leg and put her foot back on the floor, hoping he hadn't noticed.

He had.

'You've been in the wars. Got a metal plate in there, have you?'

She nodded sharply. Plus half a hardware store, she thought.

'It must have been bad to still be hurting so much. Looks like you did it a couple of years ago now.'

She wished he would shut up about it. 'Three, actually. Like I said – it's fine.'

'Okay,' he said, clearly deciding to let it rest. 'Shall we?'

Fancying he was more of a jeep man, Maddy was surprised when Ben led her to a dark-green MGB, old but clearly loved and cherished.

'It's my Achilles heel. I've got a Land Rover for most days. Truth be told I have to leave this little beauty at the end of the track to my cottage. The road is so rough it would rip her exhaust off, at the very least.'

'"Her"? Don't tell me – I bet "she" has a name too?'

'God no. That would actually be weird.'

'Tell me,' Ben said, once they were bowling along the main road, 'how did you hear Patrick was ill?'

'The hospital called me.' She remembered how her heart had crashed and leapt in her chest when the telephone in the bedroom shrilled into life. In the seconds she took to get to it, she lived a thousand lifetimes of horror. It would be her mother, she decided. Some hideous car accident. A coma. Or killed outright at the scene. Fumbling in the dark and dropping the receiver she feared she had disconnected the call, but when she answered a calmly efficient female voice had replied immediately.

'So, are you next of kin?' Ben asked.

'No. At least, I wouldn't have thought so. I don't know what relatives he has, apart from a very elderly sister in Pontefract. She wasn't well last time I heard and that was three years ago so possibly she's not even alive any more.'

She felt a pang of guilt that Patrick should have no one else to call than a so-called friend who had made no contact with him for years.

'He's sort of my honorary godfather,' she went on. 'That's what Mum told me, anyhow. An old friend of hers who I made contact with when I came here to college. He looked after me. That's all. Actually, no, more than that. We became good friends.'

Ben nodded, thoughtfully.

'But I can't be next of kin, can I?' she said, thinking that, really, she should tell her mum. That was a call she wasn't keen to make.

'In the medical context,' Ben explained, 'the patient can name anyone as next of kin. *In extremis* – and he must have been in a lot of pain – your name is obviously the one that popped into his mind.'

Her eyes filled with tears. He deserved a better next of kin than her. Come to think of it, clearly Ben was a better friend

21

to Patrick than she was. No wonder he was questioning her. He must be wondering why Patrick didn't name him, but if he was curious to know more he was discreet enough not to ask, at least for now.

He pulled into the road leading to the hospital.

'So, would you like me to drop you at the entrance or shall we stick together?'

'Let's stick together,' Maddy said quickly. 'I mean . . . I don't know where he'll be by now. We could be chasing around after each other . . .'

'Good point.' He gave her a reassuring smile.

Patrick had been moved to the cardiac ward to Maddy's relief. He had spent too long on a trolley in a bay of the accident and emergency department when she saw him that morning, grey and exhausted after being in pain all night.

When they got there, he was asleep, alone in a little side ward of four beds.

'Are you family?' asked an Irish nurse as they stood together looking through the glass and wondering whether to go in.

'Pretty much,' replied Maddy. 'I'm his god-daughter.'

'And you must be his son-in-law, then.' She turned to Ben.

'Godson-in-law, if anything,' Ben said. 'Actually, we're not – you know – together,' he added apologetically, cocking his head in Maddy's direction.

'Oh right, I'm sorry. Anyhow, if you're family,' she returned her attention to Maddy, 'you might want to have a word with the doctor who is looking after your father.'

Maddy shot a warning look at Ben, defying him to put her right, but he kept a straight, concerned face. 'That would be great,' she said.

'Not you,' said the nurse to Ben over her shoulder, grabbing Maddy by the arm and carting her off.

When she came out again, Patrick was awake and laughing at a comment from Ben, who was sitting, relaxed, on the nearest empty bed.

'Maddy, my darling,' he said, reaching to pull her in for a kiss. She saw him afresh, this afternoon, less horrifically grey than the night before but distinctly older than she remembered. Although still handsome, the lines on his face were deeper; his hair, still thick and swept back from his face, was now almost entirely white. She gave him a bear hug, alarmed to be able to feel his broad shoulders were bony.

'You're looking better,' she said brightly when she came up for air.

'I'm feeling it,' he replied, too jauntily. 'I can't say I approve of that bossy ward sister insisting you come all the way down here,' he added. 'What a fuss . . . and I suppose now that doctor has been wringing every ounce of drama out of the whole sorry episode . . .'

'That "sorry episode" was a heart attack,' she said reprovingly. 'It's no good, Patrick, the truth is you do need me down here. The doctor says you will need surgery and then several weeks to recuperate.'

'No time for that. That bloody oik Dennis has been all over the place like a rash recently.'

Ben and Maddy looked at each other, tacitly agreeing to keep his visit to the bar that morning to themselves.

'Yep,' Patrick continued, looking at the back of his hands, 'obviously I have to suck up to the little creep a bit because my lease is coming up for renewal . . . We've not been getting on too well . . .'

'Why?' Maddy probed gently. 'Other than him being an obnoxious little runt, obviously.'

He gave her the ghost of a smile and then looked away. 'Can't say we've been making the income,' he admitted. 'Working my bloody socks off but the dosh just isn't there and Top Taverns would bloody love to put my rent up. Probably can't justify it on the current figures so he's been hinting at finding a new tenant. Damned cheek.' He looked bleak. 'What I suspect they really want to do is get change of use to residential and sell the place as a renovation project – it's a big, valuable property.'

Maddy noticed, with concern, that some of his grey pallor had returned.

'Not a problem,' she assured him. 'I'll see what I can do, as long as you promise to stay in here and do exactly what the doctors tell you.'

'I'm sorry to drag you back here, Maddy. I know it's not exactly . . . I can't imagine you would have chosen to come.'

'Of course I chose to come,' she insisted, refusing to meet Ben's curious eye. 'I'm only sorry I've not been back to see you more,' she said, both of them knowing she hadn't been back at all. 'I would have, but setting up the business, work, you know . . . I've been really busy.'

'And now all that will be neglected while you sort out the self-inflicted problems of a daft old bugger like me,' observed Patrick sadly.

By the time Ben had dropped Maddy back at the bar there was no time to call home and catch up with Simon. Instead, she set herself the task of seeing how much cleaning she could get done before the customers appeared. After setting light to the fire laid in the inglenook fireplace, she took a bowl of hot soapy water and a cloth, working meticulously around the bar, damp-dusting the spokes of the chairs, the windowsills, shelves and tops of picture frames. The water was quickly transformed into a murky grey soup. Maddy got the public bar finished and was just turning her attention to the saloon bar when the door creaked open and a skinny figure slunk in out of the growing gloom.

'Kevin – how nice of you to join us,' said Maddy, hoping her acerbic manner would hide the nervous wobble in her voice.

'Yo,' he said, not meeting her eye. 'It's you,' he elaborated, on reflection.

'I take it you are here to work a shift this evening,' she continued. 'I was expecting you at lunchtime.'

'Busy,' he muttered.

She waited for further enlightenment but there was none forthcoming.

He sullenly began pulling tonic bottles out of a crate and loading them onto the shelf. Surprisingly, she noted, her nervousness at seeing him again was easy to change into irritation on Patrick's behalf. Irritation was a lot easier to deal with.

'Would you like to know how Patrick is?'

Kevin shrugged. If he hadn't then redeemed himself by looking up and waiting for her to tell him she was sure she would have slapped him.

'He's a bit better but he's going to need an operation – open-heart surgery – and then several weeks to recover.'

'You stopping here, then?' he asked, a glimmer of interest in his eye, along with a hint of – what was it? Threat? Triumph?

'I . . .' Maddy paused. Weeks? Could she really be away

from Simon and the business for that long? 'Yes,' she said at last. 'I'll be here for as long as he needs me.'

Kevin shrugged again and disappeared out the back to check the barrels.

Even with Kevin in the bar, Maddy found herself working at full stretch all night. The customers were understanding about her having closed the kitchen, especially as she promised to get it open again as soon as she could. A couple of the groups of lads brought fish and chips from the shop on the corner and were happy to eat them out of the paper while they drank their pints. Maddy was pleased not to lose the custom. The pub would not survive long without the bar takings of those coming in primarily to eat. That said, she was impressed at the amount of business for a Thursday night, although the after-work drinkers were largely gone by ten o'clock, giving Kevin and Maddy a chance to collect up the glasses and restock the shelves. By the time the bar closed there wasn't a lot to do, other than wipe tables – again – and put the chairs up ready for hoovering the carpet the following day.

Maddy was keen to be released from Kevin's mildly malevolent presence, which seemed more oppressive now the customers had all gone. She found she was painfully aware of where he was at all times and was unaccountably nervous of having her back to him.

'I'll cash up,' she said.

'No!' he blurted. 'I'll do it.' He flushed, his eyes flashing with what looked like anger. Or fear.

She blinked in surprise. 'I am simply offering because I imagine you would like to get off home,' she replied levelly.

'It's my job,' he said, going even redder in the face. 'It's my responsibility. You're not my boss.'

'No, okay,' said Maddy, her heart pounding. 'You do it, then. I'll just, er, – you'll lock up, will you?'

He nodded curtly, dismissing her.

Maddy trailed up the stairs to Patrick's flat. It was nearly midnight. Less than twenty-four hours since she received the call from the hospital but it felt like weeks.

Oh Lord, her mother! She should have given her a call.

First thing tomorrow without fail, she decided. As far as she knew Patrick and Helen had not seen each other at all for donkey's years, but telling her felt important.

Her little hastily packed rucksack was in the narrow upstairs hallway with her rolled-up sleeping bag. Thank goodness she had brought it, being far too tired for digging out clean sheets and making up a bed. That was even assuming Patrick's housekeeping standards ran to clean bedding. She poked her head around the door of the spare room where she had occasionally slept as a student when Patrick had fussed about her travelling back to her digs after a shift.

It was even more filled with random junk than she remembered but, after she had removed a pile of old vinyl records and – intriguingly – a ventriloquist's dummy in an evening suit, she uncovered a narrow single bed with a bare mattress. Fetching a feather cushion from the dusty old sofa for a pillow, Maddy barely managed to wash her face and give her teeth a glimpse of her toothbrush before falling into her makeshift bed.

Irritatingly, she then lay there, aching with fatigue and staring at the ceiling through the dark. Rather than counting sheep, she found herself counting all the things that she felt guilty about: there was her failure to visit Patrick since she left – obviously a really big guilt trip that one – right down to not yet calling her mother and deciding against checking her emails, even though she just knew the inbox would be filled with work messages, waiting for her efficient, professional response; all her worries spiralled endlessly in her head, her eyes fluttering shut despite herself, dragging her down into sleep like a drowning woman.

Consciousness returned in flashes, like a strobe light slicing through the darkness. Moments of awareness, shot through with a nameless terror. The rusty taste of the oily liquid running down her face into her mouth. Blood. She stared into the blackness, waiting for help – or for her attacker to return. Her mind nagged her about the paralysing cold, telling her to escape it or die. She groaned, moved and all other sensations were consumed by a new one.
    Pain.

Maddy woke with a start, feeling the bed shaking beneath her from the aftershock. She groaned. The dream was back, in all its intensity and horror, just like she had never been away. She quickly drifted off again but – within minutes – was fighting her way up into consciousness out of a spiralling dream where the dark, the journey there and the evening in the pub combined to create a cycle of anxiety and panic where she was desperate to reach Patrick but there were barriers in her way. Kevin's angry face suddenly confronting her in her dream jerked her eventually into grateful wakefulness, and she sat up, to shake off the last of the nightmare, checking her watch, before lying down again and floating off on a tide of exhaustion.

CHAPTER THREE

When Maddy woke again it was dawn. She took several seconds to remember where she was. As she stared around the gloomy little room, the previous day came back to her.

Summoning courage and what energy she could muster, she dealt with the most pressing task first.

'Mum?' she said, clutching the receiver of the old-fashioned bar phone too tight and winding the cord around her fingers.

'Darling, how lovely,' said Helen, who was whisking around her little house, phone in hand, gathering up her yoga kit. 'You don't usually call at this time of day. Everything alright?'

'Yeah, yeah, fine. I'm in Havenbury Magna, oddly enough,' she said lightly.

Helen dropped her gym bag and straightened, the phone now clamped to her ear. 'You are? What brought that on?'

'I had a call.' She took a deep breath. 'It's Patrick.'

There was a silence.

'Tell me.' The words came out in a little gasp, like the breath had suddenly left Helen's body. She sagged down onto the little sofa.

'He . . .' Maddy's eyes filled with tears again. 'He had a heart attack.' The last word came out with a sob attached. She wiped her eyes and took a deep breath.

'Mum?'

Helen was still silent.

'He's alive. He's in hospital. Talking, and everything . . .'

Helen breathed out at last, swaying slightly. 'He's nothing but trouble, that man,' she said angrily.

'They say he needs an operation. A bypass. Valve replacement. He's been lucky. They caught it just in time . . .'

'It's his lifestyle,' snapped Helen. 'It's his own silly fault. He's always smoked and drunk too much.'

'Not now, though, Mum,' protested Maddy. 'When I was doing my degree I never saw him smoke . . .'

'Really? It's the sins of the past, then. No sympathy required. Anyway, why did they call you?' she added, working herself up from anger to indignation. 'Being down there again, with all that stuff before. It's the last thing you need. It's selfish. He's got no right . . .'

After the call, Helen sat, unmoving, on the sofa in the pretty little red-brick terraced house – just twelve feet wide – with its tiny fireplace in the sitting room and a table just big enough for two in the kitchen, where she and little Maddy had made cupcakes when it was too wet to go out. All thoughts of her yoga class were forgotten. She stared sightlessly at her carefully tended garden, the sunny, brick-paved terrace, the generously planted pots, the honeysuckle billowing from the old garden wall, meeting and twining around the pearl-white climbing rose she chose because it had her daughter's name.

And now, after more than twenty years, she gave herself

over to remembering: the anger and hurt she had felt so passionately as a younger woman; the years of protective isolation, turning in on herself, working, saving, raising her child in the safe, predictable world she had created, followed by that tentative rapprochement some six years ago now . . . Then – of course – there was the further, unforgivable failure and betrayal when he hurt her again via the most precious thing in her world – her daughter.

'Nothing but trouble, that man,' she said again, into the silence.

As always, Maddy felt better after she had spoken to her mother. In contrast, she was pretty sure she would feel worse if she spoke to Simon. Which is why she didn't. Instead, she decided to finish cleaning the bar and get to grips with the catering. Then, when she visited Patrick later, she could give him a positive report.

With the kitchen shut, she hadn't bothered to eat the previous evening. As a matter of fact she couldn't remember eating at all the previous day, which probably did as much to explain the churning stomach as the familiar and unwelcome anxieties that were surfacing unbidden.

After a brief shower – the bathroom was none too appealing – she made a proper inspection of the kitchen. Things were not great. However, unlike the flat upstairs, the place was clean with stainless steel worktops scrubbed and clear.

It was no surprise. Patrick was uncompromising about food safety and had a cordial relationship with the food hygiene officer who always seemed to go away with a bacon sandwich and a smile on his face. Beyond that though, she was surprised at how chaotic it was. The cold store was stuffed full of vegetables but the order quantities seemed odd. There were piles of leeks but hardly any carrots or broccoli, the staples of the fresh vegetables he served with most of his dishes. By the looks of it the butcher hadn't delivered the day before, or perhaps he had tried and found the pub unstaffed like the drayman had. Examining the freezer, she found several catering packets of peas – clearly Patrick had some anxiety about running out – but there was little else other than some unidentifiable packets of food of which only he knew the exact provenance.

She scratched her head. What could she possibly order in that would pull this lot together?

An even bigger concern was that there were several unpaid supplier invoices pinned to the noticeboard on the back of the kitchen door. One was from her old friends, the local bakery, who usually supplied tarts and cheesecakes, which she also noticed were not in stock. Patrick was clearly not giving her the whole story even now. And yet the bar was teeming the previous night. Surely they were turning over a reasonable amount?

Next she went to the safe at the back of the storeroom to see if a trip to the bank with the takings was in order. It struck her that the combination might have changed after all this time, but the dial turned sweetly, and clunked open, just as it always had. She wondered how many other people were able to wander in and open it. Inside was the cash box with the float, the bundle of takings and the till rolls. Checking the till roll from the previous night, she noticed a rather smaller figure than she might have expected on the total, but what did she know? It had been such a long time, she probably felt as rushed as she had because she was out of practice, not because the bar was doing that well.

Stifling her misgivings for the time being, she got on with the bar cleaning with an eye on the clock. Without Patrick around she was assuming none of the usual suppliers had had orders placed. She would need to go shopping if she was going to be able to serve food this lunchtime.

Tying her hair back in a scarf to hide the fact it could do with a wash, she grabbed a basket and headed out. Luckily it was Saturday, which – every other week – was market day. That meant the steep main street through Havenbury Magna was closed to traffic and was given over to the market stalls of local farmers and small-scale food suppliers.

The heady scent of freshly baked bread drew her to the baker's stall.

'Those look fabulous,' she breathed, trying not to dribble as she talked, admiring a heap of fresh pains au chocolat and almond croissants.

'They are,' said the handsome, ruddy-faced baker. 'Here you go, if I can persuade you?' he added, passing her a plate of pastry samples.

'Not enough,' she admitted, picking up a whole almond croissant instead. With just a black coffee for breakfast her stomach was now groaning with deprivation.

Breaking off large pieces of the croissant and stuffing it into her mouth, she regarded the piles of fresh loaves and pies. 'I'll have six of those big rustic rye loaves,' she said through a mouthful of pastry. 'And a dozen pasties – actually, make that twenty.'

'You *are* a hungry girl this morning,' he joked. 'Where do you put it all?' he added, giving her an admiring survey from head to foot.

'Got a bit of a catering problem,' she grinned in reply. 'Need to offer lunch at the pub.'

'You're trade, then,' said the young man. 'That gets you a discount.' He tapped on a calculator and mentioned a sum that Maddy knew she could turn a decent profit on. She counted out the notes she had stuffed into her jeans pocket and handed them over gratefully.

'Here's my card.' He popped it into her basket. 'Always happy to supply the local trade. I'll get my lad to take the stuff around to you. The Havenbury Arms? Fine . . . be in the next half hour at the most, if that's alright?'

Maddy nodded, smiling as she licked the sugar off her fingers.

'You're from Pandora's Pantry,' she said, glancing at the card. It was the little delicatessen at the bottom of the high street. As a student she hadn't been in there much because the food was delicious but expensive.

'I am!' He held out his hand. 'Brendan.'

'Maddy.' She wiped her sticky hand on her jeans before reciprocating. 'I didn't realise you did the market as well. Is this all from your usual supplier?' she asked, waving her hand at all the tantalising breads and pies.

Brendan looked shy. 'Well, in a manner of speaking, yes.' He paused. 'I've actually started doing a bit of baking myself . . .'

'This is you?' she exclaimed through the last mouthful of croissant. She rolled her eyes in appreciation. 'They're amazing. You're amazing. When on earth do you find time to bake?'

'At night. Before market day it's pretty much *all* night. I'm a bit glad it's only once a fortnight. Keeps me out of

34

trouble on a Friday evening, though, I suppose . . .'

'I'm impressed. And I love the local angle too. I'm going to make sure everyone knows their pasties are freshly baked a hundred yards away from where they're eating them.'

'Thanks,' said Brendan, blushing. 'One for the road,' he added, deftly popping another croissant in a bag and twirling the corners closed before dropping it into her basket on top of the card. 'You look like you need feeding up.'

After that, glancing at her watch anxiously, Maddy quickly snapped up a big chunk of locally produced cheddar, several vines of wonderful-smelling tomatoes and some locally home-made chutney.

Back at the pub she grabbed a wet cloth to clean off the food menu on the boards. There were ten starters and a similar number of main courses with a whole blackboard dedicated to the puddings, but Maddy had other ideas. It was a struggle to find some chalk but eventually she found a couple of little stubs in a kitchen drawer. Writing quickly she replaced the pub food with her simple lunchtime menu. All fresh, local food, just soup, pasties and a ploughman's with the cheddar, which was the best she had ever tasted. She planned to serve it with the rye bread, tomatoes and chutney. As an afterthought she scribbled a single extra word: 'Chips'.

Her ankle was aching even more than yesterday. She couldn't remember having had to spend quite so much time on her feet since she left for London. Her job, other than travelling to client meetings, generally involved poring over a hot computer, putting together web-marketing proposals. When she explained her job to her friends she knew it sounded boring, but she loved what she did and her sheer enthusiasm was why Simon always sent her out as the 'frontman'.

She was surprised Simon hadn't called, and then it occurred to her it had been a while since she saw her phone.

No time to call him now but she made a solemn vow that – whatever the other priorities – she would sit down with her laptop and go through the business queries just as soon as she finished the lunchtime session.

Market day meant that trade was brisk in the bar. Beautiful blue skies had chilled the air, and people came in rubbing their hands together, praising the autumn sunshine.

The ploughman's and pasties sold as well as she had hoped and she was flattered her leek and potato soup was popular too. She had to concede it was probably more to do with the first real cold snap of the autumn than her – hardly Michelin-starred – cooking. She was relieved no one had objected to her removing the extended menu Patrick had been offering, although the sweet, skinny girl who had been selling handmade jewellery in the market was pining for treacle tart.

'I'll make you some for tomorrow – promise,' Maddy reassured her as she settled for a big plate of chips instead. It hardly seemed fair the girl was so thin, but she was too nice to resent, Maddy decided.

She was relieved when she called last orders. Her ankle badly needed her to spend an hour or two sitting down. She was just collecting glasses from the emptying tables when Ben came in.

'Am I too late for lunch?' he asked.

''Fraid so,' she said, more unkindly than she meant, as she tried not to limp on the way back to the bar. 'That is, the soup's all gone,' she added, forcing herself to feel more generous, 'but I could do you a ploughman's?'

'That'd be great. And a pint of bitter, if you would.'

Once she had got him settled at the bar with his pint and food she decided to try really hard to be polite.

'Thanks for the lift to see Patrick yesterday,' she began. 'I'm fine for this afternoon, though.'

'Glad to hear it, because I've got tutorials and a lecture this afternoon.'

'Yeah, I'm really busy this afternoon as well,' she replied, feeling silly.

'I thought I might pop in and see how he's doing this evening, though.'

'I wish I could come with you, but I'd better not leave Kevin on his own.'

'No,' agreed Ben, 'I don't think I'd want to either. Tell you what, I'll pop in afterwards and let you know how he is.'

'I thought you'd died,' snapped Simon, picking up the phone on the first ring.

'I'm fine thanks – how are you?'

'Sorry,' said Simon, not sounding it. 'How is the old guy?'

Maddy explained about the forthcoming surgery. 'They say he's not well enough at the moment, but they hope to do it at some point in the next few days.'

'How long do you reckon you'll be there?'

'Assuming he gets the surgery in the next week or so, he'll definitely need at least six weeks recovery time,' she said. 'Minimum.'

'How the hell are we going to manage that?' he replied, his voice rising to a querulous pitch. 'We've got two pitch meetings next week and I don't even have the proposal from you for Adams and Quinn. You do realise we weren't the only ones who pitched?'

'I'll do it,' she promised. 'I'll email it to you by tomorrow morning.' So much for catching up on her sleep.

Caught up in student tutorials for longer than he'd intended, Ben arrived at the hospital just ten minutes before visiting time ended.

Patrick was in bed, his head turned away from the door, staring bleakly out of the window.

'Ben!' he said, with relief. 'Damned decent of you to come.'

The men fell easily into chatter about nothing in particular as they always did, but Ben was watching his friend carefully.

'So,' he said, 'it's been a pleasure to meet Maddy. I'm a bit surprised I haven't met her before . . .'

'Ah yes.' Patrick sighed heavily. 'That.' He paused. 'I don't know what possessed me to give them her details as next of kin. Poor girl, being called in the middle of the night and dragged down here to sit about in hospital looking at me lying around the place moaning and groaning for hours on end. What a massive bore for her.'

Ben waited.

'Plus, of course,' Patrick went on, 'I was quite wrong to ask her to come back here.'

'Because?'

'Because she left here three years ago with no intention of coming back at all. And I don't blame her one bit for it, although I must admit I've missed her. There, I've said it. I miss her, and I suppose that's why she popped into my mind that night. And her mother, of course. Although even I wouldn't be mad or deluded enough to ask *her* to come,' he snorted, with a mirthless laugh.

'It's quite natural that you should think of people who are important to you,' Ben said. 'Interesting that you thought of Maddy, though . . . and touching that she came. She's clearly a friend you ought to feel you can rely on.'

'Spare me the psychology-speak,' said Patrick. 'I knew you as a spotty teenager, remember?' He gave Ben an appraising look. 'Get you now, though. So assured and full of yourself. Who'd have thought? All you were interested in when I first knew you was how to get drunk and then persuade girls to kiss you.'

'Not a good combination, as I learnt,' agreed Ben. 'And – I tell you what – psychology gave me a useful insight into the subject. I'm a damned sight better at getting girls to kiss me now.'

'I bet you bloody are,' said Patrick. 'You turned out alright in the end.'

'I had good guidance at a critical age,' acknowledged Ben with a smile. 'Anyway, back to Maddy. Whether you should have called her or not she's here now, and I can't see you getting rid of her for a while. Not until she can see you up on your feet. When I left her she was organising herself to stay for a few weeks.'

'Weeks? She can't. That'll kill her.' He plucked at the sheets agitatedly, and his breathing quickened.

'What can I do to help?' Ben asked, gently.

Patrick looked at him, then looked away. 'Actually,' he said, looking back, with a glimmer of hope in his eyes, 'maybe you *can* help her. As a matter of fact you might be the only person I know who can . . .'

'I'll try,' said Ben. 'What happened to make her leave? Is it something to do with the injury to her leg?'

'You don't miss much, do you? You'll need to ask her that.'

'That won't be easy. She seems pretty spiky.'

'Yep. Just like her mother.'

'So, I'm not sure she'll welcome my interventions.'

The older man's face fell. 'Absolutely, old chap, no right to ask . . .'

'No, no, listen . . . I'll try,' said Ben, putting his hand on Patrick's shoulder, thinking that – from what he had seen of Maddy so far – there was a good chance he was making a promise he couldn't keep.

By the time the bar started to fill in the evening, Maddy's tiredness receded with the effort of keeping busy. Kevin had made another mystery disappearance, so she had no choice but to keep the kitchen closed. By nine o'clock the bar was seething and the noise levels had reached a peak, the laughing and chatting blending to form a wall of sound, set to the backbeat of the jukebox. Maddy smiled, joked, pulled pints and whisked up and down the bar, restocking shelves and collecting glasses whenever she could grab a minute.

The students were an entirely new set from the ones Maddy had studied with, but the locals, the younger ones at least, recognised a familiar face and greeted her with casual warmth. Several of the men smiled encouragingly and offered to buy her drinks. She declined with friendly grace, sipping occasionally from a tall glass of iced water she kept by the till. The heat from the lights and the crush of all the bodies had raised the temperature to midsummer heights despite the chilly autumn night outside, and the plate-glass windows at the front ran with condensation. Maddy felt a cooling blast of air from the doorway up her back as she leant to collect a stack of glasses on a table. She leant into it gratefully and found herself pressed up against a long, hard body.

'Oops, sorry,' she smiled, turning to apologise.

'My fault entirely,' said Ben, steadying her with his hands on her shoulders as she started away in alarm. 'Wasn't looking where I was going.'

'Did you see Patrick?' she asked, allowing him to take one of the stacks of glasses from her and heading back to the bar through the throngs of people.

'He sent his love,' said Ben. 'Told me he was bored, too.'

'He must be feeling better then,' she said, loading the glasses into the machine.

'I could do with a pint.'

She drew one, uncomfortably aware he was watching her closely while she did it.

'What will you have?' he asked, passing her a tenner.

'I won't. That is, not when I'm working, thank you.'

'You don't ever drink when you're working?' he queried mildly. 'One wouldn't hurt, surely? Help you relax?' He didn't add that she seemed on edge.

'I don't like . . . not when I'm . . .' She wanted to say 'feeling vulnerable' but stopped herself.

He nodded slowly, as if he was coming to a conclusion about something.

Thankfully, customers left promptly after she called time. She remembered having to prise out reluctant homegoers with a crowbar in the past, as they tried to make their last pints last for ever as an excuse to keep the night going. Now, though, the bar emptied rapidly; the drinkers who hadn't already left for home were now keen to head off to the Sails nightclub at the bottom of town on the quay, where the bar stayed open until two in the morning at the weekends. Patrick had talked gloomily of the demise of the pub when the nightclub owner – a huge, handsome Irishman called Jonno McGrath, a formidable figure with his shaven head and his tattoos – had finally succeeded in getting his late-opening licence, but soon discovered that drinkers in the little town were still keen to start the night in the pub, moving on to the nightclub only when he had closed his doors for the night.

Soon Maddy was ushering out the last drinkers and closing the door against the increasing chill. Collecting yet more glasses on the way back to the bar she was relieved and pleased to see Ben was still perched at the end of the bar.

'Tea?' he asked.

'Bit too busy to make you tea.'

'I meant for you, seeing as you don't drink on duty.'

'You're mighty fascinated by my drinking habits. But yes, a cup of tea would be very nice. Thank you.'

She whisked around collecting glasses and wiping tables, finishing just as he came back with two steaming mugs.

'I'll do that,' he said, as she started to haul the chairs onto the tables, ready for hoovering the next morning. Maddy looked at him for a long moment, deciding whether to refuse. He gazed calmly back, an amused smile pulling up the corner of his mouth.

'Okay,' she said, shrugging. 'Thanks.'

Taking a swift gulp of tea, which was so wonderfully hot and strong she nearly moaned with gratitude, Maddy got ready to do the till.

The task was absorbing but mechanical. Quickly, she totalled up the float, bagged the notes and reconciled the takings with the till roll. Breathing a sigh of relief that the two tallied, she bundled it all up and shoved it in the safe. This time, the busy night had delivered some pretty healthy takings. She was puzzled anew at Patrick's insistence that Dennis wanted higher turnover so he could put up the rent.

By the time she finished, Ben had positioned himself back on the other side of the bar, where he sat quietly watching her.

Thinking she ought to make conversation, she blurted out the first thing that came into her head.

'You know that hypnotism thing?'

He nodded.

'Could you, like, make me do a "chicken laying an egg" impersonation, then?'

He considered her question more carefully than it merited. 'If you were – for some reason best known to yourself – secretly desperate to imitate a chicken, I could probably disinhibit you enough, using hypnosis, to allow you to do it.'

Maddy nodded, not meeting his eye.

'So, are you capable of doing anything a bit more useful?'

'I think I could probably help you,' he said carefully, cradling his tea in his hands.

She noticed he had long, lean fingers. Like a piano player.

'You did help,' she said, waving at the chairs.

'I mean with your drink problem.'

She gasped. 'I am *not* an alcoholic.'

'Didn't say you were,' he replied with irritating calm. 'What I actually said is I could help you with your "drink problem", by which I mean the difficulty that makes you too scared to drink in certain circumstances. When you're nervous. On your guard.'

'I didn't say that.'

'Didn't need to,' replied Ben. 'I'm guessing it's a fear of losing control.'

She glared at him, refusing to answer.

'Tell me what happened to you, Maddy,' he said quietly, his eyes not moving from her face.

'It's none of your business.'

'I can help.'

'No. You can't.'

'It's tempting to try and forget traumatic events,' he said, watching his hands now, but glancing up to see if he had her attention. 'That would be the easy way.' His voice was slow, soothing and low.

Despite herself, Maddy leant in, listening.

'But the trouble is,' he continued, 'in the long run, denying things have happened doesn't work. When trauma happens to us it messes with our sense of order. How the world should work. The unprocessed memories just eat away at you from the inside, you know – they can be a very powerful force.'

'Yeah? Lucky I don't have any, then.'

She marched purposefully to the door.

'Any what?'

'Any memories of it,' she replied, holding open the door and gesturing for him to leave.

He stood, with his head on one side, considering, and then he nodded as he strolled towards the door.

'Bear it in mind, Maddy,' he said, putting a warm hand on her shoulder. 'I could help – if you'll let me.'

*   *   *

Driving back home along the track by the river, Ben was preoccupied. As he had already suspected, keeping his promise to Patrick wasn't going to be easy. He knew that look: the vigilance, anxiety, fierce defensiveness. Initially he thought the fear and anger she exhibited when they first met was down to seeing Dennis. He could quite imagine the obnoxious little man could have that effect on people. And then, of course, there was her distress at Patrick being ill. But, with those few leading questions – and she hadn't liked them at all – his suspicions were confirmed. It was more than any problem Top Taverns could push her way. 'Something' had happened to her – 'something' very bad indeed . . . and then her accidental disclosure that she had damaged memories of whatever this traumatic event was? Now that was interesting . . .

He sighed as he parked his car and got out, swinging the keys in his hand absent-mindedly. She was turning in on herself. Doubtless she thought she could deal with it that way. Alone. Trouble was, he'd seen someone do that before. Someone he loved.

It hadn't ended well.

CHAPTER FOUR

Next morning Maddy was in the kitchen when she heard the door of the bar open and checked her watch. Only half past ten. What a pain. She would send whoever it was away until opening time.

'Mads!' shrieked a voice. 'It's true, you *are* here. Ohmigod it's so good to see you!'

Maddy had a vague impression of multicoloured rags topped with something exceptionally hairy swooping towards her and enveloping her in a giant, animal-smelling hug.

'Bleurgh,' she muttered, spitting out white, stringy hair. 'Blimey, Flora, what the hell are you wearing?'

'Mads!' Flora exclaimed again, holding Maddy's face firmly between her hands and giving her a smacking kiss on the mouth. 'It's so completely fantastic to see you!'

'You too, Flora, but good grief, what is it with the dead goat?'

'My jerkin?' she asked, smoothing it proudly. 'Local sheepskin, actually, straight from the South Downs and lovingly handcrafted by Jez in the unit next to mine.'

'Er, lovely,' Maddy muttered doubtfully. 'Not so "straight from South Downs" they forgot to kill it first, I hope?'

'God no; don't you like it?'

'It's distinctive,' said Maddy, 'although now you mention it, I can tell it's dead by the smell.'

'Same old Mads,' said Flora happily. 'Whatcha doing?' she added, peering at the pile of icy lumps Maddy was hauling out of the freezer.

'Disposing of unwanted UFOs.'

'You what?'

'Unidentified Frozen Objects,' she elucidated. 'I need to sort out the menus and, frankly, I can't use a lot of this because I don't know what it is and how long it's been here.'

'Hmm. I see your problem,' agreed Flora. 'I'm pretty sure this is fish pie.' She poked one cling-film-wrapped parcel. 'Or possibly apple crumble.'

'Quite,' agreed Maddy, taking it from her and lobbing it into the dustbin on the other side of the kitchen. 'She shoots, she scores,' she cried, making crowd-cheering noises. 'So, how's everyone?'

'Fine,' Flora replied. 'We've all missed you, of course, taking off like that, without warning.' A frisson of criticism fizzled and then faded. Flora gave Maddy a twisted smile. 'It was all crap,' she admitted. 'A mess. But I'm glad you're back.'

They both stared into space, remembering.

'I'm sorry . . .' they both blurted, simultaneously, and then laughed.

'*I'm* sorry,' said Maddy, 'that I didn't respond to your texts when I went to London.' She looked at Flora, appalled and remorseful to see the girl's chin wobble at the memory. 'It was unforgivable. But I just needed to separate myself completely from . . . everything here.'

She looked at Flora with pleading eyes, willing her to understand.

'I'm sorry too,' said Flora at last, twisting a beaded plait distractedly. 'I'm sorry it happened and I'm sorry you felt you couldn't stay. If I could have done something . . . I didn't realise . . .' she trailed off. 'You didn't even say you were going to leave,' she added, her voice filled with betrayal and regret.

Maddy rushed over and gathered her friend into a hug again.

'I'm so sorry,' she said, into Flora's sheepskin jacket. 'It wasn't your fault. There was nothing. Nothing you could have done differently. Honest. But I didn't mean for you to get hurt as well.'

They clung together, until Maddy eventually leant back and looked Flora in the face.

'Are we good?'

Flora nodded. ''Course.' She summoned a wobbly grin. 'Just don't go again, okay?'

Maddy couldn't answer. She knew she would, but this time she would do it right.

'Things to do,' she went on briskly after a moment. She got up, chucking the last few frozen parcels into the bin, saving only the several bags of frozen peas.

'Soup,' she explained economically. 'Talk to me while I cook? Make us a cup of tea and tell me the news.'

While Flora was filling her in, she quickly diced a bag of onions and a couple of pounds of potatoes into a big pan. After frying them gently in butter she poured in all the bags of frozen peas and added several pints of milk and some stock cubes.

While it was coming to the boil, she chucked yesterday's

French bread into the blender and whizzed it into breadcrumbs.

'Wow,' said Flora, as she watched her friend giving the soup an occasional stir whilst deftly putting together a batch of shortcrust pastry. 'You're cooking. I'd forgotten that.'

Maddy blushed. 'It's nothing complicated. Just pea soup for lunch. And treacle tart too. I promised someone.'

'I'll definitely be having a bit.' Flora's mouth watered as Maddy poured golden syrup from a huge catering-size tin into a large saucepan, adding lemon juice and a pinch of dried ginger.

'So, what's been going on here since I left? Bit of a big question, obviously.'

'How long's it been?' asked Flora. 'Must be three years? You know me and Will got together?'

Maddy nodded, checking the soup and adding double cream. 'We split up.'

'I'm sorry to hear it.'

'Yeah, well . . .' she said cheerfully. 'You know how it goes. Anyhow, me and Freddie started seeing each other.'

'Cool,' said Maddy, not actually remembering who Freddie was. 'He's nice?' she hazarded.

'He is!' said Flora warmly. 'Anyhow, that's all finished now. And then there was Steve, of course.'

'Still with Steve?' Maddy queried, but Flora shook her head. 'Oh, okay,' said Maddy, beginning to get dizzy with the effort of keeping track. 'So,' she said, worried how long this tale might take, 'who are you with now?'

'Lovely Jez,' sighed Flora.

'Jez the dead sheep guy?'

'That's the one,' she agreed happily, drawing her shaggy waistcoat more closely around her. 'You should come and see what we're all doing. There's a real buzz, you know.'

'At the farm?'

'Yes, although the farm's completely gone now. First they let us have the farm buildings, then they got rid of the dairy herd altogether. They've sold the farmhouse now, to a rich couple from London. We thought they'd chuck us out, but they didn't. They're quite nice, actually. The husband, Giles, works in London and stays up there quite often, so his wife, Serena, has to look after all his rare-breed pigs. She's really posh, all blonde and glamorous, but she swears a lot.'

While Maddy heard all about the blonde, manicured posh bird tiptoeing around in her bright pink Hunter wellies having to feed the pigs, and how the two boys Josh and Harry, both at boarding school, brought their mates to stay in the holidays, she blended the soup and put together the treacle tart. With more of the cheese from the market for ploughman's lunches again, and Brendan's pasties, which were selling really well, the menu was still short and simple. After just a few days of serving freshly made, simple food, she was gratified to see the number of lunch covers already rising every day. It would give her something positive to tell Patrick when she saw him next.

'You should come and see us after lunch,' Flora was saying. 'We've got a guy making shoes, a muralist, potter, everything. It's a really good vibe. We all muck in together.'

'I will,' decided Maddy, shoving her guilt at the work proposals and emails right down into the back of her mind. 'It does sound absolutely brilliant. I can't stay long, though.'

Flora nodded, distracted, as Maddy slid a slice of warm treacle tart onto a plate and handed it to her with a jug of thick, double cream.

'Enjoy,' said Maddy. 'I've got to open up.'

Flora was in no hurry to leave. After she had polished off her tart she ensconced herself in the window seat near Pirate, who responded by dipping his head coyly and trying to climb onto her shoulder. She watched Maddy hungrily as she whisked around. Eternally sweet and optimistic in nature, Flora reminded Maddy of a dog that wags its tail at a cruel master. With the disappearing trick she had pulled, she wondered who was the cruel master and thought – guiltily – it might be her.

The pub was pleasingly busy. A couple of people who had heard about yesterday's leek and potato soup were quickly persuaded to try the sweet and creamy pea soup instead. The treacle tart was snapped up too, with expressions of bliss and rueful regret at the effect on waistlines.

Maddy was just chatting to a jovial man in a blazer who was having a drink at the bar with his wife when, out of the corner of her eye, she saw two new customers come in and head for the bar.

'What can I get you both?' she said as she turned to them with a smile.

'Hello, Maddy,' said Ben, detaching himself from the willowy blonde at his side so he could get his wallet out. 'What would you like, Serena?'

'I'd like a *bloody* Mary', she said. Maddy took an involuntary step back.

'Really?' Ben queried, raising an eyebrow.

'Nah,' she giggled, 'I'll have a dry white wine please. I just wanted an excuse to say "bloody". As a matter of fact, what I'd really like is a "bloody Giles". It would be nice if he was here once in a while, rather than skiving off to London all week. His sodding pigs got out *again* last night. Before I bumped into you I'd spent the morning rounding the little buggers up from not one but three of our neighbours, who think the whole thing's damned hilarious.'

Ah, thought Maddy. Clearly this was the sweary posh bird.

'This is the four-month-old litter?' said Ben. 'I thought Giles had managed to sell them on to a gentleman farmer in Somerset to rear on.'

'He did! Giles drove them over a fortnight ago. I had to go and collect them again last week. They were so badly behaved he wanted us to take them back.'

Ben laughed. 'Can he do that?'

'I wouldn't have thought so, but clearly he can,' said Serena ruefully. 'There's only one naughty one, of course. He's really clever, that's the problem. He works out some Houdini escape route and his little brothers and sisters just trot off behind him. The sooner we convert the lot to bacon sandwiches the better.'

'You cried the last time they went off,' interjected Flora, who had spotted her friend and come back to the bar.

'You are mistaken,' said Serena stiffly, but with a twinkle in her eye. 'I think you must be thinking of when the boys went back to school.'

'Ah yes, you definitely cried then.'

'Don't remind me,' Serena begged, flapping her hand in front of her face and blinking rapidly. 'I don't have my waterproof mascara on. Anyhow, hello Flora, by the way . . .'

'This is Giles's wife, Serena, who I was telling you about,' Flora said. 'I was just telling Maddy she should come and have a look at what we're doing. She's a marketing whizz; I know she'll have lots of good ideas.'

'Brilliant!' said Serena, draining her glass in double-quick time. 'I've got to go back because the feed merchant's turning up pretty much now and I have to have an argument with him about his price rises. I can give you both a lift. You too, Ben?'

'Lectures to prepare for next week unfortunately.'

'Work? Even at the weekend?'

''Fraid so.'

'Just us girls, then,' she said, gathering up her keys.

'Oh, I'd love to,' said Maddy, 'but you need to go now and the bar doesn't close for another half an hour . . .'

'Not a problem, surely? There's that little weasel over there – about time he did some proper work.' Serena glared at Kevin.

'I suppose I could . . .' She thought guiltily of the client proposal Simon was waiting for. 'I'll have to take my own car, though. I've got to get over to see Patrick this afternoon too.'

'That's agreed, then,' said Serena briskly. 'You can follow me. Take Flora with you in case you get lost.'

In the end Flora didn't have to give directions despite Serena driving at a nearly unmatchable pace. Swinging off the main road into a barely noticeable side road, they barrelled down a narrow, rutted lane for nearly a mile before turning sharply into a cobbled farmyard. The space was flanked with low brick and flint buildings on three of the four sides. On two of the sides, the buildings were intact, with newly painted sky-blue window frames and stable doors, most of them with their upper half open to the afternoon sun. The remaining side of the yard was in a state of picturesque disrepair, with visible holes in the clay-tiled roofs and only a couple of panes of window glass still in situ. Maddy glimpsed inside a barn with no doors, making out cobblestone floors, gnarled roof timbers festooned with cobwebs, and the ghostly hulk of forgotten farm machinery, barely visible in the gloom.

'Hullooo,' hollered Flora, in the seemingly deserted farmyard.

'Flora! Hi! You're back, then . . . !' came the ragged reply, from various of the open doors. And then, out of the shadows, Maddy saw figures appearing, like the prisoners rising out into the light in *Fidelio*. All hailed Flora and Serena with warmth, and Maddy with benign interest.

'Got to go and berate the feed merchant, my darlings,' said Serena, excusing herself. 'Come and have a cup of tea when you're done. I'm out of Earl Grey, but the mugs will be a lot cleaner than anything you get offered out here,' she added, walking towards the house that Maddy had just noticed beyond the yard they were standing in.

'Here is my lovely Jez,' said Flora, dragging Maddy towards a dreadlocked and skinny young man with an enchanting smile and a gold earring.

Dead sheep guy, thought Maddy. Out loud she said, 'The man making the amazing sheepskin clothes!'

Soon Maddy found her enthusiasm was genuine: 'These are just gorgeous!' she exclaimed, examining the hats, slippers and gilets that filled the little stable Jez was working in. An industrial sewing machine dominated one corner, another was piled high with fleeces waiting to be transformed.

'They're all from local breeds,' he explained, following Maddy's gaze. 'There's no waste. I cut the shapes for the gilets from the fleece itself and then the offcuts are used for the ear flaps on the hats. I only need little pieces for that – see? And then the newest thing is these little baby boots,' he said, presenting her with the most adorable pair of slippers in miniature, with contrast overstitching in wool. 'Blue for a boy, red for a girl, but people can have whatever they want, really . . . I get the wool from Ursula next door; it's all natural vegetable dye she uses and her wool is locally reared on the Downs too . . .' He trailed away, looking earnestly at Maddy for her reaction. 'You should see her stuff. She does weaving mainly, blankets and throws from local wool and natural dyes.'

'I love them; I love it all,' said Maddy. 'The local thing, the simplicity, the quality. Everything really . . . it's great!'

Jez beamed. 'Show her the rest,' he implored Flora. 'I've got to get on . . .'

And Flora did.

More than an hour later, Maddy had been shown a dizzying range of products and skills, been encouraged to admire handwoven blankets and throws from thick – slightly scratchy – local wool dyed in a gorgeous range of colours. She had seen a ceramicist, Jim, hand-decorating a range of pots and tableware before sliding them into an enormous kiln; watched, mesmerised, as a glass-blower called Frank twisted and swung a hollow pole with a blob of white-hot molten glass on the end of it. He was a true showman, giving Maddy a running commentary, silenced only when he blew down the tube to shape the glass, miraculously transforming it into a wine glass of extraordinary beauty with a green stem. He then went on to attach jewel-like studs of cobalt molten glass to the bowl before setting it aside to temper, otherwise – as Frank explained – the entire piece would likely shatter as it cooled.

'There's incredible stuff going on here!' she exclaimed to Serena when she had made tea in a huge brown pot, piled home-made cookies onto a plate and related every detail of her dignified triumph over the evil feed merchant.

'Aren't they all just so clever,' agreed Serena fondly, as if she were speaking of some very brilliant achievement of a child of hers. 'And they complement each other so well . . .'

'True. I love that aspect most of all. How Jez uses Ursula's wool, and how Jonathan and the muralist – what's-his-name – did that joint commission with Jonathan's tiles in one part of the room and the mural on the other side in the same design . . .'

'Nick's the muralist,' said Flora. 'He can graffiti my walls any time he likes,' she added, smiling beatifically.

'You're right, though,' said Serena. 'There they all are, pointed at the same market, basically, but not at all in competition with one another . . . Using local materials on the whole and doing bespoke commissions as well as their off-the-shelf stuff. They all deserve to do really well,' she said. 'But they don't . . .'

Maddy noticed Serena's attention was broken, her eyes often straying to the window as she spoke.

'Why not, though?' she asked, although she instinctively knew the reply.

'It's getting to their market,' said Serena. 'They're a bit out in the sticks, let's face it. With a presence on the high street they'd all do better, but not well enough to pay the rent and rates they would end up paying. Last summer a few of them clubbed together and shared a stand at the big crafts and interiors fair in Brighton . . .'

'How did it work out?'

'Not bad, but the stands are sold by the square metre at an incredible cost so they had a really tiny space and couldn't get a lot of stock there. The fair gets the big London buyers and the interior designers attending and I know they got some good leads, but they're lucky to attract the attention of the big buyers for more than a few seconds and it's not long to really do business . . . They should probably have followed up their leads a bit better afterwards but . . .' She smiled fondly. 'You've seen what they're all like. A bit dozy. Not exactly God's gift to commerce.'

'You are, though,' said Maddy.

'Ah,' said Serena, and didn't contradict her. 'In years gone by, perhaps . . .'

'What did you used to do?'

'Nothing really,' sighed Serena. 'Actually, not "nothing"; I was sort of a buyer for a department store . . .'

'It was Heal's, wasn't it?' said Flora, dreamily nibbling on a cookie.

Maddy gasped. 'Good grief! That's amazing; you must have been brilliant.'

'Wouldn't say that exactly,' Serena demurred. 'I loved it, though. Meant to carry on after I hooked up with Giles but – you know how it is – life and its demands, the move to the country, the boys . . . So, what do you think, though?'

'About what?' asked Maddy.

'We'll help these little ones get their act together, no? Together, Flora too, we could really help.'

'You mean like – sort of – a bespoke consortium?'

'Brilliant!' said Serena. 'That's what we'll call it.'

'Fab!' agreed Flora around a mouthful of cookie. 'Let's do it!'

'I don't know . . .'

'I'll start,' said Serena. 'We'll need a business plan. I'll do the outline; you can fill in the marketing and PR bits. Give me your email,' she said, grabbing a pen and paper from a stack by the Aga.

'Okay,' said Maddy slowly, but she caught Flora's eye and grinned.

'Sorted,' said Serena with finality. As she spoke her eyes drifted to the window again and then they all heard a car slowing and turning into the courtyard.

'Here they are at last!'

Maddy and Flora were forgotten as Serena bolted out of the kitchen and appeared outside, barely waiting for the old Volvo to stop and for its cargo to disembark.

Two boys in blazers got out and headed for the boot of the car. Clearly their intention was to grab their belongings, but their mother had a different idea. Letting out something between a shout and a growl of delight she grabbed them both and gathered them to her. They submitted with resignation as she squeezed them tight and then grabbed their heads in turn, pressing kisses onto their faces, which each wiped away discreetly when her attention was turned to the other.

'Hullo, Mummy,' said the smallest one, 'I mean "Mum",' he corrected hastily.

He was perhaps eight or nine with the slight halo of fluffiness that was most definitely absent in his older brother. Otherwise they looked amazingly alike.

'Hullo, old thing,' said a balding, middle-aged man, getting out of the car with a hint of weariness. 'Here they are, both mancubs as ordered, safe, sound and all yours for the rest of the weekend – what's left of it.' He planted a kiss on Serena's face and hung his arm protectively around her shoulders as they strolled towards the house. In his fifties, with the slightly red face of a man who enjoys his wine, he had a kindly demeanour and a comfortably large stomach.

The boys ran ahead and then froze, rucksacks in hand, as they encountered the two young women in the kitchen.

'Hullo,' they both said in unison, holding out their hands awkwardly for Maddy to shake.

Flora, clearly, they knew, as she inflicted kisses on them, which were nearly as wayward as their mother's.

'My boys,' said Serena triumphantly to Maddy as she followed them into the kitchen. 'And here's my funny old husband, Giles.'

Giles didn't seem to mind a bit being described that way as he held out a friendly hand to Maddy. His hand was warm, large and all-encompassing. She could well imagine he gave very good hugs.

'So,' said Serena, 'what's the plan?'

'Pizza!' shouted the boys in happy unison.

Clearly there had been prior discussion.

Serena gave Giles a quizzical look. He shrugged his shoulders and grinned appeasingly.

'Thought I'd save you the trouble of cooking supper, old thing.'

Serena shuddered. 'Not takeaway. God knows what's in them. I'll do a quick pizza dough. The boys can choose their own toppings. I've got all sorts . . . Erm, what are you doing until then, by the way?'

'Shootout!' shouted the boys again.

Serena raised an eyebrow at the hapless Giles.

'X-Box?'

He nodded.

'Eighteen classification?'

'Might be,' he admitted. 'Mind you, it's not one of those

ghastly misogynist ones about rape and prostitution or anything . . . it's just a bit of mindless violence . . . so nothing they haven't already seen,' he explained, wincing as the two boys ran out of the room whooping at the tops of their voices. 'Or done,' he added, pulling a face at Maddy.

'My *three* boys,' complained Serena as Giles followed them out of the room. 'I'm the only grown-up in the house, as you can see.'

Maddy noticed Serena's expression as she gazed after them. It was raw hunger – a ferocious and primitive love.

'Oh no!' she exclaimed, noticing the kitchen clock. 'I'll never get to the hospital and back before I have to open the bar again.'

'I'm so sorry to have kept you. How is poor Patrick?' said Serena.

'Not brilliant. I wanted to talk to the doctors about when they'll operate. I didn't see him yesterday either. I give messages to whoever answers the phone when you call the ward but I wonder if they bother to pass them on . . .'

'Make sure to have a nice long visit tomorrow morning,' her new friend suggested. 'Take him some sweet peas! I know he loves them and the last of mine need picking.'

Chapter Five

When Maddy got to the ward early the following morning, holding the already-wilting but gloriously honey-scented flowers, she was only mildly concerned when the bed by the window was empty. She saw the bossy nurse who had spoken to her last time whisking past.

'My friend Patrick, do you know where he's been moved to?'

'He went down to theatre about an hour ago.'

'The theatre? You mean the operating theatre?'

'Well I didn't mean the Moulin Rouge. They were planning to operate. You knew that from the last time you came and spoke to Doctor.'

'Yes, but I thought they were waiting for him to get a bit better,' gabbled Maddy. 'I wasn't ready. He . . . I didn't speak to him first . . .'

The nurse patted her on the shoulder a little too hard.

'There, there, dear. Why not go down to the waiting room in the operating suite? Wait there for him.'

It was a command.

Maddy went.

* * *

The broad back and floppy hair curling on the collar was unmistakable. Maddy, conscious her nose was running and her mascara was all over her face, was just about to turn and slip back through the swing doors before they closed again but the squeak of their opening had already caused Ben to turn.

'Maddy!' He smiled as he walked towards her. Then he registered her red eyes.

'Worried? Don't be. He'll be fine.' He wrapped his arms around her and squeezed reassuringly.

He was so tall her head only reached his shoulder where it rested comfortably. She allowed herself a brief moment in his arms, but then got worried her nose might be running onto his shirt and also that, quite possibly, her knees might embarrass her by giving way for absolutely no reason whatsoever.

'I'm fine,' she snuffled, withdrawing with her head down so he couldn't see her face. 'Just didn't realise . . . I didn't manage to speak to him yesterday. Have you heard anything?'

'Not yet. They're expecting him back out again in the next hour or so, though. I was just going to go and get something to eat. Can I buy you a coffee? Breakfast? Let me take these before you squash them,' he added, gently prising the flowers out of her hand.

You had to admire a man who could march down a hospital corridor with a bunch of sweet peas in his fist without feeling he is compromising his masculinity, she mused. He dropped the little posy into Patrick's ward, charmingly persuading a ward cleaner to appropriate a vase for them, and then – firmly steering Maddy by the elbow – he planted her in the corner of the cafe. He returned swiftly with two steaming cups of coffee and an assortment of croissants, toast and muffins.

'I wasn't sure what you'd like,' he said, waving at the food.

'Any or all of them,' she said truthfully. 'But it's a bit early for me. I don't really eat breakfast.'

'Don't be silly. You've got to eat in the morning.' He opened the fiddly little packets of butter and jam, spread the toast thickly with both and plonked it in front of her. 'There you go.'

She didn't dare refuse. 'I suppose an army marches on its stomach, doesn't it?' she commented, feeling she ought to make polite conversation.

'I always found it did when I was in the field. As a substitute for sleep, remedy for anxiety and boost to morale it has its uses too.'

She washed down a mouthful of toast and jam with a gulp of coffee and felt the stomach-churning anxiety retreat like the ebbing tide. It left her weary beyond belief. She yawned hugely in Ben's face.

'Oops, sorry,' she said, clapping her hand over her mouth. 'Better not use food as a total substitute for sleep. I'll be the size of a house.'

'Any reason you're not sleeping?'

'I've just got a lot on, that's all. The London business, running the pub, Patrick being ill. It's fine.'

'Anything in particular?'

'No.'

Ben waited.

'Weeell . . .' she added, realising she was going to have to give him something: 'It's probably nothing, but . . . do you think there's something else going on with the pub? I just got the impression when I saw Patrick. He's got something on his mind, don't you think? Apart from the lease renewal thing, of course.'

Ben considered, staring into his coffee mug. He knew he

was being brushed off. Diverted. But that was fine. He could play that game.

'The lease renewal is a legitimate concern,' he said slowly. 'Plus, he's tried not to let on, but – to be honest – I think he has been feeling increasingly unwell for a while . . .'

'Of course. There's probably nothing else. It's just . . .' She thought some more, not sure where to start. 'Something about the takings in the bar isn't quite right. I think that's what it is. I'm nervous about Kevin. Can't put my finger on it and, God knows, I'm reluctant to make accusations. I just wondered if Patrick had ever confided any doubts about him to you at all?'

'He hasn't, but I wouldn't expect him to, really. He knows he can't run the pub without Kevin, although I don't think he likes him much either. I think we need to find out more about the lease renewal situation, though. We might discover something that would set Patrick's mind at rest, even if it means talking to the obnoxious Dennis. I don't mind doing it with you if it helps?'

'It's incredibly kind of you to get involved.'

'You keep saying that,' replied Ben with a hint of irritation. 'As if I'm doing more than one might expect. As if you can't think why I'm doing it.'

'I don't know you,' explained Maddy. 'Why would you help me? Us?'

'Patrick is a friend. A good friend.'

She finished off her toast and croissant obediently, feeling mildly chastised, while Ben drank his coffee.

He looked at his watch. 'I'm pretty sure Patrick will be in the recovery room soon, and then you can see him.'

'What about you?'

'I didn't want him to wake up on his own,' said Ben, 'but, now you're here, to be honest I could do with getting back to college.

I didn't quite manage to sort out all my lecture notes yesterday, plus I've got an awful lot of essays to mark and tutorials all afternoon. I'll drop by the pub for a report on how he is later.' He stood and patted her on the shoulder by way of farewell.

Maddy felt bereft when he had gone, her memory clinging to the weight of his hand on her shoulder long after he had disappeared.

Standing slowly and a little stiffly, she walked, yawning, to the recovery area waiting room and was immediately beckoned through by a theatre nurse in green scrubs.

'He's just waking up.' She smiled kindly at Maddy as she ushered her into a high, light room filled with lines of beds and equipment. 'Everything went really well,' she added, as Maddy approached the bed where he lay.

Patrick's always elegant but now even skinnier frame seemed barely to disrupt the flatness of the thin blanket and sheet that covered him. There were tubes that Maddy tried to ignore, a monitor beeping above him and a mask on his face. He was flat on his back, his arms and legs arranged tidily like a corpse.

'Patrick?' whispered Maddy, reaching for his hand.

His eyes opened and he turned his head to look at her.

'Helen,' he croaked, his eyes filling with tears. 'I'm so sorry.'

Maddy's eyes filled in sympathy. 'Patrick,' she said. 'It's me, Maddy. Everything's fine. You're fine.' But he seemed to have gone back to sleep. She squeezed his hand and he opened his eyes again.

'Helen, I've been such a fool . . . such a fool. I've done everything all wrong . . .'

Maddy was distraught. 'Patrick, please don't,' she said. 'Everything's fine. They say the operation went well. You've done nothing wrong at all . . .'

The kind theatre nurse touched her on the elbow. 'He's very woozy. You won't get a lot of sense out of him, I'm afraid.'

'Should he be so confused, though?' panicked Maddy. 'Is there something wrong?'

The theatre nurse smiled. 'They often do that. The number that come out calling their wife by their mistress's name – that causes ructions, I can tell you . . . Do you know who this "Helen" is?'

'I'm guessing he means my mum. That's her name and we do look a bit alike. Can't imagine why he's apologising to her, though. As far as I'm aware they haven't even seen each other since before I was born.'

'There, look, he's sound asleep. If I were you I'd let him rest. He'll go up to the intensive care unit until they're happy with him and be back on the ward before you know it.'

He did seem to be sleeping peacefully now, a slight smile on his pallid face. He resisted as Maddy withdrew her hand. She waited, anxiously, until his face relaxed once more and then tiptoed away.

Later, back on the ward, Patrick was furious with himself. Properly awake now he gazed miserably out of the window, remembering his confusion in recovery all too well. Poor Maddy, listening to him drivelling on at her about her mother. That was the last thing she needed at the moment. He was a soppy old fool. In all the time he had cared for her when she was studying – surreptitiously, not interfering – he made sure to resist the temptation to interrogate her about Helen; how she was, what she was doing, even who she was with – if anyone . . .

He adored watching Maddy too, the way she walked, the way she threw her head back when she laughed. He could see

Helen in her so strongly it was almost like a physical pain. It was a gift Helen had given him, letting him have just a tiny part in Maddy's life, a little glimpse of the woman he had stupidly driven away because of his idiotic behaviour. And then he had let Helen down again, allowing Maddy – her precious daughter – to be hurt . . . He deserved to be cast out of their lives. And now, with death potentially hovering, he felt desperate – not to make amends, as that probably wasn't possible – but at least to say sorry. Properly. Face-to-face. After twenty-five years it was the least she deserved and he needed to know it was done.

'Penny for them?'

'Hetty, darling.' He turned from the window, his face instantly transformed by a charming smile. 'I was simply wondering when one of you marvellous angels of mercy was going to bring me a cup of tea. And now you have, I'm a happy man.'

After the lunchtime session, Maddy made herself a cup of coffee so strong it tasted like boiled rubber tyres. Steeling herself, she put a call through to Top Taverns and spoke to Tracey, the woman Dennis grandly referred to as his PA, but whom Maddy happened to know was simply an admin assistant for about six of the regional managers and barely did anything to help Dennis on account of disliking him so much.

'Rather you than me,' Tracey remarked cheerfully as she assured Maddy that Dennis would visit the Havenbury Arms the following morning to discuss the lease renewal. 'Any excuse to keep him out from under my feet is fine by me,' she added as Maddy thanked her.

She then settled down to do the ordering but, even with the strong coffee, she found herself slumping into a doze, waking suddenly, her head on a pile of invoices, with barely twenty minutes until she had to open for the evening.

The bar was busy again, and the evening flew. It was only when she was totting up the till – another decent night – that she remembered Ben had mentioned dropping in and felt a pang of disappointment that he hadn't.

She was just putting the last glasses back on the shelf and trying not to think about the emails waiting for her to answer upstairs when there was a gentle tap at the door.

'Closed!' she shouted. The tap came again, more insistently. She peered through the patterned glass of the door, making out a tall, broad-shouldered figure. Her heart raced and her fatigue vanished as she went to unlock the bolts again.

'I thought you weren't coming,' she said, as she let Ben in.

'*I* thought I wasn't coming too. I didn't want to rock up so late but I decided it was better than not showing up at all. You look done in.'

'Thanks,' she replied with a wry grin. 'You say the sweetest things.' She couldn't wipe the smile off her face, tired as she was.

'So,' he replied slowly, swinging a chair down off the table and setting it onto the floor for her before doing the same for himself. 'I saw him. He's doing "as well as can be expected"' – he shrugged – 'but he was still quite confused and out of it. He seemed to want to see someone called "Helen". Whoever that is. Do you know?'

'My mum; at least I assume that was who he meant. We look a bit alike, despite the obvious age difference. But he hasn't seen her for years. They fell out over something; I don't really know what. Why?'

'Do you think she might be prepared to come down and see him?'

'God, I don't know. I suppose she might,' replied Maddy, confused. 'She knows he's ill . . .'

'He'd be more settled, maybe,' Ben suggested, 'and that can only help his recovery . . .'

'I'll call her. She can get the train and stay here, there are plenty of bedrooms.' She sighed. There were indeed bedrooms upstairs, but it was going to take a fair bit of work to make one comfortable for her mother. Another job to add to the growing list.

'Go in tomorrow morning and tell him,' suggested Ben. 'That'll cheer him up.'

'Can't. Got Dennis coming in to talk about the lease before I open up for lunch.'

'Have you now? Would it help if I came in and helped you set up? You can't do both at once.'

Maddy was tempted. 'No, it's fine. I'll manage.'

'If you're sure,' said Ben, standing up and replacing the chair on the table. 'Now. Are you done here?' he asked, looking around the bar.

'More or less.'

'You really do look exhausted, Maddy.' He gave her a penetrating look that made her intensely conscious of her shiny face and unwashed hair, scraped back into a ponytail. The circles under her eyes were so deeply etched she could even see them in the blurry reflection of the darkened windows.

'I just need a good night's sleep.' She tried to smile at him, but her lips wobbled.

'Okay, well, make sure you get one,' he said.

After Ben had left, Maddy went upstairs and brewed herself a revoltingly strong instant coffee. Her heart raced as she waited for her laptop to boot up and collect all her emails. It was worse than she thought. There was a message from their contact at Adams and Quinn, politely informing her that they had been impressed by 'elements' of her submission but that they were planning 'at this time' to invite proposals from other consultancies.

Fair enough. She wouldn't have engaged herself either. Simon would be furious. Yep, here was a message from him. Typically, he ranted about their having wasted their time giving out free ideas for them to use without giving him, Simon, any money for thinking them up. On the other hand, Maddy was always too keen – he said – to overdeliver before any money had changed hands. This time, he had been right.

She sighed. Simon hadn't responded to their email and she was blowed if she was going to look rude as a result of sour grapes. She quickly formulated a regretful and brief reply, inviting them to contact her again at any time in the future if she could be of any assistance. Pressing send, she noticed the time and groaned. Sending emails at nearly two in the morning didn't look dedicated, it looked desperate.

She checked through and dealt with several others and then allowed herself a quick look at Serena's draft business plan, which she'd agreed to help with. It was all looking fabulous and Serena's ideas were great – all she had to do was get down a few of the marketing strategies. The website was vital . . .

Next thing she knew it was four in the morning.

In bed at last, Maddy lay on her back with her eyes pinned open. Her heart pounding and brain racing, she stared at the ceiling, endlessly turning over problems in her mind until she fell asleep, exhausted, just as the sky was beginning to turn from navy to indigo.

Chapter Six

Her head was throbbing before she even opened her eyes barely three hours later and black coffee didn't improve matters. She couldn't face breakfast. Just as she was dragging the hoover out there was a tap on the locked door of the bar.

'You again?' she said, secretly pleased when she saw it was Ben. 'People will begin to think you've got a drink problem, the amount of time you spend trying to get in here when the bar's closed. You were sweet to offer your help last night, but I really am fine.'

'Forgot you turned me down. Must be the alcohol-related memory loss. Anyway, I thought I'd better bring you some breakfast,' he added, presenting a greasy paper bag.

'Not hungry,' said Maddy, but when she smelt the bacon roll her mouth watered. Maybe just half . . . 'Actually, it is good you're here. I've got to get the cleaning done in double-quick time so I can meet Dennis. If you help I think we can crack it.'

'Do you want me to stay for the charming Dennis too?' asked Ben. 'Give you a bit of moral support?'

She wavered. Her pride said she wanted to deal with

Dennis on her own and these were sensitive business issues, after all. On the other hand, another set of ears would be handy . . . and Ben *was* Patrick's friend.

'Yes please,' she admitted, 'but first tell me why on earth you were here talking to Dennis about buying the pub when I arrived. I'm not at all sure we're on the same side.'

'Fair point,' said Ben. 'As it happens I was just sniffing around trying to find out what had happened to Patrick when Dennis arrived. As he's so extraordinarily self-important and narcissistic, the fact that he turned up with selling the property clearly on his mind manifested into assuming I was there to buy it.'

'So he seriously asked you if you wanted to buy it?'

'Yep.'

'And you said "yes"?'

'Yep.'

'So you lied.'

'I prefer to think of it as "going along with his agenda in order to further explore his reality".'

'Do a lot of that in your line of work, do you?'

'Quite a bit.'

'Okay, so, there's to be no encouraging the little squirt to get ideas in his head this morning, if you don't mind.'

'Right-o,' agreed Ben, relieving Maddy of the hoover and switching it on, killing further conversation.

Maddy gave Ben a long look, unobserved. It was too easy to rely on his help – God knows she could do with an ally – but she wished she had overhead more of his conversation with Dennis that day. Just to be sure she knew whose side he was really on.

* * *

'Ah, how nice,' came a smug voice from the open doorway, 'a welcoming committee.'

Maddy turned with something approaching a snarl on her face.

'Dennis, good morning.' Ben leapt forward to shake his hand, giving every impression of being delighted to see him and buying her a chance to compose herself.

'Let me get the kettle on,' he continued. 'Dennis, what's yours? Tea or coffee?'

'There's no milk,' said Maddy crossly. She didn't see why he should have anything.

'Yes there is,' said Ben, annoyingly. 'I bought some, just in case,' he added, magicking a pint of milk from his rucksack.

By the time Ben had solicitously provided tea all round and sorted out the issues of milk, sugar and even biscuits, which he also had in his rucksack, extraordinarily enough, she had overcome the tremors of rage and nerves – she wasn't sure which – that had overcome her when Dennis had arrived.

'So,' said Maddy, 'as you know, Patrick has asked me – us – to cover for him for a brief period while he continues to recover. To do that I – I mean, we – thought it was important to understand precisely what this upcoming lease renewal consists of so we can make sure everything goes through smoothly.' She was determined to coolly give the impression there was no doubt about renewal.

Dennis wasn't convinced.

'That's all lovely, Maddy,' he said, dabbing his pursed, red lips with a paper napkin. 'But I am sure Patrick will have brought you up to speed with the difficulties we are facing. The lease renewal is far from a done deal, as I am sure you know.'

Maddy was at a loss, but luckily Ben stepped in. 'Of course, Dennis,' he said confidently, 'we are fully apprised but – nonetheless – I wonder if you would indulge us by running through the detail from Top Taverns' perspective.' He smiled, coolly. 'Maddy and I are keen to represent Patrick's interests in his – brief – absence and it's important that we have full disclosure from you to ensure we have the most accurate picture possible.'

Dennis blinked, and then looked enquiringly at Maddy.

'Yeah,' she muttered. 'What he said.'

'Very well,' said Dennis, shuffling papers importantly. 'You'll have seen this, of course,' he said, waving a wodge of paper with 'Lease Agreement' written on the top of the first page. Ben quietly grabbed it and started scanning through. 'So,' continued Dennis, 'you'll know that Patrick had a ten-year lease, which ends on the first of January next year?'

'Ten years?' queried Maddy. 'That can't be right. He's been running the Havenbury Arms for longer than that – from what he's always told me it must be coming up to twenty years or so now.'

Ben nodded in agreement.

'Of course,' agreed Dennis. 'But Top Taverns only bought the pub ten years ago. Prior to that it was owned by a small freeholder with an interest in just a handful of pubs. It was bought as a job lot, as I understand it, when the owner's business went bust.'

'I never knew that,' muttered Maddy, looking at Ben for reassurance. 'But Patrick has always paid a fair rent, whoever he was paying it to, surely?'

'Depends what you call a "fair rent",' said Dennis, clearly disapproving of the concept of 'fair'. 'If I'd been in charge then I'd certainly have set the terms somewhat differently . . .'

'Not in Patrick's favour, I'll be bound,' commented Ben.

'I certainly feel the terms were generous then, but now, ten years on, I can tell you Top Taverns will, reasonably enough, be looking for a somewhat better return on their investment . . .'

'I bet their "investment" ten years ago wasn't nearly as much as the pub's worth now,' said Maddy. 'And that's the key, isn't it? That's why you can't get selling out of your mind, but why on earth would a pub company want to start selling off its pubs?'

'They do, though,' interjected Ben, looking up from the lease. 'There's only a handful of huge pub companies now, whereas historically most pubs were owned by small, individual freeholders. The pub companies have borrowed such huge amounts to build these massive property portfolios, plus the value of property has risen so much since they bought, the companies are reducing their leverage by selling stuff off. Of course, a lot of the time that means the pubs close and end up being converted into residential or something else . . .'

'I can see you've done your homework,' said Dennis, clearly miffed that Ben was so well informed.

'But you're making such a lot of rent out of Patrick,' Maddy said. 'Why would you even want to sell?'

'I'm afraid we would be looking for a substantial increase in rent if we were to offer another lease,' said Dennis. 'I'm waiting for head office to confirm but, basically, you would be looking at more or less twice the current level.'

'What?' she exclaimed. 'Surely you can't do that?'

Ben shook his head. 'According to this, they can,' he said, waving the lease at her.

Dennis looked smug.

'Fine,' said Maddy. 'We can pay your poxy rent, don't you worry.'

'I'm pleased to hear that, because there has been a small issue with rent over the last few months. We cannot afford to be receiving it as late as we have been doing. I am sure you are aware,' he gave her a triumphant little smile, 'that the rent is currently two months in arrears?'

'Of course!' she said. 'It's hardly surprising with Patrick being ill. It's purely an administration issue; I'll get right onto it.' She threw Ben a desperate look.

In response he waved the papers at Dennis again. 'These beer ties are pretty frowned upon nowadays. I hope I can assume Top Taverns won't be putting such punitive terms in its new lease?'

'We are more than entitled to our beer ties. As a brewing company we are proud of our beers and it's a mark of the quality of our pubs that customers can be assured our much-loved beers will be on tap in all our premises.'

'Okay,' said Ben, 'leaving the quality of the beers to one side – although I am sure you know the Top Taverns "Golden Brite" lager is widely known as "Golden Shite", it's more about the pub companies' insistence that their publicans are compelled to buy their beer and at a hugely inflated price.'

'That's your opinion,' said Dennis icily. 'The debate on that issue is continuing and Top Taverns will respond appropriately to any legislative direction it is given.'

'So, what happens if the new draft lease is so completely pants not even an imbecile would sign it?' pressed Maddy, not entirely understanding the beer ties issue. She would need to ask Ben about it later.

'If our lease is not acceptable, then – as current company policy has it – I will be instructed to sell at the best possible price.'

'By which you mean not as a pub?' asked Ben.

'I really don't know. Certainly the building would make a very desirable family home.'

Maddy made a noise of pure disgust.

'Anyway,' he continued, 'the only other thing we haven't yet covered is the issue of dilapidations. As I mentioned before, Patrick has a full repairing lease. To be fair, I am sure we all agree the maintenance has been a little peremptory in recent years.'

Maddy and Ben took a brief look around the room they were sitting in. Even the insides of the window frames needed repainting and their shabbiness gave a fair clue as to the outside, where – in places – the remaining flakes of paint were hanging on for dear life. And then there was the ominous damp patch on the ceiling . . . She had persuaded herself it was evidence of a long-since-repaired leak but – looking again – it had definitely grown.

'I took the liberty of getting our property maintenance team in to assess the cost of repairs before I last saw you. Patrick was well aware,' he added nervously, glancing at Maddy's expression. 'We now have their estimates and, although tenants are not obliged to use our own team it would be a simple way of ensuring repairs are done to an acceptable standard . . .'

'Let me see,' said Ben, putting down the lease he was still studying.

'But that's nearly fifty thousand pounds,' he exclaimed, looking at the figures on the final page.

'Those are just the essential repairs,' insisted Dennis. 'When you neglect a property as – I'm sorry to say – Patrick has, it can add up.'

'Yes, but fifty thousand pounds,' said Maddy. 'And then you want a massive rent increase as well . . . What on earth do you want us to do?'

'You do have a little time. The lease doesn't expire until the first of January next year.'

'Whoopee,' said Maddy, 'that's less than three months.'

'You asked me to fill you in,' said Dennis, puffed up with spite. 'And I have.'

There was too much to do after Dennis left to think about it, but later – when the bar was open – Maddy found herself in the quiet before the lunchtime rush, sitting on a bar stool with her head in her hands.

'This'll cheer you up,' came a delightfully modulated voice in her ear.

'Serena!' exclaimed Maddy. 'I wasn't asleep.'

'Didn't look like you were,' said Serena. 'Well, it did a bit . . . Anyhow, I thought I'd pop in and show you the Bespoke Consortium logo stuff from a graphic designer I know. I hope you don't feel I'm rushing ahead. Loved your marketing ideas, by the way . . .'

'Not at all; these are brilliant!' Maddy said, as she spread the printed designs on the table. 'I think this one, don't you?' she continued, pointing out the least elaborate of the logo options.

'I hoped you'd say that. The simplest is always the best, and don't you think the colour palette is absolutely genius?'

'It's beautiful,' said Maddy. 'Do you think the others will like it?'

'I'm sure they will. I showed it to Flora. Did I say? She loved it and they've appointed her as official spokesperson and go-between for us and the team. I know she's a bit nuts but she's got some good ideas.'

'Good thinking,' agreed Maddy. 'She's a bright girl. Oo – and is this the website design?'

'Just a go at the layout of the home page and a sample other page,' said Serena, drawing the printout towards them both for a closer look.

'You appreciate we're going to need someone who can actually build us this website,' said Maddy, waving the page in question. 'I don't know anybody local . . . do you?'

'There's a brilliant small company in Brighton. I know they can give us good advice about making the whole online retail thing work but they won't, unfortunately, be free.'

'Ah yes,' said Maddy, deflated. 'Could the members stump up a bit, do you think? It's all about sharing the cost so they'll get more bang for their buck than they would be able to on their own.'

'Funding's another issue for another day,' she said. 'Why don't I give my Brighton lot a call?'

'Mum!' exclaimed Maddy, pressing the phone tighter to her ear. 'I'm so glad I've caught you.'

'So sorry, darling,' Helen replied. 'I got your message but I never know when to call back. You're either running the bar or out and I'm sure you don't want me calling after midnight or anything . . .'

I'd be up, thought Maddy, but didn't say.

'I've been busy,' she said, trying to inject a smile into her voice, 'but it's fine really, just a bit hectic.'

'You sound tired.'

'I'm fine, Mum, honestly,' she said, but tears were pricking at her eyes. 'I was wondering whether you'd like to come down. I haven't seen you for ages, and it's still quite sunny and warm most days. You could have a little holiday.'

'If I came it would be to help,' insisted Helen. 'And I'd be doing it for you, not Patrick.'

'Ah . . . about that . . . Patrick has been saying he'd love to see you. I think it would be good for the two of you to meet up.'

'Why on earth would we?' snapped Helen. 'What's he said?'

'Nothing, nothing . . . He's just been saying he'd like to see you. He's really quite ill, Mum,' she implored. 'You are such old friends. Won't you consider it? You could stay here, in the pub. Just get on the train and I'll meet you . . .'

'Well, if I can't persuade you to leave, get away from the place, then fine, I'll come – but remember this: you owe nothing to that man. Nothing.'

Maddy decided not to mention her mum's possible visit when she saw Patrick that afternoon. She also thought she'd better not mention the meeting with Dennis – not until she had had a chance to talk it over with Ben and – somehow – come up with some solutions.

All in all, there didn't seem a lot they could safely talk about.

Patrick's only topic of conversation was his amazement at still being kept in hospital. 'I'm as fit as a flea,' he said. 'No bleeding wonder the NHS doesn't have any money. Still, they do say I can probably leave in a few days.'

'Really? So soon?'

'Oh yes, it's all about recuperating at home nowadays. Marvellous really . . .'

Maddy didn't think it was marvellous at all, but she smiled brightly for Patrick and added his discharge to her list of things to panic about in an orderly fashion.

It was nearly opening time before she noticed a text from her mother announcing she would come down to visit the following Tuesday. It looked likely she would arrive at about the same time Patrick came out of hospital. Maddy didn't know if that was a good thing, or another complication to add to her growing list. Either way it was bound to be exciting.

Thankfully, Kevin showed up a few minutes before opening time, rather than loping in half an hour or more into the session. It was probably because it was payday, thought Maddy uncharitably. She was relieved to see him, though, because tonight was generally a big night for food. She had stuck with her reduced menu, basically a dish of the day, plus a handful of old favourites, which she rotated depending on what ingredients were fresh and available. The dish of the day was mussels, and for variety she had decided to sell them prepared with a choice of broths: a classic moules marinière with wine and garlic; a fabulous Thai version with lemongrass and coconut milk; and, another French classic, moules Normandie, with smoked bacon and cider – all the options served alongside a big bowl of chips. The broth was all quick to prepare in advance, leaving the mussels to be cooked fresh, to order. There was a decent markup to be made and, with such mouthwatering choices, Maddy was pretty sure she would sell out.

Kevin loitered around the bar, desultorily tidying the shelves and taking the last lot of glasses from the lunchtime session out of the glass-washer.

'Patrick is hoping to come out in a few days,' said Maddy.

'Oh . . . okay,' replied Kevin, not meeting her eye.

'So,' said Maddy, infuriated by his lack of response, 'I'd be interested to know your plans. With Patrick back and me here we may not need you quite so much.' It was a lie, of course; Maddy wouldn't be letting Patrick come back to work anytime soon, despite his own opinions on the subject.

Kevin's eyes widened, and he turned to face her.

Gotcha, thought Maddy.

'Is that right?' he said at last.

Minutes later, Maddy wished she had been able to resist the temptation to rile him. She was barely coping and – despite her strong and unshakeable antipathy – Kevin's presence was vital. He was also Patrick's employee, and not Maddy's, she reminded herself guiltily.

CHAPTER SEVEN

A few days later, Patrick's release from hospital was Maddy's most pressing thought when she woke. Her mother's imminent arrival was the second.

Paper and pencil in hand, she decided on a recce. There was Patrick's room, cluttered and comfortable, needing a good airing and clean sheets on the bed. Other than that, it would do for him; it was clearly what he liked.

The other large room at the front was the one where she imagined her mother would stay. It was in a worse mess than the little back bedroom she had appropriated when she arrived after Patrick's heart attack. Was it really only days ago? It seemed a lifetime . . . Taking a closer look, she made a 'to-do' list. It really just needed a good clean. The bed was basically fine. There was a little chest of drawers and wardrobe, mainly empty. Maddy was sure Patrick wouldn't mind if she bundled up the few contents in a bin bag and despatched them to the loft, which she knew was capacious. Perhaps Ben would give her a hand. Then it was just a case of finding her mother some sheets and bedding. She could even get out between bar shifts and buy a new set for her. She noticed a huge supermarket had opened up on the outskirts of the town in the three years she had been away – they were bound to sell bedding.

Feeling more cheerful, and pleased she would soon be able to share her woes and concerns with her mother, at least, Maddy went into the little kitchen and made herself a black coffee. Pirate was pleased to have his blanket taken off and be released from his cage for a wander around. After a little tour he plonked himself on the kitchen table and managed to persuade her to dig him out a handful of walnuts, which he loved. She scratched him fondly on the head as he ate and he chuckled appreciatively. He had been generally more morose than usual since she arrived and she knew he was missing Patrick quite a bit.

'You and me both,' she told him. 'Although I've got to say, I can't see life getting quite back to normal for either of you anytime soon.'

Pirate regarded her seriously, a large piece of walnut stuck to the side of his beak, presumably to be savoured later. He had taken to bar life like a duck to water and she worried – if it came to an end – neither he nor Patrick would welcome such a seismic change. Who would give Patrick a job? God help any future boss of Patrick, who had always been the one in charge. Also, where on earth would he and the little parrot live? They had both been at the pub for as long as she had known them. She imagined Patrick had no capital so it would be a rental, and who would even take pets?

'I do hope that's not breakfast,' came a familiar voice. 'Have I taught you nothing?'

Maddy turned around to see Ben ducking slightly as he

came into the little kitchen, his broad shoulders seeming to fill the doorway.

'Don't you ever knock?'

'Nope,' he replied. 'The door was open, so I knew you were up . . . I promise you'll be delighted to see me once you hear why I've come. Look at that, for heaven's sake!'

'What?'

She followed his gaze to her right hand, which was clutching the cup of strong, black instant coffee she had just made.

'You're trembling.' He grabbed her other hand and held it between his own. 'And you're sweating, even though you're freezing cold . . . That's not your first cup is it? Have you slept?'

She snatched her hand away. 'I'm fine.'

'What have I told you about eating breakfast? Caffeine is no substitute for food.'

'Who are you? My mum?'

'Good grief, I've had sixteen-year-old troops coming straight into the army from children's homes who needed less parenting than you do . . .' he grumbled, giving up. 'Anyway, what I came here to say is it's your lucky day. I bumped into Flora last night and asked her to cover your shifts for you. You've got a whole day off and the best bit of all is I'm totally at your disposal.'

'I can't!' she cried instantly. 'I can't subject Flora to Kevin all day.'

'Yes, you can.'

'That's just mean,' she chided. 'But even if I'm not in the bar, I've got consultancy work to do. Simon needs me to be available to respond to client queries.'

'There won't be any, I promise.'

'How can you know?'

'Because it's Saturday.'

'Oh,' she said. 'Fair point. Gosh, is it really the weekend again already?'

'I rest my case,' he replied. 'You've been so flat out it's no wonder you don't even know what day it is. Now, first . . .' he looked at her appraisingly, 'you are going to take a long hot bath and then get dressed.'

'Nice – so I smell, do I?'

'Not that I can tell, but do as I say because your arse, and the rest of you, is mine, soldier – that's an order.'

'Okay, okay, enough about my arse, although the mention of "soldier" is even more disturbing . . . But even if I don't have to work in the bar or do stuff with Simon I've still got that "to-do" list,' she said, waving at the paper on the table.

He craned his head to read it. 'Good grief, why don't you add "world peace" and "eliminate hunger from the surface of the planet" while you're at it? That's not a weekend "to-do" list . . . it's a New Year's Resolution pledge for the head of the United Nations – and an optimistic one at that.'

'I've got to do them all – somehow,' she muttered, grabbing it away from him.

'Okay, so, I'll let you bring it with you and we can talk it through while we walk.'

'Walk?' said Maddy, gulping. 'Far?'

'Oh yes. Very far. Now get in that bath while I do the washing-up,' he said, gesturing at the sink, piled high with dirty cups and plates. 'You live like a pig, has anyone told you?'

'Top Down? Is that where we're going?' Maddy looked in disbelief towards where Ben was pointing: a craggy, chalk hill, silhouetted against the skyline.

'It's only about five miles as the crow flies. We'll be taking the scenic route back, mind you . . . that's about another seven.'

'Is this what you do for "fun"?' she grumbled, as Ben hauled two rucksacks from the boot of the Land Rover, handing Maddy the smaller one.

'Yup. It's even more fun if you're doing twice the distance. At night. In the rain. With kit.'

By the time she had wriggled her way into her rucksack he had already shrugged his onto his back and set off briskly down the track.

'So I presume you've done the whole night-time, route march thing, being in the army,' she puffed, trotting after him.

'Yup. The South Downs are our training ground. I love it.'

'Weirdo,' she muttered under her breath.

Soon, though, she fell into a steady stride beside him and started to enjoy herself. It was a beautiful day, with barely any wind.

Soon, the exercise and the sunshine had warmed them both through, and they stopped to remove a layer of clothing. She began to regret not bothering with breakfast.

'How's your ankle faring?' he asked, looking down appraisingly at Maddy's feet.

'Fine,' she said, although it was starting to ache.

'Those shoes are no good,' he commented, gesturing at her faded high-top sneakers. 'No ankle support if you have a fall.'

'"Have a fall"!' she scoffed. 'Get you . . . Twenty-five-year-olds don't "have a fall", they just fall over. Ninety-year-olds "have a fall". . .'

'Alright,' said Ben amiably, 'try not to "fall over" then. I might have to ration your beer at lunchtime.'

'Oo, is there beer?' she said longingly, looking at his backpack. 'I could do with one of them,' she added in a wheedling tone, '. . . keep me going, that would.'

'No rest stops,' he said, his mouth twitching in amusement. 'Stop slacking; look, we're nearly there, anyhow.'

It was true, the summit was tantalisingly close and she could already imagine sitting against the sun-warmed rock, resting her legs, which were now burning with the effort.

Ben was keeping up a relentless pace. God, his backside looked good in those shorts, she thought inconsequentially. Really, the view was very pleasing indeed – and the landscape wasn't bad either. She shoved her hands into her pockets. Feeling the impossible 'to-do' list between her fingers her heart sank again.

'You're quiet,' said Ben after a few minutes. 'Worried about Patrick?'

'Worried about everything,' she admitted. 'He's coming out soon. It feels like he's a ticking time bomb . . . What if he has another heart attack? He's always been this strong, energetic man, not old . . . not frail . . . It's hard to think of him the same now it's happened.'

Ben nodded, musing. 'I honestly feel,' he said slowly, 'with Patrick we shouldn't think too far into the future . . .'

'What do you mean? That there's no point planning ahead because he hasn't got long?' She tried to sound matter of fact, like Ben was, but she couldn't help her voice wobbling a little.

'God no, far from it. I'm sure he's got years in him yet, for heavens' sake. I'm just saying do what you need to do for him now and don't meet trouble halfway. We need to help him regain his confidence, if anything. Not treat him like an invalid for the rest of his life.'

'You're right. I need to concentrate on the here and now.'

'Talking of which, we're here!'

He slipped the rucksack off his shoulder and efficiently unrolled the rug he had strapped to the back of it. Sitting out of the wind and warmed by the midday sun, Maddy stretched out her aching legs gratefully and sighed. Ben was right, there was only any point dealing with things one at a time. Tomorrow, in between shifts, she would tackle the mountain of client work still being sent by Simon for her to deal with. Next week she would worry about Patrick coming out of hospital. Her mum would be arriving on Tuesday – Maddy wasn't sure if this was a problem or a solution – but either way, she decided, she had nothing to worry about at that precise moment.

Ben handed her a roll stuffed with ham and an open bottle of beer.

'So,' he said, around a mouthful of ham roll, 'we can tick Patrick off the list for now, at least. What's next?'

'I've got a *lot* of client work to do,' she said, feeling a familiar twist of anxiety in her stomach. 'The stuff that's due for Monday I thought I could tackle between shifts tomorrow. There's five hours so I should be able to nail the urgent bits, at least.'

She didn't admit there was every chance she would be continuing for at least another five hours after shutting up the bar on Sunday evening. It was early closing, thank goodness, so she might even be able to get through it all before two in the morning.

'Load some of it back onto your bloke, what's-his-name.'

'Simon,' she said. 'It's not . . . the actual work itself; that's not really his thing.'

'Not "his thing"? So, what exactly is "his thing" if it's not getting the work done?'

'Erm, not sure really,' she said, feeling she was being a little disloyal. 'He – sort of – schmoozes, I suppose. Has the meetings and persuades the clients . . .'

'So you can do all the donkey work.'

'It's not "donkey work",' she insisted, slightly stung, 'it's actually highly skilled, and it's fine, it's just that now isn't a particularly good time to be unavailable. We've got a lot on.'

Thinking about it, Maddy had to admit they had a little less on than they had done. With a couple of pitches being unsuccessful – her fault, according to Simon – the silver lining was at least to reduce the pressure a little. Hell, if she kept letting him down there wouldn't be a business at all. That would really take the pressure off.

'I don't think he appreciates you,' continued Ben, breaking into her thoughts.

Maddy said nothing.

'And he's your boyfriend too, I gather?'

'Sort of,' she found herself saying, before pulling herself up short, but Ben was onto it like a greyhound after a hare.

'Sort of?'

'I mean, no . . . I mean, yes, he is. My boyfriend,' Maddy stammered. 'We've been together for a while.'

'Have you now,' he said quietly. 'Far be it for me . . .'

Maddy dragged her eyes up to his face. He was lying, relaxed, up on one elbow and regarding her frankly, his eyes not moving from her face, despite her meeting his gaze with uncomfortable directness.

She noticed his eyes weren't just blue, as she had thought, they had green and hazel flecks in them too. In fact, there was a solid patch of green in one eye, just like her own. She had never seen it in anyone else but herself. In fact, his eyes were mesmerising. She felt herself being drawn helplessly in until, after a long moment, he broke the connection and let his eyes lazily drift over her face, resting for a long time on her mouth, making her wonder if she had a beer moustache. She wiped her lips with the back of her hand and looked away.

'Right,' he said, with sudden energy. 'We need to pack up and leave. Seven miles to go and it's starting to look like rain . . . On your feet, soldier,' he added, reaching a strong arm down to help her up.

'Does that mean we're marching all the way home?' she complained. 'I thought this was supposed to be fun. Can't we just – I dunno – stroll . . . ?'

'You're not dressed for bad weather' – he looked pointedly again at her plimsolls – 'so I think we'd better get you back before the storm breaks, don't you?'

Within minutes the wind had whipped up but Ben's chosen route back to the car took them through a valley. It was further but more sheltered than the path they had taken to get there. For a time, they walked in silence, Ben subtly pushing the pace enough for her to feel a little breathless, making her realise how unfit she had become living in London with the Tube and buses at her disposal.

'Keeping up?' he said, turning to watch her puffing as she caught up.

'Yes thanks,' she replied, smiling through gritted teeth.

'We need to keep moving. Don't want that catching up with us.' He tilted his head in the direction of a steel-grey storm cloud that had crept up on the horizon. Sheets of rain had already softened the edges of the rocky outcrop making it fade into the sky as if it were dematerialising.

Minutes later, the rain swept over them, so heavily that Maddy was instantly drenched. *Drat*, she thought, seeing her khaki T-shirt clinging to her breasts, closely enough to show the pattern of her bra beneath. Thank goodness she was wearing one. Worse, her hair was instantly reduced to dripping rats' tails. Her mascara wasn't waterproof either, she remembered, cursing that vanity had made her put it on before they set off.

Ben barely seemed to notice the rain, keeping a steady and efficient pace, his feet surely planted at every step, despite the uneven ground.

'Watch out here,' he cautioned, turning sideways to give his feet more purchase as he navigated a chalk slope treacherous with rivulets of water and loose shingle. 'Take my hand,' he said, reaching back.

'I'm fine,' she said, wiping the make-up out of her eyes.

'It's slippery.'

'I'm honestly fine.'

He shrugged and glanced at his watch. 'Five miles to go, then back home for tea and medals.'

She wondered if he meant his home and hoped he did. She was curious to see how he lived; in a shelter in the garden probably, covered in camouflage paint and wearing one of those funny helmets with twigs and leaves sticking out of it. So preoccupied was she with her vision, she barely noticed when the slope steepened and the surface reverted from tough grass to shingle, scattered over embedded rocks.

Suddenly, her left foot slipped sideways, jamming tight into a gap between two boulders. With her foot firmly stuck, there was a sickening crunch as she lurched forward, her left leg impossibly twisted behind her.

Before she even registered what was happening he had grabbed her, holding her up off the ground. 'Don't move,' he said urgently, his hands clamped onto her arms, holding her still.

Maddy dragged a shuddering breath into her lungs and then held it, fearful it would come back out with a scream attached.

'Stay completely still,' he continued, assessing her leg's position as he held her up. 'Right, I'm going to really slowly lower you to the ground . . .'

'Don't,' she whispered, feeling the blood drain from her face.

'It'll be okay; just relax.'

He was gentle, but it wasn't 'okay'. Her foot came free with an agonising bolt of pain as he lowered her backwards onto the ground. The ankle was grotesquely distorted and a little blood was already soaking through her sock.

'Breathe,' he said. 'Or you'll pass out.'

Nothing wrong with that idea, she thought, panting obediently and wiping away the sweat that had already beaded on her upper lip, mingling with the rain, her jaw clenched tightly against making a sound.

'Shit,' he muttered, as he loosened the laces of her plimsoll, removing it with the utmost delicacy then lowering her sock to get a better view. 'It would be the one you already broke, wouldn't it?' Despite his care the knitted fabric snagged on a sharp edge in the open wound. Without looking, she couldn't tell if it was bone, or the metalwork from her previous injury. She didn't want to know.

'Is it . . . ?' she asked, through gritted teeth.

'Broken? I should say so,' he replied grimly. He looked around and glanced at his watch, running his hand through his hair before leaning down to her.

'Now listen, Maddy, we need to get you to a hospital. I'm going to run down to the car and call for help. I should be able to get a mobile signal there, if not, I'll drive 'til I can. There's no chance they'll be able to send a helicopter in this low cloud so it'll have to be an ambulance. I'll bring a paramedic who can stabilise your leg and give you something for the pain before we move you.'

'Please don't,' she implored.

'Don't what?'

'Don't leave me here . . . on my own.'

She hoped he wouldn't make her say why. She barely knew why herself, and couldn't put it into words. She looked up at him beseechingly, the familiar fear hovering in the periphery of her consciousness – the one where she was lying in the dark, cold, injured, waiting for someone or something to come, something that terrified her.

'Maddy, come on, I need you to hold it together.' He fixed her gaze with his own, putting his hand on her cheek. 'You're freezing,' he added, going to take off his jacket and draping it around her shoulders before running his eyes over her again.

'Damn,' he muttered, looking again at her leg. Seeing the concern in his face she steeled herself to look too. The skin was turning grey, the nail beds a dusky purple. It was clear her ankle was swelling dramatically quickly too. The rain lashed down, mixing with the blood from her ankle and turning the puddle beneath a rusty red.

'Okay,' he said. 'Change of plan. No time for a paramedic.

We need to get that leg seen to more urgently than I thought, so – actually – you get your way.'

'Wh-what do you mean?'

'The blood supply is compromised.'

'So?'

'So, it needs sorting fast.'

'Or I lose my foot?'

'Not going to happen,' he said, but she knew that was exactly what he was afraid of. He must have seen battle injuries. He knew.

'I'll have to take you with me now,' he said, grimly. 'It's not going to be comfortable, I'm afraid.'

Next thing she knew, he was rummaging amongst the picnic remains in his backpack.

'This'll work.' He brought out one of the beer bottles.

'We've drunk it,' said Maddy, 'and, to be honest, painkiller-wise, I was hoping for something stronger.'

'I know,' he said, with a twitch of a smile, 'but it'll make a brilliant splint. Okay,' he shrugged, 'it'll make an alright splint, but it's the best we've got.'

'I can't go to A & E with a beer bottle strapped to my leg. They'll think I'm PFO.'

'PFO?'

'"Pissed, Fell Over". I read it in an article once. Doctors, they use these acronyms on their notes.'

'Not far off the truth,' he teased, grabbing hold of his T-shirt and tearing a long strip off the bottom, all the way around. 'Drinking at lunchtime's the thin end of the wedge, I've heard.' He gave a final yank to rip through the seam.

'Steady on,' she said weakly. 'I'm not really in the mood for a striptease, thanks all the same.'

'I'm crushed – but keep talking,' he said. 'You're doing really well.'

'Sure? I thought that last one was a bit "lame", geddit . . . ?'

He didn't answer; he was concentrating totally as he laid the bottle alongside Maddy's ankle and then gently wound the T-shirt strip around them both to form a rough brace.

'Ow, ow, ow . . .' she moaned, biting her lip, tears springing to her eyes at last. Overwhelmed with a wave of nausea and pain, she slumped back onto the ground and breathed in short gasps.

'Sorry, but I daren't move you without a bit of support around it. There. That'll have to do,' he said, tying a double knot in the jersey strip. 'I'll have you know that was my favourite T-shirt too . . .'

'I'd hate to see your least favourite,' but her words turned into a gasp of trepidation as he put one arm under her knees and the other round her shoulders.

'Ready?'

She nodded.

Although he was gentle, being lifted was agony. She bit down hard on her lip again and buried her head in his shoulder.

'Tea and medals, remember,' he murmured in her ear, as he set off down the incline.

CHAPTER EIGHT

An age later, both of them bathed in sweat for different reasons, they arrived back at the Land Rover and Ben propped Maddy carefully on the back seat, grabbing a hairy old tartan blanket from the boot to wrap around her.

'Am I having a nap now?' she joked weakly.

'You're cold and in shock,' he said. 'Only I can see how white you are.'

But he wasn't the only one. She could see a reflection of her own face in the driving mirror and it wasn't great. What was left of her mascara had streaked down her cheeks with the rain and the tears she had not managed to stem. Her skin was waxy white, even her lips. By contrast, the colour of her foot was worse than ever. What if it was already too late to save it?

'It's not too late,' he said, as if reading her thoughts. 'Now hold on, I'll try not to bump you around too much, but these roads are pretty rough.'

It seemed another age until they made it back onto the main road. After that, she must have dozed or passed out because the next thing she knew, Ben was pulling up in the ambulance bay just yards from the ward where Patrick lay.

'It says you can't park here,' she protested, gesturing at the sign.

'Actually it says the bay is reserved for emergency vehicles. And that's what this is, temporarily, with you in it.'

'Fine,' muttered Maddy. 'Fight your own battles.' She was more than happy for Ben to take charge as waves of exhaustion flooded through her. Also, she had started to shake, which was a shame because keeping still was the best way of minimising the agonising jabs of pain travelling up her leg.

Still carrying her in his arms, Ben was arguing politely but firmly with the receptionist at the signing-in desk when a junior doctor in scrubs wandered vacantly towards them on the way to the vending machine.

'Look at this girl's leg,' ordered Ben.

Startled, he looked first at Ben and then, obediently, at Maddy, whose lower leg was still incongruously bound with T-shirt strips and the beer bottle. The foot, including nail beds, was now as white as lard and the swelling had spread up her lower leg to her knee.

'Right,' he said, suddenly alert. 'Come this way.' He led them to a curtained cubicle, with the receptionist's protest trailing off behind them.

'You'll need an X-ray immediately,' he said after a brief examination, 'although there's no doubt it's fractured. The orthopaedic surgeon will want to see you for sure. I'll page him now.'

Removing the makeshift splint was painful and the X-ray technician was ruthless but apologetic about moving her leg around to get all the angles she needed.

By the time Maddy was wheeled back into the cubicle,

clutching her own X-rays, she was sobbing wearily with pain and shock.

'Hey, hey,' said Ben, grabbing a tissue and wiping her face. 'You've been quite the hard-ass up until now. I've had soldiers in the field with injuries like that who would have been screaming for their mum.' He pressed a wodge of tissues into her hand and slipped outside the cubicle where she could hear him politely but firmly asking the nearest nurse to sort out some pain relief.

'Chances are she'll be going straight to surgery. They'll deal with it,' came the reply.

'That could be another hour, Nurse. I strongly suggest something needs to be done now.'

Sure enough, he returned with the junior doctor who quickly scribbled something on a clipboard and disappeared with it. Moments later, the grumpy nurse returned with a syringe and deftly taped a needle into the back of her hand. Maddy had never been more grateful to have a needle stuck into her.

'I feel weird,' she slurred a couple of minutes later.

'Not surprised. Never mind beer, you're on the hard stuff now. Better?'

She considered the question carefully. 'Not sure . . . It still hurts like hell but I don't think I really care any more.' She giggled, then clapped her hand over her mouth. 'Oops. Think I'm a bit pissed.'

The orthopaedic surgeon was a weary but kind-looking man who was more than familiar to Maddy.

'Hello again,' he said as he swept into the cubicle. 'I never forget a fracture. What on earth have you been doing to my brilliant work?' He grabbed the file of X-rays and plonked them on the light box. 'Good grief. You really don't like that leg of yours, do you?'

'Don't like it as much as I did this morning,' she agreed.

'You know I'm going to have to operate again, don't you?' Maddy nodded, meekly.

'Right,' he said, giving her an appraising look. 'I doubt you're going to remember much of this, given the look of you, but I suppose I'd better run through the technical stuff.'

He looked at Ben. 'Can he stay?'

Maddy nodded.

'Okay, so . . . first time you rocked up with your foot nigh on broken off, remember? It's all here,' he said, waving at the file. 'Not a pretty sight. Both your lower leg bones broken – tibia and fibula – with the broken ends rammed into your foot. Lovely, it was.'

Ben winced, and squeezed Maddy's hand.

'So now,' the surgeon went on, 'my work then, if I say so myself, has held up rather well. Trouble is, the metal plates on your leg have held it together but transferred the forces downwards. Different mechanism of injury too, of course, a twisting injury this time. Last time it just looked like you jumped off a cliff and landed on your feet.'

Ben raised his eyebrows but said nothing.

'So we've got a thoroughly mashed up and displaced ankle here. The talus is broken, you've doubtless ruptured at least one ligament and, despite the plate, you've got a medial malleolus fracture,' he broke off. 'Or, to put it another way, you've broken the end off your tibia. Again. You'll be in plaster to your knee and on crutches for at least six weeks.

'Lucky for you I've got a slot on my operating schedule this afternoon, or at least I will have shortly.' He turned away from them both and had a peremptory conversation with the mousey intern who had slunk in after him. 'Reschedule my four o'clock to five o'clock and clear the rest of my list. This girl needs to go in straight away to restore circulation. Actually,' he said, glancing again at the X-rays, 'cancel the five o'clock too. This is going to take a while.'

'Thank you,' said Maddy.

'You don't know how grateful you should be,' he reprimanded her. 'Doing a full repair straight away spares you having to have that fracture pulled straight before I've got you out cold on the table. Now you *should* thank me for that.'

'Out cold is definitely the way to be,' she agreed, remembering the agony three years before. Then her leg had been pulled and yanked mercilessly in A & E and then went through two temporary casts while the surgeon worked out how to piece it back together for her with all the metalwork she had now, presumably, destroyed.

'Right,' he said on the way out of the cubicle, his intern scampering behind him, 'I'd better go and have a rummage through my Meccano set for a few nuts and bolts to fix that leg.'

'He seems like a good guy,' remarked Ben. 'So you were in Sussex when you broke your leg before too?'

'Yep,' she said repressively, hoping he would leave it there. He did.

'Alright if I pop out and deal with the receptionist dragon now?' he asked instead. 'She wants me to fill in a couple more pesky forms. Which reminds me, who do you want for your next of kin? Simon?'

'God no!'

He raised an eyebrow.

'I mean, no, better not him. He's not great in a crisis; he'll just come down complaining and picking fights with everyone.'

'Your mum, then?'

'Yes, okay, her details are in my phone. Here,' she said, unlocking it and passing it over to him.

'Good,' he said, 'because also I should give her a call for you. Let her know what's going on. Better to hear from me than someone at the hospital.'

'True. That would make her panic for sure. Can you . . . ?' Maddy hesitated. 'I mean, she's coming down on Tuesday and that's fine, I don't want her coming any earlier. Tell her she should stick with her current arrangements.'

'I don't mind doing that. Why the hesitation?'

'I might need someone to give me a bit of a hand before then . . .'

'I don't mind doing that, either.'

'I mean, I'll be fine,' she added hurriedly. 'Obviously.'

'Obviously,' he echoed, with hollow irony.

'They'll let me out as soon as my leg's fixed, but, you know . . . stairs and stuff. I don't want them to not let me out . . .'

'Not a problem,' he said, putting his hand on hers briefly. 'I'll spring you out of here as soon as I can humanly persuade them to let you go. Promise.'

The porter came for her while Ben was still engaged with the form-filling and, within minutes, Maddy, still in agony, was gratefully submitting to the general anaesthetic.

She had a vague impression of her kindly surgeon reassuring her the operation had gone well and a sense of being moved through a series of brightly lit rooms, staff moving in and out of her field of vision, as she slept and woke and slept again.

Waking up properly at last, Maddy found herself in a side ward with four beds, only hers occupied. It was dark outside and the light in the room was dim. Great. There wasn't a soul in sight, so chances were she was stuck there until morning at least. She hated hospitals. Particularly when she was the patient. She wanted out with a fierceness close to panic.

'So, someone's awake,' came a kindly Irish voice, belonging to a sweet-faced nurse in her twenties. 'I suppose you'll be wanting some supper?'

'Not hungry,' said Maddy, summoning a smile. 'I'd like to go now, actually.'

'At nearly midnight?' queried the nurse pointing at the clock above the door. 'Got a pumpkin carriage waiting to whisk you off now, have you?'

'You called?' said Ben, materialising in the doorway, as if by magic.

'You're still here! Where have you been?'

'Other than popping in every hour on the hour to listen to you snoring, you mean?'

'Was I snoring?'

'And dribbling,' he confirmed. 'You're a class act . . . but, in full answer to your question, I've been hanging out in the cardiac ward chatting to Patrick.'

'At this time of night?' said Maddy and the Irish nurse in unison.

'Yep.'

'Respect to you!' said the nurse. 'The ward sister's fearsome about sticking to visiting hours . . .'

'What, you mean Henrietta?' asked Ben. 'Or "Hetty darling", as Patrick calls her . . . she was bringing us cups of tea.'

'Was she now!' the nurse exclaimed, in awe.

'And Jaffa Cakes.'

'You're clearly quite the charmer,' said the nurse, 'although I doubt your ability to charm your way into seeing this girl home tonight as she is currently insisting.'

'The charm was all Patrick's when it comes to Henrietta,' admitted Ben, 'but I'll certainly do my best with you . . . erm,' he peered at her name badge, 'Teresa.'

'Hark at you,' said Teresa, smiling in spite of herself. 'As if I've got time to help this child get dressed, get her signed off and sort out her going-home prescription on top of everything else I have to do,' she said, taking a prescription slip off the front of the clipboard and waving it in his face.

'I saw the signs for the hospital pharmacy on the way to the cardiac ward. Are they open?'

'Twenty-four seven.'

'What do you say about you getting her up and dressed, and I'll pop to get this sorted, then?' said Ben persuasively.

'And you'll need to bring her straight back in if there is any sign at all of infection,' lectured Teresa. 'Fever, confusion, anything . . . and she'll need to be brought back into the fracture clinic anyhow in a day or two.'

'Noted,' said Ben, saluting as he took the prescription from her and waved it in farewell.

Maddy was pretty keen to get dressed before Ben returned but Teresa tutted as she handed her the still-damp T-shirt she had been wearing earlier.

'And you're to get properly dry clothes on you the moment you get home,' she lectured. 'And straight to bed with you, mind. And you need to take those antibiotics your friend is getting you without fail. The whole course . . .'

By the time Ben returned with a bag full of drugs from the pharmacy, she was fully dressed and lying back on the bed. If she was honest, the effort had worn her out completely but she was keen not to show Teresa that. Or Ben.

There was a wheelchair waiting by the bed, and Teresa had even produced a pair of crutches. 'These are for use tomorrow *at the earliest*,' she had insisted, waving them at Maddy. 'You'll leave my ward in that,' she added, pointing at the wheelchair, 'and no arguing.'

'You'll get none from me,' said Ben, positioning it next to the bed and gesturing Maddy to get in, which she did, awkwardly and with his help.

Getting back into the jeep was even more tricky. Ben insisted on her lying across the back seat as she had just a few hours before.

'I don't approve,' he said. 'You'd have been better staying on the ward until tomorrow, at least.'

'But I just can't bear to.'

'I know.'

Even the short journey back to the Havenbury Arms was too long to stay awake for. The next thing she knew, Ben was gently shaking her. She felt stiff, cold and shivery getting out of the jeep, and the prospect of getting upstairs to bed was no less daunting than being told she had to climb Everest.

'Upsadaisy,' said Ben, scooping her up into his arms again.

'You'll get a hernia,' she said as she reached to unlock the door. 'I've got crutches, for goodness' sake.'

'Tomorrow. At the earliest. You heard Teresa. Now, straight to bed I think,' he continued, turning slightly sideways to get her up the narrow stairs without risking banging her damaged leg on anything.

'Why, how very forward of you. No foreplay?'

'Let's skip the sexual marathon tonight, shall we? Which one's your room?'

Maddy indicated along the corridor to the tiny bedroom that had become her home over the last few weeks. Its narrow little bed was unmade, she realised, from that morning, which seemed a century ago.

'In you get,' he said, putting her gently down.

'What, straight away?'

'You need the bathroom?'

'Yes, I do, actually. Plus I wouldn't mind brushing my teeth.'

'I'll have to come in with you.'

'You will not!'

'Oh, for God's sake, woman . . . Alright, here we go.'

Ben deposited her next to the loo, waiting until she had her hand resting on the wall for balance before he let go.

'I'll wait outside,' he announced, giving her a little bow. 'Don't lock the flipping door, whatever you do.'

Maddy took stock. She managed to manoeuver herself onto the loo but then cringed at the thought he was outside the door listening.

'Any chance you could find me some pyjamas?' she called, by way of diversion.

'Will do,' he replied, sounding reluctant.

Quickly Maddy went to the loo, flushed it, and barely hopping a couple of steps – luckily the bathroom was tiny – she was brushing her teeth by the time Ben handed in pyjamas and, cringingly, a pair of her not exactly ragged but not exactly brand-new pants.

'You pee like a horse, by the way,' he said as he dangled the clothes on an outstretched arm without even putting his head around the door.

'You listened!' she squeaked in outrage, spluttering toothpaste everywhere.

'I suppose you aren't going to let me help you change, either.'

'Nope,' she agreed, around a mouthful of toothpaste.

'Fine,' said Ben. 'For goodness' sake sit down while you do it. I'll wait here.'

God it felt good to put on clean, dry clothes. What she could really do with was a long hot bath, but she guessed he would definitely lose patience with that. In any case, it was now nearly two in the morning. He must be exhausted. She wondered if he would stay or go home, at last.

'Would you like to stay the night?' she offered primly as he carried her back to her little single bed.

'Would I like . . . ? Of course I'm bloody staying the night. I'm hardly going to leave you on your own, am I?'

Once he had helped her position her leg carefully on a pillow, he pulled the covers up and tucked them under her chin.

Crouching by the bed he regarded her sternly. 'Now listen, Maddy,' he said, forcing her to meet his eye. 'It's really important you get your head in the right place over this. It's a game-changer. You're not going to be able to just carry on as if nothing's happened.'

She gave an infinitesimally small nod. 'Got it,' she said, clutching her covers under her chin, her hands curled like paws over the edge of the duvet.

'No,' he insisted. 'You haven't. Listen, your mission, for at least the next few days, is to focus on your injury. You need to take the painkillers, okay? Never mind the side effects –

you just take them, no debate. You also need to eat if you can, or at least make sure you're getting lots of fluids. Also, the more you can sleep the better. This isn't something getting in the way of your life. It *is* your life . . .'

'Gosh, you're really bossy, aren't you?' she observed owlishly. 'No prizes for guessing you were in the army.'

'Okay, so, what did I just say?'

'You said "take drugs, drink heavily, sleep with everyone . . ." Honestly! I can just imagine you advising a teenage daughter one day.'

Ben smiled in spite of himself. 'Off to sleep with you,' he said, straightening up.

'Where are you sleeping?'

'Here,' he said, lying himself down on the floor beside the bed.

'You can't just sleep on the floor!'

'Watch me,' said Ben, rolling up his jacket and putting it under his head as a pillow. 'After a day like today I could sleep on a clothes line. There's a danger I won't hear you in the night if I'm in another room.'

'I won't call you.'

'You might,' he said, with finality. 'Now, go to sleep.'

CHAPTER NINE

Later, it must have been about five in the morning, Ben shook her gently awake and propped her partly upright.

'Open wide,' he said, steering a spoon with some clear liquid into her mouth and then handing her a glass of water.

'Bleurgh,' she spluttered.

'I know. Drink some water.'

'What *is* that horrible stuff?'

'Says oral morphine on the bottle.'

'I was sleeping,' she complained drowsily. 'The pain's okay.'

'And we need to keep it that way,' he said, lowering her back down gently. 'Can't let you sleep through a dose when it's due, you'll wake up in agony. Now, back to sleep,' he added gently, watching her for a moment and then lying back down on the floor.

Maddy slipped restlessly from one dream to another, battling to get somewhere, she couldn't remember where or why, with nameless obstacles in her path and then – suddenly and crushingly – she was back there:

Searing pain in her leg, blood running down her face, heart pounding in panic as she waited, helplessly for it – for him – whatever it or he was – to come for her. Groaning, she tried to drag herself to safety . . . The fear. The cold. The pain. And then, as if it was inside her head, she heard a calm, gentle voice.

'Where are you, Maddy?'

She tried to reply, but no sound came.

'Maddy?' the voice came again. Insistent.

'Ben?' she breathed.

'Yes,' came the reply. 'Tell me where you are.'

'It's dark,' she whispered. 'I'm in the dark.'

'Okay,' came Ben's voice, calming her. 'That's okay. I'm there too. I'm with you. You're safe.'

In her dream, she tried to talk again, but couldn't make a sound. She felt Ben near her, protecting her, and the fear was gone.

'Good grief!' she exclaimed, seeing the clock on her bedroom wall. 'It's nearly lunchtime!'

'I know,' said Ben, elbowing his way through the door with a steaming mug of tea in each hand. 'I was going to sound a bugle, I was getting so bored waiting for you to wake up.'

He sat down carefully on the edge of the bed and handed her one of the mugs.

They sipped companionably.

'I think I had a dream about you last night,' she said.

'Yeah? I get that a lot . . .'

'Not like that.' She gave him a shove. 'I mean, I was having a nightmare, I think . . .' She considered telling him

110

it was *the* recurring nightmare she always had but decided against it. 'And anyway, somehow, you were there. I could hear your voice.'

'That *is* a nightmare,' he teased, but he wasn't smiling. He was looking intently at her.

'It *was* you, wasn't it?' she demanded. 'You *were* talking to me.'

He paused, considering. 'Can you tell me what was happening?'

She sighed. 'It was this – I dunno – I get this dream . . .' she said, staring out of the window, her mug drooping dangerously. He took it from her and set it down.

'It's about when you last broke your leg, isn't it?'

'It was . . . yes, basically . . . only I can't ever remember . . .' she said distractedly, banging her fists on her temples with frustration, 'I'm just in the dark, and it's cold.'

He took her hands, pulling them gently away from her head and holding them in his own.

She looked at him. 'And I'm scared,' she said. 'I'm really, really scared, but I don't know why.'

'How did you break your leg, Maddy?'

They stared at each other in silence for an age. Eventually, she looked away and spoke.

'Nobody quite knows,' she admitted. 'I know it sounds ridiculous . . . I'd been out that night, drinking, here, in the Havenbury Arms. I was with Flora, and with some other people I knew vaguely; I mean, they weren't my close friends. Just other students, you know . . . Kevin was there, as it happens. You know him. Anyway,' she went on, staring into space, remembering, 'we were playing drinking games – like you do when you're young and stupid.'

111

He nodded, smiling slightly. 'Go on.'

'That's almost pretty much it. I remember going back to my room in student halls. At least, I think I remember . . . Other people have told me they saw me coming back. Flora was definitely there putting me to bed but the details . . . I don't know. Sometimes I even wonder if I have a memory of it *because* people told me I did, if you know what I mean?'

He nodded again, holding her gaze.

'Anyway,' she continued, 'I went to bed, I went to sleep – at least I assume I went to sleep – and then . . .'

She swallowed and Ben waited patiently, not moving.

'Hours later, in the middle of the night, I was found by a couple of students who were staying up late. I was outside on the ground, crawling around. Injured. The assumption was I'd been sleepwalking or something, and that I jumped or fell out of my window.'

He whistled softly. 'How many floors up were you?'

'My room was on the third storey, so about twenty or so feet onto concrete,' she said. 'Unlucky, really. The term before I was on the ground floor.'

'Christ,' he exclaimed quietly. 'And you were found underneath your window?'

'No, actually, quite a few yards away. It seems I'd crawled some distance, God knows why, or where I thought I was going . . .'

'With a broken leg,' said Ben, wincing.

'Yeah.'

'And you don't remember doing that?'

She shook her head. 'I remember the student bar. I remember the hospital, but even that is really confused. Like a series of freeze frames. I don't know . . . I had other injuries too. I was concussed, which probably explains the memory loss partly. It was suggested I was almost certainly knocked out when I hit the ground. It was February. Bitterly cold. Presumably I would have died of exposure if I hadn't been found.'

'I can see why it bothers you, not remembering.'

'Who says it bothers me?'

'Of course it does,' said Ben. 'It would bother anyone. Something appalling and life-changing happened and you don't – essentially – know what it is. I mean, *do* you sleepwalk ever?'

'Never have, before or since.'

'It probably wasn't that then, was it?' he said. 'And the fear,' he added, 'that's quite a consistent part of your flashback experience . . .'

'Flashback?' queried Maddy. 'You mean that nightmare I have – that dream – is a real memory of sorts? A "flashback"?'

'Oh yes, absolutely,' said Ben. 'But it's almost deliberately incomplete. It's your mind telling you there's something to remember, but another part of your subconscious is refusing to let you know what it is.'

'Why?'

He shook his head. 'I don't have the answers,' he admitted. 'It could be the concussion, simple as that. But also,' he went on, carefully, 'it could potentially be because it's too distressing – a form of self-defence. I see it with the soldiers I treat . . . they block out things until they are strong enough to process them. It's quite a clever thing the mind does, really . . .'

'How did you know it was going to happen last night, though?'

'I thought it might, which is why I stayed close while you slept.'

'So, you *were* there, in my head,' she said, wonderingly.

'I was,' he agreed. 'You were moaning. You seemed distressed. Did I help?'

'Yes.' She paused. 'I was scared – as usual – and I felt . . . I don't know, I felt that there was somebody coming – somebody who wanted to hurt me – and then, somehow, that somebody was you, and it was alright. I wasn't afraid any more.'

They both sat, musing for a few moments.

'Hang on a minute,' said Maddy suddenly. 'You say you knew I was "traumatised"?'

He nodded.

'How, exactly?'

'It's my job.'

She gave him a fierce look.

'It's fine,' he said. 'It's not like you've got it tattooed on your forehead, but I'm trained to know the signs . . . hypervigilance, emotional detachment, expressions of fear, and even anger, when someone makes reference to the precipitating event . . .'

She remembered their conversation in the bar, when he had gently enquired about her ankle and her wariness over life in general. He was right. She had been downright hostile.

He continued. 'The flashbacks are occurring as nightmares now, but it concerns me that . . . without help, your symptoms might become more intrusive, you may start experiencing flashbacks during waking hours, for example . . .'

She stared into space, horrified. Could that happen? Her eyes filled with tears.

'Come on, now,' he said, noticing. 'I've seen worse cases. You'll be fine.' He gathered her into his arms and she relaxed against him, her head resting on his shoulder.

'So,' she said, at last, wiping her eyes and nose on what remained of his T-shirt, 'could you help me? If I asked you to,' she added hastily.

'I'd like to,' said Ben, looking down into her face, so vulnerable and tear-stained, 'if you think you can let me?'

She looked up at him and gave a tiny nod. For a long moment their eyes locked and then Ben broke the contact, letting his eyes range over her face, lingering on her slightly parted lips. She arched her back, drawing infinitesimally nearer but he drew away, gently but firmly placing her back against the pillows, keeping his hands on her upper arms to lightly hold her there.

'This can't happen,' he murmured.

'Why not?' she said, dazed with longing.

'You're vulnerable,' he said patiently. 'You're in no state to be making decisions like this. Your thinking's all mixed up – with the fear, the anxiety, this – entirely understandable – preoccupation with not remembering what happened to you . . . plus you're high on morphine, for goodness' sake . . .'

She sighed, sinking back into the pillows and closing her eyes. Life was not improving.

'Now,' Ben said briskly, determined to break the mood. 'How about brunch?'

'Goodness, what a good idea,' she said, totally distracted at the thought of food. 'I am absolutely starving!'

'Not surprised,' said Ben, getting up. 'It's been an awfully long while since those ham rolls on Top Down.'

In the kitchen, he nearly groaned aloud at what he had got so close to doing. Giving in to his attraction to this woman who so clearly needed his professional help would be a disaster, not to mention that Patrick would never forgive him. But now, pushing her away, he had probably made her feel even worse . . .

As a college professor he was used to kindly but firmly rejecting the attentions of his students. Outside his teaching, things were more straightforward. Offers were plentiful and he had no problem at all with mutually pleasing encounters with little or no emotional complexity or commitment. With Maddy it was different. Not only was he drawn to her when they met in the pub that day, her traumatic leg injury and his ability to help with her flashbacks had been a fast track to intimacy and trust. It was inevitable. He saw the same intense connection amongst his men who had shared danger and trauma. But the trouble with Maddy, unlike his soldier mates, was that he was finding himself increasingly drawn to her. And that made things complicated. Even if his basic moral compass wasn't shouting in his ear, his training made the situation perfectly clear: no practitioner should combine psychiatric support with any sort of personal entanglement. It was unethical, unprofessional, immoral . . . and a downright stupid idea.

Maddy eventually persuaded Ben to help her get out of bed and into Patrick's sitting room, where they spent the day together doing what couples do on Sundays. Ben was marking his students' papers, breaking off to produce food and cups of tea at regular intervals. Maddy was alternately dozing and browsing through the pile of Sunday papers he had produced. She felt guilty at not doing any marketing work for Simon but Ben had refused to bring her laptop to her and, in any case, her concentration was so poor she could barely get through a magazine article.

'Tomorrow,' he had said firmly. 'You can do some work then. You just need to rest today. At least let the anaesthetic get out of your system.'

Kevin and his mate ran the bar together – Sundays were generally quiet anyway – and Maddy was relieved he had been able to produce a sidekick at such short notice. His mysterious friend, who she vaguely recognised from her college days, slunk around in much the same way as Kevin did: taciturn, morose and secretive.

'I don't trust him,' said Maddy to Ben again when they were alone. 'I can't put my finger on it but he makes me nervous.' She didn't say that she even wondered if he were somehow working for the ghastly Dennis, who would love to have an excuse for Top Taverns to take the pub away from Patrick.

'I'll watch him tonight,' said Ben. 'When he's running the bar.'

'What for? You won't see him doing anything. I wondered if he was stealing but, I have to admit, the bar receipts always tally. I've checked.'

'Maybe there's nothing to see . . . but there might be,' said Ben. 'You never know.'

'Cooeee!' came the voice from downstairs. 'Anybody dying for a cup of tea they don't have to make themselves?' It continued as what sounded like a herd of elephants came trampling up the stairs.

'Morning!' called Serena, bursting into the sitting room where Ben had brought Maddy before leaving for college an hour before.

'Ben gave me the key – I hope you don't mind. It all sounded very dramatic: compound fracture, miles from anywhere . . . poor you,' she continued, swooping down to kiss Maddy on both cheeks.

'Of course I don't mind. Hello, boys.'

'Ah yes,' Serena said. 'Here they are, my two little buggers. Half-term, apparently. They insisted on coming home.' She ruffled the hair of one. 'Not sure if you've been properly introduced so this is Harry – my nine-year-old,' and then, putting the other in a headlock, which was more of a hug, 'and this huge heffalump is Josh, just turned eleven. Boys, say "Hello, Maddy".'

'Hello, Maddy,' they chorused, grinning cheerfully.

'Now,' continued Serena, 'I'm under strict orders from "he who must be obeyed" not to tire you out, but – basically – we are entirely at your disposal today. So, other than the meeting this afternoon with the Brighton nerdy web boys, what's the plan?'

'Yikes, we haven't got that meeting already, have we? I haven't prepared . . .'

'Don't need to,' replied Serena. 'All sorted.'

Maddy looked concerned. 'But what about the boys?'

'Oh, they'll be fine.' She waved, airily. 'They'll wait in the car if we bribe them with a McDonald's. They'll do anything for chicken nuggets. Horrendous things,' she shuddered. 'Still . . . needs must.'

'I'm sure that's not what they want to spend half-term doing, is it?'

'That's only this afternoon,' said Serena. 'This morning they're going to work like bastard Trojans for you, aren't you, my lovelies?'

They nodded and grinned.

'Mummy – I mean, Mum?' asked Harry. 'Are we getting pocket money for helping Maddy?'

''Course we are,' chipped in Josh. 'We need to negotiate. Leave it to me . . .'

'He is his father's son,' said Serena. 'Sorry.'

'Yeah, whatever,' said Josh. 'So, we're doing chores for Maddy this morning and it's nine o'clock now. We're going to Brighton at about twelve – that's three hours . . . I'm calculating that'll be . . . a fiver,' he finished, meeting Maddy's eyes, his head tilted slightly back.

'A fiver, eh?' she narrowed her eyes.

'Each. Obviously.'

'Obviously,' echoed Maddy, stroking her chin. 'Okay, boys,' she said with a chuckle, 'you've got yourselves a deal.'

'Cool,' said Josh, offering his hand.

With minimal direction from Serena, the boys cleaned the kitchen, emptied the bins and wastepaper baskets and then dusted and hoovered the entire flat.

Meanwhile, Serena helped Maddy to have a bath, carefully ensuring her cast didn't get wet.

'Josh broke his leg last year,' she reminisced. 'He's such a liability,' she said as she rinsed shampoo out of Maddy's hair. 'He wasn't thrilled at having to have his mum help him wash, I can tell you.'

'I was dying for this,' admitted Maddy, 'but I wasn't going to ask Ben.'

'He knew that. It's partly why he phoned me. Obviously I'd have been furious if he hadn't. Now, on with your clothes.'

'Good grief, it's Tuesday tomorrow, isn't it? My mum's arriving at about four o'clock. I haven't got her room ready. I was actually going to buy some new sheets for the bed. There aren't even enough pillows . . .'

'Shopping!' exclaimed Serena. 'My absolute favourite thing. Now . . . let's get you settled in the sitting room. Ben says you can have your laptop today, if you're good.'

'Big of him.'

Serena ignored her. 'I'll sort you out with a cup of tea and leave you directing the boys while I pop down to that new homewares store. I was looking for an excuse.'

Pirate looked relieved to have some company, having been brought up from the bar again by Ben before he left. Maddy persuaded Serena to let him out of his cage for a breather while she was out. Throwing Serena an old-fashioned look – clearly he blamed her for his incarceration – he flew up to the curtain rail and mooched backwards and forwards along it, muttering to himself before crouching moodily and glaring at the two boys who tried to entice him down with bird seed and slices of banana.

Serena returned in under an hour carrying pretty white cotton bedsheets with a delicate lavender sprig pattern on them, a new pair of down pillows, tea towels for the kitchen (the others were a horror, Serena reported with a shudder) as well as two huge bunches of stocks, which she split amongst five jugs, plonking some by the newly made spare bed, some on the kitchen windowsill and the remainder on the coffee table in the sitting room.

'This is miraculous,' said Maddy, hobbling around the flat trying out her crutches. The boys were even cleaning the insides of the windows, letting the low autumn sunlight flood into the flat.

'My mum will be pretty impressed,' she added, with relief. 'And Patrick too, when he finally gets home.'

'How is the darling?' asked Serena. 'We've all been so worried about him.'

The corners of Maddy's mouth turned down at the thought. 'Okay,' she said, slightly tremulously. Really she needed to get a grip and stop all this bursting into tears. She took a deep breath and continued. 'Ben said he was in great form on Saturday night. He's recovering well from the surgery, for sure, but, I don't know . . . things are going to have to change for him now. He won't be able to keep working at the pace he has for all these years. I hadn't realised until recently, but he's in his sixties! Did you know that?'

'I didn't,' said Serena. 'He doesn't look it.'

'He sort of does now,' said Maddy.

'I just can't think of him as old. He's still an attractive man,' she mused, 'but it might be about time he was thinking about winding down a bit. Do you suppose he could be convinced to do that?'

'No chance. And also I don't know how he would. Where would he live, for one thing?'

Serena nodded, pondering. 'One thing at a time, eh? We'd better round up these boys and head off to Brighton. The traffic can be abysmal and we don't want to be late, plus we have to swing by and pick up Flora on the way.'

'Wow, you really did break it! Again!' exclaimed Flora as she flumped herself into the back of the car, beaded plaits flying, making the two boys squeeze up. 'Sad face,' she added, making a sad, clown face and blowing Maddy a kiss. 'So, serious business meeting,' she said, composing herself. 'Bring it on.'

* * *

The 'web boys', as Serena insisted on calling them, occupied a cramped office on the first floor above a stationery shop. The little office, with four desks crammed in at one end and a small meeting area at the other, was an eclectic mix of professionalism and hardcore juvenility.

The two men, both in their twenties, kissed Serena and politely shook hands with Maddy and Flora, who they eyed up shyly but appreciatively, before offering tea and coffee and exclaiming over the broken leg.

'Jules totally smashed up his leg snowboarding last year,' said Henry, fiddling nervously with the numerous friendship bracelets he was wearing, some of them practically decaying with age.

'Yeah,' agreed Jules, 'it was really gross, but the French nurses were – like – uber fit, and I totally scored with them so, you know, it was cool.'

Serena looked at them both fondly. 'Your mum wasn't too thrilled, as I recall,' she observed, and Jules went slightly pink.

'Yeah well, you know her, she was – like – panicking a bit.'

Contrary to initial appearances, the young men were hugely impressive when they got into the meeting itself. They were happy with the designs and made some useful comments about the site layout and structure.

'So, you're basically looking to create a directory site?' suggested Jules. 'Nothing to stop you having online retailing ability too – there's these modules you can just plug in – although you could do worse than encourage your members to retail via sites like eBay and Etsy too.'

'I could manage that side of things,' said Flora. 'I'm doing it all the time, anyhow.'

'It's another avenue,' said Serena, holding up her hands in agreement. 'As long as you're happy to give it the time, Flora.'

'You'll want us to make sure there's connectivity with all the social media platforms too, of course,' said Henry.

Serena grimaced. 'I suppose so,' she said. 'A closed book to me, I'm afraid. You?' she asked Maddy.

'Yes and no,' said Maddy. 'They can be real time-suckers, that's the trouble. It's a key marketing thing, obviously, but not my favourite task.' Plus – she was thinking – there was no way she would have enough time to spend on social media with everything else that was going on.

'I'll totes do that too,' said Flora, happily. 'I'm an Instagram junkie, you have no idea . . .'

CHAPTER TEN

Once Serena settled the two boys with some extraordinary-looking knickerbocker glories the three women contemplated their options over coffee.

'With those two lads on board, and Flora being such a whizz on the social media,' said Serena, 'I really think we can nail it.'

'Agreed,' said Maddy. 'So, other than some decent photography, media relations, a launch event – and we definitely still need to be at one of the big home and lifestyle exhibitions – oh, and not forgetting a major chunk of start-up funding, we're pretty much there,' she joked mirthlessly.

'What I think,' said Flora, slowly, with a wide grin spreading over her sweet, amiable face, 'is that we,' she made a sweeping gesture to include Maddy and Serena, 'are the dog's bollocks.'

'Can't argue with that,' said Maddy, infected with her enthusiasm. Holding up her coffee mug triumphantly, she declared, 'To us!'

'To us,' agreed the other two, slopping latte enthusiastically in a three-way toast.

* * *

'Anybody hungry?' came the voice, floating up the stairs. It startled Maddy out of a light doze and, before she had had time to sit up and wipe the sleep out of her eyes, Ben was there.

'Sorry,' he said. 'Didn't mean to wake you.'

'I wasn't sleeping,' she lied. 'Just resting my eyes for a moment.'

'I hope Serena hasn't tired you out. I asked her and the boys to come and help you, not drag you halfway around the country, as I now hear they did.'

'It was only Brighton. And a really worthwhile meeting, actually. I may have broken my leg, but there's nothing wrong with my brain.'

They both considered what she had just said in light of the conversation they had had the day before; the one where they both concluded there was most definitely something wrong with her brain.

'Fish and chips?' said Ben, holding up two loosely wrapped parcels.

'Yum! Tartare sauce?'

'Aren't you posh? There's ketchup but I'll see if Patrick's got any in the kitchen.'

There was half a jar in the fridge – quite possibly of venerable age – but he had a taste and proclaimed it edible.

Sitting side by side on the sofa, with her broken leg resting on a chair, they tucked in appreciatively.

'So, you spurn tomato ketchup but you're perfectly happy to eat out of the paper with your fingers.'

'God yes,' said Maddy, 'no one decants takeaway fish and chips onto plates. That's really common,' she joked.

'Good meeting, you say?'

'Really good. I don't know how we're going to pay for it, but Serena has an idea about that.'

'You know, you could really get this Bespoke Consortium idea going. It could be your job.'

'Hard to see how it could earn me any sort of living . . . At the moment, with the artisans having no budget to speak of, it's difficult to see how we can even get it off the ground, let alone put a roof over my head,' she said. 'Serena and Flora are putting loads of time into it, too. It's very much their baby as well as mine.'

'Serena doesn't need money.'

'Flora does, though. I agree, Serena doesn't, really, but she's clever and I think she very much wants an opportunity to do something that isn't chasing after Giles's pesky runaway pigs and looking after her boys – who are away a lot, anyway.'

'She was pretty senior, from what I gather of her job before she married him,' said Ben.

'Funny how she gave it all up. I'm surprised.'

'I'm not,' said Ben. 'The thing about Serena is that she does everything to the max. She hooked up with Giles reasonably late. He was sort of a second chance. Getting on for a last chance, when it came to being sure they could have children. The boys didn't come along straight away. When she had them she was so totally devoted – as you can see – the whole Home Farm thing with the Aga and the Labrador and space to run around was for their sake. No sacrifice too great, especially for Giles. Havenbury Magna is Serena's childhood home, not his.'

'Have you known her long?'

'For ever. She was like an older sister to me when I was in my teens. Not a great influence particularly . . . She's pretty wild, so generally she was encouraging me to do all the daft teenage things that I hadn't thought of myself . . .'

'And what about Giles? What's he like?'

'You've met him, haven't you?'

Maddy nodded. 'Briefly.'

'The main thing to know about Giles is that he absolutely, unconditionally adores Serena. Got her on a pedestal. Can't believe she said "yes", basically.'

'And does she love him?'

'Yeees,' said Ben, his head on one side, considering. 'No, she does, she does . . . of course she does.'

'But . . . ?'

'No "buts", it's just . . .'

Maddy waited.

'He wasn't her first love.'

'No, clearly. Serena must have been in her mid thirties, at least. Unless she was a nun . . .'

'Okay, then, let's just say that Giles isn't quite the love of her life,' he said. And then Maddy saw the shutters come down. He gave her a smile, but the message was clear: the subject was off limits.

'So,' he said briskly. 'Going back to the business, what about working for the Bespoke Consortium pro bono but subsidising it with the sort of work you are doing in London, only for local clients,' suggested Ben.

'Are you trying to persuade me to move down here permanently?'

'Yes,' said Ben simply. 'Imagine it. The landscape, the people, the cost of living must be an awful lot lower than London. You could work smart, not hard . . . 'course we'll have to get you a proper pair of walking boots when you get that cast taken off . . .'

'But it wouldn't work.'

'Why not?'

'Loads of reasons,' said Maddy, with finality. If she brought up specifics he would just suggest solutions in that annoyingly literal way that men had. There were plenty of problems to solve: the pub, the Consortium, her mother's relationship with Patrick, yikes and what about her relationship with the neglected Simon? . . . She had an idea that Ben would have an answer for them all but the insurmountable one was the constant anxiety and night-time terror, which were now inextricably linked with her presence in Havenbury. She couldn't imagine ever finding a way to live with that.

Maddy's mother's long-anticipated arrival caught her on the hop. She texted to apologise for only just realising she couldn't meet the train.

Don't worry, darling, Helen texted back. *Can hardly expect u to turn up with broken leg but wouldn't say no to bag-carrying services from hunky army boy instead . . . xxx*

Maddy duly texted the request to 'hunky army boy', who regretfully declined on the basis he would be delivering a lecture at the college when she arrived and also wasn't thirty-two a bit old to be called a boy? *Can't wait to meet your mother*, he added. *Tell her I'll buy you both supper tonight, to make up for missing her arrival.*

Thanks to careful and efficient packing, Helen arrived with just a small holdall and a rucksack, which were perfectly manageable on her own. Her walk up the steep hill from the station, in her sensible shoes, had made her quite pink in the face. Although she was racing towards fifty at speed –

something she was not keen to discuss – she and Maddy were still sometimes mistaken for sisters, to Helen's amusement and Maddy's pretend horror. Her curly brown hair, now streaked with grey, was cut in a shaggy bob, a little shorter than Maddy's but the wide-spaced blue-green eyes were the same and her neat little figure was only a little thicker around the waist than her daughter's thanks to twice-weekly Pilates and yoga classes. Next to each other, the most obvious difference was that Maddy was some six inches taller, causing her to announce that her mum was the 'bonsai' version.

It was a warm morning, almost like summer, and the familiar route, not taken for so many years, had a dreamlike quality to it as memories of that long, hot summer floated around her. She could almost feel the grit of the dust trapped between her toes in the open sandals she wore then. Her hair had been long, nearly down to her waist, and she vividly recalled how she would wind it into a heavy knot at the base of her neck to keep her cool as she worked. Those long, exhausting shifts pulling pints were buoyed by a love – an infatuation perhaps – which carried with it an optimism and excitement she had never felt since.

'Darling,' she said, throwing her arms around Maddy so enthusiastically she nearly swept her off her crutches. 'Look at you. What on earth . . . ?' she said, waving at her leg. 'That lovely Ben told me not to worry but what are they saying?'

'They're saying I need to get out of the habit of breaking it or they'll chop it off,' she joked. 'It's fine, Mum, no worse than last time.'

'That's no great comfort.'

'Really, Mum, it'll be fine; just a few weeks in plaster and a bit of physio, that's all.'

Helen gave Maddy a sideways look. 'And Patrick?'

'Ben's promised to take us in to see him in a bit. And then he's going to take us out for supper.'

'I see!' said Helen, looking smug.

'Please don't be embarrassing tonight, Mum.'

'Don't know what you mean.'

'Mrs Cross,' said Ben, kissing Helen on both cheeks. 'It's lovely to meet you. I'm so sorry I wasn't there when you arrived.'

'No need to apologise. Maddy's told me so much about you.'

'No I haven't,' protested Maddy.

'She's told me lots about you, too,' he said.

'No I haven't,' she protested again.

'We'd better get a move on,' said Ben, checking his watch. 'Visiting hours end at six. We don't want to get chucked out as soon as we arrive.'

'I doubt you would be,' said Maddy crossly, 'what with all your sucking up to Harriet, the ward sister, or whatever her name is.'

'Hetty. And it's Patrick who's got her in the palm of his hand, not me.'

'Sounds like him,' said Helen, with an edge to her voice.

'How long has it been?' asked Ben, as he unlocked the car, helping Maddy into the back so she could stretch her leg out and threading her crutches in after her.

'Goodness, I haven't seen Patrick for years,' said Helen lightly. 'Heaven knows why I'm here to see him now, other than it being Maddy's suggestion that I come.'

'Really?' said Ben. 'I got the impression you and Patrick were old, old friends.'

'More "old friends" as in "friends a long time ago", than

"friends *for* a long time",' corrected Helen. 'As a matter of fact, I haven't seen the old bugger since before Maddy was born . . .' she tried to sound offhand, but Ben noticed the tendons in her neck looked tense as she stared pointedly out of the passenger window so as not to meet his eye.

'Patrick and I were close for a time,' she went on, 'but it was only when Maddy applied for college locally I suggested she might want to get in touch. They hit it off,' she observed, smiling fondly at the thought, but then her expression tightened again. 'I was happy he was keeping an eye on her while she was away from home. Although not as close an eye as I would have liked, as it happens . . .' At this last comment, Helen clamped her mouth shut, staring straight ahead through the windscreen. To Maddy's relief, Ben took the hint and asked her nothing more.

'You are so kind to do this,' said Helen, having recovered her mood by the time they found a space in the hospital car park.

'No problem,' said Ben. 'I know how much Patrick is looking forward to seeing you. Tell you what, why don't you go on ahead,' he said, giving Helen brief, clear directions to Patrick's ward. 'Maddy and I'll pop to the canteen for a cup of tea and join you both in a bit.'

'That was a good call,' observed Maddy as he helped her onto her crutches. 'Best if they meet one to one to start with.'

'So I gather,' said Ben. 'There's history between those two,' he went on, patiently walking alongside Maddy as she sweated. Crutches were hard work and, if she was honest, walking was painful and exhausting still.

'Are you Maddy, by any chance?' said a nurse with a clipboard, who popped out of a side office like a Jack-in-a-Box, making Maddy jump and jar her leg painfully. 'I'm glad I caught you; just a bit of paperwork,' she went on, waving the board.

'Don't wait,' Maddy said to Ben. 'I'll just . . .'

'I'll go ahead and get our order in,' said Ben, taking the hint. 'I fancy hot chocolate.'

'Oo, good idea. Me too.'

'Good grief,' she said, when she finally made it over to the table he had requisitioned.

'I assumed you wanted everything.'

'You weren't wrong,' smiled Maddy, although she wasn't sure how she was going to manage supper once she had worked her way through the huge, steaming mug of chocolate, liberally topped with whipped cream, marshmallows and a swirl of chocolate syrup.

Ben was drinking a cup of coffee.

'You said you wanted one of these,' she accused, gesturing at her ridiculous mug.

'I lied, because I knew you did.'

Maddy stuck her tongue out at him. 'Your loss,' she said, scooping up a spoonful of cream and marshmallow. 'Do you think we ought to have left them on their own?'

'Probably not,' said Ben breezily. 'So what gives between Patrick and your mum, anyhow?'

'Sounds mad, but I don't really know . . .' She stared into space for a while and then continued. 'They've known each other since before I was born, I know that. But he definitely wasn't around when I was growing up. It was always just me and Mum, really. It was good. No complaints.'

'She's young,' observed Ben.

'I suppose she is,' said Maddy. 'She was only twenty-three

when I was born. Younger than I am now. I think about that a lot. I'm certainly not ready to be a mother . . .'

'It must have been hard for her,' said Ben, 'being on her own. So, if your mum knew Patrick before you were born, and he wasn't around when you were younger, what changed?'

'It was purely that I decided to study here. Mum mentioned she had a friend who lived nearby and encouraged me to find him and introduce myself. She said for me to start searching at the Havenbury Arms because he was running it when she knew him. I turned up expecting to be told he had moved on, but there he was.'

Maddy hadn't been too keen at first, she remembered. Full of the excitement of being away from home for the first time, the last thing she wanted was to have someone old and boring keeping an eye on her.

'I call him my godfather,' she explained, 'but he isn't really. Just an old friend of my mum's. An old ex-friend I suspect,' she added.

'Why?'

'Because, as far as I'm aware, in all the time I was studying here, she never actually saw or spoke to him directly. Sure she asked me whether I'd made contact, and she asked me how he was . . . things like that. I told her she should give him a call. Offered his number, but she always said "no", that there was "too much water under the bridge", that sort of thing.'

'Okay,' said Ben, piling up their now-empty cups and tidying the table, 'on that note, I think we'd better go and see how they're doing, don't you?'

CHAPTER ELEVEN

The tension was palpable in the ward. Patrick, with barely a monitoring device left on him but with the top end of his surgery scar in view above the neckline of his pyjamas, was sitting in the chair next to his bed. Helen was sitting bolt upright on the edge of the bed with her arms folded tight against her ribcage and her lips pursed.

'So,' said Ben, rubbing his hands together encouragingly, 'how are you both getting along?'

Patrick shot him a desperate look. 'We've been talking over old times, sharing memories . . .'

'Sharing memories?' snapped Helen. 'Don't recognise your version of events.'

'Okey-dokey,' said Ben brightly, rubbing his hands together again, this time with a degree of desperation. 'Time is getting on,' he continued, 'and we're expected for supper at six, so I think we'd better get going, don't you?'

'Bit early for supper?' queried Maddy.

'Yes . . . well . . . I thought your mum might like an early night,' said Ben, slinging his arms over Helen's and Maddy's shoulders. Tossing a peremptory goodbye at

Patrick over his shoulder, he marched the two women from the ward. Looking back, Maddy saw Patrick sink back in his chair with a sigh of relief and a smile for the ward sister who was bearing down on him from the other direction carrying a cup of tea. That must be the delightful Hetty, thought Maddy, wondering again at the wisdom of taking Patrick out of the comfortable, ordered hospital and plonking him down back in the maelstrom that was currently his home.

Ben had booked a table in the snug at the Havenbury Arms, although Tuesdays were rarely busy enough for booking to be necessary. Maddy had found and reinstated the cook and waiter who usually helped during the busy summer season but who were happy to have a bit of extra work and help Patrick while he was ill.

'Nice menu,' commented Ben, as he examined the card, with a carefully edited and much shorter set of options than the one it replaced.

'Not too brief?' Maddy asked, anxiously. She had spent a lot of time persuading the cook, Trevor, that the public didn't want twenty options as main courses, most of which were bought in and microwaved straight from the freezer.

'Not at all,' Ben reassured her. 'No one will miss all the deep-fried stuff. Half the time you couldn't tell one from the other.'

'Exactly,' she enthused. 'Trevor makes a mean curry so I get him to do a big batch of that once a week. And then as time goes on, we will put on a couple more choices depending on what's in season and locally available. Obviously the baked potatoes and toppings are always popular, and you have to offer chips, of course . . .'

'You're loving this,' observed Helen with surprise. 'I'm really impressed, darling. Well done, you.'

'Thanks,' blushed Maddy. 'I do love it, actually. When I was working here in the college holidays I'd always thought we should do things this way. I suggested to Patrick we should update stuff but . . .' Her voice faded away. And then she observed, 'I'm really beginning to see that it's because he's getting old and tired. I know he's only in his early sixties, but he ought to be able to wind down a bit after all these years. Running a pub's a tough old game and a heart attack's a heart attack, isn't it?'

'I doubt he can afford to retire,' said Helen acidly. 'He's never been one for planning ahead. Although I suppose he could sell this place. Must be worth a fair bit by now.'

'A fortune, but unfortunately it doesn't belong to Patrick,' chipped in Ben, filling Helen in briefly on the situation with Top Taverns and the impending lease renewal. 'He not only doesn't own the building or the business, they insist he owes them about fifty thousand pounds for repairs so, if the lease doesn't get renewed, they'll end up billing him for that too.'

'But surely they'll want him to renew his lease and keep paying them rent?' said Helen, shaking her head as she tried to take it all in. 'Especially if they have a chance to put the rent up – the greedy grasping bastards,' she added, pulling a face. 'Looks like business is booming to me,' she went on, waving a hand at the growing crowds in the main bar.

The room was filling and the noise level was rising, even though it was a weekday, with a mix of after-work drinkers and those coming in for an early supper like themselves.

'We *are* making money,' Maddy agreed. 'Patrick was worried about takings but, honestly, I've been keeping an eye, and they're not bad, especially for this time of year. Dare I say it, but he could even afford to pay the "greedy grasping bastards" quite a bit more rent, if they asked for it.'

'Do you think they actually want him to stay, though?' asked Ben. 'I've got the impression from the delightful Dennis that they'd rather close it down and flog the building with change of use on it. House prices are going up and up. An awful lot of pubs have been converted to residential now.'

'This town doesn't need another house half as much as it needs its pub,' said Maddy crossly. 'If the Havenbury Arms closes, that's it,' she went on. 'It'll be gone for ever. Okay, so there's the bar at the college – although half the students treat this place as the student bar; I always did – and there's the nightclub on the quay . . . This Johnny bloke, I haven't met yet, opened last year – dunno what Patrick makes of him but the competition doesn't help.'

'Jonno, actually,' said Ben. 'He's a decent bloke. I can vouch for him.'

'Didn't realise you knew him,' said Maddy.

'He's a mate,' Ben explained. 'We were in the army together, many years ago. Lost touch 'til I came down here a couple of years ago.'

'So you've been here a couple of years,' interjected Helen. 'And no girlfriend? Wife? Significant other?'

'Mum!' exclaimed Maddy. 'Remember we had that chat? About asking inappropriate questions . . . ?'

'Nope,' Helen replied calmly. 'Can't say I do,' she added, turning back to Ben. 'I'm a bit surprised, that's all, hunky, fit bloke like you. Are you gay?'

Maddy groaned in disbelief.

'Because it doesn't bother me if you are,' continued Helen

unabashed. 'Just be a shame, that's all. What with Maddy being here and available – and you do look good together, if you don't mind me saying so . . .'

'I don't mind you saying so at all,' he laughed.

'*I* mind you saying so,' protested Maddy.

'Oh look,' he said, to distract them both, 'here's our supper at last. I'm starving . . .'

By the time they had all despatched their food and Ben had also demolished a large portion of sticky toffee pudding with custard, pledging to go for a long run the next morning to atone, he had sneakily settled the bill under cover of returning their glasses to the bar. There he was amused and diverted to note that Kevin made him wait to pay, fussing about with restocking the shelves before eventually turning to him with a scowl.

By the time he returned, Maddy's head was drooping with fatigue and her entire leg had started up a relentless throb.

'Come on,' he said, 'time for bed.'

Helen grinned naughtily. 'There, you see. I said you made a good couple.'

'Ha, ha,' retorted Maddy. 'That old chestnut. Pass me my crutches, would you?'

'Hold onto them,' Ben told Helen as she dragged them out from under the table where Maddy had stowed them earlier. 'Fatigue, crutches and narrow staircases don't mix. I'll carry her.'

'At least let me walk out of the bar under my own steam.'

Ben hovered until she had manoeuvred herself to the bottom of the stairs. Even that short walk was exhausting and painful.

*   *   *

'Right,' he said, when he had laid her back on her little narrow bed again, leaning her crutches nearby so she could reach them. 'You'll be alright now you've got your mum here, won't you? I'd better get back home and catch up with some work. Lectures and tutorials tomorrow.'

'Of course,' said Maddy, feeling she had been a little ungracious. 'Thanks so much for all your help over the last couple of days.'

He gave her a relaxed salute and made to leave.

'Wait!' said Maddy urgently. 'When – I mean . . . when will I see you again?'

'Really soon. We've got things to discuss, remember? Although actually asking you to "remember" is probably a bit of an unfortunate turn of phrase.'

'Oh yes, that. Did I agree?'

'You sort of did, yeah.'

She was surprised at the flood of relief that she had a genuine reason to see him again soon.

'I must call Simon,' she blurted, feeling guilty at her keenness to see Ben.

'Not now. Time enough for that tomorrow. Give the guy my regards. Tell him I admire his taste in women.' He made for the door again, and then turned: 'By the way, you remember I said I was going to watch Kevin in the bar?'

She nodded, stifling a yawn.

'He doesn't always close the till between customers. Can't see why that would be dodgy. Just looked slightly weird having the till drawer open . . .'

She shook her head, wearily. 'I don't know either. Can't imagine it being a problem around here but it's not a great idea. Someone could reach in when your back's turned . . .'

* * *

139

It was the doorbell that woke her the next morning.

'Yikes,' Maddy said, looking at her watch. She swung her legs out of bed, and was quickly reminded of her injury with a breathtaking stab of pain. Damn. That was probably the postman with the materials Simon was sending her to work on. She would never get down the stairs in time, which probably meant the parcel would end up in the sorting office for collection – another logistical nightmare, which made her sob with frustration, Then she heard voices.

Thank goodness. Her mother was at the door, chatting amiably with the postman and quickly returning with a large Manila envelope.

'Love letter from the delightful Simon?' she said, tossing the envelope onto the bed.

'Ta. Sorry to sleep so late.'

'Glad you did, darling, it'll have done you the world of good,' Helen replied. 'But I was just about to wake you up, anyhow. Pancakes for breakfast . . .'

'Fab,' said Maddy. Pancakes for breakfast had been their regular weekend and holiday treat when she was growing up. She felt a rush of childish relief that her mum was really there with her, tears pricking her eyes, which she brushed impatiently away, but not before Helen had seen them.

'Come on, lovie,' she said, putting her arm around Maddy's shoulders. 'It's all going to be fine. Mum's here now.'

Over breakfast Maddy nervously confessed her conversation with the discharge nurse, naming Helen as Patrick's main carer when he came out of hospital.

'It's just a formality,' she quickly added. 'Not like they're going to check or anything. I just needed a name to put on the form, once she saw my leg . . . She caught me yesterday – you were talking to Patrick – and I panicked, basically . . .'

'Hmm,' said Helen, unconvinced. 'I'm not prepared to leave the old bugger in the lurch, not least because it'll make *your* life hard. I'm not happy seeing you here, darling. I want you back in London away from all this. And I'm not going to put my life on hold for him. I did it once . . .' she said quietly to herself, staring out of the kitchen window.

'Pirate's going to be awfully pleased to see him,' said Maddy. The poor parrot had been noticeably depressed in the last few days, refusing, most of the time, to leave his morose perch on the curtain rail, despite Maddy's and Ben's attempts to lure him down with his favourite snacks. She had started to worry the little bird was entering a terminal decline. She knew parrots had a long lifespan, but he had been around for years.

'Was Pirate already there when you knew Patrick before?'

'Yes, amazingly enough,' said Helen. 'A memento of an old love affair, from what I can gather,' she added. 'An ex-girlfriend left him with Patrick when she went off travelling. She didn't return in all the time I knew Patrick,' she recalled, 'so – as he's still here – I assume she never did.'

Pirate was sitting on Helen's shoulder, bobbing his upper body up and down and crooning happily to himself. Every now and then he would reach over and give her earlobe a tender nibble, signalling for her to pick another sunflower seed out of her muesli for him, which she obediently did, holding it up for Pirate to delicately extract it from between her fingers.

'He's got you where he wants you.'

'Oh yes,' answered Helen sourly, 'him and his master, both.' She gave Pirate's head an affectionate scratch, a hint of a smile playing on her lips.

There was a knock and, seconds later, heavy footsteps coming up the stairs to the flat.

'Morning,' said Ben, coming into the kitchen and immediately making it feel cramped.

'Who let you in?' said Maddy.

'You keep leaving the door open,' said Ben. 'Really, your security's shockingly lax. Anyhow, I am instructed to take you to Serena's,' he explained, politely declining Helen's offer of coffee.

'Ah,' said Maddy. 'Now? I've got a conference call with Simon and a client in half an hour.'

'Ah, indeed,' said Ben. 'Tricky.' He pretended to think. 'Cancel Simon?'

'Not helpful. Try again.'

'Get her to bring the stuff here?' suggested Helen.

'No can do,' said Ben. 'She's got it all set up in the barn. I'm under strict instructions,' he said, fixing Maddy with a look.

'To do what?'

'To drive you up there.'

'Mm, not great,' said Maddy doubtfully. 'Sorry, I mean it is great, thanks – but it doesn't solve the problem with the call . . .'

'Does he always do that?' he asked, distracted by Pirate, who was now delicately exploring the workings of Helen's inner earhole with his beak.

'It's a sign of affection,' explained Maddy, grabbing her laptop and opening it up to check her emails.

'I think I'm relieved he doesn't like me,' commented Ben.

'Aha,' said Maddy, skim-reading an email from Simon. 'Turns out I'm free after all. Client's cancelled. Simon's not best pleased.'

'I am, though,' said Ben. 'And Serena and Flora will be positively thrilled. Come on,' he said, handing Maddy her crutches. 'Your carriage awaits.'

'When are you going to take me for a whizz in your sports car,' said Maddy grumpily.

'I didn't think you'd be able to get yourself into the MGB,' Ben explained as he helped her up into the Land Rover.

'I'm not ninety,' she snapped.

In deference to Maddy's bad mood, which clearly amused him, Ben drove her in silence and, despite being stuck behind a tractor, they were soon drawing into the courtyard of the farm.

Serena came out to greet them. 'No MGB?'

'Ben thought I wouldn't be able to get in and out of it,' said Maddy crossly. She was trying to get out of the Land Rover with grace, but even that was difficult.

'At my school,' Serena reminisced, 'they were dead keen on teaching us silly things like how to get out of a low sports car in a short skirt without showing our knickers.'

'Really?' There had been no social graces on the curriculum at her own school, thought Maddy. 'So, how *do* you avoid showing your knickers?'

'Don't wear any,' said Serena over her shoulder as she headed for the barn.

'Wish I'd been at your school,' laughed Ben.

'So do I,' she shot back, giving him a sultry look.

'Anyhow, I should be off,' he said, looking at his watch.

'Perhaps you should,' snapped Maddy, feeling unaccountably cross at the banter between them. 'Hang on, how am I going to get home?'

'I'll collect you at lunchtime.'

'I can drop her back off home if you're busy?' said Serena.

'No bother,' answered Ben. 'I'm taking her to lunch with a friend of mine.'

'Oh?' intervened Maddy. 'First I've heard of it.'

They were both ignoring her. Which was annoying too. She was just working herself up into a steaming heap of self-pity when Serena chivvied her to the wrecked barn making up the fourth side of the farmyard quadrangle.

'Now,' she exclaimed, throwing open the door. 'Whad'yer think?'

Maddy took in the scene in silence. 'You. Are. So. Clever.' she said, her bad mood forgotten.

'You like?'

'I love,' she confirmed, moving forward awkwardly on her crutches to examine the display from a new angle.

'Mads!' shrieked Flora, making Maddy jump out of her skin, before enveloping her in the usual, all-encompassing hug.

'Isn't it completely and utterly brilliantly fab?' she asked, breathlessly, waving her arm at the display. 'I did the blankets,' she added. 'I think they look especially cool . . .'

'We've got some stuff set up in the farmhouse as well – the kitchen, mainly,' said Serena. 'Most of the ceramic and glassware stuff works better in there . . .'

'It just all looks so pulled together,' breathed Maddy, shaking her head in awe.

And it did. Serena and Flora had piled some hay bales to make a display area and had draped the handspun and woven wool blankets artfully as a backdrop to some of the smaller items. The sheepskin booties and hats looked adorable. To give it all more of the rustic, country context,

Serena had even hauled some of the old farm machinery lying about in the barn around so it set off and contrasted with the products on display.

'This is new,' said Maddy, stroking a cool, suede bucket bag with a wide, woven shoulder strap. It was multicoloured, with an emphasis on oranges, browns and moss green, but with the natural vegetable colours used as dyes the overall effect was subtle and harmonious.

'Great, isn't it? I've got Ivan to make me one too,' said Serena. 'Tilly says she can weave the strap in no time. I've picked out all the blue, aqua and green colours – they're more my thing.'

'These colours would be great for an autumn photoshoot, though,' said Maddy, enthused. 'We could do the sheepskin hats and gloves too, of course, we just need some autumn leaves and a couple of small, cute children . . .'

'I know where to borrow them,' confirmed Flora. 'I have a friend with three under five. Mad. Bloody naughty but cute as kittens.'

'Come and see the house,' said Serena, already on her way. She stood back to let Maddy in through the back door into the boot room. The last time she was there it had been a tip, with coats falling off the coat hooks, a jumble of mismatched wellies on the floor and a good quantity of honest Sussex mud on the flagstoned floor. There had even been a fair bit spattered onto the walls. Today, the transformation was astounding. The flagstones had been thoroughly washed and – the subtle gleam indicated – waxed. A carefully colour-coordinated selection of coats along with some more of the covetable sheepskin hats and gloves had been artfully arranged on a handsome new row of wrought-iron coat hooks. Another of the woven wool blankets was arranged to spill out of a handsome reed basket. The overall effect was of a ruddy-cheeked country family, having just come in from a brisk autumn walk en route to crumpets in front of the fire.

'I haven't seen these baskets before,' said Maddy, reaching down to touch it.

'Locally sourced willow. A wonderful lady in Little Havenbury. She weaves in a shed at the end of her garden at the moment, but she's dead keen to join the Consortium and says she needs more space. I've offered her the unit next to Jez. We just need to clean it up a bit and mend the roof . . .' Serena was dragging Maddy through to the kitchen as she spoke, gabbling in her excitement.

Maddy stopped dead in the doorway, making Serena cannon into her.

'Oops, sorry . . . so, do you approve?'

Maddy had never seen the kitchen table so clean. The scrubbed pine really was scrubbed nearly white. On it, laid for tea, were the chunky pottery plates, bowls and egg cups that Maddy had seen samples of knocking around in the pottery next door. There was a choice of rainbow colours, with the pleasingly handmade-looking crockery coloured on the outside only, so the cream-coloured clay was still visible on the inside. Rather than choosing a single colour, Serena had mixed them randomly so a sunshine yellow egg cup sat on a red plate, with a green bowl alongside. There was an oak chopping board with 'BREAD' carved into the side and a thick rope handle fixed onto one end – Maddy had seen that being made the last time she was there too. The rustic loaf of brown bread, with two slices cut, lay perfectly arranged on it. Two turned-wood candlesticks sat at either end of the table, candles just waiting to be lit. There was even a table runner, woven in a range of natural colours, clearly the work of the blanket weavers.

'It's like the *Marie Celeste*,' joked Maddy. 'What have you done with your family?'

'It's alright,' explained Serena. 'I haven't gone mad. Giles is staying over in London until this evening, and the boys are off seeing their grandma for a couple of days, much as I hate not to have them with me, again . . .' Her face clouded over momentarily. 'But it looks okay, doesn't it?'

'It all looks amazing,' said Maddy, waving her arm to include the stage set in the kitchen, the boot room and the barn outside. 'It just feels like there's this Boden catalogue family of ghosts, living this weird parallel life here.'

'That's the general idea,' said Serena, crossing her arms with a hint of a smug grin.

'But you haven't done it all for me?' puzzled Maddy.

'No,' said Serena. 'Obviously, we have as well . . . but no, this is all set up for Keith.'

'Who's Keith?'

'Did I not say?' said Serena, surprised. 'Oh no, I suppose I didn't, what with your leg and all, it's been a bit hectic. So, anyway, I'm pootling away on Facebook and then, suddenly, I get a friend request from Keith, so there you go . . .'

'And Keith is . . . ?'

'Ah, sorry. He's the photographer I used a couple of times when I was doing catalogues in London,' she explained. 'So . . . you know I was a homewares buyer?'

Maddy nodded.

'I was a bit of a control freak then' – Flora pulled a face, but Serena didn't notice – 'so I quite often used to make the

PR people let me attend the photography sessions. I learnt a few tricks from the stylist along the way. Fancy being paid actual money for lifestyling a few products,' she marvelled. 'I mean, it's not rocket science, is it?'

Maddy had to disagree. She saw real talent in what Serena had done. Somehow, magically, a fairly disparate range of rather random homespun bits and bobs had taken on an identity. Serena was creating a brand for the Bespoke Consortium, a set of values and references that customers would instinctively 'get' – and she was even more talented than Maddy had realised.

'And Keith? When is he coming?'

Serena looked at her watch. 'Soon,' she said. 'At least, I hope he is. It's going to take at least four hours to get all this in the can, and I've got your supper to cook too.'

'You're not cooking my supper,' said Maddy, confused.

'Not just you,' agreed Serena. 'I need you to come and chat up Giles this evening. I reckon he's good for the website-build cost.'

'You're not going to ask Giles for the money, are you?'

'No, you are,' clarified Serena. 'It'll sound better coming from you. Anyway, I've got a lot of catching up to do with Keith, having not seen him for years.'

'That's terribly kind,' said Maddy, confused, 'it's just that getting here and then home again's a bit tricky.'

'I know, I know, that's why Ben's invited too,' said Serena, waving away protest. 'And Flora, obviously.'

'He didn't mention it,' said Maddy, a little sulkily. It seemed she had very little say over the arrangements for her own life, currently.

'He was probably preoccupied,' suggested Serena.

'And he said something about me having lunch with him too. You all seem hell-bent on stuffing me full of food at the moment.'

'Can't your friends feed you occasionally?' Serena asked. 'Speak of the devil,' she went on, as she watched Ben pull into the drive again. 'Out you pop, and I'll see you at seven this evening.'

Clunking laboriously out of the house on her crutches before Ben sounded his horn, Maddy turned back to wave but she could see Serena and Flora through the kitchen window, totally preoccupied as Serena moved an egg cup, with a boiled egg in it, first a couple of inches to the left and then, holding her head on one side, back to the right again.

'So, how did that go?' asked Ben as they bowled down the lane towards the main road.

'Pretty amazing,' said Maddy, 'and I understand we're both going back for supper to persuade Giles to give us some money.'

'Count me out on the persuasion bit,' warned Ben. 'I'm happy to be your date for the evening.'

'Don't think it's quite like that,' muttered Maddy, blushing. 'But you do seem mighty keen on taking me out and feeding me at the moment. I'm going to be the size of a house. Where and why are we going for lunch, by the way?'

'Havenbury Arms again,' admitted Ben. 'It seemed simpler, and I know you like to keep an eye on things . . .'

'And the "why"?' she pressed.

'Business and pleasure,' he said, cryptically. 'Okay . . . there's someone I'd like you to meet.'

'Go on . . .'

'It's a colleague. A psychologist, like me. I think you'll take to him.' He paused. 'People do.' He glanced at her quickly, judging her reaction.

'What if I don't?' said Maddy, furious at the tiny wobble in her voice.

'It's fine,' soothed Ben. 'No one is going to make you do anything. I just thought it might be helpful to talk. It's not a consultation. He's a friend. We've done research projects together. It's just lunch. Relax.'

Maddy slumped down in the car seat, her bad mood returning. She could hardly say that she would much rather have lunch with him alone, which was what she wanted. She was perplexed. His constant presence was saying one thing and his decorous reserve something else. Again, she wondered at his motivation. Was she an interesting case – a curiosity – to be discussed with a colleague, a burden imposed by his loyalty to Patrick or a convenient way to serve some other objective? And she found herself thinking again about his interest in the pub and Top Taverns' plans. What had he been doing there that morning when they first met?

CHAPTER TWELVE

Duncan was waiting for them by the time they arrived. He had grabbed the little table in the corner. With the high settle opposite forming half of the seating it was the most private spot in the pub. He half stood up, greeting Ben with a familiar slap on the shoulders. Once they were ensconced and Ben had been despatched to collect drinks, he reached out to shake Maddy's hand.

'Ben's talked about you,' he said.

He was shorter than Maddy and had a shaven head, presumably to disguise or embrace premature baldness – she reckoned he was in his early thirties. Even in repose his face looked as if he was going to break into a smile.

'He's told you I'm a nutter, then,' she joked.

'Yeah. Well, technically, we don't use that expression.'

'No?'

'Nah. The accepted professional term is "loon",' he deadpanned. 'Anyhow, I think his fascination with your mental state was just one of the reasons he wanted the three of us to get together.'

Maddy raised an eyebrow questioningly.

'He's a good mate,' said Duncan. 'Plus we work together. Actually, that's why we work together – that and because he's reasonably clever, but don't tell him I told you – not as clever as me, obviously . . .'

'Getting on okay?' said Ben, plonking two pints and an orange juice onto the table.

'I take it that's mine,' said Maddy, reaching resignedly for the orange juice.

'You shouldn't really drink with those painkillers,' he explained. 'Besides, you need the Vitamin C. It's good for healing, apparently. There've been studies.'

'Talking of studies,' said Duncan.

'Ah yes, good,' said Ben, looking at one of them then the other. 'Has he explained?' he asked Maddy.

'Explained what?'

'About our study. Me and him. And you.'

'Not yet, but it's a relief to hear it's that, to be honest,' she said. 'I thought he was about to suggest a *ménage-à-trois*.'

Duncan blushed. 'Just saying any friend of yours was a friend of mine,' he explained. 'But yeah, the study we are working on is a protocol for treating PTSD. It's early days, but before we go for a full trial, we are planning to write up a couple of case studies trying out the new treatment. Hence . . .' he looked at Maddy expectantly.

'But surely it's soldiers you need? People who've been through proper trauma – battlefield stuff, no?' Maddy queried.

'But what happened to you,' Ben said gently, 'was clearly traumatic . . .'

'It wasn't "clearly" anything,' Maddy protested. 'It isn't clear at all. I don't even know what happened, I only know . . .' She

152

stared into the middle distance. 'I don't know what happened,' she finished simply.

'. . . and that is why we think we can help,' Duncan said. 'We treat PTSD by essentially reprogramming the memory of the precipitating event, desensitising, basically . . . That's not a particularly new idea – but that's tricky when your brain has decided to forget what it's experienced.'

'So what are you going to do?' asked Maddy. 'I mean, what would you do? In my case, I mean. If I said "yes", that is. Which I haven't, by the way.'

'Basically, I'd hypnotise you,' said Duncan enthusiastically. 'And then, while you're under, you could relive the trauma and retrieve your memories . . .'

'Wait!' said Maddy, panicked. 'What if I don't want to retrieve my memories?'

'But that's the point of the study,' Duncan said. 'It's sort of a bit . . . well – key.'

Ben noticed Maddy's thousand-yard stare had returned. She was wringing her hands until she saw him watching her, then she unclasped them and slipped them beneath her thighs, trapping them there to keep them still.

'We don't have to decide anything now,' he said. 'Moving on,' he added, studying the menu intently, 'I don't know about you but I definitely want chips.'

Duncan made as if to say something else but was quelled by a sideways look from Ben.

The two men were good company – a double act – entertaining Maddy with tales of their training. While they talked, she ate, and – having told them both she didn't want chips – she ended up eating nearly half of Ben's.

She also let Duncan talk her into a large glass of red wine. 'Essential for morale,' had been Duncan's response to Ben's raised eyebrow, 'and I speak as a proper doctor, unlike laughing boy here.'

She was yawning hugely by the time they had ploughed their way through the Havenbury Arms' treacle tart, which had become a bit famous since Maddy first made one a few weeks before. She spooned up her last mouthful and leant back groaning.

'I am stuffed,' she complained. 'And I don't know how I'm going to keep my eyes open at supper tonight,' she added. 'I can't even believe I have to eat again so soon,' she said, looking ruefully at her watch, which said it was already after three o'clock.

'The Mediterraneans have the right idea with their siesta tradition,' said Ben. 'You should have a nap.'

'It's good training,' he puffed as she protested at him carrying her up the stairs yet again.

'You'll give yourself a hernia.'

'You have gained a bit of weight,' he said, making her blink at his honesty.

'Yikes,' she said, blushing. 'That was . . . erm – direct.'

'Oh . . . no!' said Ben, realising his lack of tact as he put her back on her feet at the top of the stairs. 'I mean – you have – but I like it – I mean, it's good,' he explained. 'When we first met, I could see your ribs, here,' he said, placing the flat of his hand on the top of her chest, making her shiver, although his palm was beautifully warm. 'I could count them. Not a good look. I was wondering if it was a bit of a London thing. The girls I meet up there seem to think skinny is good and skinnier is even better . . .'

'I doubt porky is much of a fashion statement either,' she said, yawning again. 'Oops, sorry . . .'

'Bed,' said Ben. 'I'll be back to pick you up later.'

When he had gone, Maddy lay down as ordered. She was sure she wouldn't sleep, lying on her back with her hand on her chest where his hand had been, but quickly she was proved wrong.

'You've got it bad, mate,' said Duncan.

'Not following you,' said Ben.

'Maddy's case? Lovely girl, by the way . . . Can you honestly say this is really about the study? I feel a rescue coming on . . .'

'Bollocks.'

'Maaate . . . ?'

Ben held up his hands in surrender.

'She . . . it . . . feels important,' he admitted. 'She's distressed at being back here. It worries me, the direction she's going. Of course I want to . . . I dunno – stop her from self-destructing. Plus, I promised Patrick. Plus she's got a boyfriend . . .'

'Sure, sure,' said Duncan. He gave his friend a sympathetic look. 'You've got feelings for her.'

'I care,' said Ben firmly. 'But "feelings", no. I mean,' he thought for a moment, 'I've helped Jonno and I care about him too – doesn't mean I fancy him, does it?'

'So, nothing more than that . . . ?'

'Nothing more than that,' said Ben, meeting his friend's gaze.

He wasn't fooling anyone.

Wandering back to the car, he smiled at his friend's intuition. In truth, he wasn't sure how much longer he could manage to be a gentleman and, he admitted to himself with some surprise,

155

he wasn't after a quick, mutually agreeable tumble into bed and then out of it again. No, with Maddy, he wanted it to mean something – to become something more. He laughed gently at himself. What his men would think of their old leader getting so soft in old age, he could only begin to imagine. The one thing he did know is that they would be describing his predicament in some pretty unrepeatable language.

When Maddy woke, the light outside was warming into evening. She hobbled over to the window, never tiring of the view over rooftops to where the sun was slipping below the summit of Top Down.

A crash and a stifled oath from the kitchen made her jump.

Patrick? Maddy grabbed her crutches and swung quickly down the little corridor.

'Mum,' she said, in relief. 'I thought you were Patrick.'

'Sorry, darling, I was trying so hard to be quiet, but I dropped the pesky sauté pan. It's not easy making lasagne with a parrot on your shoulder. I think he thinks I'm Long John Silver.'

Maddy gave Pirate a little scratch on the crest and he bobbed appreciatively, digging his claws into Helen's upper arm as he did so, making her squeak and drop the slotted spoon into the sink with a clatter.

'I think, if anyone's Long John Silver it's me,' Maddy joked, waving her crutch gingerly in the confined space. 'Is it for today?' she asked, looking at the pasta. 'Only I'm supposed to be going to Serena's for supper tonight.'

'I know, Ben told me. It's fine. Actually the lasagne's for the freezer. It's one of Patrick's favourites, or it used to be, in any case. He can take it out in portions and bung it in the microwave after I've gone.'

'I'm really sorry,' said Maddy, putting her arm around her mother's waist and giving her a squeeze. 'Not exactly a holiday for you.'

'Wasn't supposed to be,' said Helen stoutly. 'But I can't stay much longer,' she warned. 'I'll get Patrick settled back in, then I'm going to have to go home.'

'Of course.'

'Now, you need to go and have a bath and get ready for your date.'

'It's not a date,' she said. 'I've got to pitch to Giles for funding tonight. It's work.'

By the time Ben had arrived Maddy was wearing clean jeans – she hoped it wasn't formal – her mother had ironed her favourite shirt and, with her hair clean and a bit of make-up on, she felt more civilised and together than she had done for ages.

'You look pretty,' said Ben. 'These are for you to give to Serena,' he added, waving a bunch of freesias. 'They just need a bit of wrapping or something; they're a bit drippy.'

'You think of everything,' said Maddy, partly in admiration, partly in slight irritation for reasons she couldn't explain, even to herself. 'Although I'd probably have chosen a bottle of wine.'

'Got that,' he said. 'In the car. Two bottles, actually, red and white. Thanks,' he added to Helen, who had taken the freesias from him and deftly wrapped the stems in foil before handing them back.

'Ready?'

'Yep. Oh no, hang on . . . I just need my laptop.'

'I'll get it,' said Ben, 'you start off down the stairs – it takes her a while,' he added to Helen.

'I know, bless her,' said Helen, her head on one side,

157

watching Maddy hook her crutches awkwardly onto one arm and grab the stair rail.

'It's my leg,' she muttered crossly, 'not my ears – or my brain . . .'

Travelling in Ben's MGB, with the top down so her crutches could stick out the back, the drive to Serena and Giles's farm was idyllic. They were travelling towards the setting sun, the little car's headlights sweeping the hedgerows, startling the rabbits into their burrows and raising the roosting crows out of the trees for one last swoop and wheel against a flaming pink and orange sky. Sitting in the little car, next to Ben, Maddy's heart swelled with unexpected happiness.

'Nervous?' he shouted over the sound of the wind, nodding his head at the laptop on Maddy's knee.

'A bit,' she admitted. 'I'm out of practice.'

How very far away her London business seemed – a life where sharp little suits and presentations to world-weary businessmen were an everyday occurence. Simon didn't bother asking when she was returning any more. A week ago he had mentioned on the phone a new freelancer he was using; she was called Alexis, and was very competent, apparently. More than anything, he had explained, she was there when he needed her. The clients were impressed too, Maddy had gathered.

The party was already in full swing by the time they arrived. A hugely tall and hairy man with a jutting jaw was holding forth to Flora, sitting legs akimbo on one of the farmhouse chairs, his elbows on the back and his hands waving expressively.

Serena was leaning against the Aga swigging wine and wiping tears of mirth away from her eyes and Giles was topping up the man's glass encouragingly.

'Darlings!' shrieked Serena. 'You're here.' She swooped across and swept them both up into a three-way hug. Maddy emerged feeling dishevelled and held her hand out to Giles, nearly smacking him in the eye with one of her crutches in the process.

'Hullo, Maddy,' he said, dodging her crutch adeptly and kissing her on both cheeks. 'Lovely to see you again. I understand I'm your prey, tonight.'

She patted her laptop case. 'So it seems.'

'We're not making her do work,' insisted Serena. 'Okay . . . maybe just a tiny bit, but wine first, darling. And food. I think I might have made a bit too much,' she added, lifting the lid of a huge casserole dish on the top of the Aga, which immediately intensified the delicious smells.

'Never too much, when I'm here,' said Keith, waggling an eyebrow archly at Flora, who giggled and went pink.

'Too true,' said Serena. 'For a man who's obsessed with his figure, you eat like a pig.'

'Buns of steel,' he agreed. 'My arse is the talk of Brighton clubland, I'll have you know. I've got a reputation to maintain.'

'I think the less said about your reputation the better,' said Serena. 'Keith's a shocking tart,' she explained to Maddy.

'He gets through more boyfriends than I've had hot dinners,' agreed Giles, sniffing the casserole appreciatively. 'Are we eating soon, my darling?'

'We are,' said Serena. 'Now, Keith sit next to Flora, if you promise not to corrupt her, Maddy sit next to Giles so you can get up to speed. I want you to look at Keith's photography later. He's done an amazing job. The magazines won't be able to resist.'

'Is it all done already?' asked Maddy, disappointed.

'Just the cut-out product shots to go,' explained Serena. 'We're going to rig up a white backdrop in the conservatory.'

'She's getting her money's worth out of me,' said Keith. 'And she's too mean to hire a proper studio.'

'I thoroughly approve of keeping costs down,' said Giles, leaning over to fill Keith's glass by way of appeasement. 'Remember, half of all businesses fail in the first year and the most common reason for failure is cash flow.'

'That's why we need your money, darling,' said Serena, dropping a kiss on his head as she passed. 'But enough; let's eat.'

The casserole, served with huge mounds of red cabbage and mashed potato, was delicious. They all had seconds and then regretted it when faced with pudding, which was salted caramel chocolate fondants, crisp on top, with crystals of sea salt. The little individual puddings were filled with the most unctuous chocolate sauce because they had been brought out of the Aga at the perfect moment.

'My wife is a woman of many talents,' said Giles appreciatively as he poured a thick river of double cream into the middle of his chocolate fondant. Maddy was beginning to understand the reason for his ruddy face and distinctly rounded belly. 'In the kitchen she's a chef, in the parlour she's a maid and in the bedroom she's a—'

'That's enough,' shouted Serena as laughter exploded around her. 'Now, who wants coffee?'

'Maddy and I will have ours in the library,' said Giles, getting up to hand Maddy her crutches with a little bow. 'We have business to discuss.'

'I need my laptop,' she told him. 'I've done a little presentation.'

'Oh God, spare me "Death by PowerPoint",' he said. 'Oh, go on, then. I accept my fate,' he added kindly, seeing Maddy's face fall.

*   *   *

In the end Maddy and Giles sat side by side on a saggy old leather sofa in front of the fire. He was the most incredibly fast reader, she discovered, fixing his eyes on the screen with the focus of a sparrowhawk spotting its prey. He had a way of summing up her points and then asking an incisive question, which soon made the presentation irrelevant anyway. She found herself tumbling over her words as she rushed to share their ideas. She soon learnt that Giles wouldn't waste time agreeing with her, cutting her short as soon as he'd learnt enough to answer his question and firing off another. Rather than finding it intimidating, she started to enjoy herself. He was constructive, too, making some good points about the structure of the business, which she felt sure Serena and Flora would accept.

Eventually, they got to the final page – the budget. Maddy immediately started making excuses but Giles held up a hand to silence her. Everything was costed, right down to running the office, a modest amount to kit out a little corner of the converted stables, which she, Serena and Flora had claimed as their own. She had put the website build in at four thousand pounds, which suddenly seemed a lot but which she actually knew was a good price.

He was scrolling down through the figures scribbling some notes she couldn't see without straining her neck.

'Serena tells me you're a chartered surveyor,' she said, to make conversation.

'Yes, sort of,' he said, still scribbling. 'I'm the company secretary for a land management firm,' he said. 'It's crashingly dull, or so Serena keeps telling me . . . Obviously I'm looking at this as a VC.'

'A VC?'

'I'm a venture capitalist,' he clarified. 'In other words, I'm one of those *Dragon's Den* chappies who takes a punt on new businesses – invests in return for a share of the profits. That sort of thing . . .'

'Blimey,' she muttered. 'Serena gave the impression you might just chuck in a few quid to help with start-up costs. Just because – you know – because you're her husband.'

'It helps,' he said wryly, 'but she'd be furious with me if she thought I was patronising her. Not that I'd dare. Look, Maddy,' he went on, 'these are bloody good ideas. You're clearly a bright girl. Flora's . . . erm, Flora's a one-off, and I'm sure she'll be an asset. I also hugely admire my wife and,' he flushed, 'I know how lost she feels now the boys are at school. She needs to work to be truly happy, and,' he swallowed loudly, 'I just want her to be happy.'

Maddy was shocked to see his eyes fill with tears before he looked away, studying the watercolour over the fireplace with fierce intensity, although she was pretty sure he had seen it before. She was just debating what to do next when he gathered himself together with a loud harumph and turned his attention back to the budget.

'This isn't good,' he said.

'Oh.'

'Your figures are all wrong,' he went on, grabbing the laptop from her and scrolling up and down the page.

'Have I put some things in too high?' she hazarded. 'Let's reduce the office costs. I'm sure we can do them for less . . .'

Giles ignored her. 'For a start,' he said, 'there's no salary for you and Serena.'

'No, we actually thought we could – you know – hold off, see how it goes . . .'

'Nonsense,' he said, his eyes fixed on the screen. 'If I'm

going to put my money in, I need to know you can give it the time and energy it needs.'

Without asking, he created another line in the chart and added a figure she could happily live on if she was careful and rented somewhere cheap to live.

'Also,' he said, 'your marketing budget's underpowered. You mentioned doing a London trade show for the retail buyers a few minutes ago, but where is it in the budget?'

'Ah,' said Maddy, 'we wanted to do something in year one but it costs such a lot we thought we'd probably generate some income and then do one of the big London events in year two . . .'

'Nope,' he said decisively. 'You need to hit the ground running. Again, if I'm going to invest, I need to know there is going to be reasonable impetus from the off. What are the figures for a trade show?'

Luckily she had just costed attendance at the biggest and best annual buyers' event so she came straight back with a total figure that would cover it. Just about.

Giles bunged it in and scrolled down to the bottom to total it up. The figure now displayed made Maddy gulp.

'Would you really be prepared to finance us?'

'I'll do half,' he said, snapping the laptop shut, 'in return for twenty-five per cent of the business.'

'I'll have to get back to you,' she said coolly, trying to sound confident. 'The stake is acceptable but obviously we need to have a think about how we raise the remaining fifty per cent.'

'Oh goodness,' he said. 'You don't want to worry about that. There's an enterprise fund being run by Brighton City Council offering match funding for projects just like yours. They'll be falling over themselves to fund something like this, creating local jobs, boosting the economy, rural enterprise – heavens, it fulfils more funding criteria than you can shake a stick at.'

'It does?'

'It certainly does. You'll have to fill out a monster of an application form, but you'll manage. The guy in charge is a mate of mine.'

Maddy's head was spinning and, try as she might, she couldn't stop a grin of delight spreading across her face.

'So,' said Giles, getting up. 'If that'll do you, I think we'd better get back to the others.'

When they returned to the kitchen the atmosphere was solemn. Flora seemed to have disappeared. Keith had tactfully taken his laptop to the far end of the kitchen table where he was preoccupied – or pretending to be – running through and editing the photos he had taken earlier that day. Ben and Serena were head to head over their coffee; Serena with her hand on Ben's arm, was speaking to him intently as Maddy and Giles came in. When she saw Maddy she flashed her a wobbly smile.

'Alright?' she said, letting go of Ben and giving him a comforting pat on the shoulder.

Maddy gave her a thumbs up.

'Great,' said Serena, giving herself a little shake. 'Now, enough of this,' she added to Ben, wiping her eyes and nose with a corner of the striped apron she was still wearing. 'It's the last thing Andrew would have wanted.'

'Ben's been telling me all about his research,' she explained to Giles, brightly.

'Come here, old thing,' he said, and gave her a cuddle, dropping a kiss onto the top of her head as he met Ben's eye.

Unable to work out what was going on, Maddy felt suddenly drained. She stifled a yawn.

'Time to get you home,' Ben said, pushing back his chair. 'Serena, thank you, we'll see you soon,' he said, giving her a warm and extended hug.

After peremptory goodbyes to the others, Maddy was bundled into the car, inserting her broken leg into the footwell with difficulty.

Lulled by the drive, she was soon fighting sleep.

'Who's Andrew?' she asked, in an attempt to wake up.

'My brother.'

'Didn't know you had one.'

'I did,' he said. 'I don't now.'

'I'm sorry.'

She waited. Ben drove on, seemingly having forgotten she was there.

'What happened?' she said at last.

For a moment she thought Ben hadn't heard her.

'He was in the army,' he said, not looking at her. 'Two tours of Afghanistan. Iraq. Northern Ireland. He went everywhere. Did everything. He was thirty-two when he died. The age I am now.'

'Killed in combat?'

'Might as well have been. It was the last Iraq tour that did for him. He came home a different person. Angry. Broken. He was signed off with depression, and then diagnosed with PTSD. He tried so hard to get better but he just couldn't do it. After a couple of years he was medically discharged from the army. On the day his discharge papers came through, he . . .' Ben swallowed and took a deep breath. 'On the day he was discharged, he killed himself.'

CHAPTER THIRTEEN

By this time they were pulling up outside the Havenbury Arms. The bar was dark, the curtains drawn. Maddy looked at her watch in surprise. Midnight already.

'I'm so sorry,' she said. 'Tell me about him. I'll make you a coffee.'

'That old "come in for a coffee" line, eh?' joked Ben, weakly.

In minutes they were side by side on the saggy old sofa in Patrick's sitting room.

Pirate ignored them at first, cross at having been left alone, but soon he turned back around in his cage and treated them to his best hanging upside down on his perch trick, cocking his head to check they were watching.

'He needs his blanket on,' she said. 'It's past his bedtime.'

'And yours.'

'So, is Andrew the reason you're researching PTSD?'

'He is. He's the reason I went into the army, why I studied psychology – everything really. His death blew my family apart. After losing Dad when I was young too—'

'Really? I didn't know . . .'

'I was seven,' he said. 'Pretty grim. And then Andrew, when I was fifteen. Awful for my mum having lost them both, but losing Andrew was worse, she says. Parents who outlive their children are thrown into a kind of living hell . . . Not to say it wasn't agonising for all of us. Serena too, as you saw.'

'So she knew him?' asked Maddy, sniffing away tears that had welled up at his story.

'More than that. They were soulmates. She supported him through it all, but of course, it wasn't enough in the end. Nothing was.'

'Is that why you're so close?'

'Oh, we'd known each other for years. Serena, Giles and Andrew were all in the same group and I was the bratty younger brother. I think we would have been friends anyway, but – yeah – when you go through something like that . . .'

'Poor Giles, too. I really like him.'

'Talking of Giles, how did you get on?'

'Oh, amazingly!' said Maddy, wiping her eyes. 'He's just – basically – enabled the whole Bespoke Consortium. Or at least he has if we can get the other half of the funding. And he says he can help do that too.'

He smiled at her enthusiasm. 'So, you're prepared to stay down here and make it happen?'

She glanced at him but she didn't meet his eye, instead focusing on Pirate, who was cracking pumpkin seeds in his beak whilst still hanging upside down. Every now and then he would steal a glance at her to make sure she was still watching.

'I do love it here, but I'd be walking away from a lot . . .'

'Your London clients?'

167

'Yes,' she agreed, 'but they're not just mine, they're Simon's too. We're a partnership. Not a proper, formal one, but that's where it's heading, I'm sure.'

'Ah yes,' sighed Ben. 'About that—'

'It's not simple!' Maddy burst out in anguish. 'Simon, me, the business, it's everything. It's everything I've done since . . . the thing happened.'

'You mean, you've nailed the "thing" because you've taken back control, starting up a business, a relationship, making a home for yourself. It's been, what? Three years?'

She nodded.

'And all this?' he pressed.

'It's amazing,' said Maddy, remembering her elation in the car earlier that evening. 'But it's all mixed up with the memories, or lack of them, obviously . . .' she joked.

'You belong here, though,' said Ben. 'Can you not feel it? You belong with—' He stopped himself. 'With . . . all of us. Serena, Flora, Patrick . . . me.' He paused. 'You've even got your mum here at the moment.'

'Mm, not sure how much longer that's going to be for. It's lovely having her here but they were scrapping within seconds at the hospital. Gawd knows what they're going to be like when he's home.'

'Seriously, are you sure he isn't your dad? It just fits.'

'I know he isn't.'

'Tell me?' Ben settled himself a bit more comfortably into the sofa cushions and turned towards her, ready to listen.

She sighed and began: 'Okay, well, Mum's always told me he's dead. Nothing more and I didn't ask.'

'Okay.'

'And then, I asked her again before I came here to study

because – whoever he was – I'd worked out she met him here and – yeah – when she was telling me to contact Patrick it definitely crossed my mind. All she would say was she'd had a torrid affair that summer. That he was married, they had this fling . . . and he was killed in a motorbike accident before either of them even knew she was pregnant. She left here shortly after. The end.'

Ben didn't reply. She looked at him but he seemed mightily interested in the fireplace all of a sudden. She waited. When he turned to her at last he looked strained.

'Will you let Duncan help you?'

'The PTSD study?'

She paused. 'I so admire you. Even more so now I know about Andrew . . .'

'But . . .'

'But,' echoed Maddy, with the ghost of a smile.

'You can't.'

She shook her head, biting her lip. 'I'm really, really sorry.' She turned to Ben and he saw the tears welling up in her eyes.

He pulled her into his arms, staring grimly over her shoulder as he held her so she couldn't see the devastation on his face.

Back in the car, Ben stared fixedly through the windscreen, scenes flashing through his head; his childhood, his mother, the memories he had of his father . . . He bashed the steering wheel with the heel of his hand and groaned. Belatedly he remembering the maxim 'never ask a question unless you know you're going to like the answer'. Like the opening of Pandora's box, his casual question had made her say things that couldn't be unsaid. And she didn't even know what she had done.

* * *

Maddy felt bad and it wasn't just the wine she had drunk with supper the previous night. She kept seeing Ben's face when she told him she wouldn't take part in the study. More than professional disappointment, he had looked utterly bereft. To distract herself she decided to do some work on the Bespoke Consortium website.

Keith had put all the photos online and emailed her the link so – even though she didn't yet have the money to get the web boys started – she could at least edit the photos.

Because the files were huge and the Internet in the flat was ropey Maddy had staggered down the stairs with her laptop under her arm and set herself up in a corner of the bar.

Half an hour from opening time, Kevin was mooching about, pushing a mop around with an attitude of absolute disdain. Through his body language alone he made it clear that cleaning was beneath him and that conversation was not welcome, which was fine with her.

She sighed, rubbing her tired eyes and then looking – unfocused – into the middle distance to give them a rest. After a few seconds of daydreaming she realised, with a jolt, that she was staring, unseeing, straight at Kevin.

He stopped pulling the chairs down off the tables and loped rapidly towards her, fixing her with his gaze. She felt like a mouse spotted by an eagle, a rabbit in the headlights. She looked down and pretended to fiddle with the keyboard.

'That's the same leg,' he said, nodding at her plaster cast. 'The same leg you broke last time.'

'Yes,' she whispered. 'Yes it is.'

'Funny, that.'

Maddy nodded, not trusting her voice.

'Remember what happened this time, do ya?'

She nodded again, hoping he couldn't see the sledgehammer heartbeats that shook her body. Her hands were balled into fists, her breath catching as she tried not to pant.

'Yeah,' he sneered.

She risked raising her eyes, just in time to see him leaning in, his mouth twisted into a taunting grin.

She flattened her body against the high back of the oak settle.

'Yeah,' he said again. 'Cos you don't remember nothing about what happened before, do ya?' he said unpleasantly. 'That's what I heard . . . nothing.'

She could see every pore of his sweating, pimply face. The smell of stale tobacco was overwhelming, nauseating. Her heart was crashing in her chest, her limbs frozen in the grip of terror, the rushing sound in her ears got louder, and then she was in the darkness, blind and falling through space.

Powerful hands gripped her arms, yanking her forwards, hard. She struggled, kicking her legs and scrambling away, trying to scream but nothing came. She couldn't breathe. Gasping and panting, she tried to wriggle free but, although the hands let go, they were immediately replaced with strong arms that encircled her, crushing her and pinning her down. At last she gathered her breath and screamed.

'Shush,' came a familiar voice from miles away. 'Maddy, hush, I'm here.'

She stilled, listening, clutching onto the voice for support.

'It's me . . .' the voice went on. 'Maddy? It's me. You're safe.'

She turned her head to the sound. 'Ben?'

'Hello, Maddy,' he said, more normally. Her vision cleared, and she saw the blue of his shirt, a button, a glimpse of his chest. Tilting her head up, she saw him looking down at her. His smile was warm but she could see a muscle pulsing in his jaw.

'Are you back?'

She nodded, still trembling.

Too soon, he withdrew, setting her upright on the bench and moving away decorously, to leave a foot of space between them. Confused to see him acquire an air of professional detachment she hadn't seen before, Maddy resisted the temptation to crawl back into the comfort of his arms.

'What just happened?' she whispered.

'That's what I'd like to know.'

'God, Maddy, me too.'

She turned and saw Serena, wiping a tear from her eye with a hand that shook. 'You poor darling . . .' she continued, pulling out a chair and sitting heavily. 'What did he do to you?' she said more loudly, cocking her head in Kevin's direction.

Kevin had retreated to a safe distance where he stood, slack-jawed, surveying the scene.

'I didn't do nothing,' he said, scowling.

'He didn't,' admitted Maddy. 'He didn't do anything . . . Not really.'

'See?' he snapped. 'She just went mental.' He made the universal gesture, forefinger to temple. 'She's mad. Mad Maddy, clue's in the name . . .'

Serena flushed scarlet. 'You should sack him. Horrible little weasel; how dare he!'

'Can't afford to. It's fine. He's right, anyhow. What the hell just happened, Ben? I *must* be mad . . .' Her chin trembled.

'Not mad,' said Ben. 'Just overwhelmed. Strange, though, I wasn't aware you had actual, classic flashbacks.'

172

'Is that what it was?'

'I reckon so . . .'

Maddy stared ahead, reliving it. 'It was my nightmare, basically, but suddenly real. More real than something – well – real,' she explained. 'God, how hideous. Could it just happen again?'

'Can't say it won't but I'd expect there to be some sort of trigger . . .'

'There wasn't,' said Maddy. 'I was just working on some photos for the website and then . . . as you saw . . . other than Kevin talking to me, nothing.'

Ben looked grim.

'Anyway, I'm fine now,' she said, blowing her nose on a napkin. God forbid that she had been sitting there in his arms with snot on her face.

She probably had.

'So,' she went on, 'it's an unexpected pleasure to see you both. What gives?'

'I don't know about him,' said Serena, nudging Ben. 'I just found him wandering about outside and dragged him in to keep him out of trouble, but *I've* got exciting news.'

'I could have exciting news too,' protested Ben.

'No you haven't,' said Serena. 'Not as exciting as mine.'

'How do you know?'

'Children, children,' said Maddy. 'Tell me.'

'Okay. So, Giles told me you've got him on board, of course.'

Maddy nodded.

'And . . .' she continued, relishing the moment. 'We've got this bloke in Brighton to impress double quick, cos the committee meeting for the next round of funding is coming up really soon.'

173

'The funding guy?'

'The funding guy,' confirmed Serena happily.

'But what about the application thingie?'

'It's here,' said Serena, bringing out a sheaf of closely typed paper with the legend 'Rural Business Development Funding Programme' in bold at the top.

Maddy grabbed it and leafed through. 'Cripes,' she said. 'We have to do all this?'

'Yeah,' Serena waved her hand dismissively.

'Have you looked? It's huge . . . What about this bit? "Explain in detail how your proposal answers at least four out of the eight funding criteria priorities as identified in section 3.g subsection, ii)" – what even is that?'

'Oh, you must mean the guidance notes,' said Serena, bringing out an even thicker sheaf of closely typed paper. 'Here.'

Maddy groaned. 'Look at this deadline! We'll never get this written in time.'

'Yeah we will. It'll be fine.'

She groaned again.

'It'll be fine,' Serena insisted. 'Look, come up to the farm later. We can go through it together. And in any case,' she glanced at Ben, 'there's something I want to show you.'

'Not sure I can cope with any more surprises today,' grumbled Maddy. 'Anyhow, I don't know when it'll be. Mum and I have got a meeting with Patrick's occupational therapist later. It's about his rehab, discharge, exercise programme and all that . . . It's going down like a cup of cold sick with Patrick, of course. No one's going to tell him to eat his five a day and go jogging, but as long as he makes the right noises he should be home pretty soon.'

'Brilliant!' said Serena and Ben in unison.

'And how are takings?' said Ben.

'Okay-ish,' admitted Maddy.

Patrick had been demanding to see the books but, so far, she had managed to put him off. Her excuse that she had 'forgotten' to bring them was wearing a bit thin.

'Is your mum going to stay a while?' asked Serena. 'Help him get settled in?'

'That's the plan, but I'm not sure how long they'll be able to stand each other.'

'They're fond of each other, really, I can tell,' said Ben.

'Mm, we'll see,' said Maddy, unconvinced. 'Still, I'll be there too, of course.'

'I should have thought they'll want you out from under their feet,' observed Serena brightly. 'Don't want to be all green and hairy, do you?'

'A gooseberry? Between those two?' said Maddy, incredulously. 'No, honestly, you've both got it all wrong—'

'Aaanyway,' Serena cut across her, 'you'll not want to stay in that poky little bedroom much longer.'

'Won't I?'

'Nope,' said Serena decisively. 'You won't. Will you bring her, Ben?'

'Can do,' he said, saluting. 'I'm supposed to be meeting Duncan but I'm free after that. I'll pick you up from the hospital, shall I?'

'You shall, apparently,' Maddy said, accepting her fate.

'Good,' he said, standing up and grabbing his car keys. 'It'll give me a chance to pop in on Patrick, too.'

Waving a sketchy goodbye at the two women he ignored

Kevin who stood at the bar, glaring as he left and polishing a glass with such venom it looked like he was wringing a creature's neck.

'Mate . . .' said Duncan, filling the single word with a complex combination of genuine sympathy for his friend along with a good dose of entreaty and mild reproach.

'I know, I know,' Ben replied, hanging his head and staring into his pint.

'Are you sure?'

'Short of a DNA test . . . but how many married men living in Havenbury were killed in a motorbike accident at exactly that time?'

Duncan nodded. 'Okay, fair enough. But, my God, your sister?'

'Half-sister.'

'And she's twenty-five, you say?'

Ben nodded.

'And your dad was killed when . . . ?'

'Nearly twenty-six years ago. I was seven,' said Ben, swigging his pint gloomily.

'So, you and Maddy, you haven't . . . ?'

'No! Thank goodness . . .'

'Mate . . . Are you going to tell her?'

'I don't know,' said Ben. 'I don't think I should, not at the moment. She's really not in a good place, which brings me to my next point. I've been trying to get her to accept help. It was a promise to Patrick but now – obviously – she's my own flesh and blood. I've got to help her deal with this thing or it's going to be,' he swallowed, 'well, the risk is it's going to be like Andrew all over again, isn't it?'

'Mate, for even more reasons than before, you're the

last one who should be helping her.' He thought for a few minutes. 'Is she a good subject? Suggestible?'

'I reckon so,' he said. 'I've tried a bit of "right place, right time". . . . She's pretty suggestible, although she doesn't know it.'

'Might just be because it's you.'

'Yeah.'

'Look,' said Duncan at last. 'Get her in front of me. She can be my patient. You're there as a friend only, okay?'

'You'll do it?'

''Course.'

'Now all I have to do is persuade her,' said Ben.

'If things are getting as bad as you say, you might want to get on it, mate.'

The occupational therapist was called Julie.

'He's a one, that Patrick,' she said, blushing. 'We'll be sorry to see him go.'

'I bet you won't,' muttered Helen. 'And if you think he's bad in here you should see what he's going to be like when he gets home. I don't know how on earth you think you're going to get him to do all this rehab stuff you're talking about. This mutual support group thing, sitting around drinking tea and comparing heart attacks – I mean, are you sure? I feel sorry for the others.'

'Oh, we get all sorts,' said Julie. 'Heart attacks are no respecters of people. He might even enjoy it. Anyway, you say he runs a pub; I'm assuming that means he's pretty sociable . . . ?'

'On his own terms, he might be.'

'Well,' said Julie brightly. 'He's got you to take care of

him and make sure he's making the right choices, hasn't he?'

'If he does what I tell him that'll be a first,' muttered Helen to Maddy, but she allowed Julie to hand her a sheaf of papers and leaflets, with titles like 'Eating for Heart Health' and 'Getting Back to Exercise'.

'Yikes,' said Maddy, spotting the one called 'Sex for the Over Sixties', as they walked down the corridor to the cardiac ward. 'He's not supposed to be doing that as part of his rehab too, is he?'

'People over the age of forty do occasionally have sex, you know.'

'Yeah, but . . . ew . . . not Patrick. It'd be like thinking of your parents doing it.'

Helen stiffened. 'You really are something else,' she laughed. 'I suppose you think I don't have a sex life either?'

'I know you must have done it once, to get me, but I'm assuming that was it. Please tell me it was.'

Helen smacked Maddy on the head with the leaflets, just as Ben came out of the ward.

'Woah,' he said. 'Maternal violence. You ready to pick up Patrick?'

'He's been discharged?' squeaked Helen. 'I've still got stuff to get ready,' she said, waving the leaflets.

'Oh, right . . .' said Ben. 'I popped in to see him before I came to find you. Apparently he's told them all you might as well take him home now seeing as you're coming in.'

'*That* sounds like him.' Helen clicked her tongue disapprovingly, but a little smile leaked out. 'We might pop down by the river for a coffee on the way home.'

'That's that settled, then,' agreed Ben. 'Shall we?' he added, holding out an arm to shepherd Maddy away.

'Serena's little surprise?' asked Maddy. 'I don't know now, maybe with Patrick coming out . . .' she looked at Helen. 'You'll need me to help get him settled in.'

'Nonsense,' she replied. 'Off you go and have fun.'

'Okay, well I'll just pop in and say hello.'

'You'll be seeing him back at home soon enough,' said Ben. 'Let them have their moment.'

'What moment?'

He didn't answer but Maddy watched as Helen walked through the double doors to the ward. Even her back looked disapproving but, over her shoulder, Maddy saw Patrick break into a smile as he saw her.

Chapter Fourteen

'My God, Maddy,' exclaimed Serena as they got out of the Land Rover. 'You look bloody awful.'

'Thanks.'

'Doesn't she look awful?' she implored Ben. 'I don't think I even noticed earlier,' she went on. 'What with the whole Kevin thing. Vile little man,' she added. 'You just look like you haven't slept for a week,' she said. 'Or eaten, come to that.'

'You know I've done that,' said Maddy. 'You fed me yourself last night.'

'Anyway,' said Serena, 'I wasn't going to mention it until after you'd spoken to Giles but now you have – and Ben think's it's a great idea too, by the way—'

'Mads!' The shriek cut across the idea Serena was just about to reveal at last. Maddy turned awkwardly on her crutches to see Flora barrelling towards her from the barn. There was a flurry of fur gilet, plaits and beads. Several of them thwacked Maddy in the face as Flora threw her arms around her.

'Mads,' she exclaimed, as if she hadn't seen Maddy for years. 'Soooo excited about the Bespoke Consortium thingie all being here on one spot. Sooo cool!' She carried on, working her way around the little group doling out hugs and kisses all round. 'Hmm,' she said approvingly, giving Ben's bicep a little squeeze before she put him down. 'I would,' she said to Maddy with a wink. 'Can't wait 'til you move in,' she continued. 'We can have sleepovers!'

'Erm,' interjected Serena, 'I haven't actually . . .'

'Oops! Sorree . . .' said Flora, clapping her hand to her mouth. 'Anyhoo, got to go, just helping the boy with his new pelt delivery. Pongs a bit,' she added, holding her nose. 'Must dash!'

'Allow me,' said Serena to Maddy at last.

Maddy was dying for a coffee but Serena led her not to the kitchen but to a gate leading out of the courtyard and down a steep cobbled slope.

'Watch it here,' Ben said, taking Maddy's elbow. 'The cobbles can be a bit slippery.'

'This is sweet,' remarked Maddy, as she saw the little square building beyond, with its flint and brick walls and steeply sloping clay tile roof. It was a perfect square and tiny, perhaps just fifteen feet from front to back.

'Glad you think so,' said Serena, leading her towards a wooden door not more than five-and-a-half feet high. 'Mind your head,' she said. 'Especially you,' she added to Ben.

Straightening up inside, and repositioning her crutches firmly into her elbows, Maddy looked around. 'How gorgeous! I never knew this was here.'

'Old grain store,' explained Serena. 'Giles had it all done up as an office, but he never got into the habit of working from home so I chucked him out. I thought it might be good holiday accommodation or something but – in truth – I could never be arsed with holidaymakers coming and going . . .'

Inside, the interior was cosy, with a low ceiling over the kitchen area where they were standing, but opening right to the raftered roof beyond it, where a comfortable-looking sofa covered in squashy cushions sat in front of a woodburning stove. There was dark slate on the floor with a thick wool rug defining the sitting area. The interior was saved from gloom by a wide French window in the opposite wall that opened onto a verandah with a bistro table and two chairs. Beyond was the most stunning view of the Sussex countryside. From the little room you could imagine there wasn't another house for miles, just rolling hills, mainly fields with patches of woodland and a silvery stream running through the valley below.

'It's absolutely beautiful,' said Maddy when she had taken it all in.

At that point, she noticed the ladder leading from the sofa area to the little loft area where she could just see a low bed platform piled high with plump pillows, and one of the Bespoke Consortium's checked woollen blankets.

'There's a bed on the mezzanine, of course,' said Serena, following Maddy's eyes. 'There's not a lot of headroom, but it's enough, and there's a shower room behind it. The plumbing and drainage was all there already because Giles had put the kitchen in. We improved it a bit, of course,' she continued, looking around the little apartment with an appraising eye. 'So, it's not much,' she said, holding her hands out to the sides, 'but it'll do you good to get out of that cramped little bedroom at the pub . . .'

'Me?' said Maddy disbelievingly. 'I can really have this?'

'Of course,' said Serena. 'That's the point: it's for you. Oh, but silly me,' she exclaimed, misreading Maddy's look of disbelief, 'you're worried about your leg. Of course that's a nuisance but Ben and I have thought it through. That's a sofa bed,' she explained, waving at the little sofa. 'It's a reasonably good one. You'll be comfortable enough until you can manage the ladder. And luckily the loo's downstairs,' she added, checking around to spot and eliminate any other issues Maddy might be concerned about. 'It'll be no fun washing in the kitchen sink, I appreciate, but you can pop into the house whenever you like and have a really lovely soak in the bath. And the cast is coming off soon enough, isn't it?'

'It's not that, it's not . . .' said Maddy. 'It's absolutely amazing but – I mean – I can't . . .' she trailed off and then continued, 'Giles has made me put a salary in the budget for the first year of the Bespoke Consortium – did he say?' she asked Serena, not waiting for the answer. 'It's wonderful to have an income, of course, but it doesn't run to renting a lovely place like this.'

'Good grief, are you mad?' exclaimed Serena. 'You don't have to pay rent! Of course you can't afford to on the tiny bit of money you'll get for the first year. I jolly well hope you'll be making more by the end of it . . . No, I want you to live here as our guest. Actually, not even our guest, let's just say it's part of the deal in return for your contribution to the Bespoke Consortium. It suits us all for you to be here. It makes perfect sense.'

Maddy looked around again. 'It's just simply the loveliest place I've ever seen,' she said quietly.

'Anyhow,' continued Serena, 'Ben says you *have* to move here. For your health.'

Ben shuffled his feet. 'I didn't exactly say that. What I actually said is that I suspect your condition might deteriorate unless we can get you away from the pub, which does – for some reason – seem to be triggering.'

'Ah,' sighed Maddy. 'Here it comes.'

'It's not just this morning,' he went on. 'You've said yourself that your sleep is becoming more disturbed. Then there was the flashback. These are all signs that uncomfortable memories are resurfacing . . .'

'I thought I was *supposed* to be remembering stuff.'

'I didn't exactly say that. I think what's happening at the moment is that the trauma is resurfacing in an uncontrolled and potentially damaging way. Your mind is telling you that – in the environment you are in – it can no longer suppress the memories it was keeping a lid on while you were in London. Its strategies to keep you in denial are breaking down and it's distressed. You're distressed, Maddy,' he added gently.

She was conscious of his gaze but couldn't lift her eyes, which were unaccountably filling with tears. He was right, dammit. She was cracking up. She rubbed her eyes furiously, and – instead of looking at Ben – she turned to Serena with a bright smile.

'I absolutely love it. I'd love to be here. But only when I know Patrick and Helen are okay without me.'

Serena sighed with relief. 'Fantastic,' she said, giving Ben a triumphant look. 'You can be in by the end of the week.'

Bumping along the country lanes in Ben's Land Rover, Maddy started getting nervous at the thought of Patrick and Helen having spent a couple of hours on their own. If one had murdered the other her money was on Helen. Patrick didn't stand a chance.

'Come and have supper with us tonight?' she asked. 'Mum's made lasagne and I think I might need your peacekeeping skills.'

'Didn't manage to achieve much in Bosnia, so with Patrick and Helen I've got no chance,' he said. 'Anyway, I can't this evening, I'm afraid.'

'Work?'

'Nope. Got a hot date, actually.'

'Oh!' she exclaimed. 'Okay . . .' She turned to look out of the window, pretending to be fascinated by the advertising hoarding by the railway station. Of course he had a date. She swallowed her disillusionment and turned back to discover him grinning at her.

'A "hot date" with Jonno, my mad, bald, pot-bellied and tattooed army buddy who is calling in his God-given right to a wild night with his old mate painting Brighton town red,' he said. 'It may be my most dangerous mission yet.'

'It's no concern of mine who you see.'

'Sorry,' he said, seeing her prim expression, as he drew up outside the Havenbury Arms. 'I shouldn't tease. Now wish me luck – I may not make it through the night.'

Maddy leant in to give him a peck on the cheek but he put his arms around her and gathered her in for a far too brotherly hug instead, the gear stick digging into her hip, and her plastered leg sticking out awkwardly. Uncomfortable as it was, pressed up against him she nearly groaned aloud with the pleasure of his embrace. The only girl she wanted Ben to have a hot date with was her. Failing that, she wanted to just stay here, in his arms, feeling his warmth and breathing in his smell . . . Disappointingly, after one final squeeze, he released her and drew away. Reluctantly, she grabbed her crutches.

'Take care, Maddy,' he said. 'Stay out of trouble, and try to get some sleep.'

* * *

To Maddy's relief, Patrick and Helen were both sitting companionably at the little kitchen table over mugs of tea and a plate of biscuits, now empty except a few crumbs.

'Were your ears burning?' asked Helen, waving a mug at Maddy in enquiry.

'Yes please,' said Maddy to the offer of tea. 'My ears are fine,' she added, pretending to check. 'Why? What have the two of you been plotting?'

'Patrick was just saying that he's been getting good feedback about your contribution to the food menu. Your Trevor's doing a great job with the new menu, and the locals are loving the whole simple, local produce thing,' said Helen, patting Patrick on the shoulder. 'So I'm telling him there's no rush to get back to the kitchen.'

'He's a sweetie,' agreed Maddy, 'but I'm frustrated this' – she rapped her knuckles on her plaster – 'has meant we needed to bring someone in.'

'Just what I was saying,' said Patrick. 'I'm perfectly happy to go with the new menu and suppliers but we just can't be splashing money around that we haven't got paying wages now I'm back.'

Helen raised her eyes to heaven. 'Get him,' she said to Maddy. 'He was three-quarters dead a few weeks ago and now he's Superman.'

'Near enough,' said Patrick, 'and if you're keen to see me wear my underpants outside my tights you only have to ask.'

'What makes you think I want to see your underpants under any circumstances?' retorted Helen. 'Tell him, Maddy.'

'I wouldn't dare,' grinned Maddy, chickening out. 'Although it would be a shame to overdo it.'

Patrick's shirt was unbuttoned just far enough for her to

see the top couple of inches of a livid red scar, which now divided his chest. As always he was smiling but Maddy noticed how he shifted uncomfortably on his chair, holding his ribs as he turned.

'It's about time you had a rest,' snapped Helen, noticing too. 'I'm going to get you to bed,' she said, standing and holding out her arm.

'Steady on, woman,' joked Patrick. 'I thought I wasn't supposed to be overdoing it.'

Helen didn't move.

'Alright, you bossy woman,' he said. 'Perhaps just for half an hour.'

'Must you do that today?' Maddy asked as she clumped noisily into the kitchen for her first cup of tea of the day. Patrick was already up and dressed, sitting at the table, working his way methodically through a large pile of post. With a mug of coffee to the side of him, he was slicing envelopes with the butter knife and dumping the majority of the proceeds into the waste bin beside him. It was already overflowing.

'No time like the present – although it would have been nice if you'd brought them to me in hospital, like I'd asked.' He peered at her over the top of his glasses but Maddy was unmoved.

'The nurses told me not to,' she lied. 'Anyhow, I'd be very surprised if there was anything important.'

'There's this, for a start,' he said, picking up an A4 envelope with a 'Top Taverns' frank on it.

'I haven't seen that before,' she said, reaching for it.

'Actually this one only came this morning,' he admitted, snatching it back out of her grasp. 'Make us another cup of coffee, darling,' he pleaded. 'I can hear your mum's up now so she'd probably like one too.'

With Maddy's attention elsewhere, Patrick slid the knife across the top of the envelope and slid out a sheaf of papers with a letter paper-clipped to the front. Laying the papers carefully to one side, he held the letter in both hands and read, with concentration.

When Maddy turned back to the table, with a mug in each hand, just about managing to rock the couple of steps on her cast, she saw that Patrick was sitting completely still, staring unseeing at the letter. His face was grey and beads of sweat were breaking out on his forehead.

'Patrick!' she exclaimed, plonking down the mugs, oblivious to the coffee slopping onto the table and onto the edge of the sheaf of paper, which Patrick had laid to one side.

'Nothing to worry about, my lovely,' said Patrick, through stiff lips. 'I'm completely fine . . . just need my spray if you could . . .' He gestured to the worktop behind him.

Shaking, Maddy clumped over to the other side of the room putting her full weight on her broken leg but barely registering the stab of pain that resulted. She scrabbled through the bottles of medication Patrick had brought back from the hospital with him. Amongst them was a slim white canister with a spray top.

'This?'

Patrick nodded, staring with concentration at the table as he held onto the edge with both hands.

Fumbling with the lid, Maddy stumbled back to him. She watched anxiously as he sprayed it twice under his tongue and then looked up at Maddy with what he clearly hoped was a reassuring smile. It was more of a grimace.

Tears sprang to her eyes. 'Shall I call an ambulance?'

Patrick shook his head. 'Wait.'

She sat down opposite him and watched intently. Over a couple of minutes, his breathing eased and colour seeped back into his face.

'I'm fine,' he said at last, with a more convincing smile.

Maddy brushed away tears, and reached for the letter. 'Is it this?' she demanded. 'What do they say? Please let me see . . .'

Patrick shook his head with resignation. 'It's fine. Not a surprise, just a bit of a blow, that's all . . .'

Maddy skimmed the letter rapidly, exclaiming rudely at intervals. Getting to the end and practically spitting in fury at Dennis's ridiculously grandiose signature – it nearly took up half the page – she made herself read it through carefully again from the beginning.

'Wanker,' she said at last, with feeling.

'Language.'

'He is. Can he do this?'

'He's doing it.'

'So, basically,' she said, waving at the lease on the table, 'this is what they want you to sign or they'll chuck you out after Christmas.'

'That's about it.'

'And they want how much per week?' She rifled through the papers until she found it. 'This is ridiculous,' she said, throwing it back down on the table in disgust. 'The pub can't possibly pay that.'

'The beer ties have got a bit more onerous too,' said Patrick, grabbing a pencil and circling a paragraph on the next page. 'I barely sell enough of the stuff to suit them as it is.'

'Why not?'

'Because it's bloody awful.'

'Language,' joked Maddy mirthlessly.

They sat in silence.

'I'm spent,' said Patrick.

Maddy shook her head frantically, the corners of her mouth turning down. 'No.'

'I am,' insisted Patrick. 'I'm too old for this game.' He pushed the lease papers away. 'It's not the same as it was and I don't like the new rules one little bit. Even if I didn't have the whole heart thing I should probably be calling it a day. Leave the whole local publican thing to a younger man – like that Irish bloke down on the quay. Johnny or something. A jumped-up Irish boozer with ambitions to run a monopoly, I don't doubt . . .'

'Where will you live?' asked Maddy.

'I don't know,' he sighed. 'I'll admit it's damned hard to imagine living anywhere else. I can't persuade myself Pirate will enjoy the change.'

They both fell silent again, listening to Helen in the sitting room, chatting to Pirate as she took the blanket off his cage and his squawk of greeting.

'He'll miss the company,' Patrick went on. 'And so will I.'

CHAPTER FIFTEEN

'Compulsory beer ties aren't legal any more,' said Ben.

'How the heck do you know that?' said Maddy, stirring the cream into her hot chocolate to stop it looking quite so much like a Mr Whippy ice cream. 'I feel like a six-year-old,' she complained mildly.

'You love it like that,' said Ben. 'I even asked for extra marshmallows.'

'Back to beer ties, Mastermind,' said Maddy. 'I had no idea they were your specialist subject. What gives?'

'So,' said Ben, 'I was talking to my mate Jonno last night, as you know.'

'I knew you were seeing him. I didn't realise you were quite so stuck for conversation. I thought it was a bender?'

'He doesn't drink, actually. I was just winding you up. Anyway, he was telling me there's legislation forbidding the mandatory inclusion of beer ties in leases offered to publicans by the pub companies.'

'Okay,' said Maddy. 'Never mind how *you* know, how does *he* know?'

'He is sort of in the business . . .' said Ben.

Then, the penny dropped. 'Your mate Jonno is that Jonno McGrath bloke from Sails nightclub?'

'One and the same. Don't you remember him from your student days?'

'He arrived after I left,' explained Maddy. 'Like you did. Oh dear,' she went on, 'don't tell Patrick you've been talking to Jonno McGrath about our troubles.'

'Not a fan?'

'Not really,' Maddy went on. 'It's fair enough. Jonno represents the enemy. Patrick's been known to describe him as "that jumped-up Irish boozer", which is a tad unfair if – as you say – he doesn't drink. Isn't that a bit unusual for a publican, by the way?'

'You remember I said Jonno was ·one of my ex-army mates?' explained Ben. 'What I didn't say was that, as far as work goes he's also one of my moderate successes.'

'PTSD?'

'With knobs on. He's very open about it, otherwise I wouldn't say. Basically, although he's better than he was, his anger issues don't mix with alcohol but do seem to improve with physical exercise, so he's the cleanest living, hardest-running bloke you'll ever meet. As for the insomnia, it's a plus given the hours he keeps with the nightclub, which is partly why he took it on. Nowadays he only feels safe to sleep in the daytime so that's when he does it.'

'So, thanks to your help he's now a cross between the Terminator and a vampire. Good job! Can't wait for you to fix me.'

'I can only help if you'll let me.'

'Anyway,' she said, breaking his gaze, 'I'm not sure your Jonno is exactly the ally we're looking for, although the beer tie info's helpful.'

'He's a good bloke,' insisted Ben. 'You need to learn to trust people.'

'It's interesting to know, though,' said Maddy. 'The loathsome Dennis has sent Patrick a draft lease for approval definitely including the beer tie, so we should chuck that aspect back at him for a start.'

'Okay,' said Ben, 'so Patrick needs to calculate whether it works out cheaper to buy all his beer from Top Taverns in return for a lower rent or whether he'd be better off paying more rent and being allowed to sell what he wants.'

'Can't imagine a beer tie pays,' mused Maddy. 'That Golden Brite stuff's terrible. I'm amazed anyone drinks it . . .'

'And yet they do,' said Ben. 'Listen, tell Patrick what Jonno said but maybe don't tell him Jonno said it. It's up to Top Taverns to propose a "rent only" alternative but he had better ask quick because his lease expires just after Christmas and we need to know where we stand.'

'We may as well face facts,' said Patrick, when Maddy relayed the news. 'Whether Top Taverns are allowed to enforce the beer tie or not, the main issue is they want more money out of the Havenbury Arms than the turnover can generate, and if I can't afford to give them their pound of flesh then they'll either offer the lease to another publican or just sell the whole place from under me.'

'I think Maddy's right,' said Helen. 'You should at least ask Top Taverns to propose a lease without it. Then we can look at your sales and work out which deal is better for you.'

'Fine,' said Patrick gloomily. 'Maddy, will you ask for me? I don't think I can face a conversation with that little Turk just at the moment. And that reminds me of another pressing issue . . . The sales info we need will come out of the annual stocktake and it won't be long before my bookkeeper lady comes knocking on the door for it so she can do the year-end stuff. Surrounded by bossy women, me . . .' he added.

'So, what do we have to do?' said Maddy, rubbing her hands.

'To help with the stocktake?' said Patrick. 'That's the last thing you'd want to do, I should have thought. Dead boring. Plus, there's the leg thing,' he said, gesturing at Maddy's plaster.

'I'll do it,' said Helen firmly. 'Maddy can take notes and you can give instructions.'

'Aren't you keen to get home?' said Patrick hopefully.

'With you and Maddy in this state?' said Helen. 'Not remotely. And if I don't do it myself I'm pretty sure it'll end up being some silly sod not a million miles from here humping boxes around and generally doing things he shouldn't.'

'Many of our tenants are hugely appreciative of our beer tie deals,' insisted Dennis. 'They constitute a very attractive business proposition, especially for our newer publicans looking for lower fixed costs while they build their business.'

'Yes, well Patrick is hardly wet behind the ears, is he?' said Maddy. 'He's been filling Top Taverns' pockets for nearly ten years and he just wants a chance to look at all the options.'

God, even talking to the oily little man made her want to hold the phone away from her ear and give it a good wipe. 'Anyway, the point is, you're supposed to be giving publicans the choice, beer tie or full market rent.'

'Alright, alright . . . fine. I'll email an alternative version of the lease without the beer tie.'

'Good.'

'It's all very well quoting your rights, but I very much

doubt Patrick will like the new version when he sees it, either.'

'That's as may be,' replied Maddy with dignity, 'but we would like to see it, nonetheless. We will speak again when we've considered all the options.'

'And while you're considering "all the options",' said Dennis, 'I should have thought Patrick would do well to add "graceful retirement" to his list.'

Maddy had begun to enjoy her new life. The work was hard – especially with plaster on her leg – but there was a routine to the days. She adored having her mother and Patrick there, for all their bickering and Patrick's complaining. He was infuriated by his weakened state and desperate to take the strain away from Maddy but she took pride in getting the pub running right, with food the customers appreciated. If she was too highly tuned to visits from Ben, who tended to pop in at least a couple of times a week, then she hoped she didn't show it and if fear for the pub's future had not quite abated, the little team were learning – after Patrick's near-death experience – to live in the moment and be satisfied with that.

Despite having dreaded it for days, the stocktake was simple enough. They needed a record of every bottle, cask and packet of crisps in the storeroom so their book-lady Libby could work out how much of Patrick's money was tied up in stock at the year end. Helen made Maddy sit down and handwrite the figures she was shouting out as she worked through the shelves and cupboards.

'Libby'll be in soon,' said Patrick, looking at his watch. 'She usually drops the pay packets in around now.'

'She won't be thrilled with this scrappy old list,' said Maddy, holding up the paper she had been jotting on. 'I'll have to drop it all into an Excel file and email it to her, won't I?'

'I never have,' said Patrick. 'She's had a handwritten stocklist from me for years.'

'She's too kind to insist you join the twenty-first century.'

'You know what they say about old dogs and new tricks,' he retorted. 'Ah, speak of the devil, there you are, Libby. Tell this cheeky young woman a handwritten stocktake is fine.'

'A handwritten stocktake is fine,' parroted Libby, a slim, blonde woman in her late twenties. 'Is it done?' she said, holding out her hand for the list and shooting Maddy an understanding grin. 'I'll just drop the pay packets into the safe and I can pop back home to bung them into the stock sheet. Jack's at nursery until midday today, thankfully.'

'Not sure you should be spending a rare free morning crunching figures,' protested Maddy.

'It's fine,' said Libby. 'Mostly I do it at night once the children are in bed. I'll be able to sit up and watch telly tonight instead.'

'Let me make you a coffee and you can do it here,' said Maddy. 'Would it speed things up if I read stuff out to you?'

'Yes, actually,' said Libby gratefully. 'I've got what I need,' she added, fumbling in her bag in a welter of spare nappies, baby wipes, bottles of water and packs of mini rice cakes before finally bringing out a slim, battered laptop.

'Young mums are famous for carrying everything but the kitchen sink,' said Helen. 'I always did.'

'What makes you think I forgot the kitchen sink?' joked Libby, plonking a sheaf of papers, a calculator and a couple of biros on the table next to the computer.

'There we go,' she said, just minutes later. 'A complete record of stock bought and sold over the last twelve months.' She took a swig of her latte and pressed save with a little flourish. 'I don't suppose you've got the time sheets, have you?'

Maddy fetched them and watched in awe as Libby inputted them, her right hand tapping in the figures without looking whilst she used her left-hand index finger to guide her eyes down the handwritten columns of the time sheets.

When she finished and was sitting drinking her coffee, Maddy had a thought: 'You know that stock sheet?'

Libby nodded.

'Do you have them for previous years too?'

'Absolutely. I've definitely got them for the last couple of years, anyhow. When I took over the job I set up my own spreadsheets from scratch, really: stock, takings, time sheets, the whole thing . . .'

'I don't suppose you can, sort of, compare them, can you? I mean to previous years, but also – to each other?'

'Sure,' said Libby, draining her coffee and returning to the keyboard. 'What do you want to know?'

'Not sure,' admitted Maddy. 'I suppose I want to see anything that's surprising. Is there any change in the last year that there isn't an obvious explanation for, especially in the last few months or so? Since Patrick's been less involved in the day-to-day running of the pub . . .'

Libby nodded twice sharply, and then sat with her hands poised over the keyboard.

'Okay,' she said, 'for a start let's compare the stock turnover year on year.' She clattered at the keyboard for a bit, toggling between two files and rapidly tapping in formulas. 'Let's see it as a bar chart,' she muttered to herself, tapping a few more keys.

'There. Pretty,' she said, swivelling the laptop to show

Maddy the screen. It was a mass of vertical red and blue stripes.

'So, what am I looking at?' said Maddy, perplexed.

Libby leant around and pointed. 'Look, so here's this year's stock in blue, divided category by category – snacks, casks, spirits, mixers and so forth – and last year's equivalent stock categories in red. See?'

Maddy did see.

'Funny, though . . .' added Libby, frowning.

'What?'

'Hmm,' she said. 'We know turnover has dropped – I show you that in a minute – so obviously that will be visible in the amount of stock we've got through, right across all the categories, right?' She looked at Maddy to check she was following.

Maddy nodded.

'First, it's generally not, which is surprising in itself but on the other hand . . . look at the spirits category, here,' she pointed again. Maddy peered at the screen.

'It's *much* lower,' she exclaimed.

'Exactly.'

'So, we know turnover has fallen because the takings at the end of the nights that I have seen have definitely been a bit lower than expected, but from here it just looks like people have dramatically cut their consumption of gin, whisky, vodka . . . but not, say, snacks.'

'Exactly,' said Libby again.

'It's not like they're suddenly drinking more beer instead,' mused Maddy, looking more closely at the bars in the chart. 'In fact, they're drinking a little bit less, if anything.'

'Hardly surprising,' commented Libby. 'I don't know a single devotee of Golden Shite – sorry – Golden Brite lager. Plus it's about a quid per pint more than at Sails down the road.'

'Jonno doesn't sell Golden Shite – Brite – at Sails, does he?'

'No fear,' said Libby. 'He's mostly got the ales from Blackdown Brewery up the road. Their lager's brilliant. Plus it's cheaper. It doesn't bother me because I drink wine mostly, but a lot of my friends say they wish Patrick would stock some decent beers on tap.'

'Mmm. Funny you should say. That's quite the topic *du jour* at the moment . . . Okay, what would be the reason for us suddenly selling fewer spirits?' Maddy asked. 'The markup on them is pretty good so it's a big hole in the profits if it's true. Also,' she went on, 'if we were selling fewer spirits you'd expect us to be selling fewer mixers – you know, tonic, orange juice, ginger ale – but those sales are almost identical to last year.'

'So . . . what does it mean?'

'I don't know yet. Okay, tell me this: is it possible to see what we sell in relation to who's been working for each shift over the whole of the previous year? Temporary staff too?'

Libby shook her head. 'The data isn't there for that, but I could give you the turnover per shift against the staff on the rota – would that be any good?'

'Yes, it might be,' said Maddy. 'And I'd really like to know the shift-by-shift turnover year on year too.'

'That last one's easy,' said Libby. 'Hang on a mo.' In less than a minute she twizzled the laptop to show Maddy again.

'Blimey,' said Maddy.

'Quite,' agreed Libby. 'Kind of falls off a cliff, doesn't it?' They both looked again.

'And that's around the time Patrick started to withdraw,' said Libby, pointing. 'He was really ill with some sort of bug around May and, after that, he just really wasn't around much. No coincidence?'

'No coincidence,' agreed Maddy.

'Okay,' said Libby slowly. 'You were wanting a closer look at takings in relation to the staff rota. It's not obvious, but I think . . .'

While Libby worked it out, Maddy made them both another coffee. By the time she had got back to the table carrying the two mugs precariously in one hand and limping with her crutch in the other, Libby was looking pleased with herself.

'Here you go,' she said. 'I mashed the staff rota data in with the daily turnover data. Check it out.'

Maddy looked again. 'Talk me through?'

'So,' said Libby, 'here's the turnover when Adam was on shift.'

'Adam?'

'Sorry, forgot,' said Libby. 'Patrick did less and less from May this year and Adam started about the same time. He was lovely,' she said. 'Nice arse. Anyhow, he left in September to go travelling. Just a few weeks before Patrick had his heart attack. When he was here, he and Kevin split the shifts fairly evenly between them. So, here, you can see turnover on Kevin's shifts,' she pointed, 'and here are the shifts Adam worked.' She pointed again.

'Kevin's are lower,' said Maddy.

'Yup,' said Libby, 'by quite a bit.'

'Doesn't surprise me,' said Serena when she and Ben popped in later. Maddy took them upstairs to the flat, even though the crutches made it a faff. She wanted to make sure they weren't interrupted. 'Surely just looking at his spotty face would put customers off and make them spend less.'

'Not nigh on twenty-five per cent less,' Maddy reasoned.

'I don't see why not. I just look at him and I want to poke him in the eye. I've always known he was up to something.'

'That's not exactly what she said, though,' interceded Ben.

'Low turnover in itself isn't proof of anything criminal.'

'It is when consumption has stayed the same. And then there's the thing about the spirits,' said Maddy. 'That's definitely dodgy. I just can't quite work out what the scam is . . . and, of course, I have no proof it's him that's done something.'

'How frustrating,' said Serena. 'Shouldn't we ask Patrick? He must know the common dodges by now. Time was he'd have spotted it a mile off.'

'Not yet,' said Maddy. 'Libby's promised to take a closer look at everything. Let's see what she comes back with.'

'Don't we need to watch the little weasel, though?' insisted Serena. 'Whatever he's doing, he's doing it right under our noses.'

'Hmm, true,' said Ben. 'But when I sat and watched him recently I couldn't see him do anything that meant anything to me,' he admitted. 'I told you, Maddy – didn't I – that he sometimes left the till drawer open in between customers?'

'You did, but I don't suppose it's as simple as someone just leaning over and grabbing a few notes when people's backs are turned. Maybe he has an accomplice . . .'

'I think I'd have noticed that,' said Ben.

'And also, the till would have been out,' said Maddy.

'Out?' queried Serena.

'When you cash up at night,' Maddy explained, 'the till roll gives you a total figure for all the transactions you've rung in throughout the shift and that figure – whatever it is – should be the same as the amount of money you've got in the till. Minus the float, of course.'

'Does it always add up?' asked Ben.

'Usually,' said Maddy. 'Occasionally it'll be a few pence out; that just means you might have given someone slightly the wrong change. Actually, the annoying thing is when it's exactly a tenner down, and then you know you've given someone change for a twenty when they only gave you ten. And of course it can work in your favour too, if you've made a mistake the other way – although customers let you know pretty quickly if you do that. Anyway, that's not the kind of thing we're talking about here. I've been impressed at how precise Kevin's cashing up is. The amount in the safe is always exactly what the till roll says it should be. He's uncannily accurate, if anything.'

They all thought silently for a minute.

'Anyway,' said Ben, standing up and stretching. 'I'll leave you girls to it – got to go and mark essays again. Going to be a late one.'

'I'm not going to be keeping this child up for long,' said Serena to Ben. 'She needs her sleep.'

Ben nodded. 'There are lots of studies on sleep and healing,' he told a sceptical-looking Maddy. 'The general finding was you need lots of the first to facilitate the second. Remember, you've got the appointment where you're hopefully getting rid of your cast in a couple of weeks.'

'Am I?' said Maddy. 'Yay!'

'Sleep,' said Ben, giving Maddy a hug. 'And don't think about Kevin.'

'Ah, but you see now I'm thinking about Kevin. It's like when people say "don't think about elephants" and then all you can think about is elephants.'

'Fine,' said Ben. 'Don't think about elephants, then.'

Chapter Sixteen

Hunched over Maddy's laptop, she and Serena discovered they were a better match for the funding criteria than Maddy had first thought.

With trepidation and a sense of fatalism she attached the document to the email address and pressed send.

'Do you think we'll get it?' she said, sitting back in her chair with a sigh.

'Definitely,' said Serena. 'I've never been surer about anything in my life.' She paused. 'Except what a great couple you and Ben make, of course.'

'We're not,' protested Maddy, blushing.

'Then you should be,' said Serena. 'I'm very fond of you both and I just happen to think you're very well matched plus – I admit – I'd dearly love to see Ben settled.'

'That's so maternal. You can't feel motherly,' Maddy protested. 'You're not old enough.'

'I blinking am,' Serena insisted. 'I'll have you know I was very precocious – and very naughty too. I could easily have had a baby in my teens and he or she would be your age. Lucky I didn't, though.'

'I don't think of you as my mum's age. She had me in her early twenties,' said Maddy. 'Actually, when I first saw you and Ben together I was a tiny bit jealous,' Maddy confessed. 'I thought you had a thing.'

'Me and Ben!' hooted Serena. 'He's like my little brother.'

'Ben told me about Andrew. I'm really sorry.'

'I know. It was crap.'

'But at least you've got Giles.'

'Yeah,' said Serena. 'I have.'

They were silent for a moment.

'So,' said Serena, brightening, 'what gives between your mother and Patrick, then?'

'You're quite the matchmaker, aren't you? Honestly, there's nothing . . . whatever you and Ben would like to think. He's about fifteen years older than her, for a start. I hadn't even met him until I came here to study. Mum just said he was an old friend from when she was younger, that they'd lost touch but that I should look him up and he would look after me. And he did. That's all.'

Serena pursed her lips, knowingly. 'Just keep telling yourself that. Personally, I think there's more.'

'Yeah well, you think me and Ben are an item too and we're not – so your strike rate isn't great, is it?'

'You'll see,' said Serena.

Maddy didn't share Serena's confidence about the funding. In her mind's eye she could imagine Giles's contact coming into work, opening his email and opening up their application. What if they had entirely missed the point? Not done enough? Failed to impress in some fundamental and irrevocable way? She realised, sipping her coffee, that she minded failing with the Bespoke Consortium very much indeed. It wasn't just the thought of letting down all the artisans she was creating a platform for, it was – she admitted to herself – the crushing disappointment she would feel if this, the most exciting project she had ever worked on, flopped. Patrick was improving daily and, with luck, her efforts to renegotiate a lease for him would be successful . . . By Christmas, just a few weeks away, her reason for staying in Sussex, within a community she felt increasingly at home with, would have disappeared. She would have no purpose. No excuse to stay.

She was also hurt that Patrick and Helen were so enthusiastic about her moving out.

'What about you?' Maddy had said to Patrick. 'You don't want to be here on your own, do you?'

'I don't need a nursemaid,' he had said brusquely. 'And even if I did,' he had added, 'I've yet to get rid of your mother.'

Maddy was packing. When her phone rang, she scrambled for it, finding it under a folded pile of clothes just before it went to answerphone. It was Libby.

'You'll never guess,' said Libby.

'Probably not,' agreed Maddy. 'What?'

'Okay, so . . .' Libby stalled, for dramatic effect, 'I think we've got the little git.'

She paused again.

'Go on,' said Maddy. 'Spit it out!'

'Okay, okay,' she relented. 'So, I took the stocktake and we already had the clue that turnover for Kevin's shift was lower than it should be, so that made me think . . . what about if I compare the retail value of the entire year's worth of stock sold against the entire year's worth of turnover and guess what?'

'What?'

'The retail value of the stock exceeds the turnover. Quite a lot. Several thousand pounds, in fact.'

'Oookaaay,' said Maddy, scratching her head.

'So-o,' she went on, 'that tells us there's a hole in our turnover.'

'Someone's been stealing stock, maybe?'

'Possibly,' said Libby. 'But to my mind it's more likely they've been selling everything but not all the money is making its way into the turnover figures, which also explains why it looks lower than it should be, given your hunch that the bar actually seems quite busy . . .'

Maddy slowly ran it over in her head.

'But how?'

'That's the final piece of the puzzle,' said Libby. 'You physically can't put money in the till or give change unless you've keyed in the transaction because it won't be open.'

'Ah,' said Maddy at last. 'Bingo! Did I mention it's been noticed that Kevin has a habit of keeping the till drawer open? We couldn't work out why.'

'We know why now, alright,' said Libby grimly. 'If he's taking money for drinks and not ringing it into the till, then all he has to do at the end of the night is make the money match the till roll and then pocket the extra.'

'No wonder the takings look as if they're low,' said Maddy. 'And no wonder he insists on cashing up himself,' she added.

'So, now we get him,' said Libby. 'Is he onto us, do you suppose? If he knows we've done the stocktake he'll guess.'

'Actually, by sheer lucky chance, I don't think he does,'

said Maddy. She had been irritated at his message on the answerphone claiming to need a day off to attend his grandmother's funeral. She strongly suspected Kevin was working his way through a positive rugby team of grandmothers but it meant he was unware of the stocktake.

'Don't breathe a word to anyone,' she said to Libby. 'Not yet.'

'Wouldn't dream of it,' agreed Libby. 'I want you to get him, though. I've always hated that man. He's evil.'

'I trusted that little shit,' said Patrick, flushing with annoyance. 'And this is how he repays me.'

Patrick relaxed visibly when Maddy outlined the likely figure stolen by Kevin over the last six months.

'That's the kind of money we *should* have been making,' he said. 'I knew it! Top Taverns might get their outrageous rent after all.'

'Have you had the revised lease?' asked Maddy. 'You never said.'

'It came this morning,' admitted Patrick, rifling through the papers on the kitchen table and handing the A4 envelope to Maddy. She slid the papers out impatiently and flicked through to the page she was looking for.

'Bloody cheek,' she said, when she saw the sum they wanted. 'Makes the one with the beer ties look like a good deal.'

'It *is* high,' agreed Patrick, 'but if the kind of sums Kevin has been helping himself to actually stayed in the business, we could afford it. Just.'

'Plus you get rid of the ghastly beer tie.'

'Quite so,' said Patrick, his eyes alight with the possibilities. 'If I get in beers that taste better *and* have a higher margin, I reckon we could increase our profits, even with the higher rent. I could get in guest beers, a beer of the month . . . Plus, with a bit of money in the pot we could actually hire a band every once in a while. Live music always draws the crowds . . .'

'One other thing, though,' said Maddy. 'Now we've got him on that, maybe you can explain something else.' She told him about the apparently low spirits consumption.

'That old trick!' exploded Patrick. He shook his head. 'Can't believe I didn't spot it . . . of course! I can't remember the last time I had to place an order for spirits, but it just didn't occur to me, what with all the other stuff to worry about . . .'

'What?' asked Maddy.

'Oh,' Patrick waved a hand dismissively, 'it's the oldest pub trick in the book. A dodgy barman will sell his own spirits and hive off the income. The markup's good, you see?'

Maddy didn't really.

'And,' Patrick went on, 'I bet I know where he's buying it from. We occasionally get blokes showing up flogging cheap vodka and Scotch. It's probably counterfeit. Could be anything. Could be laced with antifreeze, anything . . . I just send them packing, obviously.' He looked concerned. 'If there's any chance we're selling counterfeit spirits we need to sort it out.'

'One thing at a time,' said Maddy. 'We can't arouse his suspicions; not yet.'

'Fine, one more night and he's out. I'm more than ready to get back to pulling pints,' said Patrick. 'And it wouldn't do your mother any harm to lend a hand for a few days. Just like old times, it'll be.'

'Did she work here before?'

'She did,' said Patrick, staring into space and smiling fondly. 'It's how it all began. She turned up with her sandals and her hippy smocks wanting a summer job. I said yes and, my goodness, we worked hard. There was a music festival that year, I remember . . .'

'. . . and a heatwave,' said Helen, coming into the room and putting her hand on Patrick's shoulder. 'We all absolutely boiled. The pub was so rammed we set up a temporary bar in the car park, just to give us a bit more space. Do you remember?'

'Ah yes, I remember it well,' sang Patrick, tilting his head to look at her.

They didn't want to arouse suspicion by turning out in force that night. Patrick had been persuaded to stay upstairs with the argument that he would give the game away too soon if he exploded in rage the first time Kevin did it. Ben had the idea that they might need objective proof. That stumped them all for a while, until Maddy remembered the camera trained on the door.

'We have to have them on the outside of the pub, just in case, but when Patrick got them installed he decided to have one inside too, trained on the door to catch people who run away without paying for their food. Not that many people do, I might add.'

Ben stood on a chair to take a look.

'It's easy enough,' he said. 'If I unscrew it and put it the other way around it'll cover most of the bar. If I get the angle right it will just about see whether the till drawer is open. It's not ideal, but I think it'll do and I can't imagine Kevin will notice anything's changed.'

'I'd not noticed it at all until now,' Helen said, 'but he will if he sees the screen showing the footage, won't he?'

'Actually,' admitted Patrick, 'the monitor broke a couple of years ago but I think the footage is saved onto a hard disk or something highly technical. If I ever needed it – and I never have – I could retrieve it providing I do it within twenty-four hours. It automatically deletes after that to make room for the next lot.'

'I'm impressed,' said Maddy, at this show of technical know-how.

'Oh yes,' said Patrick. 'I'm not just a pretty face, you know.'

'Not *even* a pretty face,' said Helen. 'Shouldn't we just check we can get the footage off the hard disk?'

'No time,' said Ben, jumping down off the chair. 'He'll be here in a minute. You lot skedaddle and Maddy and I will pretend to act casual.'

CHAPTER SEVENTEEN

The evening session started off quietly. A few of the local shopkeepers popped in for a post-work drink and were quickly on their way home to supper, but by about seven o'clock the bar was beginning to fill. Maddy was bringing Ben up to speed on her and Serena's application for funding.

'It's a great idea,' said Ben, 'and I'm sure he'll see that.'

Neither of them wanted to stare too fixedly at what Kevin was doing.

'Ridiculous that we're the ones feeling guilty,' commented Maddy. 'What if we confront him and he goes mad?' she asked.

'We don't have to do anything tonight. Getting the evidence is enough for now.'

'I don't trust Patrick not to blow a gasket on him once we know.'

'Tonight it is, then,' said Ben, taking Maddy's hand and giving it a squeeze. 'It'll be fine. He's hardly going to compound the situation by doing anything silly.'

'Should we involve the police?'

'We could, but just sacking him solves our problem. We've

got no realistic chance of getting the money back, whether he gets convicted of theft or not.'

'What do you suppose he's spending it all on?'

'Gambling? Drugs?' suggested Ben. 'It could easily be drugs. Look at the state of him.'

'I'd never thought,' said Maddy. 'But yes, he does look very unhealthy. I suppose I knew he smoked dope from when I was here before,' she mused. 'It didn't occur to me it was anything stronger.'

'Even marijuana can be pretty destructive,' observed Ben. 'He'll have access to anything and everything, working in a pub. I reckon he's on the hard stuff too.'

'Here we go,' said Maddy, grabbing Ben's arm. Her eyes were fixed on the till. 'Drawer open. Don't look.'

Ben casually rested his head on his hand and sneaked a glance before turning back to Maddy.

'What now?'

'Just watch, Keep it cool, keep it cool . . .'

They both waited. Then Kevin took the customer's ten-pound note, walked to the till, put it in the drawer and grabbed the change. He loped morosely back to the customer and tipped the change into his hand.

Maddy and Ben looked at each other.

'He didn't ring it up,' they said simultaneously.

'Got him,' said Ben.

Maddy's stomach lurched. 'Let's wait a little longer, see if he does it again . . .'

The bar was busier now and Kevin was moving swiftly, dealing with customer orders, collecting glasses and loading the glass-washer machine. Most of the time he would ring up the transactions in the normal way but – now they were watching – it was clear to see that approximately every fourth transaction he would fail to close the till. The next time he took money he would hand out change without having tapped anything in.

'He's planning to keep something like a quarter of the money,' said Ben in amazement.

'Yep, that's about it,' said Maddy. 'According to Libby it's around twenty-two per cent down year on year. So, with inflation, a quarter is about right. And I'm not talking a quarter of the profits, I'm talking a quarter of the turnover.'

'Must be nigh on all the profits then, after costs,' mused Ben. 'No wonder Patrick's been in despair.'

'So, what do we do now?' asked Maddy.

'Insist on cashing up?' suggested Ben. 'That'll provide a bit more evidence, won't it?'

'Yes,' agreed Maddy, 'but I—if I do that . . .' she trailed away. 'What might he do? I'll be . . .'

'I'll obviously stay here,' said Ben.

'What if . . . ?' Maddy clasped her hands together to stop them shaking. Ben put his hand over them and gave them a reassuring squeeze.

'You can do this.'

Maddy took a deep, shuddering breath and nodded.

To kill time until the end of the shift, they went upstairs to Helen and Patrick, who were getting ready for bed, and told them what they planned to do. It also gave them a chance to check out the CCTV footage and – after a bit of head-scratching and fiddling – Ben managed to save extracts onto a data key, picking out a couple of examples where it illustrated clearly what Kevin was doing. 'I'm so frustrated I didn't work it out weeks ago,' commented Ben. 'I saw him do it; I just couldn't see why, or understand what was so significant about it.'

'You have to be crooked to spot criminal behaviour,' said Patrick, yawning. 'Anyhow, it's not your responsibility, it's mine. The little git. To think I paid him a bonus last Christmas. I even gave him a pay rise, even though I couldn't afford to. I just felt it was the decent thing to do with me not pulling my weight like I used to.'

'You will again,' said Helen. 'Nothing would give me more pleasure than to know he won't set foot behind that bar again, and I'm looking forward to getting back behind it myself,' she said. 'At least for a while . . .' she added to Maddy and Ben. 'You will be careful, won't you?'

'Yep,' said Maddy, wiping her sweating hands on her jeans and trying to relax on the sofa. They still had an hour to go. It was worse than waiting for the dentist.

'It's not exactly Starsky and Hutch, is it?' she joked as Ben helped her down the stairs later.

'More like Starsky and Crutch,' agreed Ben. 'What are you going to do if he makes a run for it?'

'Scream like a girl and wait for you to rugby tackle him?' suggested Maddy. 'Or I could bash him over the head with this,' she said, waving her crutch around.

'Maybe not,' said Ben, ducking. 'More dignified to keep to the moral high ground. Plus, I'm not sure I want to be raising bail for you. Right,' he said, peering through the glass panel of the door to the bar. 'Customers are all gone; let's go.'

'Kevin,' said Ben loudly, coming through the door and reaching back to move Maddy in behind him as he went. 'A word.'

'Busy,' said Kevin, gesturing to the tables covered in empty glasses.

'We'll cash up, then, shall we?' suggested Ben. 'Share the load and all that?'

Kevin threw him an evil look. For a moment Maddy thought he was going to face Ben down and then, as she watched, his face suffused with rage.

'You can't prove anything,' he said.

'Interesting choice of words,' said Ben. 'Don't remember mentioning that I needed to. Maddy?' he added, gesturing towards the till. 'Would you?'

'I would,' she said, pulling the till tray out onto the bar. Initially her hands were shaking but – as she worked her way through the familiar actions, printing off the till roll, scooping out the change and the notes, counting it out into piles – she became calmer.

Kevin, after staring furiously at her for several seconds, got on with gathering and washing the glasses, going on to restock the shelves as she finished.

'It's out,' she said to Ben, as she finished, tipping the coins that made up the float back into their little sections in the tray.

'That happens,' said Kevin defensively. 'You know it does.'

'Not by this much.'

'So I made a mistake,' he said. 'Gave the wrong change.' He glared at Maddy, his hands tightening into fists.

'No mistake,' said Ben. 'It's over, Kevin.'

'You've got no proof.'

'Ah, but we have,' said Ben. 'All the proof we need,' he added, pointing up at the camera over the door.

Kevin's eyes went to where Ben was indicating. For the

first time he noticed the adjustment and he scowled, his upper lip rising into a sneer.

'What are you going to do?' he said, shrugging almost casually and strolling towards them both. Ben, checking out Kevin's clenched fists, took a step towards him simultaneously grasping Maddy by the shoulders and moving her aside.

'Well,' said Ben calmly. 'That depends . . .'

The two men squared up to each other. Ben was taller, broader, and Kevin, his chin jutting, had to look up at him.

'I could pay it back,' said Kevin.

Ben tilted his head, pretending to consider. 'That would be very nice,' he said, as if Kevin was offering him a cup of tea and a slice of cake, 'and if you want to avoid prison I should have thought that would be a very good idea indeed.'

'You going to call the police?'

'Er, well, I thought I might,' said Ben, raising his shoulders and holding his hands out to the sides in mock surprise.

'Fine,' spat Kevin. 'Put me in jail and see where that gets you,' he sneered. 'You'll never see a penny of it if I'm inside, and you needn't think I haven't got mates,' he added threateningly.

'I would imagine the kind of mates you've got are already inside,' said Ben. 'And, as for the money, I'm not holding my breath anyhow,' said Ben, 'but – I'll tell you what I'll do for you,' he said, as if he was proposing a compromise solution in a tricky business matter, 'you walk out of that door and never come near this place ever again and I might just consider not handing over our evidence to the police. Of course, if there's the slightest hint of trouble, either from you or from anyone in your delightful little circle of friends, we will ensure that charges are pressed for every theft, drug deal, pub fight and parking ticket you've ever swung. Do you understand?'

As Ben had been talking his voice had been dropping in volume and growing in intensity until his face was an inch from Kevin's.

Recoiling, Kevin took a step back and then another.

'You'll be sorry for this,' he hissed, looking away from Ben to Maddy who had been standing stock-still behind the bar.

He pointed his finger at her. 'You . . .' he spat, his face contorted with hate. 'You stuck-up bitch. This is down to you. Posh cow . . . you think you're better than everyone, don't you? I know what you are, even if you can't remember,' he sneered. 'I know what you did.' He paused. 'What *we* did.'

He watched her face closely, for her reaction. 'Yeah . . .' he sneered again. 'You weren't a posh stuck-up cow then, were you?' He gloated at the effect he was having on her. 'I reckon we should do it again sometime, don't you?' He raised his eyebrows in query. 'Maybe when you're least expecting it, eh?' She shook her head, trying to back away but the shelves were pressed up against her spine. 'Yeah, let's do that,' he said. 'You disappeared for a bit, didn't you? Ran away. But I know where to find you now.'

She stared at him, frozen, her lips pressed into a thin white line, her pupils dilating with fear, until her eyes were like black pools. She saw Ben lurching towards Kevin, fist raised, and it broke the trance.

'No,' she shouted to Ben. 'Don't do it. Let him go . . .' she gasped for breath. 'Just . . . get him out of here.' Turning away, she grabbed the money bag and till roll and walked, stiff-legged, her crutches wobbling unsteadily, to the office to put the money in the safe. Her heart was pounding so hard, her whole body was swaying with the impact of every beat.

When she came back in, Ben was alone. He reached up and shot the bolt in the door closed before walking towards her, arms held out to the sides.

'You're okay, Maddy,' he said quietly, intently, meeting her eye and holding her gaze. 'You're fine.'

Maddy nodded, but she was gasping too much to speak.

'This is just adrenaline,' he went on, reaching her and grabbing her arms. 'Just a physical reaction. That's all it is.'

'I know . . . I know . . .' she sobbed. 'I just . . . I can't . . .'

'Yes you can,' said Ben. 'Come here.' He encircled her with his arms, tightening them around her as she tried to turn away, instead pulling her head against his shoulder. 'Breathe with me,' he went on. 'Maddy!' he said sharply, commanding her attention. 'Breathe with me. Now.'

Feeling his chest rising and falling against her own, Maddy closed her eyes and tried to mirror him. In. Out. In. Out. Every third breath she took an additional gasp, the urge to pant for air was overwhelming.

'There you go,' said Ben steadily, after a few breaths. 'You're doing fine.'

It wasn't true, but as the minutes passed, Maddy's heart slowed. Gradually, though, violent trembling overtook her and her limbs seemed to turn to water.

In response, Ben turned her in his arms and lowered her gently to the floor, so she sat, with him behind her, leaning her back against his chest.

Slowly but surely the world returned and the panic receded. She could feel his body heat warming her icy limbs. She realised she was freezing even though she was simultaneously drenched in sweat.

'Better?' murmured Ben into her ear, at last.

Maddy nodded. 'Just adrenaline, eh?' she said shakily.

'Uh-huh,' he replied. 'Oxytocin's pretty much the direct antidote for it. It's known colloquially as "the cuddle hormone". My holding you like this has just made your body release enough of it to calm you down.'

'Oh,' said Maddy, straightening. She was thinking of Ben's actions more as an emotional response than a chemical experiment. 'Anyway, I'm fine now,' she added briskly. 'It's amazing what a bit of adrenaline can do to a girl – awful, really.'

'Could have been worse,' said Ben.

'How?'

'Incontinence,' he said dryly.

'Lovely,' said Maddy. 'You mean you go around hugging people – purely in a medical capacity, obviously – and in return they wee on you.'

'Yep,' said Ben, 'and worse. Believe me, I've been there.'

'Oh, I do,' said Maddy, pushing herself up off the floor, awkwardly balancing on her good leg. 'Anyhow, I really am fine now,' she said, brushing herself off, and avoiding meeting his eye.

'Thanks,' she said.

'You're welcome.'

'I thought you were going to hit him.'

'So did I.'

Maddy noticed there was a muscle pulsing in his jaw.

'He knows what happened,' she whispered, a tear escaping from the corner of her eye. 'And I don't,' she went on. '*He* knows. It was him.' She swallowed. 'And he knows where I am . . .'

'No, he doesn't,' said Ben grimly. 'Because you're getting out of here. Tonight.'

* * *

219

Patrick and Helen had already gone to bed. Ben had a brief and terse-sounding conversation on his mobile and then joined Maddy in her bedroom to help her finish her packing.

'I can bring the rest of this stuff tomorrow,' he said. 'Just take what you need for tonight and for your meeting tomorrow.'

'Yikes! My meeting. I've got nothing to wear.'

'Serena will help.'

'Is that where we're going?' asked Maddy.

'It is,' said Ben. 'They're waiting up for us.'

'I can't just leave Patrick and Helen on their own.'

''Course you can. They're not children.'

Reluctantly, Maddy scribbled a note for them and left it on the kitchen table with the pepper pot on top of it.

'What if he—? Do you think he'll come and – I dunno – do something?'

'I don't even seriously think he'll come back and do anything to *you*,' said Ben, 'let alone Patrick and Helen. He may be a despicable toerag, but he's not as stupid as he looks. You just need to be out of here,' he said. 'Admit it, even the thought of Kevin coming back and challenging you is enough to cause harm, the state you're in.'

'No one's ever been worried about my mental state before.'

'Really? You surprise me. Now, come on . . .' he added, grabbing her rucksack and holding out his arm.

Chapter Eighteen

It was nearly one in the morning and, just as they drove out into the country, the street lights, all on timers, switched off behind them, making the town disappear into the night. It was like a ghost town, only real when they were in it, like *Brigadoon*.

'Do you ever miss London?' asked Ben. 'The city that never sleeps and all that?'

'I think that might be New York,' said Maddy, yawning. 'I do like the countryside; I like that it's properly dark at night and that you can notice the seasons changing. In London, there's such anonymity I sometimes I feel I might be invisible . . .'

'Will you stay here?'

Maddy sat up straighter in her seat.

'More and more, I think I would,' she said. 'But not with this awful thing . . .' she gestured, remembering how she was half an hour before. She turned to look at him. 'Would you like me to?'

Ben stared straight ahead at the road. 'I would,' he replied.

* * *

Serena and Giles were waiting for them. Before Ben had even switched off the engine they were out in the courtyard. Giles was fully dressed still, despite the late hour. Serena looked as if she had just got out of bed, with pyjamas, a fleece top and a pair of green wellies that she ditched in the porch as she led Maddy into the kitchen, clucking and fussing over her.

'I'm so sorry,' Maddy said.

'Don't you *dare* apologise,' replied Serena. 'I will not have you apologise for anything to do with that *vile* little creep,' she went on, grabbing Maddy and pulling her into a fierce hug.

'We're on furniture-moving detail, old man,' said Giles to Ben, who took the torch Giles was offering and made to follow him outside. Turning back to Serena, he said, 'You need to try and get some food into her. Her blood sugar is probably on the floor after everything she's been through.'

'Cheese sandwich?' she offered. Maddy shook her head. 'Beans on toast? Bacon bap? Sausage roll? Chocolate cake? Come on, Ben'll kill me . . .' she pleaded. 'I know!' she exclaimed. 'Hot chocolate and a piece of toast?'

'Oh, go on, then. No toast, though, thanks.'

Relieved, Serena grabbed a little saucepan and filled it with milk.

'It's perfect that you're here. We can run through the proposal again tomorrow – actually today – but I mean after we've slept,' she said, glancing at the kitchen clock, 'and then we can go to Brighton together.'

'Are you nervous?' asked Maddy.

'Not remotely,' said Serena. 'And neither should you be.'

Maddy was draining the last of the hot chocolate when Ben and Giles came back.

'Right, come on,' said Ben, holding out his hand. 'Your boudoir awaits.'

'The Grainstore?'

'Of course,' said Serena. 'I just hope it's not too cold. We lit the woodburner as soon as Ben called.'

There was a fine drizzle falling as they made their way the few yards to the Grainstore by torchlight. The slick, rain-soaked cobbles made Maddy nervous and she was grateful for Ben's arm around her waist, steadying her.

'It's fab,' said Maddy, overtaken with the charm of the little space all over again as she ducked through the low doorway. With a table lamp on the floor by her improvised bed – the men had somehow dragged the mattress and bedding down from the mezzanine – and the flickering light from the woodburning stove, the room glowed with cosiness and warmth.

'I didn't want you having to use the sofa bed; it's a bit small,' said Serena. 'Especially if there's two of you,' she added naughtily.

Maddy gave her a sideways look and didn't dare glance at Ben.

'Righto,' said Giles, rubbing his hands together. 'That's you sorted, then.' He reached for Serena and shepherded her away. 'Come on, old thing, time for your beauty sleep.'

'Are you staying?' Maddy asked Ben.

He yawned and rubbed his face. 'I should get back, really,' he said. 'But I'll admit, I'm bushed. Would you mind?' he said gesturing to the sofa.

'Of course I wouldn't,' said Maddy. 'Although I'd be insulted if you didn't just lie next to me here, like Serena suggested,' she said. 'No funny business, mind.'

'Definitely no funny business,' agreed Ben, with a little too much emphasis for Maddy's liking.

Within minutes they were respectively in the bed and on the bed, Ben insisting he was perfectly happy fully clothed with one of the Bespoke Consortium blankets over him.

The glow of the fire made an outline of Ben's profile. Maddy lay gazing at it, tracing the strong jaw and full lips with her eyes.

'I'm so relieved we've nailed the pub losses,' she said at last.

'Me too,' smiled Ben. 'Although I don't think we should count our chickens . . . I don't trust that Dennis as far as I can chuck him.'

'I think dwarf-chucking's outlawed nowadays.' Maddy sighed, feeling the tension drain out of her, replaced by a gentle but mammoth wave of fatigue.

Yet again, she felt tears spring to her eyes.

'Maddy?'

'I'm fine,' she said, but her voice cracked on a sob. 'Oh bugger, I wish this would stop happening,' she muttered, dashing her forearm over her eyes.

'What is it?'

'Dunno . . . relief?'

'Okay.'

'Yeah?' said Maddy, turning her head to look at him.

'Sure,' he said. 'Think about it, all these problems . . . we're nailing them one by one, aren't we? Patrick's improving, he's getting on with your mum, the pub looks like it can climb out of its financial pit, your cast is coming off soon and tomorrow your funding for the professional part of your whole new life down here is going to be one step closer to dropping into place. All sounds pretty good to me.'

They lay in companionable silence, watching the reflected light from the flames flickering on the vaulted ceiling above them.

'Sleepy?' asked Ben.

'Not really. I think my oxytocin levels are falling a bit low again.'

He leant over her and pulled her onto his chest.

Looking up at him, Maddy gazed at his lips, just inches from her own but he pulled his head back and turned away. To take the sting out of the rejection he curled his arm around her more firmly and gave her a hug. 'You have no idea,' he said in a low voice, 'how much I would like to . . .'

'I wouldn't mind,' pleaded Maddy, propping herself on one elbow so she could slide a hand between the buttons on his shirt. Mm, his chest was so warm and firm, with exactly the right amount of hair, she thought.

In response, Ben took hold of her hand, removing it gently but determinedly from his chest and holding it in his own. 'We can't,' he said. 'Believe me.'

Maddy groaned, but desisted. There was only so much rejection a girl could take.

'Are you going to go to sleep?' he murmured after a minute or so.

'Nope,' said Maddy, but with his body warmth and his heartbeat thudding slow and regular in her ear, her eyelids quickly drooped.

Alone at last, Ben sighed. It wasn't getting any easier keeping her at arm's length. In any other circumstance he would just stay away altogether – give himself time to get his head straight – but with Maddy in the state she was in he dared not. His mission, his promise to Patrick, his need to protect his own flesh and blood meant he was in it up to his neck and the sooner he could persuade her to accept help from Duncan the better. That said, the escalation in her distress worried him; the flashback and then tonight's panic attack – both involving Kevin – made him wonder just what the hell had happened that night. Perhaps his and Duncan's plan to unveil her memories, far from resolving her fears, might lead to more harm than good. Was Kevin telling the truth or were his comments tonight just the cruel taunts of a creep lashing out in revenge because he'd been caught out?

The coffee machine was what woke Maddy the following morning.

'Sorry,' said Ben, seeing she was awake. Expertly, he flicked buttons and held a jug of milk under the steamer. 'It'll be worth it, though; give me a minute.'

By the time she had dragged herself to sitting and wiped the sleep from her eyes, he was crouching beside her holding a delicious-smelling mug.

'Latte,' he said, handing it over carefully so she could grab the handle. 'Double shot, no sugar.'

'Perfect,' she said, taking a grateful sip. 'Is it late?'

'Nearly ten,' he said, pulling aside the floor-length curtains that hung over the glazed door to the terrace.

'Yikes. We've got our meeting in Brighton. I've got to iron something. And wash my hair,' she said, raking it back off her face with her fingers.

'You're fine. Serena's going to sort out some clothes for you.'

'You're wet,' she said, looking at his hair.

'Yep. Amazing shower upstairs. Rainforest head. You're going to love it when you can get up there.'

She looked at the stairs leading to the mezzanine. They were more of a ladder. 'Can't you give me a shove?' she asked. 'A leg up?'

'Erm . . .' He pretended to think, finger to temple, 'that would be a "no".'

'Oh go on. I'm really grubby.'

'I can't smell anything. Anyhow, there's a better plan. Serena's running a bath for you in the house. Bubbles and everything. I've been detailed to get some breakfast into you and then send you over.'

As he spoke he was clattering around with plates and cutlery in the little kitchen area under the mezzanine. He came out with a pile of warm, flaky croissants. There was butter and two kinds of home-made jam on the tray too.

'Wow. Where did you spirit this up from?'

'You'd be amazed what us soldiers keep in our rucksacks. But that's a story for another day. Actually, Serena gave them to me.'

'You're not having breakfast?' she asked, disappointed to notice there was only one plate.

'It's alright for you part-time self-employed people. I've got lectures to deliver,' he said, grabbing his car keys from the coffee table.

Maddy held up her face in the hope of a kiss but Ben just dropped a peck on her forehead, simultaneously giving her an awkward pat on the shoulder. And then he was gone.

'Aha!' said Serena, waggling her eyebrows, 'I see lover boy spent the night. How nice. Do tell Auntie Serena . . .'

'"Nice" nothing. I am entirely unravished. Not for want of trying on my part, I hasten to add. Truth is, he turned me down.'

'Ouch. Silly boy. I shall have to have words . . .'

'By all means; I've done my best. Now, any chance I could borrow an iron?'

'Every chance,' said Serena, 'if I can remember where it is. But you're bound not to have much from your business wardrobe down here. I was wondering if you'd like a rummage in my drawers?'

'And that's not an offer you hear very often,' interjected Giles, on his way past with a cup of coffee. 'I can't remember the last time I got to rummage in my wife's drawers.'

'Ignore him. I do,' said Serena. 'Now, walk this way . . .' she added, doing a funny walk and leading Maddy up the stairs.

'I've got my own funny walk, thanks,' said Maddy, using the banister to pull herself up. 'Nothing's going to make me look that sharp with this flipping thing hanging off my leg.'

'Nonsense, I'm sure we can make you look smart – from the waist up, at least.'

Rifling through a packed wardrobe, Serena chatted over her shoulder. 'I'm a couple of sizes bigger than you now, but – believe it or not – I was an eight to ten when I was working,' she said, pulling out an unexceptional-looking grey jacket with matching skirt. 'This one might work. Try it.'

Maddy shrugged on the jacket over her T-shirt.

'I was going to dig out a shirt but, actually, it really works with that top.'

Maddy looked in the mirror. Her simple scoop-necked T-shirt looked cool and unfussy beneath the jacket. She buttoned it up and looked again.

'Wow,' said Serena. 'Perfect.'

Maddy scooped up her wavy hair and gathered it into a loose, low knot making her neck look positively swan-like.

'Yes,' said Serena. 'Just like that. I'll find you some hairpins in a mo.'

'Not sure about the skirt, though.'

'Mm,' agreed Serena. 'I see your problem. We might be better off with trousers. As long as they're wide enough to go over that.' She dived back into the wardrobe, chucking random garments over her shoulder periodically.

'Bullseye,' she said, emerging triumphant with a pair of trousers over her arm. 'I'd almost forgotten, I wore that jacket so much I actually went and got matching trousers made. Hardly ever wore them, though. Too keen to show off my legs, if I'm honest.'

'Blimey,' said Maddy, looking at the jacket with new respect. 'Is it bespoke?'

'It certainly is,' admitted Serena. 'I was earning a fair amount in those days. Had to look the part.'

The trousers were wide, going over the clumpy cast and draping beautifully, although they pooled on the floor a little too much.

'I might break the other leg.'

'What size feet?' she asked. 'Me too,' she said, when Maddy told her.

She delved back into the wardrobe, before emerging, ruffled, with a high-heeled boot.

'Bugger, wrong foot,' she said, examining it more carefully. 'Hang on.'

This time the scrabbling took a little longer, but eventually there was a muffled cry of triumph.

'Here you are,' she said, handing Maddy the matching boot to the one already discarded.

It was the softest grey calfskin with a towering chrome heel, which Maddy would be mortified to scratch. But there was another more ergonomically challenging problem too.

'I'll have to balance on one leg,' said Maddy doubtfully. The built-in heel on her plastered leg was not nearly high enough.

'You'll be fine,' insisted Serena. 'We'll just wheel you around and plonk you where he can admire the jacket. You look much more of a city slicker than I ever imagined,' she said, picking out hairpins from amongst the expensive designer scent and make-up scattered on her dressing table.

'There you go. The transformation is complete.'

CHAPTER NINETEEN

'Maddy was amazing,' said Serena, as they held the meeting post-mortem around the kitchen table later that day. 'I never knew! There she was, cool as a cucumber, doing the PowerPoint thingie, with the pointer doodah and the profit-and-loss stuff . . .' Serena did a little demonstration of Maddy's ball-breaking businesswoman persona for Flora's benefit.

Maddy shovelled in a bit of cake. 'You'd better hope so,' she said, swigging it down with a large gulp of tea. 'God, I'm going to be the size of a house if all our meetings are like this . . . because we'll be stuffed if they say "no".'

'I would never have thought to even apply,' said Flora. 'I can't believe they might be prepared to give us all this money.'

'"Might be"?' said Serena. 'It's in the bag, I tell you . . . Definitely.'

Maddy saw the bright-yellow notice stuck on the front door of the pub just as soon as Giles dropped her off.

'What the hell . . . ?' she was saying as she arrived at the top of the stairs.

'Hello, darling,' Patrick called from the kitchen. 'I gather you've seen . . .'

'Mum?' she said, coming into the room. There was another copy of the bright-yellow paper on the table.

Helen, sitting opposite Patrick, was mirroring his attitude of despair, one hand clasped over his on the table. The other was holding a damp tissue, which she used quickly to wipe her eyes before throwing Maddy a wobbly smile.

'Hallo, darling,' she said too brightly. 'How did it go?'

'Never mind,' she said, waving it away. 'What's all this?'

'Ah,' said Patrick, with a thin smile. 'This is what is known as one of those "so near but so far" situations.' He waved his hand at the sheet of paper.

'I just don't get it. "Planning application HB238/49 Stana Developments, for the reclassification and development of the 'Havenbury Arms' into residential use" . . . shit.'

'Language,' said Patrick automatically.

'Sorry, but . . . seriously,' said Maddy, clutching her head. 'What on earth?'

'I know!' said Patrick. 'And I just signed and returned the lease this morning.'

'So that's it, then,' said Maddy. 'You've signed. It's a done deal – and they can't . . .' She waved her hand at the paper.

'I said *I'd* signed it. Obviously Top Taverns have to sign it too.'

'That little shit,' said Maddy, and this time Patrick didn't bother to reprove her.

'Does that mean they've actually sold it out from under us? They must have done . . .'

'Actually, no,' said Helen, sniffing and sitting up straighter. 'It doesn't at all. As a matter of fact, anyone can apply for planning permission for whatever they like. They don't have to own the property at all.'

'Yes, but they'd hardly spend money on something like this if they weren't at least planning – and being encouraged – to think they can buy it. Hang on a minute . . .' Maddy slid her rucksack off her shoulders and got out her laptop.

'What's the planning reference again?'

In less than a minute, the three of them were poring over the plans. Maddy was right. Money had clearly been spent. The proposal was to knock down the pub and replace it with a terrace of no fewer than four three-storey townhouses. There were detailed layout plans and some fancy watercolours showing the exteriors with mock-Georgian sash windows and fancy pediment porches over the front doors.

'That's ridiculous,' said Patrick. 'Why on earth would they knock the place down? It's outrageous. And it beggars belief that they can even fit four houses on, even terraced ones.'

'It's not a bad-sized plot,' admitted Helen. 'And modern houses are always as small as they can get away with making them.'

'Well,' said Patrick crossly, 'they're not getting away with these ones. I'm calling that prat Dennis, right now.'

'Tell him I don't give a monkey's backside if he's having his lunch,' Patrick was saying to someone in Dennis's office. 'It's the publicans like me who pay his goddamned salary and I want to speak to him now.'

Helen and Maddy could only hear Patrick's side of the telephone conversation but it wasn't hard to get the gist of Dennis's contribution.

'The new lease is signed,' Patrick was insisting. 'I know the existing one is still current . . . yes, I know Top Taverns have still to agree, but it was their goddamned lease, for heaven's sake. Why offer it if they're not prepared to commit to it? . . . I don't give a damn if poxy Stana developments have "made a generous offer", this pub is not for sale.' At that, Patrick slammed down the phone and placed both palms flat on the table, breathing deeply through his nose.

After a few moments he took a deep breath. 'So,' he said, 'obviously it goes without saying that Top Taverns are a bunch of double-dealing, weasel-worded, unprincipled toerags.'

Helen and Maddy nodded their agreement.

'But it does appear that all is not necessarily lost. Yet. The pub is still owned by Top Taverns. Can't say I ever imagined myself saying that's a good thing . . . but my guess is they intend to put it up for sale. By auction most likely. Naturally this Stana lot will be in the front row. And there isn't a lot we can do to stop it.'

'Okay,' said Helen briskly. 'Let's see what we've got here. But first, who wants another cup of tea?'

Once all three of them were sitting at the table, each with a full mug, Maddy with her laptop and Helen with a large pad of lined paper and a newly sharpened pencil, they set to work.

'The first thing I want to check is whether Top Taverns – having provided the replacement lease – are actually entitled to refuse to sign it,' he began.

'Good point,' said Helen, making a note on her pad of paper. 'I'll ask my friend at home. She's a property lawyer; she knows about leases and things, although I think mainly she does conveyancing.'

'Sounds like she could answer a few questions, not just that one,' said Maddy. 'Patrick, isn't there something in your existing lease, saying that you are entitled to renew?'

'Yes, there might be,' said Patrick. 'Good point, but – if there is – I've got a feeling it's connected with a requirement for me to bring the property repairs up to date, and Dennis reckons there's fifty-grand's-worth of those,' he said, looking gloomy again.

'Okay,' said Helen. 'That's the next thing to look at, then. And I think we should show the repairs and dilapidation list to three local builders to get quotes. I bet it doesn't have to cost fifty thousand.'

'Wouldn't matter if it was half that,' said Patrick. 'I still don't have it.'

'Okay, well, we'll look at it anyway,' said Maddy. 'What I want to know is whether this Stana – you do know that's an anagram for "Satan", don't you? – Property Development company are likely to get their planning permission and if there's anything we can do to stop them. They won't want to buy unless they have it.'

She looked at the application again. 'It's still in the consultation stage. That means we can write letters of objection.'

'We will, then, but it's not much good if it's just us doing it,' said Helen. 'We need to get lots of other people to write too.'

'How long have we got?' asked Patrick.

'Deadline for comments is ten days away,' said Maddy, gulping. 'That's not long.'

'Those houses really are hideous,' mused Patrick. 'Can't we object on aesthetic grounds? After all the high street is quite an architectural feature. I remember a big group coming in once for lunch. It turns out they were architecture students on a field trip. The high street has been here for centuries, and the way all the architectural styles have evolved and been joined together makes it really special, apparently . . .'

'That's another point to explore, then,' said Maddy.

'I bet that Jonno bloke from the nightclub on the quay'll be thrilled, though,' said Patrick gloomily.

'Not going to happen,' insisted Maddy, deciding not to mention Ben's connection with him and his feedback over the beer ties. 'We need to get something printed out. A flyer or a poster or something. We can have them on the bar. We could put them through people's letter boxes, actually. This flaming cast . . .' she said, looking down at her leg in frustration. She hoped, with this appointment Ben reminded her of, the X-rays would show it could come off but she had a feeling it would have to stay on longer. She hadn't exactly been the perfect patient.

'I can do leaflet drops,' said Patrick. 'I'm supposed to be getting fit.'

'Yes, but not overdoing it,' warned Helen. 'I'll do that bit.'

'You will not,' protested Patrick immediately. 'What about that great long list you've got there already?' he said, waving at the pad of paper.

'No point arguing,' said Maddy swiftly, seeing her mother take a deep breath to answer Patrick back. 'We can all do it. Together. There. I'll put something together now. It need only be A5. I can email it straight down to the print shop on the quay. They'll only need a couple of days.'

'Excellent,' said Patrick. 'There, I told you it'll be fine.'

With a bit of brazen arguing and finger-crossing, Maddy had persuaded the orthopaedic team the leg was fine but, with the plaster finally prised off, she examined her leg with a sinking heart. Like before, there was a livid scar stretching across her ankle and up her leg. The surgeon had kindly followed the same line as he had done previously but, this time, it was longer and uglier. It didn't help that the stitches had had to stay in for weeks. The nurse tutted sympathetically as she quickly removed them with tweezers and a scalpel. 'Those surgeons have no idea,' she said. 'As if a young girl like you wants a great, red scar up her leg.' She deftly wrapped up the tray and popped it in the bin. 'Now, isn't that better?' she added.

Looking at the livid red line, dissected with stitch marks, along with the flaky skin and horrible dark sprouting hairs all over her leg, Maddy wasn't sure it was, much. Her calf, too, was noticeably thinner than the other. Exercise, a long bath with a razor and a good exfoliator would improve things a lot, though. She knew that from experience.

'It's fine,' pronounced the kindly surgeon when he examined her. 'You're young and you heal well, but I'd be awfully grateful if you could possibly avoid doing it again. Twice is more than enough, for one leg. Maybe see if you can land on the other one next time, just for a bit of variety.'

Maddy smiled. 'In the nicest possible way,' she said, 'I hope we've seen the last of each other.'

'In the nicest possible way,' he replied, 'I agree. It'll be feeling incredibly stiff,' he went on, 'but you know all about that. Get it moving, make sure to go to all your physio appointments and do what you're told. I fully expect you to make a good recovery. Again.'

'Thanks,' said Maddy.

'And don't overdo it,' he called after her as she went out of the door.

...
collect the ... flyers from ... quay ...
should be ...

Chapter Twenty

Maddy's plan was to jump off the bus at the bottom of town to collect the flyers from the printer on the quay. Getting around was so much easier without a big, bulky cast on her leg. She was grateful she had decided to wear her comfortable old plimsolls. Although her calf was wasted, her left foot seemed to have spread a bit inside the cast and, at the hospital, she had had to loosen the laces just to get her shoe on.

'These look great,' she said to the tall, spotty youth working in the printers who was giving her a strange look, she noticed.

Along with the key information about the threat to the pub and the call to action over the Development Committee meeting Maddy had quickly sketched a little picture of the pub with a large 'CLOSED' sign fixed to it, which caught the eye nicely.

She looked doubtfully at the two large cardboard boxes.

'I can drop them off if you like?' the youth offered. 'It's no trouble,' he added, gazing at her meaningfully.

Maddy wondered if he was quite alright in the head.

She thanked him but took two large wodges out straight

away. As she was walking up the high street to the pub to collect her car and see Patrick, she might as well shove some through letter boxes.

By the time she arrived at the Havenbury Arms, all the shops in the high street had posters and flyers, but it had taken two hours and Maddy was limping badly and sweating a little from the pain.

Pushing open the door to the bar, she was pleased to see the two boxes with the remaining materials had arrived. She was even more pleased to see an unmistakably broad back, topped with wavy dark-blonde hair standing in front of the sink behind the bar.

'Ben!'

'Hullo,' said Ben, turning, smiling, towards her, with a bottle of Scotch in each hand. He was pouring the contents down the sink. 'I know it looks like I've gone mad,' he said. 'Patrick's orders: he's concerned about poisoning people with fake liquor. I'm pretty sure this is the real thing, though,' he said, sniffing the fumes. 'Single malt. What a tragedy . . .'

Plonking the bottles in the recycling bin he came towards her and his smile faded abruptly.

'Maddy?' he said, his gaze switching rapidly from her face to her feet. 'What on earth . . . ?'

'It's fine,' she said, biting back tears. 'Nice to have the cast off at last.'

'Sit,' he said, yanking out a chair and pushing her down into it. Sitting opposite her, thighs spread wide, he lifted her leg, cradling her foot tenderly in his hands.

The laces were stretched tight and the double knot had gone tiny with the pressure from her swelling foot.

'Might have overdone it a bit . . .' she muttered.

He gave her an incredulous look, shook his head and, transferring her foot to his left hand, he produced a penknife, flicking it open to reveal an evil-looking blade.

'It seems an awful shame to amputate after all this effort . . .' she joked nervously.

'I should,' he replied, instead sawing gently through the laces.

'Oi! I like these shoes. I don't have any spare laces, either.'

'If you hadn't been wearing stupid shoes like this in the first place, none of this would have happened.'

'I like plimsolls.'

Ben said nothing, concentrating on carrying out his task without hurting her.

'These are – were – my favourites,' she complained again.

'You're going to need some better ones,' he said. 'There you go,' he added, gently removing her shoe and tossing it on the floor. 'Now, wait there.'

She watched as he filled a plastic bag with ice cubes from the ice-making machine, tied the top and then looked around him. 'What can I . . . ?' he muttered to himself, before disappearing into the kitchen. Coming out with a rolling pin he placed the half-full bag on the bar and proceeded to beat it with the rolling pin with what Maddy felt was quite unnecessary violence.

'That should do it,' he said, as he grabbed a bar towel from the bar, wrapped it around the bag of crushed ice and then moulded it gently but firmly around Maddy's swollen ankle before laying her foot carefully on the chair seat.

'Don't move,' he said.

She didn't want to. The ice felt like heaven.

He disappeared and came back a few minutes later with

a steaming mug of tea and two round white tablets, cupped in his hand.

'Here,' he said, handing her both.

'Are they strong?'

'Yep,' he said, standing over her as she took them.

Within minutes she felt the slight, heady rush as the painkillers kicked in. She sighed with relief.

'I've got no shoes now,' she complained. 'I've taken all my clothes over to the Grainstore already.'

'When's your birthday?'

'Not for a couple of months.'

'Fine,' he said, getting out his phone. 'Early birthday present, then.'

'Mate!' he said to the person at the other end of the line. 'When are you closing today? I don't suppose you could stay on for a bit, could you?' he went on, looking at his watch. 'We're not far but we aren't walking particularly quickly.'

'And,' mouthed Maddy, 'we – don't – have – any – shoes!'

'Only the Havenbury Arms,' explained Ben. 'That would be brilliant, mate. Thanks.'

A knock on the door, and a young man with a beard that made him look older, sidled his way in with a stack of large shoeboxes in his arms.

'Here we go,' he said, plonking them on the table.

Maddy, acutely aware of her horrible flaky and hairy leg, was busy making sure her jeans were down as far as they could go.

Ian – which turned out to be the man's name – produced five near identical pairs of chunky, brown walking boots, with heavy-tread soles and high-laced, padded ankles.

'Don't you have any other colours?' protested Maddy.

'Why would you want other colours?' he asked. 'Look, they may all look the same, but you'd be surprised. There's always one brand that suits customers better than another.' He looked at Maddy's feet with eyes narrowed in appraisal.

'Mm. High instep. Narrow feet . . . I think . . .' He grabbed a pair and deftly removed the laces altogether before starting again in a different pattern. 'This is how you need to lace them if you have a narrow foot,' he explained. 'Better support. See?'

Getting the boot on her right foot was fine. He expertly adjusted it, wrapping the excess laces once around the back of her ankle before tying in a double knot.

For the other one, he made sure the laces were much wider, gently easing her foot into the boot and grimacing at the scar.

'What happened?' he asked.

'Hillwalking in stupid shoes,' Ben informed him before Maddy had a chance to reply.

Ian tutted. 'Wear these next time,' he said, tying the bow with a flourish. 'There. Want to give them a try?'

She got to her feet gingerly. Contrary to what she had thought, the boots were light and comfortingly all-encompassing, holding her foot and ankle in place while thick padding, which was responsible for the bulky, unflattering look, meant they didn't press or dig in anywhere.

'Nice,' she said, trying a few steps. 'Surprisingly nice, actually,' she brightened. 'My new favourite shoes, potentially . . .'

'Happy birthday,' said Ben.

'Right,' Ben continued, when Ian had been thanked again, paid and despatched. 'About your car. Shall we have a look?'

'Yes please! God . . . am I a complete pain?'

'Yeah,' he said. 'You are a bit.'

'Sorry,' she muttered, glancing up at him. His jaw was set and he seemed to be avoiding meeting her eye again. She missed their easy camaraderie now replaced by a dutiful concern that left her feeling like an irritating kid sister. She needed to stop looking for more from him. It clearly wasn't going to happen.

After several weeks sitting unused in the corner of the pub car park, the battery in Maddy's little car was completely flat.

'Not a problem,' he said, rummaging in the back of his Land Rover and producing a set of jump leads.

'What haven't you got in there?'

'Not much. Now, bonnet up . . .'

In seconds, Ben had attached the leads and started the Land Rover engine. Maddy, sitting in the driver's seat, managed to start it first time. He quickly detached the leads and closed the bonnets. She was desperate to go and give her scaly, reptile leg a long soak in Serena's bath.

'Thanks for everything,' she said to Ben, shutting the driver's door and winding down the window.

'Oh no, you don't,' he said, opening the door again. 'Budge over.'

Maddy climbed awkwardly over to the passenger seat.

'I don't care what the surgeon said,' he continued, 'you're not driving today.'

'Then you'll be stuck at Serena's.'

'I need a run,' he said. 'From Serena's house back to here'll do nicely.'

'Try this,' said Serena, coming into the bathroom with a bottle of something pale pink and expensive-looking. 'Apparently it's an exfoliating, brightening, moisturising thingie,' she said, peering at the label.

'Mm, smells lovely,' said Maddy, giving it a sniff when Serena handed her the bottle. 'Are you sure?'

'Absolutely. Wasted on me.'

Serena perched herself on a low stool and looked on approvingly as Maddy squeezed some of it onto a loofah and scrubbed at the horrible, scaly skin on her leg.

'At least it's not hairy now,' Maddy said, with a shudder, holding her leg up above the bubbles to check progress. The first thing she had done when she got into the huge roll-top bath was to borrow a razor and deal with the dark layer of fuzz.

'You'll have to put lots of moisturiser on when you get out,' said Serena. 'And how about a pedicure?'

'Definitely. Although I'm no good at painting my toenails.'

'Ah, but luckily, I'm brilliant.'

'It's pretty puffy still, isn't it?' said Serena disapprovingly, as she inserted cotton wall balls to hold Maddy's toes apart. 'No wonder Ben told you off.'

'He's always telling me off.'

'He cares about you,' said Serena. 'He worries . . .' She held up two bottles of nail varnish, jiggling them about. 'Which one?'

'Turquoise please,' said Maddy.

'Good choice.'

'Is he like Andrew?'

'Ben? Yes, in some ways. In a lot of ways, actually. He's changed. Got more like him, I think. Steady. Loyal. When Andrew died he grew up pretty fast, and of course the poor boy had already lost his father . . .'

'I know. It's so awful,' said Maddy. 'Do you mind talking about him? I don't want to make you sad . . .'

'You can't make me sad. I already am . . . I mean, there's a bit of me that's deeply, deeply sad, and always will be . . .' she trailed off, staring into space.

'I'm sorry.'

'No! Don't be. "Better to have loved and lost", and all that.'

'But you love Giles, of course?'

'I do,' said Serena, brightening. 'Funny old Giles, bless him.'

They were silent, while Serena concentrated on Maddy's toenails.

'It's like the film *Sliding Doors*,' she said at last, putting the lid back on the little bottle. 'You know, there's the moment where the heroine misses the train by about two seconds because she stumbles on the stairs. Only in this other version of her life she catches the train . . .'

'I saw it,' said Maddy. 'And then it's all about how things can take a different path from that moment – true love, success, good friends, happiness in one life, and then a cheating boyfriend, job loss and all sorts of other disasters in the other . . . I forget which one's which now. Does she need to miss the train or catch it?'

'I can't remember either,' admitted Serena. 'But that "parallel life" thing . . . that's what it feels like for me.'

'How did you and Giles get together?'

'Oh, it was just one of those things,' said Serena. 'Not romantic, I'm afraid. After Andrew died I just immersed myself in my work. First I did it because it helped and then I was doing it because the rest of my life fell away and it became everything. I was travelling, living out of a suitcase, working insane hours, getting promoted . . . One day I looked up and

245

work was all I had. I was in my late thirties and it just felt like I was hurtling towards a life that I had never imagined for myself. No children, no family . . . just a stellar career. I say "just" but I loved my job . . .' Serena paused.

'And Giles?' she prompted gently.

'Giles was just . . . always there,' said Serena, 'part of our group, but I never noticed him, I confess, never saw him in "that" way, and then, one weekend, he took me off for a walk without the others and proposed. Well, it was more of a business proposition, really. He was getting on a bit. I was getting on a bit. We were both consenting adults with similar backgrounds and we both wanted kids before it was too late, so why didn't we give it a go?'

Maddy blinked. 'Seriously?'

'Yep. Mind you, once I'd said yes to the general principle he wooed me in the time-honoured manner. He's a traditionalist is our Giles . . .'

'But that's so odd.'

'Yes and no,' said Serena. 'For me, no one was ever going to be "Mr Right" because that was Andrew. Giles understood that. What I settled for was the man who adored me and who offered me everything I wanted. The man who was prepared to do that because he wanted me. He knows the score,' she added, registering Maddy's shock. 'And look at me now. I've got Giles, the boys, this house, this life – I'm lucky, I know I am – but there's a bit of me that wonders about my "other life". The one where Andrew is still alive. Where somehow we manage to save him . . . Plus, of course, I feel hellishly guilty because Giles is a sensational man, and I fob him off with second best. He deserves all of me and what he gets is – basically – what's left.'

'Giles really, really adores you.'

'He does,' she replied briskly, sitting up and putting her hands on her knees. 'Now, time for the topcoat.'

When she was painting Maddy's nails again, concentrating on her feet, she continued on her theme.

'Ben's very special,' she said. 'And he cares deeply about you. I know him. I can tell.'

Maddy stayed silent.

'The thing is, my darling,' she said, sitting back to admire her efforts and meeting Maddy's eye, 'you have to decide. Are you going to catch the train?'

'Sliding doors . . .' mused Maddy. 'I don't know. I mean, put like that, it's a no-brainer, but you're asking me to leave my London life, where I'm – fairly – successful and,' she swallowed, 'on the whole, I'm okay. I mean, the thing that happens . . . that happened to me here, the nightmares and . . . things – I don't get that in London.' Her eyes filled with tears. It was true, in London she was the person she had invented after she left: the businesslike, polished professional with the shiny-new boyfriend, and the flat bought together in an up-and-coming area. She and Simon did the things successful young professional couples did: they went out for cocktails after work, they went to trendy new restaurants, to concerts and festivals and – at the weekend – they held barbecues for their friends in their teeny, tiny garden and had conversations about property prices and overcrowding on the Underground.

There were few nightmares, no flashbacks, no panic attacks sweeping the ground from beneath her feet, knocking the wind out of her. Not in London.

Maddy sighed as Serena carefully removed the cotton

wool from between her toes and gathered up the bottles to put them away.

Here, on the other hand, she had her dear, dear friends, the Bespoke Consortium, which was the most exciting work thing she had ever been involved in, she had Patrick – at the moment she also had her mother, which was a bonus – and, of course, she had the intrigue and excitement of her growing relationship with Ben, although his recent distance and reticence, presumably because of her continuing relationship with Simon, was a worry. His ability to close himself off from her so tactfully and kindly made her wonder what else he was capable of hiding.

It was a shame she also had the hideous recurring nightmares stealing her sleep, the frank terror of not knowing what was going to spark a flashback next with the risk of bumping into Kevin around every corner, and the general, terrifying sense that she was falling into a bottomless pit, out of which she would be lucky to escape with her mind intact.

Which future, in her 'sliding doors' life, should she choose?

CHAPTER TWENTY-ONE

The move from the Havenbury Arms to the Grainstore had been a fine idea, thought Maddy, but – delightful though the little apartment was – the nightmares inexplicably worsened there, waking her again and again through the night until, her eyes gritty and her body heavy with exhaustion, she was relieved to see the dawn.

It was a fine morning and the low winter sun streamed into the building through the French windows, reaching golden fingers across the platform bed where she lay awake, staring at the ceiling. Her most recent encounter with Kevin had been added to her repertoire of nightmares and she was driving herself insane, trawling through her fractured memories to decide whether his latest taunts were true. Had he been there? She even started to wonder if she was beginning to invent memories, piecing together the scant facts into a narrative, just to make sense of something senseless. She would have liked to have asked Ben but – since that first night in the Grainstore – he seemed to have disappeared, presumably caught up with his college work as the autumn term drew to a close.

She dragged herself out of bed and straight under the

shower before the momentum wore off. She inched the temperature dial around by tiny degrees until it was as cold as she could bear, hoping it would refresh her energy levels a bit. Serena would be banging on the little door soon, keen for Maddy to join her and Flora for work.

Maddy pulled on trousers, boots and a cosy sweater. Luckily her swollen ankle had gone down enough to get her trusty London boots on and she barely even limped if she put her mind to it. She looked longingly at the walking boots Ben had bought her. She had hardly taken them off since, but they were clumpy and ugly. She needed to raise her game.

She looked at herself appraisingly in the mirror. It wasn't great. The dark circles under her eyes were more obvious than ever and it didn't help that all trace of a summer tan was now gone. Added to that, her smart black work trousers that fitted so neatly before were now hanging so low on her hips they trailed on the floor.

She must have lost nearly a stone. Either that or her legs had got shorter, she thought to herself as she threaded a belt through the tops of the trousers and hoicked them back up, tightening the belt as far as it would go. She would need Jez the leather worker to make another hole in it soon.

A quick slick of blusher and a bit of mascara was as much as she was prepared to do to her face. In a last-ditch effort she grabbed a beautiful Bespoke Consortium turquoise and green scarf. She was just knotting it neatly when Serena knocked and came in.

'Morning, lovely,' she called. 'Blimey, do be careful with those stairs,' she added as Maddy came down from the bed platform backwards because it felt safer. 'Have you had breakfast?'

'Yes,' Maddy lied, to disguise having woken so late. 'I wouldn't mind a coffee, though.'

'I've laid out the brochure proofs on the kitchen table and popped some croissants in the oven. Flora's there.'

Serena and Maddy went over to the farmhouse, where Flora was singing to herself and dipping a finger into each open jam jar in turn.

'Hi, Mads,' she said. 'Yum. I think the ginger and rhubarb's my favourite. You know, we should sell jam too . . .'

'I think we've got plenty to do already,' said Maddy. 'But it's a good idea for the future . . . Wow, they're beautiful,' she said, catching sight of the proofs laid out on the sideboard. She pored over the double-page spreads of the brochure lined up on the kitchen table, trying and failing to avoid getting croissant crumbs all over them.

'You don't have any copy,' she said guiltily, noticing the words were just the graphic designers' standard Latin text, '*Lorem ipsum dolor sit amet . . .*'

'True, although I rather like the Latin,' Serena said. 'I've always wondered what it meant – something absolutely filthy, one hopes . . . I was sort of trying to lift the copy you wrote from the website but it didn't quite work. Would you have time to do something?'

'Of course! When do we need it by?'

'Erm, end of today?' Serena said apologetically, licking a blob of cherry jam off the corner of her mouth.

'No problem. When are we doing the mailing?'

'In terms of orders, nineteenth of December is the last date for first class UK posting if we want things to arrive for Christmas, so we need to work back from there,' said Flora.

Maddy blinked with surprise. She wouldn't bank on Flora

even knowing what day of the week it was, let alone knowing Christmas posting dates.

'So, if you get the copy done as soon as possible today,' said Serena, 'and we send it to the printers tonight, you sign off the proofs tomorrow morning, then they'll deliver by Friday and we can mail on Saturday morning.'

'Who needs sleep?' agreed Maddy.

'Flora thought we should call a meeting,' said Serena. 'So we can bring people up to speed.'

'While we're doing it, they can stuff envelopes,' added Flora. 'Perfect, yeah?'

Serena was loading the dishwasher and Maddy was getting started on the copy when the letter box clattered.

'It'll be all Giles's boring stuff,' said Serena, but she went to collect it, wandering back with a small handful of envelopes which she sorted onto the kitchen table.

'Giles, junk, Giles, Giles . . . ooh, Rural Enterprise Funding,' she said, brightening. Dumping the rest, she quickly slit open the envelope and unfolded the single piece of paper inside.

Maddy and Flora watched.

'I was so sure,' said Serena quietly, as if to herself.

'Yeah, yeah,' said Maddy. Serena had caught her out too often in the past with her little jokes. 'Nice try . . . give it here.'

She quickly scanned the letter. '. . . "we regret to inform you" . . . "high standard of applications". . . Shit.'

'No money,' said Serena again, disbelievingly, as she, Maddy and Flora comforted themselves with Serena's home-made carrot cake, even though it was barely an hour since breakfast.

'Well, not *no* money,' said Maddy, trying to look on the

bright side. 'We've still got Giles's money to keep us going, and there will be other grant opportunities, somewhere, I'm sure . . .'

'True,' said Serena, breaking off a large chunk of cake and cramming it into her mouth. 'Shame it's too early for a stiff drink,' she mumbled with her mouth full. 'I feel like I need it after that.'

'It'll be fine,' said Maddy, in tones designed to convince herself, let alone Serena. 'It's a timeline issue. We just need to push back a couple of things, like the brochure mailing, perhaps . . .'

'We can't!' protested Serena. 'Not the brochure mailing. It's a critical part of our pre-Christmas push. We won't have a chance to shift stock like that again for months.'

'Alright, not the brochure mailing,' agreed Maddy reluctantly, 'but definitely the trade show. I mean, if we scrap the trade show and book into that summer one instead, we're pretty much sorted. It was going to be pretty painful doing it so close to Christmas, what with everything else that's going on.'

'Ah,' said Serena guiltily, after she had swallowed her mouthful of carrot cake with a gulp. 'About that . . .'

'Go on,' said Maddy, her heart sinking.

'I might have forgotten to mention it,' said Serena, 'and I know you've been really busy with the whole pub closure campaign, so – erm – I got a call from the exhibition organisers . . .'

'Ye-es . . .'

'It was an amazing deal. Too good to miss. They had a little stand come up at the last minute – another company cancelled, went bust I think – and they offered it at half the rate if I said "yes" there and then.'

'So you did.'

Serena nodded guiltily. 'Looking at it another way, we saved ourselves more than four grand.'

'But we've also spent six grand we now don't have,' said Maddy in desperation. Then she relented. 'Don't worry. You're right; it was the right thing to do. Probably,' she said. 'At least . . . we'll make it work somehow.'

It was the last thing they needed at this fragile early stage, though, she thought to herself. As Giles had said, too many brilliant new companies go under because of cashflow problems, and the funding gap raised the chances of that happening to them to stratospheric levels.

Plodding on, they distracted themselves with one last check to make sure all the prices of the products were right before Maddy finished the copy. They couldn't afford mistakes.

Because the job was boring and the women were feeling disconsolate, the meeting quickly degenerated into a morose, biscuit-eating session.

'I can't believe all that stuff about Kevin stealing from Patrick,' said Flora, talking around a large mouthful of chocolate chip cookie.

'Believe it,' said Maddy.

'It's funny, though, isn't it?' said Flora. ''Cos you kind of get used to certain people just being in the background, don't you? Part of the furniture? You sort of ignore them because you don't think they're actually – well – *doing* anything.'

'I can't ignore Kevin,' insisted Serena. 'I don't even know him really but, ever since Patrick first started employing him, I just can't look at him without wanting to stamp on his toe. I don't know what it is . . .'

'Tell me again about what Ben did,' said Flora excitedly. 'Did he punch him? Was he heroic?'

'He was,' said Maddy, with a smile. 'I don't know what he said to him outside the pub, but I'm given to believe we won't be seeing him again, if he knows what's good for him.'

Just as they had reluctantly returned to the pricing, there was a sharp rap at the back door.

'Who actually knocks around here?' muttered Serena, but before she had a chance to shout 'Come in!', the door opened and the doorway was filled with a sturdy, serious-looking man with an irreproachable short back and sides, a baggy grey suit and an extremely cross expression on his face.

'Ah,' said Maddy, in a voice filled with guilt, regret and a certain acceptance born of inevitability. 'Simon,' she said. 'How nice.'

'Not sure "nice" is the word,' he replied, as he came, uninvited, into the kitchen and stood towering over them all. 'I've been all over the shop looking for you,' he went on. 'Spoke to your mother – not an entirely positive experience – she didn't seem pleased to see me, but at least,' he conceded, 'she had the grace to tell me you might be here. What the hell have you done with your phone?'

'Ah, you've got me there,' said Maddy, bobbing down in her chair. 'I kept meaning to look for it. The battery's flat so I can't call it. I think it might be down the back of the seat in the car.'

'When you finally find it I suggest you might not want to bother with all my messages and texts,' said Simon. 'Especially the more recent ones. I haven't been best pleased.'

Serena stood, charmingly introducing herself and Flora to Simon and – in the same interaction – made it clear that she and Flora would be making themselves scarce.

'Don't go,' said Maddy, standing too. 'We'll go to

the Grainstore,' she insisted, grabbing Simon's arm and propelling him firmly out of the room.

'So *that's* Simon,' she could hear Flora saying as she left. 'I don't think I like him, do you?'

To Maddy's relief, Serena's reply was inaudible.

She quickly got the two of them settled on the little verandah with a couple of bottles of beer. It was cold, but the sun was out.

'Nice view,' he acknowledged. 'Decent place you've got here.'

'I'm lucky.' She stole a sideways glance. Poor Simon had jettisoned his suit jacket and undone the top button of his pressed, stripy shirt, but he clutched the beer bottle awkwardly in his fist. She couldn't help but imagine Ben sitting in the same seat, his bottle of beer doubtless hanging from his fingers with casual ease.

'I'm sorry I've not been in touch,' said Maddy. 'There's been a lot going on.'

'There's been a lot going on in London. I've been working my arse off covering for your absence.' He stopped himself with visible effort. 'I'm sorry, Maddy,' he said. 'I'm not here for that. In truth, even without the lost phone, it's about time we talked properly, face-to-face.'

'About us?'

'Um, yeah. Yeah of course . . . and work too, obviously.'

'Obviously,' she replied dryly.

'So,' he said, clearing his throat. 'I've been thinking about taking the company forward. And I'd like you to come on board.'

'Gosh,' she said with heavy irony. 'Would you?' She was wondering when exactly she hadn't been 'on board'.

'Yeah, so, I've been thinking we incorporate and . . . despite your poor performance in the last few weeks – although obviously that would have to be addressed – I'm prepared to offer you a seventy–thirty split. Partners. You and me. What do you think, eh?'

'Wow. That's a generous offer, but I'm just wondering whether you would truly be happy with just thirty per cent of the business.'

'Wha—? No, darling,' he went on, 'but I hear where you're coming from.' He gave her a heavy wink, waggling his finger at her. 'How about I say sixty–forty and that's my final offer. You've got to admit, it's pretty attractive. Forty per cent of a dynamic communications company developing quite a reputation. There are no limits, baby . . .' He toasted her with his beer and took an awkward swig, dribbling it down his chin slightly.

She gave him a considering stare. 'I'm entitled to fifty–fifty.'

'You're not even there.'

'It's my business as much as yours.'

'Do some bloody work, then.'

There was a brief silence.

'What do you need?' she said reluctantly.

'Thought you'd never ask,' he said. 'I've got us a chance to present to Clifford and Hayes in a fortnight. It's the annual strategy meeting of the board and they're looking for fresh ideas. If we impress them, it's a two-year contract with a fee to blow your brain. We could afford offices, staff, decent salaries . . .'

'And us?' said Maddy quietly.

Simon looked awkward. 'We're alright, aren't we?'

'Can you honestly say we would have got together if we hadn't been setting up the business and both needing somewhere to live at the same time?' she asked. 'It almost literally came down to deciding on a one-bed flat rather than a two-bed, to save money and get your leg over in one convenient package.'

'Well,' he huffed, 'I think that's a bit harsh.'

'I'm not getting at you. It was both of us.'

There was a silence while they both sipped their beers reflectively, gazing at the view. It was almost peaceful.

'Have you found someone else?' he asked.

She glanced at him. There was no sign of distress.

'Yes and no.'

'What does that mean?'

'It means I think I may have fallen in love with someone else,' she elucidated. 'It means I am beginning to understand better what it's supposed to feel like when you meet someone who's truly important . . .'

'And does he feel the same way?'

'Don't think so,' she replied, with a tiny tremor, which she clamped down tight. 'I think – I know – he cares about me,' she went on. 'But he's made it pretty clear, one way and another, that that's as far as it goes.'

'I'm sorry,' said Simon.

Maddy looked at him and he turned to meet her gaze, his face as open and honest as she had ever seen it. 'I *am* sorry. Truly. I have to admit, you're right about us. It's a rubbish relationship. We're not right for each other – not personally, anyway – and life's just too short, isn't it? I hope you can convince this guy or I hope you can maybe find someone who feels the same as you do . . .'

'Thank you,' said Maddy, touched.

'But – notwithstanding all that bollocks,' he went on, 'business-wise we're a winning team. Let's do that presentation. Let's win that contract. I'll email the details and, when it's done, we can sit down and sign the papers. I don't mind where you work and where you live – I can see you've got something good going here,' he gestured around him.

'We can do this,' he said, jutting out his chin like he did in sales pitches. 'You and me,' he declared, holding out his hand to shake hers.

Patrick was in high spirits. He had turned the little flat's sitting room into an operations centre. The dining table had been cleared and was filled with stacks of paper, including the 'SAVE THE PUB' campaign flyers Maddy had had printed. There was a whiteboard fixed to the wall, with writing in several different colours, marking out the plan of action.

'So . . . what's happening?' asked Maddy, giving him a hug.

'Cup of tea first,' he replied, marching to the kitchen and shouting over this shoulder. 'I'm glad you've turned up. I've been needing to brief you . . .'

'"Brief me", eh?' she said quizzically to the empty air.

He soon returned with two steaming mugs and Maddy took hers gratefully.

'So,' he said, retrieving a whiteboard marker pen from behind his ear. 'The key issue is this,' he said, rapping the whiteboard with his pen. 'We need to prove the Havenbury Arms is a community asset. I've been taking advice and it's a legitimate planning argument that the pub should be retained as making a valuable contribution to the community . . .' He paused. 'Actually, I've just thought . . . we need to bring in the support of the market stallholders. Lucky the market is this Saturday. We can lobby them then . . .' He made another scribble on the whiteboard and then drew another line from this to another part of the board with a confident scythe of the arm.

'Blimey,' said Maddy. 'Let battle commence, eh?'

'Darned right,' he said, his eyes blazing. 'I'm not going down without a fight . . . Now,' he went on, 'the other issue is funding.

I've been having long discussions with other pubs who've faced closure. The one in Edenford is community-owned now. Have you been there recently?'

She shook her head.

'Me neither,' he admitted, 'but it's brilliant, apparently. Two hundred community members put in a minimum of a grand each and now they are all directors, running the pub as a community enterprise. There's a post office in there, they have a doctors' surgery in there once a week too . . .'

'But we've already got a post office in Havenbury,' she argued, 'and a doctors' surgery.'

'Yeah,' he admitted, 'but still . . . I like the idea of the community raising funds in return for shared ownership, don't you?'

'I'm not sure I can see you handing over your pub to a random bunch of locals,' she admitted. 'But I think community ownership sounds a darned sight better than Top Taverns owning it . . . The question is: will they sell?'

'They're keeping their options open,' he said, setting his jaw with irritation. 'They want it every which way. A couple of weeks ago all I would have wanted was a new lease from them. Now, I don't think I'd take it if they paid me.'

'Which I doubt they will,' said Maddy. Then she relented. 'Patrick, what you're doing is amazing,' she said. 'I honestly don't know if we can do it, but a community-owned pub and no houses sounds like a goal worth fighting for.'

'And the first battle,' he said, 'is to persuade the Development Committee to refuse the planning application for the houses. With any luck the town council will turn it down flat, which they bleeding well should but you don't want to make any assumptions; they're a pretty dim lot.

Also,' he added, 'there's still time for comments before the Development Committee meeting, which is the one that really counts. So, we've got a lot of work to do.'

'We certainly have,' muttered Maddy, rubbing her painful leg wearily.

'Ben'll give us a hand.'

'I dunno that he will . . .' said Maddy. 'He seems pretty busy. Anyway, talking about Ben and the pub, what do you know about his friendship with that Jonno McGrath?'

'Friends, are they?' mused Patrick. 'Hmm. I don't think I trust that Jonno. Mind you, I really don't know him . . . They've been talking, you say?'

She nodded.

'About all this?'

'Think so.'

'Hmm,' said Patrick again. 'Have they, indeed?'

He shook himself. 'That said, I've been meaning to mention, your mother and I thoroughly approve of your seeing Ben.'

'I'm sorry to disappoint you both,' said Maddy, not missing the 'your mother and I' line, 'but we're not seeing each other. As a matter of fact, I haven't seen Ben for days. He's gone to ground.'

'What's the matter with you? Both of you? It's a match made in heaven, I tell you.'

'How long have you known him?' said Maddy, changing tack.

'A long time. Serena used to bring him in to the Arms as a young lad. Too young to drink, technically, but I'm not saying he didn't end up with the odd pint . . . Mind you, he was in a bit too often once he came of age – doing all that ridiculous macho stuff, seeing how much he could drink without either falling over, starting a fight or generally making a prat of himself. Usually he ended up doing all three. He was a bit of a slow learner as it happens . . .'

'He's not like that now.'

'No. Andrew's death changed him. And his time in the army had an impact. He came back a man.'

'So now you're playing matchmaker – you and Mum?'

'Absolutely.'

'Talking of which, where is Mum?'

'She's out posting flyers through doors,' he said, his eyes lighting up. 'God, she's a wonderful woman.'

'Glad you approve,' she said, giving him an appraising look. 'Talking of all this "your mother and I" stuff,' she added, carefully, 'what exactly is going on between you and Mum?'

'About what?'

'You know perfectly well "what"! Are you – well – together?'

'That's the million-dollar question.'

'It is a bit, isn't it?' said Maddy. 'If you don't know, then I'm sure I flipping don't.' She took a swig of tea and a deep breath.

'Look,' she said, 'tell me about before,' she went on. 'When you knew her. You know, before I was born.'

'I love you, Helen,' came a voice.

'Out of the mouths of babes,' said Maddy, laughing. Pirate was hanging upside down off the top of the curtain, turning his head in that alarmingly flexible way, so he could see Maddy the right way up.

'I love you, Helen,' he said again, apparently keen to make his point.

'So, clearly you've been talking,' she pressed, giving Patrick a beady look. 'If you wanted to keep it a secret you might have done it when Pirate wasn't around.'

'He's got a gob on him, that bird,' he complained, giving

Pirate an exasperated look. 'It's not really my tale to tell.'

'You were there, weren't you?' she said, determined to take no prisoners. 'How is it "not your tale"?' Plus she knew pressuring Patrick to spill the beans was going to be a darned sight easier than getting her mother to talk.

'Okay, look,' he said, spreading his hands in submission and sitting heavily at the table. 'Helen came to work for me,' he said. 'It was summer time. An amazing summer . . . It seemed to go on for ever,' he stared into space, misty-eyed.

'Get on with it.'

'Fine,' snapped Patrick. 'We had a "thing". It was a serious "thing", I hasten to add. Not just a casual shag – or at least it wasn't from my point of view . . .' He looked at his hands, curled around his mug of tea. 'I probably shouldn't have let it happen,' he continued. 'Helen was – is – about fifteen years younger than me. I was in my late thirties at the time . . .' He smiled. 'She mesmerised me. So beautiful, so clever, determined . . . God . . . When she made her mind up about something . . .'

Maddy softened. 'Go on,' she said, 'what went wrong?'

'I don't really know,' he admitted. 'Not now – not even then . . . but I know it was my fault. I was so determined that it had to finish, for her sake. We argued, I remember. She called me a coward for ending it.' He wiped his hand over his face and sighed. 'I've gone over and over it a thousand times. I've had years, after all . . .'

'Have you had a relationship with anyone since?' she asked.

'Of course I have, darling,' he snapped. 'I'm a human being, for goodness' sake.'

'Not recently, though.'

'No,' he admitted. 'I haven't wanted to. And even when I did – in the past – it was never anything like the thing I had with your mother. After a while, I accepted that I would never recapture that with another woman. I suppose that's why I stopped trying.'

'What did you argue about?' pressed Maddy. 'Go on, you must remember.'

He glanced up at her and then looked down again at his hands. 'I started it deliberately,' he said. 'I was trying to push her away, and I succeeded.'

'But why on earth would you?' said Maddy. 'You've just told me you loved her. Love her . . . What were you trying to achieve, exactly?'

'I was trying to do the right thing.'

'The right thing?'

Patrick leant back in his chair. 'I don't know . . . She was so fresh and young and full of promise. Me? I was a pub landlord. Not even my own pub. I was drinking too much, I'll be the first to admit. Until your mother came along I was having a high old time picking up pretty girls – they seemed to be prepared to let me, goodness knows why – whenever they took my fancy. I was scared to change. I was no good for her.'

'She loved you,' said Maddy. It was a statement, but he waved it away.

'She thought she did,' he said. 'She didn't really, I could see that. She was just – I don't know – infatuated. I knew if I pushed her away, she'd go off and fulfil her potential. Live her life. She'd be happier without me, meet someone her own age, get married, build a career. She was – is – so bright and determined, she could achieve anything she set her mind to. She didn't need me holding her back.'

'So you decided for her.'

'It was the right thing,' insisted Patrick, willing her to understand.

She could tell he didn't believe his own words, though. Not any more.

'How old was she?'

'When she left?'

'Yes.'

'It was just a couple of weeks before her twenty-third birthday,' he recalled. 'The fourteenth of October was the last day I saw her. The last time I set eyes on her until a few weeks ago . . .'

There was no ignoring the next question. It was in the room with them, tangible, irritating, like it was tugging on Maddy's sleeve.

'So, my birthday is . . .'

'. . . the sixth of June,' finished Patrick. 'I know. I've thought about it a million times, since you came here to study.'

'Were you . . . ?' she swallowed. Paused. 'I mean, you were definitely together . . . ?'

'Of course, why?'

'Because . . .' she hesitated to hurt him. The words felt like lead weights, so reluctant was she to lift them to the light. 'Because Mum told me – before I came to college here – that my father was a married man. Someone she was having an affair with, who was killed in a motorbike accident.' She steeled herself to look at him.

To her amazement, he was shaking his head. Laughing in disbelief.

'What, Mike?' he said. 'You must be kidding! He would never have cheated . . . and Helen – your mum – would never have cheated on me, either.'

Maddy blinked, as years of preconceptions shifted, like tectonic plates.

'Mum lied?'

'Looks like it,' said Patrick gently.

'How can you be so sure?'

'I've never been surer of anything in my life. The only man Helen was sleeping with before she left Havenbury was me.'

She could so easily stop it here. Let him be.

'So . . . are you my father?' she said, staring at the floor.

It came out louder than she intended, ringing in the air, hanging there, almost visible among the dust motes, which were dancing in the low, autumn sun slanting through the window.

Even Pirate righted himself, sitting bolt upright on the curtain pole, and looking at the two of them with fierce interest.

As if her head weighed a tonne, she slowly looked up, and saw Patrick's eyes fill with tears.

'I can't say,' he replied in a whisper.

'I think you bloody can,' said Maddy, suddenly angry, 'because I'm damned well asking and you owe me an answer.'

'Of course,' he said, holding out his hands towards her across the table. 'You deserve an answer, and – well – perhaps, at long last, despite all my sins, so do I.'

Maddy reached towards him and he caught her hands, squeezing them fiercely with his own.

'I can only tell you what I know, and' – he swallowed – 'what I hope . . .'

'Okay,' said Maddy, reluctantly withdrawing her hands to reach for the tissues. She handed one to Patrick and pulled out another to wipe her own eyes.

'Shoot,' she said, with a wobbly smile. 'I'm listening.'

'The first thing I have to make you understand . . . you *have* to know, Maddy,' he looked at her desperately.

She nodded, reaching again for his hand, to comfort his distress. 'What?'

'I – didn't – know,' he said. 'I didn't know about you, because if I'd known . . .' he clenched his fist, regaining control with difficulty. 'She had every right to keep it secret,' he said, 'but if she'd told me, things might have been different.'

'Do you think I look like you?'

He smiled. 'Thankfully, you take after your mother,' he said. 'Look at us both. There's nothing obvious, is there? If the question was who your mother is, though, there wouldn't be any doubt . . . The main difference between you is your extra six inches in height. That could be from me. I'd like to think so.' He gazed at her so proudly she cried even more.

'When she called me after all those years to say you were coming here to study and that she wanted me to keep an eye on you – look after you . . . I did the maths, of course. I knew there was every chance . . . And then, when I first met you' – he smiled – 'you just blew me away, Maddy. So beautiful. So much like your mother . . . I could barely take my eyes off you. I felt so proud, even though I didn't know . . .'

'Surely you asked?'

'I wasn't entitled to. I made her leave, remember. Hurt her terribly. I gave up my right to be a father. I'd have done a rubbish job, anyway. I was a selfish, boozing, deluded idiot. And then,' he smiled at the memory, 'there she was, asking me to – in a sense – *be* a father to you, just a tiny bit, perhaps prove myself . . .' His face darkened. 'But . . .'

'But,' echoed Maddy sympathetically, 'the thing happened.'

'You were in my pub that night, for goodness' sake. Right under my nose. Drinking with your mates . . .'

'They weren't my mates. Not really. Apart from Flora.'

'No,' he agreed. 'God knows what actually happened and who did what, but they certainly didn't look after you,' he said. 'And neither did I. When I heard . . .' He wiped away a tear, blowing his nose gustily. 'For heaven's sake look at me! What a mess. I'll tell you what, though, I've learnt how to cry over the years. Your mother would be impressed at that, at least. She called me a cold, unfeeling bastard before. But – of course – I let her down again, in the most horrific way possible, letting you be hurt . . .'

'It wasn't your fault.'

'Helen thought it was,' he said, remembering the terrible moment when he had to phone and give her the news. 'And it *was* my fault,' he added. 'She was right. Again. She's always right. She gave you to me – the most precious thing in her life – to look after and look what happened.'

Getting up, Maddy went around the table and leant down to hug him. Soon her tears were soaking into his shoulder as he clung to her with one arm and gently rubbed her back with the other.

'So,' he said shakily at last, 'to answer your question . . . I devoutly hope that I am your father, and I strongly believe that I am. That said, it's down to your mother to tell us both whether I am or not, and – now you know what I know – I think the time has come for you to ask, don't you?'

CHAPTER TWENTY-TWO

The spotty youth in the printers dumped a sheaf of A3 paper on the counter as soon as he saw Maddy coming in through the door.

'They're ready? My God, you're a lifesaver,' exclaimed Maddy. 'We've got to have them for the meeting on Friday.'

'I know,' he said, giving her a wry smile. 'Talk about cutting it fine . . . Cup of tea?' he offered, as she sat down at the little table to spread out the pages and take a forensically good look for any last-minute typos.

'I wouldn't say no,' she said gratefully.

'What's your name?' she said, as he returned with a steaming mug a couple of minutes later.

'Freddie,' he said. 'And you're Maddy. You don't remember me, do you?'

Maddy took a sip while she took a shifty look at him.

'I'm so sorry,' she said. 'I'm hopeless at this . . .'

'You were in the third year when I started,' he prompted. 'I was doing graphic design. We didn't mix much, obviously.'

'Of course,' said Maddy, striking her forehead. 'How fantastic! And – so – presumably you've graduated . . .'

Freddie nodded.

'And now . . .' she tried to make it sound like a triumphant career move, 'you're working here! How fab.'

'Yeah, well, it's a start,' he said, looking a little nervous at her enthusiasm. 'I just wanted to say hello.' He paused, looking at her as if he was gauging her reaction. 'I was really sorry about the whole thing, with the . . . with that "accident" thing. I mean I would have said so at the time, but – you know – I didn't know you and anyway, obviously, you left and all that.'

He had blushed to the roots of his ginger hair as he spoke, tugging awkwardly at his ear lobe. It worried Maddy that he might dislodge one of his many piercings so fiercely was he pulling at it. She instinctively reached towards him to take his hand away like a mother might do to a toddler picking its nose. Just in time she turned it into an unconvincing stretch.

'So,' she said, using every ounce of will to keep her body language and tone of voice relaxed. 'Were you actually there? I mean, in the bar where we were? Or in the student halls later, perhaps?' She tried not to look as if it mattered either way.

'In the bar,' he said, eager to prove his credentials. 'I was there with some year-one graphic design students, because – you probably don't remember – Patrick was doing a student night. It was a big bowl of chips with every round of drinks and free soft drinks for the drivers.'

'I do remember,' said Maddy fondly. Patrick was always doing that by the time she met him, far from the louche hard-drinking publican he described himself as before Maddy was born. Not content with fussing over Maddy when she was working, making her stop and eat supper, lending her his scarf to cycle home when it was cold, he was also a mother hen over the other students too. Rather than enticing them in with cheap alcohol, he was instead running promotions based on feeding them and keeping them safe.

'So anyway,' said Freddie, 'we were there; we were being reasonably quiet, you wouldn't have noticed us,' he went on. 'Although us graphic design students can be pretty wild, as you know,' he joked, with a lopsided grin.

She grinned back but said nothing, not wanting to distract him from his memories of a night where her own were in short supply.

'Tell me . . .' she said. 'Everything . . .'

'Okay,' he glanced at her for reassurance and continued. 'So, like I said, it was me and some mates . . . we were at the table next to yours. In the little annexe place at the back? You know.'

She nodded.

'Of course,' he apologised. 'You were there . . . Anyhow, your lot were playing that drinking game that was all the rage at the time. The one with the penny. It's impossible, but that's just an excuse, obviously. You were . . .'

'Go on.'

'You were completely out of it, weren't you?'

'I was.'

'It was like . . .' Freddie went on, gaining confidence, 'it was like they were ganging up on you a bit. They were egging you on. I didn't like it. That Kevin bloke was there, I remember. He works in the pub.'

'He doesn't now . . . Never mind, go on.'

'Okay, so you know who was there, anyhow. It was Kevin and his mate, and then some of the others from your year that I don't know the names of. Although Flora was there too, wasn't she? I know her,' he said, blushing again.

'She was.' Flora had been there, being her usual ebullient self, Maddy remembered fondly. Everyone would always remember when Flora had been there, she thought.

'I saw him do it, actually,' said Freddie.

'Who? What?' said Maddy, returning from her recollections. 'Saw who?'

'That Kevin bloke. Filling up your glass under the table he was, wasn't he? That's when he did it.'

'Did what?' said Maddy, trying to keep calm. Not wanting to prompt – what was it they said in those crime dramas? One mustn't 'lead the witness'. She waited, poised.

'When he spiked your drink,' said Freddie, hanging his head. 'It was an acid tab; he held it in the drink under the table and then dropped it on the ground. I saw him. People the next day were talking about it. It was common knowledge – or at least rumour. I thought loads of people must have seen, not just me, but now I realise . . . I'm sorry.'

'Why?'

'I dunno. I didn't do anything. I'm really, really sorry . . .' Freddie brushed his eyes with the back of his hand.

Maddy was surprised at how calm she felt. 'You're not to blame,' she managed to say. She reached out and put her hand on Freddie's arm. 'It's not your fault.'

'But it was so awful,' he muttered. 'When I heard you were so badly injured, I thought it must be to do with it. But then I thought you knew by then. Pretty much everyone knew. It seemed like it wasn't for me to tell.'

Maddy shook her head. 'I didn't know,' she said truthfully. 'But it wasn't for you to tell. You – are – not – responsible,' she insisted. Although the truth of the matter was, his eyewitness testimony would have made all the difference in the world, but it was surely too late now. And anyhow, what was done was done. What mattered to her more now was her missing memories and her horror of what they might be. Freddie couldn't help her with that.

'Look,' she said, gathering herself together, 'never mind all this for now. I really appreciate your telling me but I need to get these proofs signed off.' She shuffled the pages together and stood up. 'I think I might just pop to the trattoria to check them through.'

In the trattoria at the bottom of the high street there was a warm, comforting fug of Italian coffee and breakfast. Maddy contemplated food but her churning stomach persuaded her otherwise. She settled for a latte and drank it slowly as she meticulously and methodically checked through every inch of the proof pages. Reading backwards as well as forwards to stop her brain automatically filling in what should be there, rather than what was there – she had learnt that trick from an old hand years ago – she spotted and ringed a couple of missed capital letters and crossed out an unwanted comma. Other than that, they were pretty near perfect. She leant back in her chair and swigged her milky coffee. She signed the bottom of the last sheet and breathed a sigh of relief. If they went to print today, they should have them just in time.

Draining her mug she got ready to leave, stacking the money for her coffee neatly next to her empty cup.

'*Ciao, bella,*' shouted Chris, the owner, as she went. She grinned and waved, acknowledging their little in-joke. He said it to the tourists, who loved it because it made him sound authentic, and to Maddy because she knew he was born and bred in Scunthorpe and was no more Italian than Winston Churchill.

She had missed all these funny little interactions, she realised sadly. Leaving when she did, and for the reason she did, was like ripping a plant out of the ground before it had had the chance to flower. She had trashed her degree and dipped out of her friendships . . . just because she had been shafted by a single person who was clearly an irredeemable shite.

Dropping off the proofs she paused on the pavement to gather her thoughts. Gazing up the street, she saw two familiar figures, standing talking at the top of the hill. Dennis and Ben were unmistakable and made a comic pair, with Ben so tall and broad standing next to Dennis, with his short stature and bald head. The third figure was less familiar but was surely Jonno from the nightclub on the quay? She peered at the threesome and wondered what they were doing. She was dying to offload her confusion and distress at what Freddie had said. She wanted a hug and to be helped to make sense of it all. As she set off up the hill, Ben broke away from the group and started to walk towards her. She was just about to raise her arm in greeting – they were too far away to call out – when Ben stopped abruptly, turned and headed back up the hill. Maddy watched in confusion as he briefly acknowledged the other two men again and then turned left, out of Maddy's sight.

Fine, she thought, surprised at her lurch of disappointment.

The only other person she could turn to in distress was her mother and – while she was about it – she remembered they had another pressing matter to discuss.

Helen was just coming out of the flat with a bag of rubbish as Maddy arrived at the Havenbury Arms.

'Hello, darling,' she said warily, the bag drooping from her fingers.

'Mum.'

They stood, looking at each other for long seconds.

'Let's get out of here,' said Maddy suddenly, rummaging for her car keys. 'I need to . . . I dunno . . . walk.'

'Okay.' Helen crammed the rubbish bag into the dustbin and dusted off her hands. 'Let's go.'

Neither of them spoke as Maddy negotiated the narrow one-way streets that took them out of the top of town, past the castle ruins and into the Sussex countryside. She swung the car into the little car park at the edge of the woods. There were two footpaths: one downhill, into the forest towards the pond and one climbing steeply along the edge of the ploughed fields to the top of the Down.

With a look they made a silent agreement and headed for the hill climb. The sky was high and blue, with frost still riming the ground in the shadows and the thin winter sun catching the dew on the cobwebs in the hedgerows.

They were soon puffing clouds of condensation – Maddy more so than Helen – making her realise how unfit her broken leg had made her. She stole glances at her mother as they climbed, side by side. Her body was still youthful and firm, honed by years of Pilates and yoga but, in the bright winter sunlight, the thin wires of silver in her hair gleamed and the crow's feet tracing across her face tracked right across her cheeks to her temples, the stark generational gap sweeping away the sisterly resemblance that could be seen in softer light. For twenty-five years Maddy had been looking at her mother's face and now, for the first time, she felt like she didn't know her at all.

There was a wooden bench at the top of the hill, a reward for walkers prepared to make the climb. They sat, side by side, with three feet of space between them, and gazed down into the valley below. There was Havenbury Magna, its busy, chattering streets reduced to a toytown model. The mist still hovered in the valley below them, blurring the edges of the town and lying thickly over the river as it snaked its way past the bottom of the town and continued, across the coastal plain, like a sinuous, silver ribbon, all the way to the sea.

Maddy took a deep, sighing breath. She glanced at her mother and then looked straight ahead.

'Do you hate me?' said Helen at last.

'No,' said Maddy automatically. 'Nooo!' she said again, with anguish. 'Of course I don't.'

Suddenly, she felt like she was four years old again. All the security, warmth and certainty that her mother had created for her felt fragile, and – even at twenty-five – she was cold without it.

'I need to understand,' Maddy said, her chin quivering and her voice wobbling hopelessly.

'Come here,' said Helen, shifting to close the gap and wrapping her arm around her daughter's shoulders. She opened her coat and wrapped it around Maddy as far as it would go, enclosing them both tightly.

'I remember when I could scoop you up and hug you on my knee,' she said, with a sad smile. 'I used to hold you here, inside my coat, and rest my chin on the top of your head. It feels like yesterday. And I still want to do it, you know,' she said, turning to look at her. 'I still wish I could wrap you up and keep you safe.' She dropped a tender kiss on her daughter's cheek, kissing away the tear that was tracking its way down her face.

Maddy, desperately trying to suppress her tears, gave a little involuntary hic, making Helen hug her even closer.

'You lied,' she said.

'I did,' Helen admitted. 'I'm so sorry . . . but everything I did and said,' she went on, gazing out over the countryside laid before her, 'every decision, every mistake, every muddle and compromise we all get into when we try to be good parents . . . it was all with love and good intentions. I just want you to know that.' She turned to look at Maddy again. 'Alright?'

Maddy nodded frantically and gave another little hic, not trusting herself to speak.

'When I left, and then, when I realised I had you,' she went on, 'my own feelings stopped being important. What I wanted for myself stopped being important. All I knew was that I had to protect you and care for you.' Helen squeezed her again. 'I found a job, found our tiny little house and created a safe space. You were all I thought about, cared about, for years,' she said.

'You were a great mum,' hiccuped Maddy. 'You *are* a great mum,' she added, her shoulders heaving.

'Not what you were saying when you were a teenager,' joked Helen.

'No . . . sorry about that.' She steeled herself. 'Was there anyone else, just after you left Patrick?' she asked, hardly daring to hear the answer.

'God no,' said Helen. 'I was in no state.'

'And the motorbike man?'

'Not true, I admit. Although there was such a man. His

name was Mike and he was lovely – a friend of Patrick's. He really was killed, leaving two young boys and his wife a widow. It was just before I left and we were all so shocked . . . The first time I really grasped that life could end in a heartbeat. An end to innocence, really . . . When you asked me, after all those years, it was the first thing that popped into my head. I'm so sorry.'

'So,' Maddy took a deep, shuddering breath, 'Patrick *is* my father?'

'Of course!' said Helen. 'Of course he is . . . and – listen – you want to know why I didn't tell him, involve him in your childhood . . . why I lied when you came here to college? Of course you want to know, and all I can say is this: when I thought about Patrick, I didn't think about his rights as a father, or how he might be hurt if I didn't tell him. I just thought about how he had cast me off, causing me so much pain, and how I didn't – ever – want you to experience that rejection for yourself, from your own father. I couldn't risk it. Wouldn't.'

A deep peace filled Maddy, closely followed by a fresh wave of snotty, hiccupy tears. 'It's just that you never told him . . . us . . .' she spluttered, or at least that was what was meant to come out but she was crying so hard, it was more of a wail. Luckily, Helen understood the language of 'wail' quite well.

'I have told him now,' said Helen calmly. 'Patrick and I have been having a good talk. Twenty-five years overdue, mind.'

'Why didn't you tell him I was his when I came here to study?'

'He didn't ask,' said Helen simply. 'I waited, I wondered if he would, but he didn't ask. Mind you, I understand that better now too.' She sighed. 'It's all been a bit of a balls-up really,' she added, stroking her daughter's hair. 'But we are where we are,' she said. 'It is what it is.'

'Will you and Patrick stay together now?' She couldn't quite make herself call him 'Dad'. Not just yet.

'I hope so. I really think it might work. He's changed. I've changed. The love is still there. It never went; there were just too many things in the way.'

'What about the house? Your job?'

'Oh, I've resigned,' said Helen in surprise. 'Did I not say?'

'Erm, no, actually. What about the mortgage and all that?'

'Paid off last year. Funny how taking it out was so huge – such a stretch – it seems a tiny amount nowadays . . .' Helen mused. 'Anyway, point is, I've been quietly paying it off for twenty-five years and now, here we are! I got the house valued a few months ago. Unbelievable, really, what it's ended up being worth. Of course, if Patrick and I stay here I can rent it out, generate a bit of income. Or I could always sell it, of course . . .'

'Did he talk about marriage?'

'Actually no. Why?'

'Well,' said Maddy, 'he said to me he wouldn't ask you if he lost the pub. He seemed pretty determined,' she added, remembering how vehement he was.

'He's a stubborn man,' said Helen, unmoved. 'We'll see.'

Chapter Twenty-Three

Patrick was talking to a tall, swarthy man who towered over him, partly because Patrick was slumped into the most abject attitude of defeat Maddy had ever seen him in.

'Who's that?' she whispered to Helen, who was gathering up glasses after the busy lunchtime shift.

'Turns out the town council have backed the residential planning application,' explained Helen. 'That's Zach – Lord Havenbury,' she went on. 'His family have pretty much owned Havenbury Magna since the dawn of time.'

'We've lost the battle not the war, Patrick,' Zach was saying. 'Don't waste your energy on the town council. We've got the Development Committee coming up in just a few days and that's what counts. I'll speak if you'd like me to?'

'I would, Zach,' said Patrick, with visible relief. 'I was going to do it myself but I'm not sure I can keep my counsel.'

'That's decided, then,' said Zach. 'I'll pop around tomorrow and go through what we can say.'

At that, he turned and left, barely glancing at Maddy.

'There, you see,' said Helen encouragingly. 'We've lost the battle not the war, like he says, haven't we, Maddy?'

'Absolutely.'

'Come upstairs and have a cup of tea?'

'Can't, Mum,' she said regretfully. 'The Bespoke Consortium meeting's tomorrow night. We've got lots to discuss and I've promised Serena a few figures and things.'

The brochures were looking beautiful, Maddy was relieved to see when she collected them the following morning. She thought they would do a great job – as long as they could get them out in time.

It took a few hours for her to prepare the figures Serena had wanted, along with a brief PowerPoint presentation. They needed to know that the financial situation was parlous and good Christmas sales were absolutely critical if the Consortium was going to avoid failing before it even got going.

Once they were done, Maddy had a really hot shower to warm herself up and put on as many layers as she could, finishing off with her trusty walking boots. Looking in the mirror, she barely thought make-up was worth the bother. Foundation just seemed to emphasise her grey, lifeless skin with such huge dark circles under her eyes she looked like a panda. Lipstick looked like she was trying too hard, so she wiped it off again, and blusher made her look like a clown. Sighing, she decided she would just have to go au naturel.

Because she knew she would be out all evening Maddy hadn't bothered to light the little woodburning stove, so the Grainstore was chilly and she knew she would be grateful for the blankets Serena had used to decorate the little apartment. For the last few days she had been using them as extra covers on the bed, not that they had helped her to sleep. Actually getting to sleep wasn't the problem, but continually waking with the familiar nightmare had made her form a habit of getting up and drinking tea on the sofa wrapped in blankets so she could watch the dawn gradually lighting the landscape.

She would miss the view.

The thought of leaving and returning to London routinely brought tears to her eyes during her dawn vigils. She hadn't shared her thoughts – or Simon's offer – with Serena or anyone else yet but – increasingly – the thought of being able to sleep without terrors, and to go about her daily business without anxiety about bumping into Kevin and his cronies, had made the bleak decision of returning to London feel like a form of relief.

CHAPTER TWENTY-FOUR

Serena and Giles's kitchen was – as always – filled with warmth, light, colour and noise, and Flora was doling out cups of tea from Serena's huge brown teapot.

'Here's yours, Zach,' she said, kittenishly, handing him a mug where everyone else had to make do with a little teacup.

He thanked her briefly and then made his way over to Maddy.

'You're Maddy,' he said, holding out a large, tanned hand to shake. 'I'm sorry I didn't say "hello" properly yesterday. I gather it's you and Serena who have cooked up this escapade together. I'm looking forward to hearing more.'

'And Flora too,' said Maddy. 'I'm glad you're here – erm – my lord.'

'Call him Zach, for God's sake,' Serena said. 'We don't want him getting too big for his boots,' she added, rubbing his upper arm in a familiar manner. 'How are things up at the Manor?'

'Oh God, parlous as ever,' he replied. 'Dodgy gutters, leaky roofs . . . Looks like this conference company we're talking to will actually go ahead and sign a lease on the place, so then we'll have some money at last. Fingers crossed.'

'What about work?'

'I've got some good commissions . . . an amazing one to create a pair of gates, twelve feet high . . . I just need a bit more time to do them. The trustees seem to be on a mission to get me in a suit and into boring meetings all the time.'

Serena turned to Maddy. 'Zach's the most amazing artist blacksmith,' she explained. 'He made those beautiful wrought-iron coat hooks in our boot room, and I wondered if we might want him to do a range for the Bespoke Consortium.'

'Sounds great,' said Maddy.

'Don't rush to decide whether you want me,' said Zach. 'Perhaps you'd like to come and see what I do? I've got a workshop up at Havenbury Manor. You're welcome any time.'

Luckily Giles was there to sort out the IT stuff as Maddy was struggling to get her laptop to work with the projector so she could beam her presentation up onto the blank wall above the Aga.

Eventually, after an age of shuffling around and scraping chairs, the group was settled around the scrubbed kitchen table. Each participant had a cup of tea and a hunk of cake chosen from the selection in the middle of the table. Serena had excelled herself, making brownies, ginger cake and some sort of Victoria sponge with gorgeous yellowy-green home-made greengage jam in the middle.

After taking them briefly through the agreed product range, showing the fabulous photos Keith had taken, she got down to the detail and she spared them none of the harsh realities: 'Sales will inevitably fall off a cliff in the new year. The time to get money in to fund all our fantastic plans for the future is now. Actually, all we're really trying to do is get sufficient funds to keep ticking along,' she admitted. 'The grand plans need to be carefully timed,' she added. 'But we will get there. I think the Bespoke Consortium has a great future. Potentially.'

'Yeah,' came the ragged reply as with whoops and applause they showed their approval. Maddy blushed.

'Well,' she said, glancing at Serena for confirmation, 'can I suggest we take a pee break, grab some more tea or whatever, and then settle ourselves down to thrash out the detail for the next few weeks. We've got a lot to do.'

After ten minutes or so, Maddy called the meeting back to order, but, before she could start talking, Jez held up his hand.

'Maddy,' he said, standing up. 'We've been having thoughts and first of all, we just all want to express our appreciation to you and Serena for all you're doing . . .' What he said next was drowned in a chorus of whoops and table thumping. When it had died down, he continued: 'We all wouldn't have the first clue how to do what you're doing for us and we can see it's all really sensible stuff so, to help, we would all like to add a further thirty per cent to the twenty per cent commission you are due on each sale. Basically, if we make sure Bespoke Consortium gets a full half of all the turnover for the next four weeks then that should hopefully help get things a bit more secure.' At this he sat down again and shyly bowed his head during a further chorus of approval.

'Jez – all of you –' said Serena, 'that's just amazing, but that basically means most of you'll just be working for your materials with no profit at all for your time. Are you sure?'

All heads around the table nodded vociferously, other

than Zach, who sat, taking in the scene calmly, with a considering expression.

'That's just amazing,' said Maddy, touched to the point of tears. To hide it she had to turn her back to compose herself, clattering around with the teacups by the sink until she could face them all with a smile.

After that, the real work began. Flora piped up to report on her social media promotion. 'I've got a few thousand followers on Twitter . . . more on Instagram – we seem to be popular on that. Nice photos, that's the key . . .'

'What do you do with them?' asked Serena incredulously.

'I post stuff about the process, for example,' Flora explained. 'When Ursula was dying her yarns the other day – goodness it stank,' she held her nose in demonstration, 'I did a series of posts on it. They got a really good response, actually. Obviously I was including links to the website . . .'

'Last Tuesday?' said Maddy.

Flora nodded.

'You're amazing,' she said, in genuine awe. 'The website figures show a spike; I was wondering what it was.'

'There you go,' said Serena, laughing. 'I frankly have no idea what you're both talking about, but it sounds great to me.'

'Moving on,' said Maddy, glancing at the clock, and knowing how much more they had to do, 'this kitchen is campaign headquarters,' she said, noticing Giles was looking a little alarmed, 'so by the end of the week we are going to have a whiteboard here' – she pointed at the wall by the door – 'charting our sales along with the sum we absolutely have to achieve, without fail. That way, we will all know at a glance whether we are succeeding or . . . erm . . . not.'

'The brochures are our key marketing tool,' went on Maddy, pleased to see they were being so closely examined and widely admired. 'We've printed about five thousand of them.' There were wolf whistles at that, but she went on. 'It may seem a lot but it's actually quite a small amount,' she explained. 'We have a mailing list and we need to get them out really soon. The rest will just be on our stalls whenever we are out and about.'

'And that,' said Serena, 'is pretty much it for Christmas sales so – fingers crossed – we will be packing up an awful lot of orders on this kitchen table over the next couple of weeks.'

Giles looked even more unhappy at that, but manfully hid his dismay by putting the kettle on again and gathering up dirty crockery for the dishwasher.

For the envelope stuffing, Zach came into his own and Maddy watched, impressed at his natural air of authority, as he organised the rabble into a production line, and the finished envelopes were soon accumulating in teetering piles.

She was annoyed with herself that they had had to resort to first-class stamps rather than second class. They really would be lucky to get in enough revenue to move forward. She slumped wearily at the table, bowed down with the size of the task. The rest of them seemed quite merry, which simply meant she had failed to impress on them how tough things were looking.

'Here,' came a deep voice, making her jump, as a plate with a large slice of Victoria sponge and a fresh mug of tea arrived in front of her. 'You did a good job of talking while we ate,' said Zach. 'Now you need to catch up. I don't suppose you've had any supper.'

Nor any lunch, thought Maddy, but didn't say.

'Thanks,' she said, wondering how she could disown it without him noticing. 'I'd love to see your stuff,' she said.

'Wait 'til the new year,' said Zach. 'It looks like you've got your work cut out for you until then.'

Maddy felt another pang of regret. If she took up Simon's offer, she would be gone by then. Even if she was still working for the Bespoke Consortium somehow, that sort of work would all be done by Serena.

'I'll see you at the Development Committee meeting,' added Zach, and then he was gone.

One by one, predictably, people made their excuses and left.

Wearily, Serena, Flora and Maddy plodded on, with a fresh pot of tea to sustain them.

Flora was happily sticking Christmas stamps onto the envelopes, taking the time to choose a design for each one, which wasn't ideal in terms of speed and – with discussions of the Bespoke Consortium at an end – Maddy brought up her conversation with Freddie from the printers.

'Lovely Freddie!' Flora exclaimed. 'I don't remember him being there that night, though – was he really?'

'He was,' said Maddy. 'And he saw Kevin spike my drink.'

'The little shit. I knew it . . .' exclaimed Serena.

'But we kind of all knew that, anyway,' blurted Flora.

'We did?' said Maddy.

'Why were the police not called?' Serena went on. 'It beggars belief. Flora, did everyone really know that's what he did?'

Flora looked uncomfortable. 'OK, well we didn't "know" know . . . It was a rumour. The next day, people were saying that he had been bragging he'd done it that night, but no one was sure whether to believe him. He shut up quickly enough when we heard Maddy was hurt and anyway he was always saying stuff like that, wanting attention . . . When I put Maddy to bed,' she explained to Serena, 'I thought she'd just had too much to drink. I never suspected. I'd never have left her if I'd known . . .' Her chin crumpled as she remembered. 'I'm so sorry, Mads,' she said. 'It was – like – sooo awful! I never liked that Kevin. Even though,' she reflected, 'actually, I pretty much like everyone. But not him. He's a creep.'

'Okay, so I don't understand why the hospital didn't call the police,' persisted Serena.

'They didn't know a crime had been committed, I suppose,' said Maddy. 'They didn't even test my blood, so that opportunity to gather evidence was missed. They were too busy patching me up. I do remember this doctor guy asking me at one point whether I had taken anything, but I said "no" so I suppose they just assumed I was lying and imagined they were doing me a favour by letting it drop.'

'Your mum must have been wanting an investigation, though?'

'Ah, well, that was the funny thing,' said Maddy, thinking back. 'Mum came storming into the hospital like the wrath of God, determined to sweep me up and take me home, practically before they'd even set my leg. By the time I was making sense of things for myself, she'd been persuaded by the college principal that it was a case of least said soonest mended. Basically, I'm sure he just didn't want the college dragged into any reputational damage.'

'But what about when you got back to college?' insisted Serena. 'Even if your mum . . . Surely when you got back . . .'

'I never did get back to college. Mum suggested I come straight home – just to recuperate, or at least that was the initial idea – but I never went back . . .'

'We packed up your room for you at the end of that term,' Flora said. 'Your mum came down to help. She was nice. She was quite cross with Patrick,' she added. 'I remember that. We had to break into your room to get your stuff. We had to break the door down, literally . . .' she looked awed at the memory. 'Actually, it wasn't us it was the caretaker guy – what's-his-name, Andy?'

'But why didn't you just get a key from the warden?'

Flora sighed. 'No, obviously we got the warden to unlock the door,' she explained. 'But because you had bolted it from the inside, we still couldn't get it open.'

'It was locked on the inside?' said Serena sharply.

'Yeah, course,' said Flora. 'Maddy did it herself. When I put her to bed that night she was going on about people getting in. She had this idea that someone wanted to get into her room and so I told her to lock it and bolt it after I'd gone. I heard her do it before I left.'

'So,' said Serena, looking at Maddy, 'no one got into your room that night, did they? Not if the door was still bolted.'

Maddy stared into space. 'True,' she said.

'So that revolting Kevin can shut the hell up about his nasty insinuations and suggestions,' said Serena. 'Whatever caused you to get up and go out of your window that night,' she went on, 'we now know there wasn't anyone in your room but you after Flora saw you safely home.'

By the time they finished all the envelopes Flora had fallen asleep on the table, her head on her arms, mouth slightly open and snoring sweetly like a child. Wearily Maddy and Serena shuffled the last pile together to wedge them in yet another cardboard box. Maddy glanced at the clock as she carried the first one out to the car. It was nearly one in the morning. Maybe she would be too tired to dream, she thought as she made her way to the Grainstore, unsteady with fatigue. The night sky was clear and the stars so bright she took a moment to tip back her head and admire their clarity. It made her head spin. She would miss this in London where the skies were never truly dark.

As she arrived in Havenbury Magna the thick, purply-grey cloud rolling in from the sea threatened snow.

The 'one hour only' parking slots near the post office were taken by Christmas shoppers so, cursing mildly, she drove into the car park at the bottom of town. The boxes were an awkward size. It was going to take ages one box at a time, and her ankle was going to hate it. Grabbing the first and balancing it while she tried to close the boot, she cursed again.

'What poetic language,' came an amused male voice, as she dropped the box on the floor. 'May I?' Ben leant down and picked it up effortlessly, balancing it on one arm and reaching into the boot for another. 'Need a hand?'

'Breakfast?' suggested Ben as they handed over the final box to a surly post office worker behind a heavy metal grille.

'Dunno about breakfast,' said Maddy, 'but I could seriously do with a latte.'

'You need to eat,' said Ben, giving her a piercing look. 'You're losing weight. Quite a bit, I'd say.'

She made a non-committal noise because he was right and

she didn't want to admit it. She looked at her watch. 'Ah, can't do it, I'm afraid,' she said with false regret. 'I only put twenty minutes on the car.'

'Easily sorted,' said Ben. 'Come on.' He grabbed her arm and marched her back to the car park. 'Hurry up. I'm starving, even if you're not.'

Even as he was walking he was excavating his pockets for change and quickly shoved in a random handful before pressing the button for a ticket. 'That'll do,' he said, handing it to her without looking at it.

In no time at all, she was ensconced in one of the window seats in the trattoria while Ben sorted out some food. She was soon glowing and drowsy with the warmth and with the soothing hum of chatter, interspersed with the whoosh and crackle of the coffee machine. He plonked a huge latte in front of her and sat next to her, his long, muscular thigh pressed up against hers on the cramped bench, athough she noticed, depressed, that he did his best to edge away as far as he could.

'So,' he said. 'Haven't seen you for days; what gives?'

'Quite a bit, as it happens,' she replied. By the time she had brought Ben up to speed with the latest revelations from Freddie and then from Flora, his light mood had completely passed.

'This is huge,' he said.

'It is?' asked Maddy. 'I mean, yes, it is.'

'Of course it is,' he said, running his hands through his hair, in a gesture she was getting to know so well. He thought intensely for a moment. 'It's significant, Maddy. Not least because – even three years on – surely Freddie's and Flora's testimonies now fill in the gaps in your memory almost completely? Where before you had these emotional memories – the abstract terror and pain – now you have facts to tie them to, don't you?'

'Go on.'

'Well, here's the narrative, I suggest; you went out drinking, your drink was spiked with God knows what – LSD you say? – I think, on some level, you must have known that Kevin had done something to harm you, which explains why being around him makes you so nervous. Anyhow, you went back to college that night, Flora put you to bed, critically you *locked your door from the inside*. That means you know that when you woke up and decided to jump out of the window, you *must* have been alone. Your fear and paranoia, your sense that you were being pursued? Totally explainable by the drink spiking. Monsters under the bed, and all that . . .'

He looked at her, waiting for her to register her acceptance.

'Okay.'

'So,' he said, 'you broke your leg, you probably knocked yourself out, you came round, crawled about a bit and then you were found and – well – you know what happened from there, don't you?'

'It's horrible,' said Maddy.

'Yeah, it is. It really is,' he squeezed her arm reassuringly, 'but it's a "known" now. No more gaps, no more nameless terrors.'

She thought. He was right.

'So, now it's all out there, will my nightmares and panic attacks stop?'

His face clouded. 'Probably not,' he admitted. 'Not without help because your fear response is so entrenched now. Here's a thought,' he said at last, swivelling to face

293

her. 'If you can bear me playing the psychologist again.'

'Go on.'

'Given that we now know, objectively, that Kevin is a sad, sorry, inadequate little runt who is angry at the world because he is ignored by those he seeks to impress,' he said, pausing for agreement, which Maddy gave with another nod. 'You can challenge your thinking. Why – actually – is it that Kevin frightens you so?'

She shrugged.

'Is it worth considering that your fear, which is undoubtedly terrifying but is without form, and without – perhaps – literal reason,' he paused, raising his eyebrows, 'has somehow been attached to the really not terribly impressive Kevin as a way for your mind to give it a hook to hang itself on.'

'He did spike my drink, though,' said Maddy. 'We know that now.'

'Yeah, but overwhelming, ongoing, paralysing terror? The drink spiking was the random act of a pathetic little creep, who, realistically, you could pick up and tuck under your arm, should you so wish . . .' said Ben. He paused. 'Just a thought.'

'Is that – like – a psychology trick?' hazarded Maddy.

'Yeah,' he admitted. 'A little bit.' He paused, gauging her reactions. 'I want to speak to Duncan about it,' he said. 'Will you let me?'

'Yeees . . .' said Maddy. 'Why?'

'Look,' he said, 'basically, you're going to need some more help and I'm just not able to do it. There are ethical issues. But Duncan has agreed to take you on. It's legit. He'll write to your GP and everything.'

'But,' Maddy's chin wobbled, and she pressed her hands to her face, furious with herself. She loathed how just thinking

294

about all this made her break down and cry. 'I don't think I can bear to talk to anyone else about it. I just want you . . .' She wiped away a tear and hung her head. 'God, I hate all this,' she muttered.

'How's your sleep?' he asked gently. 'Rubbish,' he answered for himself, looking at the deep, dark circles under her eyes. 'And your anxiety levels?' he added, noting the trembling in her hands.

Maddy shook her head, hopelessly.

'Look,' he said, trapping her hands between his own, warm, strong ones. 'I've said it before, you don't have to suffer like this. You can beat this and what you've just told me makes me even more certain that you can. Let Duncan help you, Maddy. I can even be in the room, if you want me. If that would help?'

She nodded, her head bowed, sniffing back the tears.

'Maddy, I need you to trust me to help you sort this out. Do you trust me? Can you do that?'

She thought, seriously. He had been a good friend. He was heroic, carrying her down off the mountain, protecting her from Kevin . . . of course she could trust him, couldn't she?

She nodded, dubiously.

'So, I'm telling you, the way to go forward with this is to see Duncan. Will you do it?'

'I'll think about it.'

'Okay,' he said. 'Let's leave it there. For now. Here,' he added, handing her a paper napkin to blow her nose, which she attempted to do with as little honking as possible.

At that point, two enormous plates of food arrived. Ben's was a full English breakfast and Maddy ended up with a plate too.

'What's this?' she asked, daunted at two mounds covered in a yellow, creamy sauce.

'Eggs Florentine,' said Ben. 'Poached eggs, hollandaise and spinach. You need protein,' he said. 'And iron, by the look of you. You're terribly pale.'

He pushed her knife and fork towards her, but she didn't move.

'Just start,' he said. 'Sometimes you don't know you're hungry until you're actually eating.'

She sighed, feeling the tension draining out of her, and picked up her fork.

'Anyhow,' said Ben, shovelling in a large mouthful of fried egg and sausage, 'what else? Haven't seen you for ages.'

'I know! I was beginning to think you were avoiding me.'

'Sorry,' he said, blushing. 'It's . . . I've been a bit . . . busy.'

'There is something else as it happens,' she said. 'Much as I regret having to admit you were right, it turns out Patrick is my father after all.'

Ben froze, his fork halfway to his mouth. 'Tell me,' he said, putting it down and turning towards her.

So she did. Mentioning her conversations with Patrick and then her mother, their love affair, its end, her mother's decision to raise her alone, Patrick's guilt over her fall, his desperation to make amends, and their current obvious happiness.

'And the whole motorbike man thing?' he asked, his voice tight with tension. 'What about that? All forgotten now, is it? Conveniently brushed under the carpet?'

She looked at him, nervously.

'Patrick is my father. I absolutely know that now.'

'Well that's just peachy then, isn't it?'

'It is?'

'Don't you think?' he said, incredulous. 'I mean – all I'm saying is, your mother has a bit of a record, doesn't she? First she tells you you essentially don't have a father, then it seems convenient to tell you a story about a random affair with a married man, *then* a few years later we're onto a third version where Patrick is – drum roll – your father after all.' He broke off, scowling.

Maddy edged away from him. She had never seen him so angry.

Ben took a deep breath. 'Sorry,' he said. 'I'm not . . . It's just a bit weird, don't you think?'

Maddy shrugged. 'I believe her,' she said simply.

'Of course you do. Of course. It's none of my business, anyway.' He took a deep breath and let it out. 'And they're happy with each other now? All's well that ends well?'

'You'd think, wouldn't you?' said Maddy, relieved the fury she had somehow triggered was gone again. 'However, Patrick has already said that if he can't be this whole ridiculous male protector thing, supporting her financially, putting a roof over her head, that he will refuse to be with her altogether,' she said, her brow furrowing. 'I really worry that if he loses the pub, he genuinely will throw away the only other good thing in his life . . .'

Ben polished his plate with a triangle of fried bread and popped it in his mouth, chewing thoughtfully.

'They'll work it out,' he said.

'That's your professional opinion, is it, Mr Psychology Guru Extraordinaire?' said Maddy, looking with amazement at her empty plate.

'It is. Like you said yourself, they love each other. Plus – whatever I might personally think of your mother – they're kind of getting wiser as they get older . . . Have faith; love will find a way. So,' he said, stretching widely, nearly knocking the baseball cap off the market trader sitting behind him, 'we should wish them well, I suppose.'

'I'm pleased you're pleased,' she said. 'Anyhow, to change the subject completely, what's with you and Jonno meeting with Dennis and looking thick as thieves?'

Ben's face went blank.

'Ah . . . can't talk about that. Sorry.'

'Really?'

'Really. No, listen, I wish I could – but I can't . . . not now.'

And he wanted her to trust him, thought Maddy. That was rich.

CHAPTER TWENTY-FIVE

With the Development Committee meeting looming, Patrick and Helen were on a mission. The whiteboard was looking increasingly complex and Helen was being kept busy with paperwork. Her legal contact back at home was drawing up a Memorandum and Articles of Association to form the community company that would own the pub, assuming they managed to buy it, and Patrick had taken charge of the lobbying and recruiting of community members to co-own the business.

With a shared cause, they were barely even arguing.

Maddy, Serena and Flora had their own whiteboard at Home Farm and were generally stuck around the kitchen table drinking too much coffee, working the Bespoke Consortium figures and monitoring their marketing activities anxiously, waiting for the 'flood' of orders, which would hopefully come in and scoop the whole enterprise out of the 'new company' danger zone. When they had run out of other things to worry about, Serena would google 'new business failure rates' and relate them to Maddy and Flora until they begged her to stop. One morning, the three of them gathered around the whiteboard gloomily.

'It's not bad,' said Serena, waving her coffee at the sales figures.

'But it's not enough,' insisted Maddy. 'If we don't hit our turnover targets by January . . .'

'We could find more funding?'

'Not soon enough.'

'What about the trade fair?' asked Flora.

'You're right,' said Serena. 'We're in it up to our necks with the expense of it. I know, I know . . . my fault . . . We've got to make it pay.'

Flora and Maddy said nothing.

'We just need to meet one major buyer there,' said Maddy at last. 'It's an outside chance . . .'

'But it's the best chance we've got,' said Serena.

Simon had emailed the pitch he and Maddy had to prepare for the massive two-year contract. As always, he had her down as half of a double act, the operations guy to his strategic genius, whilst cunningly making sure most of the work was hers. She worked hard on her presentation, knowing preparation was the one thing that stopped her being paralysingly nervous. Their slot was down first thing, so she would be driving up or catching a train early in the morning, getting up in the dark, which always made her feel depressed.

Maddy was relieved when the day of the Development Committee meeting arrived. She drove Patrick and Helen there and arrived early so they could sit near the front.

Other people drifted in, most of them giving Patrick a

wave of greeting, although Maddy recognised only a few. Zach had planned to meet them there.

'That loathsome Dennis is here,' Maddy whispered to Patrick. 'Don't look now, but he's talking to a greasy-looking bloke in a suit. Do you suppose he's the property developer who wants the land?'

'Does he look like a property developer?'

Maddy checked him out. Shiny suit, red face, greased-back hair. 'Yep.'

'Do we know if or when the property is up for sale?'

'Nope.'

The Committee were now filing in, looking pleased with themselves.

Maddy flicked through the printed agenda, copies of which had been left on the chairs.

'This is absolutely vast,' she said, her heart sinking. 'They're hearing about fifteen applications before ours. It's alphabetical, by the look of it.'

'Lucky we don't come even further down the alphabet, then,' said Patrick. 'Zach did warn me. You don't have to turn up at the beginning, you can just come in for your bit, but it's a dangerous game working out when that is.'

Given Patrick's agitation, Maddy really hoped Zach didn't play it too close to the wire.

As if he was reading her mind, Lord Havenbury slid around the door just as it was closing for the meeting to start.

'Sorry,' he said, as he slid in next to Maddy. 'Trustee meeting. Nightmare.'

Despite the stress and the high stakes, Maddy found the whole tenor of the meeting deeply soporific. Interminable discussions about development plans and reports from highways seemed to accompany every planning case. Zach occasionally leant over to whisper explanations and comments to Patrick and to Maddy as they went along.

'You know an awful lot about it all,' whispered Maddy.

'Land management,' he whispered back. 'It's having an estate to run that does it.'

'What's this bit?' asked Maddy, pointing to the recommendation at the bottom of each application. Generally, the 'recommendation' was to 'approve'.

'That,' whispered Zach grimly, 'is the steer from the paid planning officers. Basically, they're telling the Development Committee what to do.'

'Do they listen?'

'Almost always.'

She checked the recommendation for their one. 'Approve', it said. Her heart sank a little more.

He gave her a grim smile. 'Just the battle not the war, remember,' he murmured, but she thought they were losing an awful lot of battles recently. It would be nice to have a win for a change. Maybe they were saving up their luck for the auction, whenever that was going to be. That was really the bit that counted.

Then they were on. Zach was the first up to speak and was commanding. He swept his gaze across the entire room and also gave a brief nod acknowledging the councillors sitting on the stage. Then he spoke. 'I would simply like to observe,' he said, 'that the Havenbury Arms has been so named after my family, and serving the community as a hostelry since the seventeenth century. The present incumbent,' he gestured to Patrick, 'has been running it with nigh inexhaustible energy, for at least the last thirty years, despite being – in more recent years – weighed down by the frequently unreasonable demands of the pub company who have taken control over the last decade. This extraordinary and unattractive application to convert this key town centre plot to a residential building site does at least indicate that Top Taverns may be ready to relinquish control and put up the property to auction. We must exploit this opportunity to return the Havenbury Arms to those who put the community first, preserving it as a community asset and ensuring its continued viability into the future. One cannot overestimate the importance of maintaining the diversity and energy of our high street. It is an organism that cannot survive if any part of it is taken away. It is a credit to the strength of community feeling that our landlord here has managed, in a staggeringly short period of time, to obtain financial promises from community members amounting to just over two hundred thousand pounds. I am delighted to use today's event to confirm that I am prepared to contribute a further one hundred thousand pounds to that sum, providing the community control is maintained.'

Maddy was watching Dennis's face when it came to that bit and was pleased to see him puff up with rage.

There was only one other speaker and – surprise, surprise – it was the oleaginous property developer who presented a slick and, Maddy felt, almost entirely untrue argument about the wide range of licensed restaurants and bars remaining in the town if the pub were to close and how they were answering housing need with high-quality design respectful of the high street's unique heritage . . .

'Blah, blah,' muttered Patrick. 'Just creating some hugely expensive, totally unaffordable Frankenstein building with every stylistic feature you can think of doesn't make it classy or relevant.'

'"Gob-ons", they call them,' replied Zach, in agreement. 'When they chuck pastiche features onto crappy brick boxes.'

Surely the Committee won't have their heads turned by that silly nonsense, thought Maddy.

'Any more representations?' said the Chairman. 'I'm afraid we really don't have time to hear everyone . . . You, sir,' he said, pointing to a red-faced, belligerent-looking man in the front row.

Maddy winced. She wouldn't have chosen him herself.

'Lord Havenbury makes a damned good argument,' he said forcefully, jabbing his finger at the committee. 'You lot are up there to represent us. I propose you hold a vote in the audience *before* you decide.'

'Hear, hear,' came the murmur rolling around the room like thunder.

'No . . . no . . .' said the Chairman nervously. 'Now, that – that's not quite right,' he said. 'It's not that we are supposed to "represent" you – well, no, we *are* supposed to represent you – what I mean is that we don't have to . . . at least, we represent you by making my – our – own minds up. Yes,' he nodded sharply. 'That's what we're supposed to do.' He took a swig from a glass of water and smoothed his tie.

After a further brief bit of self-important faffing, the Chairman invited the councillors to vote. A kind-looking, grey-bearded guy immediately voted against the application. The others squirmed, whispered to each other and then – extraordinarily – with nervous glances towards the audience, the others, one by one, voted: in favour.

There was a brief, stunned silence and then a surge of

noise as the audience realised what had happened.

'Unbelievable!' burst out Patrick. 'Absolutely unbelievable. You've got a lot to answer for,' he said, jabbing a finger at the town council chairman – a slimy little man who Patrick knew vaguely from town events. He shuffled in his seat and refused to meet Patrick's eye.

'Come on,' said Zach, catching Helen's eye without Patrick seeing, 'time we weren't here.' Ushering Maddy ahead he gave Helen his arm and led her out, giving Patrick no choice but to follow. As they made their way down to the door at the back Maddy saw that – again – Jonno and Ben had snuck in and were standing at the back of the hall. Jonno was nodding at something Ben was saying. They both looked cheerful enough at the outcome but Ben, seeing Maddy, limited himself to a brief wave as he and Jonno slipped out of the room ahead of them. When the little group got to the foyer the two men had already gone.

'Did you see him?' said Patrick. 'That Jonno chap from the nightclub? I bet he's bloody loving this. Take me out of the equation and he's laughing, isn't he?'

Maddy didn't know what to say. She didn't even know what to think.

Just as she thought she and Zach might be able to get Helen and Patrick out of the building without anything else happening, the odious Dennis came out of the room, obsequiously holding the door open for his little property developer mate.

'Ah, Patrick,' he said cordially, as if they'd met at a cocktail party. 'How are things?'

'That's a bloody good question coming from you, isn't it?'

Helen raised her eyes to heaven.

'What else have you got up your sleeve?' he continued crossly. 'I take it you appreciate you can't just knock down the pub and build whenever you like,' he said, this time addressing the developer. 'You may have got your theoretical building plot, but there is the small but important matter that it doesn't belong to you.'

'Doesn't belong to you either,' interjected Dennis.

Maddy and Helen groaned in unison.

Patrick went a further shade of purple. 'But I am – you seem to forget – still in possession of a current and legitimate lease.'

Disappointingly, Dennis seemed unmoved. 'Aaaanyway,' he went on, with extraordinary courage under the circumstances, 'we will see what tomorrow brings because – as you may know – it is more than possible to sell a property with an incumbent tenant, especially with a lease which is just about to expire.'

'When?' interjected Zach sharply.

'When?' echoed Dennis, turning his attention to Zach for the first time.

'Yes, when? When is the pub up for sale?' Zach repeated, with heavy patience.

'The auction is tomorrow, as you well know,' said Dennis.

'As we well know?' exploded Patrick again.

'Don't give him the satisfaction,' muttered Helen, putting a calming hand on his arm.

'The property is being auctioned tomorrow?' repeated Zach.

'Of course!' said Dennis. 'Did I not say?' He didn't bother waiting for a response. 'I suppose I assumed the office might have informed you, otherwise I'd have mentioned it myself – but no matter, the auction lists have been out for weeks so the information has been "in the public domain",' he said, doing the rabbit ear thing with his fingers, which made Maddy want to punch him even more than she usually did.

'Fine,' said Zach, again grasping Patrick's arm and leading him away. 'Fine,' he repeated, over his shoulder. 'We'll see you there.'

'Tomorrow, for God's sake,' blurted Patrick as they stood outside.

'Tomorrow's fine,' said Helen. 'We're as ready as we'll ever be. I'll be glad to settle the matter one way or another,' she said to Patrick. To Maddy and Zach she added, 'Patrick needs to know where he stands; he can't cope with much more of this.'

'I'm not deaf, woman,' said Patrick. 'I'm right here.'

'I've got nothing to hide from you,' said Helen. 'I just don't want you getting ill, that's all.'

'You might have me well and truly on the scrapheap by this time tomorrow,' said Patrick gloomily. 'I'll be no good to anyone with no pub, no livelihood and no roof over my head. Never mind "ill", I might as well be dead.'

'Don't you dare say things like that,' said Helen crossly. 'Where would that leave me?'

'Ah, young love,' said Zach, smiling at Maddy. 'Bless 'em, eh?'

It was a relief to get back to Serena to help with packing the orders.

'It's not looking good,' Maddy commented to Serena, checking out the whiteboard on the way into the kitchen. The line showing the sales they had to meet and the sales they had so far were still a long way apart.

'Oh, I don't know,' said Serena, 'it could be worse . . . The deadline for first class post is tomorrow – gosh, less than a week 'til Christmas! – but there's always Special Delivery. Makes a hole in our profits if we resort to that . . . Also, I think I rather overestimated the amount of packaging, though.'

'You're not kidding,' said Maddy, surveying the scene. Every flat surface, including the floor, was covered in boxes of stock, rolls of brown paper, stacks of cardboard boxes and clouds of woodshavings.

Serena was battling with parcel tape and address labels, ticking off on a printed list once a parcel had been packed and despatched.

'How many more to do?' asked Maddy.

'This many,' said Serena, handing Maddy a dauntingly long list.

'It may not be enough to dig us out of a hole but, from a packing point of view, it actually seems like quite a lot,' said Maddy, with a sigh. It was clearly going to be a long night. 'Any chance the team could give us a hand?'

'I don't like to distract them. I had a word with Flora about it, but they're working so hard to produce stock. We need samples for the exhibition too, remember.'

Maddy did. Straight after the property auction tomorrow she and Serena were going to have to start getting ready. It was going to be an exhausting couple of days.

'Right then, where do you want me?' she said, squaring her shoulders.

'Making tea,' said Serena. 'I'm parched.'

But before Maddy could lift the kettle onto the stove, the kitchen door burst open with a crash. Giles ran in looking grim-faced.

'Phone,' he barked, pointing to the work surface.

'What is it, darling?' said Serena, frightened, as she reached behind her and handed him the handset, but Giles didn't reply, just jabbing the emergency number and then clamping it to his ear.

'I need an ambulance,' he said. 'One casualty. Head injury. Probably other injuries too. It looks serious.'

As he was talking, he was grabbing Serena by the arm and lifting her out of her chair. 'You need to come with me,' he said to her before returning to his call. 'It's Josh.'

Maddy followed them both out of the kitchen door with a stomach-churning sense of foreboding.

Stopping dead, she clapped her hands to her face in horror.

'Talk to him,' Giles was saying to Serena as he led her towards Josh, who was lying, deathly still, on his back, underneath the oak tree at the top of the horses' field. He was white, like a corpse.

Serena ran over on unsteady legs and fell to her knees beside him and grabbed his hand in hers, using the other to stroke his face.

'Josh? Josh . . .' she was saying, over and over, tears running down her face.

Giles, meanwhile, was still on the phone. 'He's eleven. Yes, usually. No, he's not been conscious at all . . .'

At last, he spoke to Serena again. 'They're sending a helicopter. It's the quickest way, and they can land right here.'

Serena let out a wail, but Giles intervened. 'You need to stop that,' he said. 'You need to talk to him. Come on, darling, reassure him. He may be unconscious but he might be able to hear and he doesn't want to hear this.'

Serena looked at her husband and rubbed her eyes as if she

was seeing him for the first time. 'Of course,' she said, taking a deep breath. 'Quite right.'

Maddy suddenly noticed Harry, standing, rooted to the spot, a few yards away. He was pure white too. Even his lips. She hurried over to him and put her arm around his shoulder.

'Let's go inside, my lovely,' she said.

He seemed barely aware that Maddy was there, but he allowed her to lead him away. Giles briefly nodded his approval. 'I'll come and speak to you in a minute,' he said, before returning to his call where he was giving coordinates for the helicopter to land in the nearest safe location, which – he was persuading them – was the horse field just adjacent to the farmhouse.

CHAPTER TWENTY-SIX

'He fell,' said Harry faintly, as Maddy sat him at the kitchen table and drew up a chair next to him.

'Out of the tree?'

Harry nodded. 'He went really high. He always does. Higher than me. And then, when he was coming down, he slipped. First I thought he was going to be alright but then he fell some more . . . and then he fell all the way down to the ground. And then he didn't move. He didn't get up and I went over and he was . . .'

Harry's eyes were blank as he relived what he had seen. 'I thought he was dead,' he blurted.

God help him, thought Maddy. What if he truly had witnessed his own brother's death?

She gathered him into a hug, rubbing him to warm him, but he barely responded.

'Look,' she said, 'Josh's alive. He's not dead but,' she chose her words carefully, 'he is hurt. He needs to go to hospital so they can look after him and make him better. Accidents like this happen all the time. People do fall out of trees. We have to not worry . . .'

Just then, Giles came into the kitchen, ruffling Harry's hair reassuringly as he met Maddy's eye over his head. His expression was grim.

'They're airlifting him straight to the trauma centre in London. It's his best chance. Better than the local hospital and quicker too, if they fly him.'

Maddy nodded.

'I need to drive Serena up there by car. No room in the helicopter. Okay if we just go?'

'Of course,' she said, getting up and giving him a quick, intense hug.

Harry and Maddy watched the helicopter take off from the horse field and wheel in the direction of London.

'A trip in a helicopter, eh?' said Maddy. 'He'll be gutted to have missed it.'

'He can always do it again when he's better,' said Harry. 'Both of us, though, not just him.'

'Of course both of you,' she said, smiling at the tiny hint of sibling jealousy.

'Right,' she said, when the noise of the helicopter had died away completely. 'Come on, we've got work to do for Mum.'

The parcel packing was perfect for keeping Harry busy and distracted. Maddy kept an eye on the time and at about seven-thirty she made him beans on toast with ice cream to follow. Sensing weakness, he asked for Coke but she made him settle for lemonade instead, which she was sure Serena would think was nearly as bad.

The kitchen clock ticked away the minutes and then the hours, still with no news of Josh. She kept Harry chatting about school, riding and the latest computer games. He was a sweet boy, she discovered, and she felt he was enjoying having her undivided attention. She suspected he got to say less than he wanted to with his confident older brother around.

Maddy had her phone on the table next to her and was constantly checking for a text, although she would hardly have missed the alert. When it did sound, she grabbed the phone with trepidation but was relieved when she saw it was from Ben, commiserating on the Development Committee result. It felt like something that happened days ago. She yearned to text or call him back, to tell him the news and have him hurry to her side, but – remembering his and Jonno's mysterious apparent interest in the pub's fortunes, and his refusal to explain more – she thought perhaps she wouldn't. Not until the auction was over. Which, she realised with a start, was tomorrow morning. What if she was still looking after Harry? She wasn't going to bother Giles and Serena with childcare problems.

'Come on, you,' she said to Harry, who was now fiddling with the parcel tape gun. 'You've done a fantastic job! Look, we're all done,' she said.

There was a mountain of carefully stacked parcels awaiting courier collection by the door and the boxes on the other side of the kitchen, with the stock in, were now seriously depleted.

'Time for bed, I should have thought,' she went on, pointing at the clock.

Harry stood up floppily and went to slouch out of the room and then he stopped. 'You won't leave me on my own, will you?'

'Of course not,' she said brightly, although she hadn't thought what she was going to do. 'Will you show me your room?'

Harry and Josh's room was large and shambolic, with a pair of single beds, one against each wall and a daunting mess of what appeared to be Lego, socks, railway tracks and Meccano in a pile between them.

'Mummy wants us to clear this up,' he said apologetically, 'but Josh won't help me, and I don't want to do it on my own.'

Suddenly his face screwed up and went red. Maddy reached for him and pulled him towards her. At first he resisted and then he pushed his head fiercely into her tummy and threw his arms around her, squeezing her surprisingly tightly for such a little boy. She waited. At first he held his breath, but then – after a few seconds – he began to sob, wrenchingly and painfully. She held him until his grip loosened and the sobs had resolved into occasional hiccups.

Maddy steered him onto what she guessed was his bed and sat down next to him. He rubbed away the snot and tears with his forearm, slumping exhausted against her. There was a floppy brown dog on his pillow, which he picked up in both hands, clutching it to his chest.

'What's his name?'

'"Doggy". Josh says I'm too old for him now.'

'I don't think you are,' said Maddy. 'I've still got my teddies and I'm very old.'

'Really?'

'"Really" have I still got my teddies, or "really" am I very old?'

'Teddies,' said Harry, clearly feeling the other was obvious.

'Yep,' she said. 'One teddy in particular. He's called "Teddy", oddly enough.'

Harry thought for a bit.

'Don't tell Josh I cried,' he said. 'He'll call me a baby.'

'I won't,' she said. 'And you're not a baby. You're really brave.'

By the time Maddy had got him into pyjamas, washed and into bed it was nearly eleven o'clock. Not wanting to leave him alone, she lay down on Josh's bed, with her phone in her hand, intending to get up when she was sure he was sleeping.

Within minutes, reassured that he was soundly asleep, she tiptoed downstairs and opened her laptop. She had an email to write and she needed to write it and send it before she chickened out.

'*Dear Simon . . .*' it began, and – in it – she tried to explain her innermost thoughts: her absolute certainty that – however, she lived her life, wherever, and with whoever – she knew she would not be doing the right thing in taking up his offer of partnership in the business. Like their relationship, she tried to explain, habit, convenience and coincidence were not enough. She was certain he would find better people to work with by striving longer and compromising less.

It was still several days to the bid for the contract. She had prepared the presentation, which she attached to the email, wishing him well and saying she looked forward to hearing how it went. She pressed 'send' and then, despite the acute stresses of the day and her concern as to what the next day held, she lay down, in her clothes, on Josh's bed, and fell immediately fast asleep.

When the text signal came in she woke instantly. Sitting up, she looked over at Harry. In the light from the hallway, she could see he was fast asleep, mouth open, head back and his Doggy tucked tightly under his chin.

She stole out and closed the door quietly. It was fourteen minutes past two in the morning and there was a new text from Serena, a brief message asking her to call, which she did with trembling fingers. After a single ring, she heard – not Serena – but Giles.

'Maddy?' he said curtly.

'Yes.'

'Look, Maddy, Serena and I can't thank you enough... How is everything at your end?'

'Harry's fine. Fed and fast asleep, but how are you all?'

'Josh's in surgery.'

Her heart sank.

'Why?' she said faintly.

'They need to relieve the pressure in his skull. It's touch and go for the next twenty-four hours, I'm afraid.'

'Has he woken up?'

'No,' he said, 'but they've got him in a drug-induced coma now, anyhow. He's on a respirator. We won't know anything until they wake him up. That'll be at some point in the next day or two, if all goes well. Poor chap's broken his arm, it turns out, so they've set that too, although obviously it's the least of his troubles.'

'Serena?' asked Maddy. 'Can I speak to her?'

Giles hesitated. 'The poor old girl's in a bit of a state at the moment,' he explained. 'I'll get her to call you when she's a bit more together . . .'

Tears sprang to Maddy's eyes. 'Give her my love, won't you?'

'Absolutely,' said Giles. 'Now listen, we need to talk logistics here. How are you placed for looking after Harry? I'm grateful you're there for him tonight but what about tomorrow?'

'Erm, it's fine,' she said, thinking guiltily of the pub sale. 'Of course I'll be with him if it helps.'

'I know you've got the property auction,' said Giles, cutting across her, 'so I've put a message in to Flora. She's hopefully going to relieve you at breakfast time and make sure Harry gets off to his piano lesson. He goes on the bus

316

into Havenbury for it luckily. He's done it before – part of Serena's training to make them independent. Best to keep things normal. With luck, Serena or I will be back with you by the afternoon. How does that sound?'

Weird, thought Maddy. She suspected that, even if Josh recovered, nothing would ever be the same again, not for Giles and Serena anyhow, their marriage changed irrevocably into a new relationship forged – or perhaps broken – on the anvil of terror that parents share when their child comes to harm.

'Fine,' she said.

After her brief nap she didn't sleep at all, mainly because she was worrying about Josh and wondering about Simon's reaction to her email. She was wearily making herself a cup of tea at around seven in the morning when Flora burst in.

'God, Mads,' she exclaimed. 'This is just awful. How is he?'

She told Flora what she knew and impressed on her the need to keep to Harry's routine.

'God, yeah, absolutely,' she said, staring into space. 'Bloody awful. Poor Serena.'

Maddy placed a large, strong cup of tea in her friend's hand and offered sugar, which Flora spooned in copiously.

'Are you alright to get Harry up and off to school?' she said. 'I really need to go and get myself cleaned up and dressed.'

Flora nodded but didn't move.

Maddy had to assume the nod was sufficient, so she left.

The atmosphere in the function room of one of the larger town hotels was electric.

There was a podium with a lectern branded prominently

by the auction house hosting the morning's event. There were several pages of lots to be auctioned. The Havenbury Arms was one of the first.

Maddy looked around the room from her vantage point at the back. There was a nervous-looking couple with a very young baby and several older retired couples who looked as if they spent much of their lives on cruises and had presumably turned up to add to the property portfolios that funded them. She could see Patrick and Helen at the front of the room. Patrick, clutching a folder of paperwork, was pacing like a lion and Helen was trying to get him to sit down.

Just as she was resolving to join them, the door beside her opened and Jonno came in, followed by Ben.

She turned away. Whatever gave between her and Ben – his apparent hatred of her mother, his mysterious pact with Jonno – she realised suddenly the last thing she wanted to do was tackle it now.

Ben had other ideas.

'Maddy,' he said, pulling her into a hug. Feeling his strength and warmth, her knees went weak and her eyes filled.

'I heard about Josh,' he said, into her ear. 'Are you alright? Have you spoken to Serena today?' He released her and looked down into her face.

Maddy ducked her head to hide her sudden tears. 'Yeah, yeah,' she said. 'I'm fine. It was awful, though . . . I talked to Giles last night, not Serena. We don't know anything yet.'

'I might go up there after this,' he said. 'Do you want to come?'

'Yes,' said Maddy, with relief, partly because she wanted to see how Serena was, partly because she loved the idea of spending a couple of hours in the car with Ben, drawing strength from him and sharing the horrors of the previous few hours with him. 'I'd love to come. Let's do that.'

'Excellent,' said Ben. 'Right, let's get this over with eh, Jonno?'

He and Jonno then took up their places near the back and Maddy, reluctantly, went to the front to join Patrick and Helen.

'Ready?' she said, as she sat down beside them.

'As we'll ever be,' said Patrick, patting his folder of paperwork and waving his auction paddle. 'We can go to three hundred and twenty-three thousand – a damned fair price. It's not worth more.'

'Not as a pub, it's not,' said Helen, giving him a frustrated look. 'But if that property developer is here . . .'

'Which he is,' said Maddy, looking behind her and spotting him, along with Dennis, his obsequious and permanently present lapdog.

'Well, then,' said Helen, frustrated. 'You *know* he's going to bid up the amount,' she said to Patrick. 'It's worth more than three hundred grand as a building plot. You need to . . .' she stopped, shaking her head with irritation.

'What's going on?' said Maddy, looking from one of them to the other.

Patrick looked mutinous and said nothing.

'Patrick won't let me join the community funding syndicate.'

'Why ever not?' asked Maddy.

'That's hardly what your mother is referring to,' said Patrick tetchily. 'I wouldn't mind if she was proposing chucking in a grand in return for voting rights, but that's not what she's talking about at all.'

'Mum?'

Helen looked away and tutted. 'Look,' she said, 'I have

319

simply proposed that – if Patrick and I are seriously going to give our relationship a chance – I would dearly like to invest some money in the Havenbury Arms. I'd sell the house and put perhaps a hundred thousand pounds into it. But this man won't contemplate having a useful extra hundred thousand to add to a potential bid – purely' – here she shot him a furious look – 'because it's me doing it.'

'I will not be a kept man,' he muttered, crossing his arms and his legs with finality.

'And that,' she said, 'is that. Apparently. So we had better hope the three hundred and twenty whatever-it-is thousand is enough, hadn't we?'

She turned away from Patrick and, like him, crossed her arms.

Just as Maddy was wondering what on earth to do or say, the auctioneer bounded onto the stage and picked up the gavel.

It turned out the young couple *were* after a renovation project. They bid bravely on a near-derelict three-bedroom cottage against a couple of hardbitten builders and were tearfully triumphant. Maddy silently wished them luck and hoped they hadn't spent their entire budget on buying the property in the first place.

Other lots, a flat above a chip shop, a row of garages and several shabby ex-council houses went swiftly under the hammer and then – before any time seemed to have elapsed at all – the Havenbury Arms was next up.

Dennis, Maddy noticed, sat forward in his seat, licking his lips, as the auctioneer whizzed quickly through the details. He started the bidding at one hundred thousand pounds and Patrick jumped in strongly with the first bid. After that, others seemed reluctant to come forward and Maddy wondered – for a mad moment – whether it would go for that. Then the property developer raised his paddle and they were off. The bidding rose quickly to two hundred and seventy thousand pounds, rising in tens of thousands of pounds. At three hundred thousand, Patrick's bidding became more hesitant and the auctioneer, responding, reduced the increments to five thousand. Maddy watched, on the edge of her seat as the price rose – three hundred and ten thousand, three hundred and fifteen thousand, three hundred and twenty . . . She looked at Patrick in despair. He, in turn, was staring desperately at the auctioneer. Behind him the property developer's paddle was whisking up again and again, showing no sign of stopping. Just as Patrick, anguished, steeled himself to raise his paddle for what must be his final bid, the auctioneer's eye was caught.

'And we have a new bidder at the back of the room,' he announced. 'Do I hear three hundred and twenty-five thousand pounds?'

There was a shuffling sound as everyone, including Maddy, turned to see the new bidder. Maddy twisted around just in time to see Jonno confirm the bid with a sharp nod. Ben sat, impassive, at his side. He didn't look at Maddy or Patrick.

She then watched, horrified, as Jonno and the property developer went head-to-head. The bidding raced to four hundred thousand . . . five hundred thousand . . . Maddy couldn't even bring herself to look at Patrick and Helen as the final death knell of the bidding resolved, with the lot being eventually knocked down at five hundred and ninety-seven thousand pounds.

To Jonno.

Jonno and Ben, without looking at Patrick, immediately got up and went to seal the deal with the paperwork. Dennis's face was contorted, Maddy noticed, as he simultaneously commiserated with the property developer – who was looking very cross indeed – and failing to wipe the smug, triumphant look off his face at the size of the final figure. He would probably get a fat bonus from Top Taverns for this. Didn't Ben once say that the pub companies were just masquerading at pulling pints, being far more interested in playing the property market? Suddenly, the memory of her first meeting with him flooded back into her mind. He had been there, with Dennis, playing the part of someone who was interested in buying the pub. Or so he had told her.

Maddy's stomach churned and fierce tears at the betrayal sprang to her eyes.

She faced front again. The auctioneer was well away with the next lot so they couldn't even get up and leave. Patrick was rigid beside her, facing front, a muscle ticking in his jaw. Helen, on the other side of him, was bright pink, choking back tears.

At last the next lot was knocked down and the three of them rose to leave.

Thankfully Dennis had already gone but Ben was still outside, waiting.

'How could you?' said Maddy, furious that he was seeing her tears, which she dashed away angrily.

'Maddy, I—'

'It's been that all along, hasn't it?' she asked. 'You and your mate Jonno.'

'No, listen . . . I'm sorry.'

'All's fair in love, war and business, I suppose,' she observed bitterly. 'Was the whole pretending to be interested in stopping Kevin thing just part of the plan? I suppose you were wanting to see whether the business could be profitable – sizing up whether it was worth Jonno buying it . . . I might have guessed . . .'

'Maddy,' said Ben firmly, grasping her upper arms, 'you need to let me explain. We can talk on the way to the hospital.'

For a moment Maddy wavered, then Helen's voice pierced her concentration.

'It's not, you stupid man,' she was shouting. 'You just think it is, because you're a stubborn, proud, reactionary old dinosaur. You always have been, and you always bloody will be. I don't know why I bother . . .'

Patrick replied, too low for Maddy and Ben to hear and then Helen's voice rang out again.

'Fine,' she said, making a flinging motion with her arm. 'The feeling is mutual.'

'I have to go,' said Maddy, pulling away from Ben and turning her back. 'I have to help the people I can still trust.' Her voice wobbled on the final words and she stalked away.

'Go for it,' Helen was saying. 'Knock yourself out. Throw away everything that ever mattered.'

'I'm not throwing anything away,' said Patrick, beating his head in frustration. 'The pub has been *taken* away. I have nothing to offer. Nothing to give you. I am not prepared to drag you into my problems, woman. Just go.'

He stared at Helen fiercely. Helen stared back in exasperation and then she seemed to sag.

'Get me out of here,' she said to Maddy. 'Please.'

CHAPTER TWENTY-SEVEN

Not knowing what else to do, Maddy brought Helen back to Home Farm. She took her into the Grainstore and made her a cup of tea. Her mother was swinging wildly between fury and tears and Maddy sat, patiently, doling out tissues, wondering how Serena and Giles were getting on and who was looking after Harry. Presumably Flora was there with him. She should go and check. She imagined briefly how Ben must be at the hospital by now, holding Serena, offering comfort, doubtless bringing them up to date on his and Jonno's triumph in taking the Havenbury Arms away from poor Patrick, thereby ruining his life and Helen's. Thinking about it was too awful even for tears. She envied her mother's ability to cry.

'Even if he had accepted your money,' Maddy offered at one point, 'it still wouldn't have been enough. Jonno's paying nearly six hundred thousand for it, isn't he? You could never have raised that.'

'Doesn't mean we couldn't still be together,' countered Helen. 'We had options, even without the pub, but – of course – he refuses to be with me if he can't support me. I mean how ridiculous is that in this day and age?'

The conversation continued in a circular vein, with Helen apologising, quite unnecessarily, on Patrick's behalf for being a deadbeat father and useless partner. 'Thank goodness I haven't wasted the last twenty-five years on him,' was her constant defiant refrain, closely followed by heartbroken bouts of crying.

After the third cup of tea, a near whole box of tissues and much repetition, Maddy excused herself to go and check on Harry. She discovered him and Flora holed up in the little television room, side by side in a nest of cushions and throws on the sofa with crisp packets scattered all around. They were binge-watching a box set of *Breaking Bad*, which Harry was hugely enjoying, mainly because he knew his mum would be horrified at all the swearing and violence.

Having established that Flora would, eventually, feed him something slightly more nutritious for supper, Maddy returned to the Grainstore to discover her mother curled up, exhausted and asleep on the sofa. She covered Helen with a throw and chucked another log into the stove as quietly as she could. Then, deciding not to bother with food, although she'd eaten nothing all day, she went back to the farmhouse and occupied herself with plans for the London trade show, which she was clearly going to have to manage without Serena or Flora.

Back in Serena's kitchen, checking stock and ticking off the list was therapeutically absorbing. She was worried about the new challenge of getting everything into her car and sent a prayer of thanks for her foresight in having got the display boards produced in one-metre sections, which would stick together with Velcro. She and Serena had chosen just three photos from Keith's portfolio and had them blown up huge. The impact should be brilliant.

They had planned to bring some straw bales to display the samples and brochures on but that really wasn't going to be feasible with just Maddy's little car. She made herself a cup of tea on the Aga and leant against it thoughtfully. Hiring furniture from the exhibition organisers was a possibility, but the choice on the exhibitor website was pretty dire and even a couple of small tables or plinths were astonishingly expensive. She tapped her teeth. The cardboard boxes she was transporting the stock in weren't a bad size and shape, as long as they were strong enough. She took a few, emptied them and experimented. Even empty, once they were taped shut they sat on top of each other pretty well. Grabbing a couple of the beautiful woven, vegetable-dyed woollen blankets, she draped and folded them to cover the boxes and stood back appraisingly. Not bad.

'Harry?' she called.

She heard a faint reply and footsteps. 'Yes,' said Harry, coming into the kitchen and brushing his hair out of his eyes.

'Darling, does Mummy have a sewing box at all? I need some pins . . .'

'She's not really a sewing sort of mummy,' Harry admitted. 'She does do my Cubs badges. She's not very good. I think her stuff's in the study.'

Maddy smiled. 'You need to do your sewing badge,' she suggested. 'Then you can do your own.'

By dint of rummaging, she and Harry found a small stash of sewing materials in a desk drawer.

'Eureka!' said Maddy, spotting a clear plastic box of safety pins.

After a bit more experimenting in the kitchen, folding and safety-pinning the blankets so they draped neatly and securely, she was happy enough.

Rather than wait until the last minute, she got the car loaded, with Harry's help, right down to the exhibitor pack, the brochures, Blu-tack, scissors, Sellotape, a book for visitors to give their contact details and a box for business cards. By the time they had got everything in and ticked it all off her list it was evening. With Flora having left to go back to Jez at last, it was clearly down to Maddy to sort out some supper for Harry and her mother.

Deciding that sending a text to Serena would be less intrusive than calling, she reassured her that all was well with Harry and the organisation for the exhibition and that she need do nothing other than worry about Josh. She signed off with her love. She didn't mention Ben and hoped Serena wouldn't think it strange. Presumably Ben would have now told her that, thanks to him and his friend, everything was over for Patrick and – consequently – for Helen. She wondered whether Jonno intended to close the pub to kill the competition or perhaps keep running it. Maybe Ben was getting a kickback for his role. Chances are the knocking down and replacing with houses option was the most profitable, so she assumed that was what the two men were intending. Either way, she was pretty certain there was no role for Patrick in Jonno's plans.

Maddy had a rummage in Serena and Giles's larder. Luckily Serena ran a pretty organised household and she had no trouble rustling up pasta with a tomato and olive sauce, along with a big salad and some garlic bread. Harry had huge amounts of grated cheddar cheese on his and ate masses. Even Helen, who Maddy had fetched from the Grainstore, was persuaded to eat and to polish off a large glass of red wine. She was calmer now, still tear-stained but far too stoic to cry in front of Harry. Instead, she chatted to him engagingly, telling him stories about the naughty things Maddy got up to at his age, many of them exaggerated, if not totally made up, much to Maddy's pretend outrage.

She gave her mum a smile and poured her another glass of wine.

'Let me get this one to bed,' she said. 'And then we can relax.'

Harry seemed to be bearing up pretty well. He was happy to choose a book to read to himself and to submit to lights out after fifteen minutes. The only wobble came when – again – he was checking he wouldn't be alone.

'Will you sleep there again?' he said, pointing at Josh's bed.

'Would you like me to?'

Harry nodded.

'Then I will,' said Maddy. 'Actually I might go and put *my* pyjamas on before I go to bed tonight.'

Downstairs, her mother had other plans.

'I can sleep in Harry's room, darling. You've got to get some proper rest tonight, if you're going to get up at the crack of dawn to get to London. I'll need to look after Harry tomorrow, anyhow. I may as well be in the farmhouse with him when he wakes up.'

Maddy hadn't thought of that. 'It would be brilliant if you would, Mum,' she said. 'But . . .' she hesitated. 'What about Patrick?'

'What about him?'

'Really?' said Maddy. 'Don't you think you ought to go back? To the pub? You need to talk . . .'

Helen sighed. 'I'm not sure we do. It's just impossible, darling. It was impossible twenty-five years ago and it's impossible now.'

She looked at Maddy and saw the bleak look in her daughter's eyes.

'This doesn't stop you having a relationship with him,' she said. 'He's your father, God help you. Now you know . . .'

'Do you love him?'

Helen thought. 'Yes,' she said at last. 'Always have. Probably always will. But look at us, for goodness' sake. Before he pushed me away, supposedly for my own good, and now he swears he's doing the same thing again. There's no talking to him.' She took a mouthful of wine and swilled it around thoughtfully before swallowing.

'I'm going home,' she said, 'back to something solid. Something safe. So I know where I stand.'

'Please don't,' implored Maddy. 'Stay. Talk to him. You've got to try.'

'No point.'

'You're both as bad as each other,' snapped Maddy, frustrated. 'Look,' she went on, 'stay at the Grainstore. Just for a few days. I'm in London tomorrow. After that . . .'

'What?' pressed her mother. 'What about you and Ben?'

'There is no "me and Ben",' protested Maddy. 'There never was,' she said. 'And there definitely isn't now.'

'Will you stay?'

'No,' said Maddy. 'Why would I?'

Maddy found her mother some pyjamas and a spare toothbrush and then went back to the Grainstore alone.

The first nightmare woke her at three in the morning. This one was about the pub; the shrieking laughter, the distorted faces and the panicky desire to get out and be alone. Staring out at the moonlit countryside she quelled her fear and waited for her heart rate to slow. Drifting off again the next nightmare woke her immediately. This was the old one about the dark, the fear and the pain.

It took hours and all his diplomatic skills for Ben to persuade Patrick to sit down with Jonno and talk. By the time he felt he could safely leave them it was late and he still had to get up to London to sit with Serena and Giles at Josh's bedside. Before he went, though, there was one more conversation he needed to have. Turning off the main road into the narrow track that lead to Home Farm he crossed his fingers that Maddy would have gone to bed and that he could get Helen on her own.

Helen was making herself a cup of tea after making sure Harry was still sound asleep.

'You're the last person I want to see,' she said, when Ben came in.

'I understand that,' said Ben. 'Although I should have thought Patrick would be the very last person, surely?'

'Don't get smart with me,' she snapped, glancing at the ceiling and consciously lowering her voice to a furious hiss. 'You've betrayed my family, destroyed my relationship and God knows what you think you're doing to my daughter. Doubtless there's some Machiavellian plan to damage her too, you turncoat . . . over my dead body, by the way.'

'What?' said Ben, his diplomacy deserting him at last. 'Me Machiavellian? That's pretty rich coming from the woman who casually had an affair with a married man, whilst maintaining a relationship with someone else, with no thought of the consequences to his family.'

'I have no idea what you're talking about. Patrick's not

330

married and he never has been. I'm not surprised, mind you. I can't imagine anyone who'd be stupid enough to marry him.'

'This isn't about Patrick. This is about my father. And Maddy's.'

'Well then it is about Patrick, isn't it? He's Maddy's father, as I'm sure you now know.'

'So it suits you to currently say,' said Ben acidly. 'So if Patrick's now the daddy – which is all very convenient, isn't it? – then how do you explain cheating on him with my father twenty-five years ago.'

'What?' she said incredulous. 'I've never cheated on Patrick. For all his sins I never would, and I don't even know who your father is.'

'Mike? Motorbike Man? Ring a bell . . . ?'

Helen looked at him uncomprehendingly, for a moment, and then her face fell. 'Good Lord,' she whispered, 'what have I done? What have I done . . . ?'

He looked down at her for a moment and then, quietly, he pulled out a chair and sat heavily next to her at the table.

'You're Mike's child?' she said wonderingly, her eyes roaming over his face. 'He had two sons, didn't he? I remember the older one . . . Andrew.'

'He died.'

'I'm so sorry.' Her face crumpled and she reached out to put a hand on this arm. 'I didn't know. You poor boy. Losing your father and then . . .' Her eyes welled in sympathy. She reached for a piece of kitchen towel and rubbed them impatiently. 'Ben, I have done a terrible, terrible thing to you – I know I've hurt and confused you and I am so, so sorry – but, you have to believe . . . your father never cheated with me. To my knowledge he never cheated with anyone. He was a decent, lovely, honest man who loved his wife and sons dearly and was a loyal friend to Patrick. That's my memory of him. We were all devastated when he was killed. It was weeks before I left. My memory of those last few days here is of this deep, deep sadness . . .' She stared into space, remembering. 'I think that's why he popped into my head when Maddy was asking before she came here. I'm so sorry to have lied. It was just . . . I was wanting to protect her. It was spur of the moment and I panicked. I didn't mean to hurt you and I'm sorry I have.'

'But me and Maddy, we *must* be brother and sister,' said Ben. 'We've both got Dad's green eyes; Patrick's are brown.'

'Mine are green,' said Helen, impatient now. 'Look,' she said, leaning forward and pointing, quite unnecessarily, at her eyes, bloodshot with crying. 'Green. It's not so desperately unusual, you know.'

'So,' Ben was processing slowly, hardly daring to believe, 'if Patrick really is Maddy's father . . . then . . .'

'You poor darling,' said Helen. 'You've been torturing yourself all these weeks. No wonder she says you've been behaving oddly.' She looked at him with such pity and compassion Ben nearly laid his head in her lap.

'I care about her so much,' he said, his voice cracking.

'Makes two of us.'

'I'm glad she's not my sister.'

'So am I,' she laughed. 'But I'm hugely glad you met. She loves you. You do know that, don't you?'

Ben nodded, not trusting himself to speak. He looked at his watch. It was late. 'I've got to go to Serena and Giles,' he said. 'They need me.'

'Of course. But let me make you something to eat. Bacon

332

and eggs? And perhaps have a coffee before you drive . . .'

'That would be amazing.'

'And then,' she said, standing up and reaching for the frying pan. 'You seriously need to talk to my daughter.'

Another nightmare woke her and she switched on the bedside light. It was four o'clock. Wearily Maddy dragged herself out of bed and into the shower. Putting on her scruffy but comfortably familiar clothes an idea came to her.

She shivered as she walked to the car. The freezing rain fell lightly and she hoped that, at Olympia, she would be able to unpack the car under cover. Glancing again at her watch – coming up to five o'clock – she drove through the gate and away, switching on her radio and the car heater as she went.

Soon, on the main road, with the warmth and the comforting familiarity of the shipping forecast, her spirits lifted. The roads were clear except for the haulage trucks and the occasional police patrol car. She would take no time getting to London at this time of day. As the dawn broke, she thought back to when she made a similar journey, driving at dawn, to see Patrick in the hospital those few short months ago. Fearful and not knowing what to expect, her anxiety had heightened as she got closer to Havenbury. This time, driving towards London felt like a relief, with every mile taking her further away from the pressure cooker her life had become there.

It was time for a new start – but first she needed to tie up a few loose ends.

CHAPTER TWENTY-EIGHT

Arriving in Chiswick at around half past five in the morning, Maddy needed to kill a little time. She stopped at the garage on High Road, filled up with petrol and bought a vending-machine coffee to drink in the car. She looked at the unappetising food on offer and grabbed a bag of wine gums instead.

It was still only quarter to six when she pulled up outside hers and Simon's maisonette in their pretty little road off the high street. Miraculously there was a space directly outside the house, and she had a good view of the front garden and sitting-room window as she sat sipping her coffee. The scarlet geraniums she had planted in the window box had been allowed to die, a few withered leaves still clinging to skeletal stems. Behind them, on the windowsill inside, there was a large orchid with fleshy leaves and bright-pink flowers. Not Maddy's sort of thing. And not Simon's either, she would have thought.

Finishing her coffee, she looked at her watch. Just past six o'clock. That would do.

She checked her reflection in the driver's mirror. Not

good. Ah well. Getting out and locking the door, she walked confidently to the bright-red-painted front door and knocked. It seemed presumptuous to use her keys.

Nothing happened. She knocked again, rapping hard with the knocker three times. This time, she saw shadows moving in the obscured glass panels and the familiar rattle of the chain and locks.

The door opened and Simon was standing there, ruffled and bleary in his boxers and T-shirt.

'Oh my God!' he said, rubbing his eyes.

'No need to deify me,' she joked weakly. 'Just "Maddy" will do.'

No kiss of greeting was offered.

'You might have called.'

'I might, but it was a bit of a last-minute thing,' she explained. 'May I?' she added, gesturing. It was her flat too, after all.

'Yeah,' he said slowly, and then gathered himself. 'Yes, of course, do. We – I – was in bed.'

She raised an eyebrow.

'Well . . .' said Simon defensively as they went through to the kitchen at the end of the hallway, 'you can't reasonably expect . . . We talked. Your email . . .'

She could hardly criticise. She may have failed to get Ben into bed with her, but it wasn't for want of trying.

'I'm not blaming you,' she told Simon. 'Look, I'm not here to be awkward . . . to make trouble . . . and I'm sorry for just showing up too,' she said.

He nodded his head sharply. 'Yeah . . .' he said, clearly examining and liking the position of 'aggrieved ex-boyfriend' better than being cast as the guilty party.

'Coffee?'

'I'm fine, thanks. So, do I know her?'

'No, don't think so. We met through work. She's the one I was telling you about. Alexis. She came in to help when you – er . . . became sort of "absent without leave".' He shot her a look.

Maddy nearly laughed. He had always been lazy. The idea of deciding the freelance worker could also slot into the absent girlfriend role to save him the bother of looking elsewhere was typical of him.

'So clearly Alexis is a woman of many talents,' she teased. 'Sorry,' she added. It was hardly the girl's fault and – after all – she was taking something Maddy no longer wanted.

At that moment, there was a shuffling noise and a pretty, tousle-haired, sleepy-looking woman wearing one of Simon's T-shirts appeared in the kitchen doorway.

'You must be Alexis,' said Maddy, standing and holding out her hand. 'I'm so sorry to disturb you both so early. I'm Maddy.'

Alexis immediately stiffened, halfway through the act of holding out her hand to shake Maddy's. She shot a look at Simon and then back at Maddy.

'It's fine,' said Maddy. 'I appreciate it's all a bit ad hoc, but I'm just really aware I've left people dangling a bit over the last couple of months and I'm here to sort things out.'

'Are you staying in Sussex, then?' asked Simon.

'Actually no,' said Maddy with a pang, blinking back the tears that sprang to her eyes. 'I'm going to come back here.'

He shifted uneasily on his seat.

'Not "here" here,' she clarified. 'That's what we need to sort out. I'll need to get my own place.'

'Fine,' said Simon, with relief. 'You'll have to let us all know when you're settled.'

'Mm . . . sorry to be the bearer of bad tidings but it's a bit more complicated than that. I'm going to need to sort this place out with you. My name's on the lease, remember, and half the deposit is mine too. I'm going to need that back, I'm afraid.'

'Yes, yes, fine. I'll have to deal with that. Next week do you?'

'Brilliant,' she said, relieved. Funds in her account were now so low, the deposit return was in danger of being swallowed up in living expenses.

'And what about your stuff?' he asked. 'We could do with the space, to be honest . . .'

'Sure, no problem. I was wondering if I could grab some of my clothes. I'll arrange to collect the rest as soon as I can. You don't have a couple of bin bags by any chance, do you?'

Alexis rummaged in a drawer and handed her a roll. 'Let me give you a hand,' she said.

It was odd going into the bedroom where she and Simon had slept for nearly three years. Alexis's clothes were scattered around the room. Maddy was sure Simon would have a problem with that. The bedding was new, too – a fussy Chinoiserie print she couldn't imagine he would have chosen. None of the make-up and other clutter on the dressing table was Maddy's.

Alexis saw her looking. 'Sorry, your stuff . . . Look, I just put it in this drawer.' She opened it and they both looked inside. It was a pretty paltry effort in comparison with the top. Alexis was clearly a much more glamorous woman than Maddy was, or would ever be.

'I don't need this stuff right now,' she said. 'But the clothes . . . ?'

Alexis went swiftly to the wardrobe. 'Here,' she said, opening the furthest door to the right on the wall of wardrobe space, which Simon had been impressed by when they viewed the flat. 'Plenty of storage,' he had said to the letting agent, as if he was selling to her and not vice versa.

Maddy's clothes were shuffled up, on hangers, to the far side of the space.

'And here,' she continued, lifting the lid of the blanket box at the end of the bed.

'I'll get all this out of your way.' Maddy lifted armfuls out of the wardrobe and folded them into a bin bag, hangers and all. She then scooped the contents of the box into another two bin bags and she was done.

'So,' said Simon, who had now showered and got dressed, rediscovering his bullish demeanour, 'thanks for your email about the pitch and the partnership. Obviously disappointed not to have you on board and all that . . .'

Alexis looked at Simon sharply. Maddy wondered whether he had shared the whole business plan idea with her. Probably not.

'I appreciate your understanding,' said Maddy. 'I hope the presentation draft was helpful.'

'Yeah, it was a start,' he said ungenerously. 'We'll let you know how we get on, shall we?'

'Do.'

'And I'll get onto the lease thing, pronto, and all that . . .' He trailed off, looking around the flat vaguely.

'I'll leave you to decide whose is whose,' said Maddy, who genuinely, she discovered with surprise, really didn't care about splitting their possessions.

Her eyes lighted on the large wooden duck she had bought when they had both gone to Indonesia. They used it as a doorstop for the sitting-room door that had an annoying tendency to swing shut. Simon had pronounced it hideous at first sight. Maddy consequently haggled and bought it, defiantly lugging it around for the rest of their trip.

'I'll take this, shall I?' she said, picking it up and tucking it under her arm.

'Be my guest,' said Simon, with a genuinely warm smile at last. 'I really do wish you well, Maddy,' he said, sweeping her into a cautious hug.

She hugged him back with the arm that wasn't holding the duck. 'So do I, Simon. So do I,' she said, her smile wobbling only slightly.

He then crammed the bin bags of clothes in and around the exhibition stock and display materials. The duck had taken up residence on top of Maddy's paperwork on the front seat, where it stared glassily through the windscreen.

Alexis and Simon stood in the doorway, arms around each other's waists, to wave Maddy off. She could imagine them breathing a sigh of relief as soon as she turned the corner out of sight.

CHAPTER TWENTY-NINE

On the main road the traffic had increased substantially. Maddy looked at her watch. Already seven o'clock and she still had to get to Olympia, negotiate the unloading issues, set up the stand and change into clothes, which currently lurked in one or more of the bin bags.

The traffic crawled and Maddy's stress levels rose. She switched on the radio to distract her but the jolly, high-energy breakfast programme felt too frenetic and the frequent traffic reports and time checks just added to the tension. She switched it off and concentrated on the car in front.

The dawn had given way to a gloomy winter's day, with a steel-grey sky producing frozen rain, which fell intermittently, making her switch her windscreen wipers on, then off again, every few minutes.

At last, her satnav guided her into the exhibition centre where she was greeted by a jovial security man, who checked out her paperwork and explained where to unload and park.

Serena had done well with the stand position. It was to the left of the main entrance, opposite one of the cafes and far enough in not to fall foul of the human tendency not to focus on what you are looking at for at least the first few metres. It was small, though, just two metres deep and three metres across the front.

The aisle space in front of the stands was crammed with stock and materials, and people stepped over each other's stuff to set up their own stands. Thanks to the Velcro dots Maddy had pre-stuck on the display boards, they all went up without a hitch and looked great. She took a quick picture on her phone and texted it to Keith the photographer and to Serena. Then, she got on with setting up the products. She was glad she had practised in Serena's kitchen. She saw a couple of the other stand holders looking askance at her pile of cardboard boxes but, once they were carefully draped with the blankets and had the other products laid out on them, Maddy thought they looked just as good as the other stallholders' much more elaborate and expensive solutions. The straw bales would have looked great, though. They could do that next time. If there was a next time.

Right, Maddy thought to herself, the stand was looking appreciably better than she was, with her hair on end and the scruffy jeans she had put on what felt like aeons ago. She made one last trip out to the car and, this time, rummaged in her bin bags. Extracting a charcoal-grey trouser suit and an uncreased burnt-orange camisole top that would subtly echo the Bespoke Consortium brand colours, she rummaged again through the one which contained her shoes for a pair of ankle boots with killer heels. She moved the car to the outside car park and trudged back with her bundle of clothes and her handbag through the icy rain to the ladies' loos nearest her stand. In a tiny cubicle she shimmied her way into her smarter clothes, grateful that the suit trousers had a belt with

341

sufficient holes in it to stop them falling down. She tightened it three holes more than the mark showed she had before.

The orange camisole leant a little colour to her face, thankfully. As she put on make-up, smearing foundation to eliminate her freckles, she noticed her cheekbones seemed to have emerged, needing less blusher than usual to disguise her round face. Taking care to make up her eyes with sharply defined liner, several coats of mascara and a neutral eyeshadow with chestnut brown shaded carefully into the socket, she stepped back to assess the effect. A slick of a dark lipstick she hardly ever wore completed the look. Wetting her hair to get it smooth, she wrestled it into a small bun at the nape of her neck, pulling it straight so it came back off her face completely. This was the severe, polished look she had got used to wearing in her London life. It was time to reacquaint herself with it.

'Wow,' came a voice when she returned to the stand, tip-tapping on the floor with her killer heels. 'You scrub up well.'

'Camilla,' said the owner of the voice, who was standing in front of the stand next to Maddy's. She held out her hand and Maddy shook it with a smile.

'Thanks,' she said. 'I needed an overhaul after this,' she waved her hand at her own stand.

'That scrubs up well too,' said Camilla. 'Your first time?'

Maddy nodded. 'Not my first exhibition, but this is a new thing. You?'

'Third year running. It's the only one I do – they're all so expensive, aren't they?'

Maddy nodded again. 'But you come back,' she said, 'so this is worth it, presumably?'

'I always get something,' said Camilla. 'I cover my costs and more,' she said. 'Still waiting for the big break, though, obviously. Got to be in it to win it and all that.'

'So true,' said Maddy, looking at Camilla's stand.

'Are these your designs?' she asked. Camilla had a series of single wallpaper strips decorating her stand. There was a samples book on the table too. Maddy made a note to take a look later. 'They're great, and they do look familiar . . .'

Camilla ducked her head modestly. 'I've got a few bits and bobs – cake tins and stuff – in John Lewis and I'm talking to another high street chain, which must remain nameless, about some bedding, which is really exciting.'

'It is!' said Maddy. 'Can I get you a coffee?' she asked, waving at the cafe opposite, where there was now a queue of exhibitors wanting refreshment before the doors opened to the visitors.

'That would be brilliant,' said Camilla, scrabbling in her back pocket for money. 'Double-shot cappuccino, please. We can take turns and mind each other's stands. I'm on my own today too.'

'Don't worry about money; it's on me this time.'

By the time they had both drunk their coffee, the game was on. There was not so much a sudden rush but a growing trickle as the exhibition visitors piled in. It was a trade show so the visitors were primarily buyers, ranging from the big, high street stores to many, many small retailers who Maddy was also very keen to court the attention of.

After just half an hour of catching people's eyes and smiling warmly at them all, handing out brochures and engaging in small talk she was already exhausted. Thank goodness it was only one day. Actually the briefness of the event had been one of the attractions for them all, although they hadn't been thrilled at how close it was to Christmas. *Less than a week*, thought Maddy, *and goodness knows where I'll be spending it.* Most likely back at her mother's house, just the two of them with their dual broken hearts, hers over Ben and her mother's over Patrick. She would be just another statistic, a boomerang kid, slinking back to parents after a failed attempt to be a grown-up, she thought gloomily.

By lunchtime, Maddy was pleased with her progress. She had filled a page and a half of her book with email addresses and other contact details. It was really important that the Bespoke Consortium had a regular e-newsletter and blog, she decided. She just hoped Serena and Flora would be prepared to accept her working in London. They could still meet regularly. Hopefully not in Havenbury but perhaps somewhere halfway.

Maddy was just idly wondering if the cafe had anything for sale that she a) would want to eat and b) could afford to buy with her dwindling finances when a sweet-faced young woman wandered onto the stand, gazing at the photos and paying a flattering interest in the sample goods on display. She picked up the little sheepskin moccasins, felt the wool blankets and ran one of the soft, woven scarves through her fingers, looking impressed.

'Hi there,' said Maddy. 'What do you think?'

'Very nice,' said the woman slowly. 'Yes, very nice indeed. And,' she gestured at the copy on the display boards, 'I like your story too. Local, authentic, bespoke . . . very good. Very much the sort of thing I'm looking for, in fact.' She paused and looked around again before seeming to make a decision.

'I'm Abby,' she said, holding out her hand. 'I'm a buyer for Liberty. May we talk?'

Maddy, registering what the woman said a millisecond after taking her hand, crushed it convulsively, making her jump and take a step back, leaving her hand behind in Maddy's vice-like grip.

'God,' said Maddy, letting go a second later and leaping back too as if she'd been electrocuted. 'I'm so sorry; are you alright?'

Abby rubbed her hand ruefully but laughed. 'Fine, thanks. I'm sorry, it's my fault; I do seem to have that effect on people. I really like your offer. Shall we go and grab some lunch and have a chat?'

'That would be lovely,' said Maddy slowly, 'but . . .' She looked around the stand, ruefully.

'Or we could eat here?' suggested Abby. 'I could go and grab something and bring it back?'

'Don't worry,' swooped in Camilla, who had been lurking nearby with her ears flapping. 'I'll do your brochures and contact book for a bit, if you like?'

Maddy moved over to her gratefully. Camilla grabbed her arm and hissed, 'Do you know who that is?'

'Yes,' whispered Maddy. 'I do now.'

'Go, girl,' said Camilla. 'Take as long as you like.'

Abby and Maddy had left it rather late for lunch so the queues weren't bad but the choice was. They settled themselves at a little table with some dubious-looking falafel and a couple of chocolate brownies. Abby efficiently stacked the rubbish left by previous occupants – clearly the waitresses had not yet caught up after the lunch rush – and removed them to a neighbouring table.

'Right,' she said, taking a swig of her water. 'Let's talk.'

She then explained that her bosses at Liberty had asked her to create a new range in the store, focusing exactly on the kinds of things the Bespoke Consortium valued, the local, natural materials, designer-makers, small volumes, bespoke finishing . . . Maddy listened to her talk with growing excitement.

'I want to place a smallish order for certain aspects of your range,' she said, using the brochure to mark off the goods that interested her.

'We're developing all the time,' said Maddy. 'We hope to have an artist blacksmith soon,' she explained, 'making coat hooks, fire irons, that sort of thing . . .'

'Brilliant,' said Abby. 'I want to see everything like that as it comes through. This is a working partnership I'm proposing here. A two-way street.'

'You should come down,' said Maddy.

'I'd love to. In the new year?'

'Perfect,' said Maddy, wondering where on earth she would be by then. Never mind, Serena and Abby would get on brilliantly. Serena was a buyer too, of course, plus she had Flora. They didn't need her.

Eventually, they agreed to keep in touch over the next few days with a firm first order from Abby by Christmas, which would give them a chunk of income pending, hopefully enough to secure the enterprise into the first few months of the new year.

By the time Maddy got back to the stand, she was euphoric. Camilla gave her a grin as she returned.

'That went well,' she said, as a statement of fact, rather than a question.

346

Maddy nodded. 'Think so,' she said. 'Who knows . . .'

'Nah,' said Camilla. 'It looks like a blinder to me. If you get nothing else out of this exhibition, I should have thought that one will justify the cost and time right there.'

Maddy suspected she was right. Looking at her watch was a relief too. Just an hour to go until they were allowed to pack up and call it a day. She picked up her phone to text Serena and then decided to give her a call instead.

She waited nervously as it rang. What if they were right in the middle of some crisis to do with Josh? What if the mobile phone signal did something awful to the equipment. Weren't people supposed to switch off their phones in hospital?

Just as it was about to go to 'message', Serena answered, sounding breathless.

'Maddy?'

'Oh God, Serena,' said Maddy. 'How's Josh?'

'I still don't know,' said Serena. 'It's been awful. We haven't slept. Giles has been a complete hero, managing everything. Asking all the questions. Josh has just been taken off his drugs and we're waiting . . .' She paused to compose herself. 'We're waiting to see if he wakes up or . . .'

'I'm so sorry,' said Maddy, 'the last thing you want is to hear from me. I was going to text.'

'No,' interrupted Serena, sounding stronger, 'I want to talk to you. I want to be able to talk about something else. How's it going? I'm so sorry you've been on your own.'

Maddy reassured her and then told her quickly about Abby. Serena was thrilled, shooting questions at her and then interrupting the answers. Maddy told her as much as she could and they both savoured the possibilities.

'Anyhow,' said Serena. 'Ben's here.'

'Ah,' said Maddy. 'I see.'

'You don't, actually. I really don't think you do. Look, the thing is, we're only a few miles away so Ben's coming.'

'What? No!'

'Yes,' said Serena. 'He's just setting off now. You two need to talk.'

'We do not.'

'Yes, you do,' insisted Serena. 'Anyway, he can give you a hand with the stuff.'

'I don't want a hand,' said Maddy, but Serena had hung up.

CHAPTER THIRTY

'Bugger,' said Maddy, and looked at her watch again. There was a chance, if the traffic was bad, which it almost certainly was, that she could get packed up and out of there before he arrived. Even though visitors were still straggling through the hall, she started surreptitiously packing up bits and pieces.

Just as she was starting to think about taking down the boards from the walls, she saw him walking towards her, his hair flopping over his forehead, a worn red polo shirt faded practically to pink because it had been washed so many times and an equally faded pair of jeans.

He was making eye contact from yards away but when he finally stood in front of her neither of them could think what to say or do.

'Wow,' he said at last, looking her up and down in her impeccable charcoal suit with her sleek hair and make-up. 'You've gone all cosmopolitan.'

'This is London me,' said Maddy. 'It's the real me.'

'I'm not sure that's true,' he said, reaching for her but she put up a hand and took a step back.

'No.'

He put up his hands in submission. 'Okay,' he said gently. 'No touching.'

There was another pause.

'How is Josh?'

Ben's eyes softened. 'He's amazing. Just before I left – after you spoke to Serena – he woke up. He's had a rough time, but he's in there. He's himself. It's just going to take a while. Basically he complained a bit and then told us all he's taking up skydiving as soon as he's old enough.'

She smiled at that. 'Sounds like Josh,' she said. 'At least he'll be wearing a parachute.'

Maddy's smile dissolved suddenly into tears. Ben pulled her towards him, into a reassuring hug.

'No,' she sobbed, into his shirt.

'Yes,' said Ben, holding her tighter and putting his chin on her head, because it was just the right height. 'I'm not put off by sleek, suited, sophisticated Maddy. That doesn't wash with me, I'm afraid. We love you. All of us. And we want you back.'

'You don't love all the people I care about,' protested Maddy, muffled by his chest.

'I know it seems that way . . .'

'Seems that way?' she exclaimed, making a fresh attempt to wriggle free. 'It's damned hard to see it any other way, frankly. You and your little mate Jonno have meticulously dismantled the life and livelihood of my father, ruining his relationship with my mother in the process, I might add. And,' she paused to steel herself to say it, 'obviously, as a result, that means I hate you.'

A laugh rumbled in Ben's chest, vibrating against her ear.

'Ah,' said Ben, 'about that . . .'

'I do! I hate you.' This time, when she struggled, he allowed her to pull away.

'Listen,' he said, this time grave-faced. 'It was terrible not being able to tell you what Jonno was trying to do. It was important to keep our plans under wraps – and in any case, it might not have worked out.'

'It bleeding well hasn't "worked out",' she pointed out furiously. 'In what sense does Jonno pushing up the bid price and snatching the pub out from under Patrick's nose constitute things having "worked out"? I mean,' she went on, 'I'm sure they've "worked out" for Jonno in some way. God knows what his plans are – to run the pub, run it down, knock it down for houses . . . either way, he holds all the cards now, doesn't he?' she finished, breathless with outrage.

'And I can't imagine a better man to be holding all the cards,' he said calmly, unmoved by her rage. 'Listen, Maddy, I don't expect you to take it from me, but hear this: Jonno is, as we speak, having a meeting with Patrick and Zach to talk about the way forward for the Havenbury Arms.'

'He is?'

Ben nodded. 'He is. Now, I'm not saying what's going to come of it, but believe me when I say Jonno is a decent man. His intention is to find a way for the Havenbury Arms to go forward with Patrick – and the community – taking some sort of role in its future.'

'Why all the secrecy, then?'

He tutted with irritation. 'He's a businessman,' he said. 'It's how these things go. The situation with Top Taverns was seriously dodgy and Jonno had an opportunity to get control. He took it. Now you,' he pointed at her, 'have to relax and let him sort stuff out.'

She took a deep breath and let it out. 'Okay,' she said. 'Fine.'

'So, can I take you home, please?'

'No.'

'Because . . . ?'

'I want to be here,' she said. 'In London. Like this. Being my London self . . .' she trailed off, helplessly, but Ben nodded.

'I get that,' he said. 'I do.'

'You've got your psychologist face on.'

'It's just my face,' smiled Ben. 'Honest. Although, I do admit, I've been talking to Duncan . . .'

'About me?'

'Yep. About the drink spiking. And the door being locked on the inside.'

'What about them?'

'Duncan thinks it's about time we sorted it out,' said Ben. 'And so do I.'

'I know how to do that too,' said Maddy. 'Be here. Do my London life thing. I've been fine here.'

'You mean going back to Simon?'

'Not exactly, no.' She explained briefly.

'And how does that make you feel . . . oops, sorry,' he said. 'I mean, well, what do I mean?'

'It was okay,' said Maddy. 'It was fine.'

Their eyes met. In the end it was Maddy who looked away. 'You'd sleep with me now, wouldn't you?' she asked. 'Now your scruples about Simon have been dispensed with.'

'Mm,' said Ben. 'It's not quite as simple as that.'

She sighed and then, without warning, she sank to the floor in the little exhibition stand, putting her head on her knees and wrapping her arms around them. Ben crouched down next to her, not touching her. Not speaking. Just waiting.

'I'm so tired,' she said at last, fat tears of self-pity welling up. She didn't just mean the last few nights of broken sleep, either. She was bone-tired. Tired of months where nightmares haunted her every night, where the fear of a panic attack dogged her, where she was responsible for the happiness of so many people: her mother, father, Serena and the Bespoke Consortium, even Ben . . . Down there on the floor, she almost drifted off to sleep, somehow feeling that with Ben beside her she could finally hand over – or at least share – everything she had been carrying since she first received the call that night in the autumn, telling her Patrick was so gravely ill.

Eventually, he pulled her gently to her feet.

'Come here,' he said, leading her over to the little cafe. He sat her down at a table in the corner and went to the counter. In magically quick time he returned with a steaming cup of tea and a chocolate muffin.

'Give me your car keys and get that into you.'

She handed them over and watched, in a daze, as he deftly and methodically deconstructed the stand.

She found that giving in to her fatigue had led her into a near-catatonic state. She could see her teacup but the strength and motivation to actually lift it to her lips had deserted her. She could barely feel her body as she sat slumped in the chair. She was vaguely aware of Ben lifting unfeasible numbers of boxes in his arms and disappearing to load them into the car before returning for more. He also took a load for Camilla, who turned to Maddy to give her a conspiratorial wink and thumbs up before staring blatantly at Ben's bum as he walked away.

'Let's go,' said Ben, suddenly in front of her. She must have drifted off. The stand was stripped back to its original state and many of the exhibitors had already made their escape.

He took her hand and she allowed him to lead her to the car. She went to get in the driver's door.

'Erm, I don't think so,' he said, steering her around to the other side.

'I like your duck,' he observed, picking it up off the passenger seat so Maddy could sit down and lobbing it into the back without ceremony.

'I can drive,' she protested.

'I highly doubt it. You're exhausted. In no fit state . . .'

'What about your car?'

'I slipped that nice man in the booth a twenty,' said Ben. 'He's going to look after it for me. I'll pop up on the train tomorrow.'

'I can't let you do that.'

'I insist,' said Ben who, bored with Maddy's protests, had inserted her into the passenger seat, taken up his position in the driver's seat as they discussed the matter and was already manoeuvring Maddy's car out of the car park.

'Please,' she said desperately, her words slurring with fatigue. 'Please don't take me back there.'

He didn't answer for a moment, concentrating on the mammoth roundabout he was negotiating in heavy traffic, having to change lanes repeatedly to follow his route out of London. The usual commuter traffic was augmented by all the people who travelled into town by car to do Christmas shopping. The Christmas lights were up and everywhere the shop windows had taken up the Christmas theme with enthusiasm.

'Look,' he said, 'I appreciate what you're saying about taking yourself out of the environment that you find so triggering but I truly, truly believe we can do something better than that for you.'

He reached over and took her hand. Such was her exhaustion it just laid limply in his, like a dead fish.

'Let us try and help you. Me and Duncan. Make it so you can make the choice for yourself. London or Havenbury. You decide where you want to be, don't let this crap decide for you. In Havenbury you have people who care about you. Don't turn your back on that.'

He withdrew his hand and returned his gaze to the road. They were still negotiating heavy traffic, edging their way down and across to the road that would take them home.

Maddy made the mammoth effort to move her head so she could stare out of the passenger window. It took several goes.

Time passed. The traffic thinned and the car's speed increased a little. Soon they would be out of town, travelling along the darkened country roads back to Havenbury.

'Okay,' she said.

'To what?'

'I'll see Duncan. But it has to be tonight.'

'I don't know about that. You're really shattered. He might not be free . . .'

'It has to be this evening. I can't go through another night . . .' she said, anguished, staring at Ben with pleading eyes. 'I just can't.'

He took his eyes off the road and looked at her.

'Okay,' he said. 'Let me see what I can do. Are we going back to the Grainstore?'

'My mum's there. She and Patrick have fallen out.'

'Ah, I'd forgotten that. Looks like it's my place, then.'

Steering with one hand, Ben pulled into a side road and got out his mobile. Duncan answered straight away.

CHAPTER THIRTY-ONE

The next thing Maddy knew they were braking sharply.

'Sorry,' said Ben, seeing he had woken her. 'Car in front. Caught me by surprise.'

She sat up to see they were at the red lights at the bottom of the Havenbury Magna high street, just past the docks and Sails nightclub.

'That's okay,' she said, her fists balling in tension. The whole Jonno, Patrick and Helen situation came flooding back, with – of course – the underlying fear that had dogged her all the months she had spent there. Tears rose and her heart quickened.

'Anxious?'

'Same old, same old,' she said, taking a deep breath and trying to let it out slowly.

'Nearly there.'

'I actually don't know where you live,' she said. 'Which is weird when you think about it.'

'Not really,' said Ben. 'I've been trying to be the perfect gentleman, remember.'

'You mean you're going to stop being the perfect gentleman now?' Hopefully he was.

They were bumping down a rough country road she didn't recognise now, with the river on one side and the lonely marshes on the other.

'It's a bit rough, I'm afraid,' said Ben. 'Does nothing for the MGB, I can tell you.'

'Not sure my little car's exhaust is up to it either,' said Maddy, straightening up and smoothing her hair, which had more or less escaped the tight little bun it had been in all day. She fiddled for a moment or two and then, frustrated suddenly, she took out the clips and shook it loose instead.

'That's better,' said Ben, glancing sideways.

'I didn't realise there were any houses down here,' said Maddy. The confines of Havenbury Magna were sharply delineated by the wetlands at the foot of the hill it perched on. The marshes were unsuitable for building which kept them safe from development on the whole. Or so she had thought.

'Is this it?' she said, as they came across a little wooden one-storey building with a pitched roof on the river side of the track.

'It's a boathouse,' he said. 'At least it was. I've converted the inside now. It's basic, but it's home.'

She could make out little detail in the dark, but there were lights on and a car she assumed was Duncan's was already there.

Ben squeezed Maddy's car in next to it and got out, coming around her side to help her out.

'I'm not ninety,' she complained.

'No, but I don't want you to trip in those heels,' he said patiently. 'The ground's a bit uneven.'

She was glad of his arm as they walked the short distance to the door. She shivered in the cold, damp air and that, coupled

357

with her having been newly reunited with the anxiety that dogged her in Havenbury, made her unsteady on her feet.

There was a sweet little wooden porch canopy over the doorway, illuminated with a fisherman's light, and Maddy noticed the roof was clad not with the red clay tiles most buildings had around there but with cedar shingles.

'It looks like a little gingerbread cottage,' she said, charmed.

'It needs painting,' said Ben. 'Wooden buildings are a constant maintenance headache it turns out.'

The door opened onto one large room, which was open to the wooden rafters of the roof. Limed floorboards were partly covered with a large kelim rug and kitchen units ran along one wall. There was a series of tall, floor-length windows along the wall facing the river, each currently covered with thick grey, watermarked silk curtains that pooled on the floor. A small scrubbed table with four wooden chairs sat in one corner, and a low, comfortable-looking sofa, flanked with armchairs, was arranged to make the most of the daytime view. Tonight, though, lamps on low tables and a giant floorstanding anglepoise lamp created intimate pools of light. A door in the far wall led, presumably, to a bedroom and bathroom.

Duncan came forward and shook Maddy's hand with a decorous formality at odds with his casual manner at their last meeting in the pub. 'Hello, Maddy,' he said. 'How are you?'

'Fine,' she said, clamping her jaw shut to suppress her chattering teeth. 'Thanks for coming.'

'Ben said you needed to see me tonight, urgently, so I'm more than happy . . . although I'm not sure . . .' He gave her an appraising look. 'Come on,' he said, making a decision. 'Let's sit down and have a chat.'

He settled himself in the chair opposite her and rested his hands on his knees. This was clearly the professional Duncan, calm, in control, his gentle grey eyes watching her with intelligence but no judgement.

'So, first of all, what makes you feel I need to try and help you tonight?'

'I didn't want to come back here,' Maddy explained. 'I just feel like I can't go through another night. I can't. Not if I have to be here.'

'That's okay,' said Duncan. 'I can go with that. We can talk, tonight, and then we can decide what we are going to do next. No pressure. Sound like a plan?'

So Maddy went through the whole thing again: the story of what happened that night including her memories and also her new knowledge; her departure from Havenbury, her new life in London and then her return to look after Patrick, triggering panic attacks that then escalated after she broke her leg again. And now, the impossibility of even being in Havenbury because of the constant, crippling fear and anxiety that was seemingly only reduced by being somewhere else.

Duncan listened, nodding and taking notes. Eventually Maddy came to the end.

'Okay, listen,' he said. 'Like I mentioned before, Ben and I have been developing treatment strategies for soldiers with PTSD. We think we can help you with hypnosis.'

'Okay,' said Maddy, her heart beating a little faster.

'That approach is nothing new or unusual. What Ben and I are looking at is the mutable quality of memories.'

'What do you mean?' asked Maddy.

'Our memories are actually quite open to change. Not fixed and absolute like we might have thought before. Studies have shown that people, under the right conditions, can be persuaded to remember all sorts of things that haven't actually happened to them.'

'So, do you think my nightmares are memories that haven't actually happened to me?' said Maddy, bristling.

'No, no,' Duncan said hastily. 'I'm actually coming at it precisely the other way. I'm saying we are looking at how we can take a distressing memory and we can – under the right conditions – make it less distressing by, basically, attaching it to a new thought, a new "memory", which can halt this endless loop of distressing remembering by, sort of, giving a happy ending to the story, if you like.'

'Okay,' said Maddy slowly. 'I can see how that *might* work, but – in my case – I'm not sure I can actually remember enough of whatever it is that terrifies me to even create a happy ending.'

'Actually,' said Duncan, 'I think you're an excellent case. We now know that your drink was spiked, which certainly explains the nightmarish and disjointed quality of the fragments of memory you have of that night.'

'Plus, of course,' added Maddy, with wry humour, 'I fell on my head.'

'Yeah, that too,' acknowledged Duncan, with a smile. 'All this adds to the confusion. And – if we accept that you, somehow, ended up going out of your bedroom window . . .' he looked at her for confirmation and she nodded, 'then it's pretty useful to know the door was bolted from the inside.'

'In other words, that it was just my drug-induced dementedness that made me jump, fall, or whatever and not any real person pursuing me,' said Maddy. She had played with these thoughts before but, somehow, going through it all with Duncan there, she was able to look at it all in a more clear and objective way, and a little of the tension she had held in her for years, and certainly for the last few months, ebbed quietly away.

'Exactly,' said Duncan, noticing. 'That's good.'

'So, what now?'

'Well,' he said, looking at his watch, 'perhaps not necessarily now, but – now we've discussed it . . .'

'No!' Maddy's vehemence surprised both of them. Ben, in the kitchen, even glanced over at the sound.

'I mean,' she said, wiping her tears away with her fingers. 'Please can we do it now?'

'Okay,' said Duncan. 'How much do you know about hypnotism?'

'Stage shows, mainly. Rod Stewart impressions with mop handles as mike stands? That sort of thing?'

'Right.' He smiled. 'Well. It's nothing like that.'

'Okay.'

'What it is,' he explained, 'is the kind of mind state our brains go into quite often and naturally, when we're doing a repetitive task perhaps, or just daydreaming, letting our minds wander. It's basically a state of profound relaxation and enhanced suggestibility. In it – guided by someone like me – you can examine stuff. To be honest, it's easier to do than explain,' Duncan broke off, holding his hands apart. 'Shall we?'

She swallowed, nervously.

'Can we . . . ?' She paused. 'I mean, I know, with Ben, because he's a friend and stuff, it's weird.'

'It's not weird. Because it's not Ben. It's me.'

'And you're not a friend?'

'Nope,' said Duncan. 'Can't stand you.'

'But can I have Ben with me? When we – do this?'

'Yeah, of course. I don't have a problem with that. Mate,' called Duncan. 'You're on. We're doing it.'

Ben strolled over, taking a seat on the end of the sofa nearest Maddy, and giving her a reassuring smile.

Duncan turned to Maddy. 'Now, the thing about a hypnotic trance is that if you don't want to go into one you won't and there's nothing magic I can do to make it happen. Equally, if you want to stop at any time, you can. You're in control, got it?'

'Okay,' said Maddy nervously.

'Ready?'

She nodded, and Ben quietly leant back in his seat, watching her face closely, alert for any signs of distress.

'So,' said Duncan in a calm but normal voice, 'all I want you to do is relax and listen to my voice . . .'

Maddy sat back and let her mind drift, allowing Duncan's suggestions to gently wash over her. Quickly her consciousness narrowed. Her body felt heavy and formless and her eyelids began to droop.

'Your eyelids are feeling heavy,' came Duncan's voice, 'and soon, they start to feel so, so heavy, you might start to feel that you can't keep your eyes open any longer, so you might just want to let them close . . . like that . . . Just letting your eyes close now . . . That's good, Maddy, you're doing really well . . .'

Duncan and Ben shot each other a look. As Ben had guessed, she was hugely suggestible. He could see from the pulse in her neck that her heart rate had slowed. She was unmoving in the chair, her face smooth and expressionless.

He nodded to Duncan. They were there.

'So, Maddy,' said Duncan conversationally, 'I want you to take yourself back to the night you had your accident, but what I want you to do is stand to one side, okay? I want you to imagine you are in the corner of the room, just watching yourself doing the things that happened that night.'

The two men watched her carefully; she looked entirely relaxed. They waited, and then – almost imperceptibly – her head twitched to the side and a tiny frown formed on her brow.

'Where are you, Maddy?' asked Duncan.

'In the bar.'

'Who's there with you?'

'Kevin.'

'Who else?'

'Flora.' Her mouth twitched in the tiniest semblance of a smile.

'Who else?'

'Patrick,' said Maddy. 'Fussing. Patrick's always fussing. Dunno the rest . . .'

The men waited.

'Drinking game,' she said suddenly. 'Stupid game . . . Keep losing.'

'Tell me what you see.'

'My turn again. Kevin's fault. Keeps being my turn.'

'What is Kevin doing.'

'Filling up my glass.' Maddy paused. 'Filling my glass. Under the table.'

She frowned. Several seconds passed.

'What's happening now, Maddy?' Duncan prompted.

'Want to go home.' Her voice was still low and slurred but now slightly tearful.

Ben looked at her sharply but Duncan held up a pacifying hand.

'Who's there now, Maddy?'

'Flora,' murmured Maddy, calmer. 'In my room. Want to go to bed now. People outside my room. Shouting. Scared. Don't want them in here.'

Then, Maddy seemed to fall asleep for a few moments. The men waited for a while.

'Maddy,' said Duncan at last. 'What's happening now?'

'Sleeping,' she murmured drowsily.

'Are you still watching from the corner of the room?'

Maddy gave a tiny nod.

'Good, Maddy, that's good,' said Duncan. 'Are you alone?'

Another tiny nod.

They waited. Maddy's body twitched. She gasped. Once, Twice.

'What's happening now, Maddy?'

'What's that?' she said breathlessly. 'Someone in my room.'

'Okay, Maddy,' said Duncan. 'Stay in the corner of the room. Watch and tell me what you see?'

'Waking up, getting up . . . someone there,' she panted. 'Looking around. Door bolted. Good. Checking room. Under bed . . .' she was gasping continuously now.

'Do you see anyone, Maddy?' said Duncan urgently.

'No,' said Maddy. 'No one but . . .' she gave several short gasps of panic. 'Got to get out . . .'

'How are you going to get out, Maddy?'

'Not the door,' she said. 'People in the corridor. Shouting. Don't want them to see me.'

'So how are you going to get out?'

'Window.'

364

Ben winced.

'What are you doing?'

'Climbing up . . . Got to get out.'

As the men watched the drama unfolding, Maddy gave a huge gasp. And then went limp.

Duncan observed her intently, holding up a hand for Ben to stay back.

'Maddy?' he said.

Nothing. Her breathing was even, her body relaxed and her eyelids flickering barely perceptibly.

'Maddy?' he said again.

She screamed.

Both men jumped and Ben reached for her but Duncan held him back.

'My leg,' she wailed, anguished, eyes still closed.

Ben gave Duncan a look, but he shook his head. 'It's fine,' he whispered. 'Just a little longer.'

'Maddy, try and tell me what's happening. Remember you're just watching. Can you do that?'

At that, some of the tension went out of Maddy's body, and she nodded.

'My leg,' she whispered. 'It's dark . . . I'm cold . . . really cold.'

'Are you alone?'

'Yes,' she said, and then, 'no . . . I don't know.'

'Someone's there with you?'

'I don't know. I've got to hide,' said Maddy. 'I've got to get away . . .'

'What are you doing?'

'Crawling. My leg . . . Got to get away . . .'

There was a pause.

'Someone's there,' she said at last. 'Hiding in the dark . . .'

She was panting again now, her head moving from side to side. She said nothing more but her fear was evident.

Duncan looked at her thoughtfully. Then, he turned to Ben and nodded.

There was a pause, the silence of the room broken only by Maddy's terrified gasps and sobs.

'Maddy,' said Ben quietly.

Her head turned to the sound of his voice and she froze, listening.

'Maddy,' he said again softly.

'Ben?'

'Yes, it's me.'

'Are you the one?'

'The one?'

'Are you the one who's hiding in the dark?' Maddy asked, her eyes closed, head turned towards him.

Ben glanced at Duncan.

'I am,' he said. 'You're safe.'

'Safe,' she repeated, drowsily now, the panic gone.

Her breathing slowed. Her face smoothed out once again, her head drooping to the side. Ben watched the pulse in her neck slow until it was thudding, steadily, in time with his own.

Duncan waited for a few moments more and then he spoke: 'Maddy, I'm going to count to ten. As I count you are going to steadily become more alert and when I get to ten you are going to be fully awake and relaxed. Here we go . . .'

'Wow, that was amazing,' said Maddy, opening her eyes. 'I don't think I remembered anything I don't already know, though.'

'I didn't think you would,' said Duncan. 'I suspect the

point, with you, is that your memory is not so much blocked but confused because of the drugs you inadvertently took.'

'Okay,' said Maddy thoughtfully. 'I actually don't feel scared,' she admitted, with surprise and relief, 'but – I mean – do we *really* think I'll be better now?' she held her head on one side.

'Who can say?' said Duncan, not at all insulted at Maddy's scepticism. 'How do you feel?'

'Mm. Pretty okay, actually.'

'So that's good?'

'Yep,' admitted Maddy, yawning. 'Oops, sorry.'

'Not at all.' Duncan laughed. 'I'd expect you to be relaxed and sleepy after that.'

He glanced at Ben. 'Tell you what,' he said to Maddy, as if it had only just occurred to him, 'why don't you maybe have a little sleep now and see how you get on? With the nightmares, I mean . . . I think you could do with a rest. It's definitely past *my* bedtime,' he added, glancing at the clock in the kitchen. It was nearly eleven o'clock.

'I might just do that,' she said equably. 'Although, frankly, I'd be amazed if you've done anything to fix me that quickly.'

The room leading off the sitting area was a calm, spacious bedroom with very little in it other than a large double bed and a rag rug on the floor. There were smooth, white sheets and plump feather pillows. The room was cool but there was a cosy-looking grey blanket on top of the duvet. Maddy could think of nothing better than snuggling down into it and closing her eyes.

'Bathroom through here,' said Ben, pointing to the door in the corner of the room. 'Hang on a mo . . .'

He disappeared briefly into the bathroom and came back with a fluffy white towel and a toothbrush. 'Here you go. We're fully equipped for emergency guests.'

'I'm sure you are,' teased Maddy. 'Get many of them, do you?' As soon as she said it she felt a pang of jealousy.

'I live in hope,' joked Ben as he rummaged in drawers. 'I don't stretch to guest pyjamas, but you're welcome to sleep in these. More comfortable than what you've got on, anyhow . . .' he added, handing her a well-worn T-shirt and a reassuringly new-looking pair of boxers. 'Help yourself to shower and stuff. Tell you what, I'll just see Duncan out and then what do you say to a large mug of hot chocolate? Whipped cream and marshmallows?'

'Absolutely.'

'Cool.'

'Thanks, mate,' said Ben as he showed Duncan out.

'No worries,' said Duncan. 'Pretty satisfying, that was. I reckon we've nailed it, don't you?'

'Wouldn't be surprised.'

'Now we know the facts, the damage for Maddy was in being stuck in that loop of terror. It's a nameless fear because the thing she was scared of didn't happen. Kevin didn't turn up and do anything horrific . . .'

'So we implanted a resolution.'

'Yep,' agreed Duncan. 'You represent safety. Now her mind thinks you were there, making her safe, and it stops spinning off into nightmares every time she closes her eyes or sees her nemesis walking down the street. Simple.'

'Grand job. I can't thank you enough.'

'She's a great girl.'

'And you are – of course – a towering genius,' added Ben with a salute.

'I know,' agreed Duncan, slapping his friend on the back and then rummaging in his pocket for his car keys as he walked out to the car.

Closing the door, Ben made good on his promise and went to the kitchen to rustle up the biggest and best mug of hot chocolate he had ever made.

Knocking softly on the bedroom door, he heard no reply. Edging around the frame with the near-overflowing mug he smiled to himself. There, in his bed, in his boxers and T-shirt and looking absolutely adorable, was Maddy, her hair wet from the shower and curling around her face as it dried.

She was fast asleep.

CHAPTER THIRTY-TWO

'Tea?' said Ben the next morning as Maddy opened her eyes. She rubbed them and sat up, looking around her. She took the mug gratefully, and pushed her hair out of her eyes. It was daylight and the curtains were open, the rays of the low winter sun playing across the lime-washed floorboards and Maddy's bed.

'It's so beautiful here,' she said, looking out of the window. 'Wow, we really are right next to the river here, aren't we?'

'This side of the room's basically over it.'

'Don't you worry about flooding? At high tide and stuff?'

'Stilts,' was Ben's economical reply. 'May I?' he said, gesturing at the bed.

'Of course,' she said, shuffling up to make room. The duvet was still millpond smooth, despite her having spent the entire night under it.

'Goodness, I slept well. That's amazing.'

'I know you did. I was right next door with the door open, just in case . . . I literally don't think you stirred for eight hours.'

'Nope.'

'So,' said Ben, leaning on an elbow and looking at her intently. 'Tell me. How do you feel?'

Maddy thought.

'Safe,' she said, with an air of surprise. 'I feel safe.' She sank back against the pillows and wallowed in the unfamiliar feeling. 'Was it the hypnosis?'

'Probably.'

'Will it wear off?'

'Nope. But if it does I'm sure Duncan will be standing by.'

'What did you guys do? I'm not going to suddenly launch into the Funky Chicken dance at inopportune moments, am I?'

'God, I hope not,' said Ben in mock horror. 'I'm not sure I could cope with a girlfriend who did that.'

'Aha!' she said in triumph. 'So, what was it that won you over in the end, eh? My devastating charm? The news that my ex-boyfriend is now officially defunct? The fact that – it would genuinely appear, as of last night – I am no longer mental . . .'

'None of the above so shut up,' said Ben, smiling, then leaning down and giving her lips the gentlest brush with his. He would never tell her Helen's lie had made him think she might be his sister. What would be the point? That was over now.

Maddy sighed with happiness.

'Why didn't you sleep here last night?' she said. 'I feel awful for chucking you out of your own bed.'

'You were fast asleep. I didn't have your consent.'

'You have my consent now.'

'Ah,' he said teasingly, rolling away, 'but my college lecturer always told us, "Don't settle for consent, gentlemen. Hold out for enthusiasm."'

Maddy reached up and pulled him down on top of her, wrapping her legs around him and pressing her body against his.

* * *

'Is that enthusiastic enough for you?' she said later, sleepily, as they lay in each other's arms.

'I'm persuaded.'

Outside, on the river, a pair of swans drifted serenely by, allowing the current to pull them downriver.

'Swans mate for life, don't they?' she mused, lying with her head on Ben's chest.

'So I gather.'

'Is that something you want?' she asked, lifting her head and looking at him.

'It's definitely an aspiration. With you, that is . . .'

'Good.'

They slept again after that. Maddy couldn't remember the last time she had slept so much and so soundly, but then – after the last few months – she had some catching up to do.

'Yikes,' she said, when she woke up to discover Ben lying awake next to her, not moving for fear of disturbing her. 'This is shocking! It's nearly one o'clock and we're still in bed.'

'What's shocking,' said Ben, amused, 'is that we haven't even had breakfast yet, let alone lunch. Could you do a bacon sandwich?'

'Absolutely,' said Maddy. 'I'm starving. But, what about the time? Don't you have to be in college or something?'

'Holidays,' said Ben. 'It's Christmas in a few days, you do realise . . .'

'No! That's terrible; I haven't done anything . . . no Christmas shopping or anything.'

'We can go Christmas shopping, if you like, but surely the Bespoke Consortium has got something for everyone?'

'Phew, of course it has,' she said, relaxing back on the bed and thinking about all the sample boxes stacked up in Serena's kitchen. 'Will you settle for a pair of sheepskin slippers?'

'Sounds great. But I want your presence, not your presents.'

'That's appalling,' she groaned, but thinking of Serena's kitchen made her think of all sorts of other things, like whether the Liberty order had come through and would it be enough to bale them out, whether Josh was okay, whether Helen and Patrick were still at each other's throats. Where would they all be by Christmas? Sadly not in the Havenbury Arms, it would seem. Her brow lowered and her fingers picked at the bedcovers, anxiously. She should get up. Do stuff . . .

'Hey,' said Ben, grabbing her hands and holding them in his own. 'What's wrong?'

She explained, in a breathless rush, but – after a moment – Ben swept her into a hug and shushed her.

'I happen to know there is an important – er – gathering, in the pub tonight. The plan is for Jonno and Patrick to have worked things out to their mutual satisfaction by then. They'll be announcing their conclusions and I think you'll find there will be a few others there keen to bring you up to date . . . It's not till six o'clock, so relax.'

'Not till six, eh?' she said, stretching luxuriously. 'Hurry up with those bacon sandwiches, then. You'll need to keep your strength up with the plans I've got for you until then.'

CHAPTER THIRTY-THREE

Maddy drove to the Havenbury Arms that night because Ben's car was still in the exhibition car park in London.

'My poor little car isn't going to survive our relationship unless we do something about these potholes,' she complained as they bumped down the track to the main road.

'That's a summer job,' said Ben complacently. 'I'll do it then – and paint the boathouse. You can help.'

The heavy grey sky had darkened with purple-tinged clouds by the time night came. As Maddy joined the main road and started towards Havenbury Magna, frozen rain was lashing the windscreen. She shivered and turned up the heating.

'I suppose a white Christmas is too much to ask for.'

'With everything else working out okay, I wouldn't rule it out,' said Ben. 'I think you'll be surprised at how good life can be down here.'

As she drove into the bottom of town and turned up the steep high street, she examined her state of mind. No wobbles? No sweating palms? No gasping for breath?

Nothing. Just a profound sense of calm, safety and a swell of excitement at what the future held.

The pub was already full by the time they got there. Maddy drove past the windows, which were glowing with light, and found a parking space in the street outside.

'Mads!' came a familiar voice as they went through the door. Flora galloped towards them with a tray of canapés – which arrived miraculously unspilled – and gave them both a kiss.

'This is soooo cool,' she said, indicating the crowd in the bar. 'And Serena's dying to talk to you, by the way. Fab news,' she said, tapping the side of her nose.

'Quite a party!' Maddy exclaimed to Patrick as he came towards her for a hug.

'We've got a lot to celebrate.'

She raised her eyebrows enquiringly but he declined to say.

'Jonno will explain in a moment.'

Maddy was relieved to see that Helen was there, and apparently chatting happily.

Spying Serena, swigging from a glass of champagne and smiling up at Giles, who was leaning up against the bar, she gave Ben's arm a squeeze and went over to speak to her.

'Maddy!'

When they eventually unravelled themselves from each other both were wiping tears away.

'Ben told me about Josh. I was so relieved. How is he now?'

'Oh, amazing,' said Serena. 'They're planning to chuck him out in time for Christmas. I can't wait.' She turned to Giles, her tears gathering pace. 'It's just because I'm so happy and relieved,' she wailed, looking around desperately for a tissue.

'Come on, old thing,' said Giles, leaping to the rescue with a Christmas cocktail napkin, 'we don't want all that again, do we?' He pulled her to his side and gave her a squeeze. Serena looked up at him with gratitude and admiration in her eyes.

In a few moments, after another encouraging squeeze from Giles, Serena womanfully pulled herself together and gave Maddy a wobbly smile. 'The other thing,' she said, with tears threatening to overwhelm her again, 'is that I got an email from the Liberty buyer today.'

'Abby?' said Maddy, eagerly concerned that – given Serena's tears – it might not be good news.

Serena nodded, gulping.

Maddy waited.

'So she placed an order,' Serena said, 'and – well – it's just amazing . . . They're being really flexible about delivery dates because we're new and small but it's already put our turnover where we expected to be in eighteen months.'

Maddy gasped. It was more than they could possibly have hoped for in a million years.

'And,' Serena continued, 'they've taken all Keith's photos with a view to running a print advertising and PR campaign timed to hit the lifestyle magazines in the early summer. They're going to do a June launch event in store with all their best customers . . .' Serena drew breath, 'so – basically – it looks like we couldn't bugger up the Bespoke Consortium now if we tried.'

'I'll drink to that,' said Maddy, although she hadn't actually managed to get a drink yet.

'Here you go,' said Giles, handing her a full champagne glass and then grabbing the bottle to top up Serena's. 'We've got a lot to drink to tonight, and I couldn't be more proud of my wife,' he said, smiling down at her. 'Now,' he said, pushing himself away from the bar. 'Do forgive me, I'd better mingle . . .'

Serena did a little twirl, and toasted Maddy with her glass.

'Do you know,' she said consideringly, 'I don't think I could be any happier.' A cloud crossed her face momentarily. 'I've spent too long . . .' she said, pointing at Maddy intently.

She realised that Serena was a little drunk.

'I've spent too long hankering after what might have been,' she said. 'The whole Andrew thing, the whole "I could have had another life" thing,' she went on. 'It's a waste, thinking that way, Maddy. No more "sliding doors" stuff. I love my boys, I love my life, I love my work and – more than anything in the whole wide world,' she said, looking at Maddy to check she was listening, 'I absolutely, completely and utterly . . . love my husband. He's been "second choice" for too long, Maddy. I've done him a terrible disservice. He's been a complete hero over Josh. He's my one and only,' she said, jabbing Maddy in the chest. 'I don't want anything I can't have any more,' she said. 'It's done.'

Maddy put down her glass and hugged her friend. 'I'm so glad, Serena. I just hope my mum and dad can be as sorted as you and Giles are one day . . .'

There was a tinkling of glasses, calling the party to order and, turning, Maddy saw Jonno, climbing up on one of the tables near the door.

'Ladies and gentlemen,' he said quietly, and the noise in the room dropped into hush, instantly, such was his authority.

'Thank you,' he said. 'Now, I'm not going to go into detail tonight. Now's not the time, but I would like to quell the rumours and announce the good news.' He paused, and the occupants of the bar waited expectantly. 'As you are all aware, I put my shirt on the Havenbury Arms earlier this week at the property auction. Currently, I own the pub outright, so it is safely out of the hands of Top Taverns once and for all.'

There was a cheer, which Jonno quelled with a raised hand.

'Buying the pub has – I'll be honest – stretched my finances to, let's say, an "uncomfortable" degree,' he rolled his eyes comically, raising a laugh, 'so it is with great relief that I can confirm the second part of my necessarily "secret" plan has now come to fruition.'

He wiped his hand theatrically across his brow, raising another laugh, and then indicated for Patrick to join him, which he did, climbing onto the table with the help of several jovial partygoers.

When Patrick was alongside him, he continued: 'I am relieved and delighted to confirm that Patrick here, and his considerable band of supporters who pledged money to buy the pub for the community, have kindly agreed to my request to buy me out of fifty-one per cent of the value of the pub, leaving me with a forty-nine per cent stake.' He paused for people to digest the maths. 'Put simply, as was always my intention, the Havenbury Arms will be run in the future, as a Community Interest Company with me and Patrick as joint directors, and the remaining investors invited to become members with voting rights over all major decisions.'

There was a cheer as this information sank in and Jonno, with no further ado, proposed a toast to the new endeavour.

'To Patrick and Jonno,' they all cried, and slapped each other on the back.

Ben, by this time, had worked his way back to Maddy's side. 'Relieved?' he said.

'You knew!' said Maddy reprovingly.

'It might not have worked out,' said Ben. 'Touch and go.'

'Mum!' shouted Maddy, seeing her within grabbing distance at last. 'Are you okay?' she said, searching her mother's face.

'I will be,' said Helen. 'Wish me luck.'

With that, she walked off towards Patrick, who was holding forth to a couple of local investors. 'Decent bloke, that Jonno,' he was saying. 'Can't judge a book by its cover, got some good ideas, and has his head screwed on – 'course it helps him that I've got the industry experience he lacks . . .'

Helen tapped him on the shoulder and then, when she had his attention, she dropped to one knee. Maddy started forward, thinking her mother had fallen, but Ben held her back.

Jonno, still standing on the table, saw her and tapped his glass for silence again, gesturing towards her as people looked at him.

Into the silence, Helen said: 'Patrick. Never mind the business deals, *I've* got a proposal for you . . .' At this, there were whoops and cheers.

Someone shouted, 'Go on, Patrick, about time you made an honest woman of her,' but Jonno gestured for silence and Helen continued:

'We've done it all back to front. We have a beautiful daughter, and I've spent twenty-five years away from you, doing what you insisted was best for me. I know what's best for me; what's best for me is to spend the rest of my life with you. No more wasted time, Patrick. Will you marry me?'

Patrick reached for her hands and clasped them both in his, lifting her to her feet and drawing her close. To the frustration of the crowd, he murmured softly to her, wiping the tears gently from her eyes, and then going back to clasping her hands. She listened, smiling, occasionally breaking into a sob of laughter. Tears were running freely down Patrick's face too, as they talked – too quietly for anyone to hear – their eyes fixed lovingly on each other.

The crowd grew restless. 'Go on, Patrick, don't leave us in suspense,' one person cried. 'Yes, come on,' shouted another. 'The poor woman's waited twenty-five years for this.'

Patrick and Helen ignored them all until – eventually – Helen wiped away the mascara from under her eyes and turned to the crowd.

'He says "yes",' she said quietly.

As the cheering went on around them, Ben spun Maddy towards him and tightened his arms around her.

'Merry Christmas,' he said, kissing her softly and lingeringly on the lips, before turning her bodily to face the window.

'Looks like you got your wish, too.'

Outside in the high street, as their friends in the pub chatted, drank and cheered, the snowflakes drifted silently, crowding down from the sky and falling softly and thickly onto the ground.

ACKNOWLEDGEMENTS

It is a privilege to be in a position where I am not only allowed to write but am actively instructed to do so. It is a solitary pursuit but never lonely – partly because of my characters' voices in my head and partly because I have such a fantastic and supportive team around me.

This is all the fault of my agent and friend Julia Silk, who encouraged me to create the world of Havenbury, into which I escape most days. I thank her and all at MBA Literary Agency, for their skill, enthusiasm and knowledge.

I also want to acknowledge the extraordinary support of all my family and friends, who provide gin and laughs and even take the trouble to read the damned thing – Alex, Claire, Clare, Kate, Nancy, Carolyn, Charlie, Catherine, Georgie, Sarah, Anna, Vicky, Kim, Helen, Sharon, Lisa et al – you know who you are . . . to say nothing of my stalwart husband and children, who have to endure all those late and hastily cooked suppers.

I am grateful to the several clever people who keep me writing by preventing bits of me from dropping off. They are all amazing – Louise, Hannah, Petra, Kevin, Carole – goodness what a lot of you there are! Special thanks to osteopath Jon, who doesn't bat an eyelid at being asked exactly which bones you might break under various violent circumstances.

And finally, a million thanks to the entire fabulous Allison & Busby team, including my lovely editor Lesley Crooks, Susie Dunlop and Kelly Smith, and the marketing team who – fortunately – know so much more about 'that sort of thing' than I do.

I salute you all.

After obtaining a degree in music, Rosie Howard pursued a career in PR, campaigning and freelance journalism but realised her preference for making things up and switched to writing novels instead. She lives in a West Sussex village with her husband and two children in a cottage with roses around the door.

rosiehoward.co.uk

@RosieHowardBook